LUV (UN)ARRANGED

LUV SHUV #3

N. M. PATEL

Copyright © 2024 by Nilika Mistry

All rights reserved.

No part of this book may be reproduced in any form or by any electronic or mechanical means, including information storage and retrieval systems, without written permission from the author, except for the use of a brief quotation in a book review.

This book is a work of fiction. Names, characters, places, and incidents are either products of the author's imagination or are used fictitiously. Any resemblance to actual events, locales, or persons, living or dead, is entirely coincidental.

Development Editor: Kristen's Red Pen

Editor: Editing4Indies

Proofreader: Vanessa Esquibel (Kat's Literary Services)

❦ Created with Vellum

DEDICATION

To my chaotic, hilarious, crazy, and perfectly imperfect family.

TRIGGER WARNING

Instances of fat-shaming from the heroine's mother.

1

Song: Woh Ladki Hai Kahan
- *Kavita Subrahmanyam and Shaan*

Kriti

Marriage might not be all bad, but the journey *to* marriage was slowly ruining my life, one arranged meeting at a time. Like the one I was getting ready for.

"Stop making that face, Kriti. You look like we're forcing you to get married." Maa carried three dupattas draped over her arm as she entered my room. She gently laid them on the bed and handed me one after the other, looking to see which suited my salwar kameez the best.

"You're clearly forcing me to meet this guy *today*. I told you I had to go to Meera's place. She needs me." I draped the bright pink dupatta with thin golden lace along the edges over my shoulder. Usually, I didn't mind these arranged marriage meetings, but my best friend, Meera, needed me today. She was finally paying off the loan shark who had been hounding her for years, and I had promised to stand by her side.

Maa came behind me and pinned the dupatta to my light pink kameez. She tied the string at the back of my kurta and muttered, "If you follow the diet I tell you to, you could lose more weight. But no. No one listens to me in the house."

I wasn't the slim-and-trim girl that was the most common requirement of all the men and their moms in the arranged marriage market. Most of my clothes came from the large section, and I didn't mind it. The only one who had a problem with it was my mother. The moment I turned twenty-one, Maa had been trying to put me on a diet. Whether it was sending me bland tomatoes and cucumbers for lunch or putting less sugar in my chai, she never missed an opportunity. But the more she insisted on her ridiculous antics, the more Pappa snuck my favorite foods to me.

So I didn't concern myself with her complaints. I'd been hearing them for over five years now. "Maa, if a guy doesn't like me, he's free to reject me. I don't need the pressure and negativity."

"Rashmi told me they're coming to the village just for the day. And the boy's biodata seems good. Rashmi even messaged me his picture. His father was born in our village too. You know, Meera's father was a friend of their family."

Rashmi is my mother's point of contact for all the gossip in town as well as my self-appointed matchmaker. Maa kept going on and on with her list of reasons the guy would be a great match, like she did every time, while I applied some light makeup, barely paying attention to her spiel. Just because I wasn't in the mood to meet this guy today didn't mean I wanted to look unprepared. I expected a guy to bring his best to these meetings. After all, we didn't get more than three to four meetings before making the final decision.

First impressions were everything.

Maa was still going on about the guy's family when the doorbell rang. I turned to her in shock, thinking that the guy and his family had arrived already. Maa shook her head. "It's your pappa. I'd sent him to get some snacks. His hands must be full."

She shouted, "Rati, Kartik, open the door. Now."

Maa and I were in my bedroom upstairs. But within a few seconds, hearing the excited chatter of my sixteen-year-old siblings had me itching to go downstairs. Pappa would've gotten some good snacks.

Maa was arranging the bangle combinations, which could easily be done downstairs. I checked my kajal, put a small bindi on my forehead, and I was good to go. "Let's go downstairs, Maa. You can arrange the bangles at the dining table too. I want to eat something before everyone arrives."

Maa complained a little about the inconvenience of carrying all the bangles downstairs, but I quickly plucked her bangle pouch and ran to join the others. Her shout followed me all the way to the kitchen.

Opened newspaper packaging covered the kitchen countertop. I opened each package wider to find aloo samosa in one, kachori in the next, and fafda with shaved papaya chutney in the last one. My stomach rumbled, and I picked up a plate from the drying rack near the sink and started filling it up.

"Didi, can you please bring the packages to the dining table?" Kartik asked, his words jumbled because of the food in his mouth. Didi is a proper form of address for an older sister.

Before I could agree, Maa entered the kitchen. "We have guests coming soon. We don't have time to sit and have snacks. Your brother can eat more with the guests. You can eat while you make chai. And don't forget to add some ginger to the chai."

Before I could argue and convince *her* to make the chai and let me eat in peace, she gave me the classic "mom stare." She only had to turn her unblinking eyes at me to get no arguments. I sighed, took a big bite of kachori, and started preparing the chai.

Seeing things were in control, Maa left the kitchen and went to sit at the dining table. I poured the coriander chutney and tamarind chutney into my samosa and kachori. With my attention on the boiling chai and my one hand busy eating, I opened the biodata of today's guy that Maa had sent me. Biodata is just another word for résumé but for the marriage market.

BIODATA

Name: Aakar Mishra
Height: 6' 0"
Birth Date: 28 December 1993
Birth Place: Ahmedabad
Birth Time: 7:12 a.m.
Religion: Hindu
Caste: Brahmin
Education:
Master of Business Administration (MBA) in Product Management from L.D. College of Engineering
Bachelor in Textile Engineering (B. Tech) from L.D. College of Engineering
Work: Manager at Mishra & Sons Textile Group
Family Background
Father: Pravin Mishra, Co-Founder of Mishra & Sons
Education: Bachelor of Science in Mathematics
Mother: Shilpa Mishra, Homemaker
Education: Bachelor of Commerce

. . .

What a boring biodata—no hobbies or a summary of his dreams and goals, not even anything that could indicate his interests—that he clearly put together under pressure from his parents. But then I opened his picture.

Dark brown eyes stared at me with the smallest smile hidden behind the neatly trimmed beard, accentuating his sharp jaw. His shirt stretched tight across his broad chest with the top button opened, revealing a hint of bare skin. This man might be the hottest man I'd ever seen in my life, let alone for an arranged meeting. Maa had definitely upped her game.

The hiss of the overflowing chai touching the flame made me jump in panic. I quickly turned off the stove and checked how much chai I'd wasted while distracted by that handsome face. Thankfully, not much. I poured the chai into our fancy kettle, reserved for these arranged meetings, and resisted the urge to look at his photo again.

Aside from his looks, he and his parents were educated. Hopefully, that meant they would also value my education and be open to letting me continue working. The fact I started looking for positive qualities about him right after seeing his photo was purely coincidental. I wasn't that easily swayed by a pretty face. Not at all.

As I polished off my plate of samosa, kachori, and fafda with half a cup of chai, I couldn't help but wonder who would disappoint whom in the meeting.

If not, we might actually end up married.

∽

Aakar

The day I agreed to let my mother find a wife for me was the day I signed away my life for her entertainment. This past year had been an endless loop of meeting women, realizing my mother knew absolutely nothing about me or my expectations for a future wife, and trying to find a good enough reason—just one good reason, as my mother would call it—to reject the perfectly good women she introduced me to.

I agreed to give arranged marriage meetings a chance for two simple reasons. First, to compensate for helping my younger sister get together with her American boyfriend against our parents' wishes. Second, my life didn't offer many opportunities to meet new women. College was different, but ever since I'd joined the family business, I hadn't found the time to meet anyone new. This was as good an opportunity as any.

"Did you read the biodata I sent you last night, Aakar?" Maa asked, startling me.

We were on our way to our ancestral village. I informed Maa that I needed to help out our family friend Meera a week ago. Maa managed to find a single woman through the village grapevine and arranged a meeting with her and her family.

"Maa, all the biodatas are the same. I don't really care about her date of birth or her entire family history. Just tell me what she does and if she's educated."

After reading over twenty biodatas, I'd stopped caring about that sheet of paper. It told me absolutely nothing about the woman I was going to meet.

Maa made a chiding noise and pulled out her phone. Ria, my cousin who's as close to me as a sister and only a year older than me, gave me a teasing smile from the passenger seat in the front. Maa and I sat in the back seat of our car while my younger brother, Abhi, took the wheel. Abhi didn't particularly care about all the arranged meetings; he was here to help Meera out. Ria, on the other hand, usually came along with me and Maa to these meetings.

Maa scrolled through her phone. "Look at her photo."

And before I could protest, she handed me her phone.

I looked at the phone and stilled. If only for a moment.

"Her name's Kriti," Maa piped in.

She was beautiful. Her dark brown hair was lush, and her full lips were curved in a soft smile. But her eyes had me transfixed. Bold and lined with thick kohl, her gaze was fixated on the camera, challenging me to look away. I couldn't.

Maa continued, "She's a teacher in the local government school and has been teaching for the past five years. I know she's not very young or slim, but Aakar, you gave me only a week's notice."

No wonder her eyes posed such boldness and authority but also warmth. Of course, she was a teacher.

"I didn't give you any notice. I informed you I was going to the village." I didn't know why I was arguing about that when I couldn't take my eyes off the picture. Yes, she wasn't slim like all the women I'd seen until now.

She had curves men only dreamed of.

"I'm not exactly young either," Ria said, teasing my mother.

Maa looked at Ria. "You're a little older than Aakar, beta. Maybe you should start looking at arranged marriage prospects yourself."

I couldn't stop the chuckle. "Yes, Ria. When was the last time you went to see a guy? Aren't you missing the delightful conversations you have with the guys? Are you ready to cook and clean for your in-laws before leaving for work and serve them dinner after you return home?"

Ria poked her tongue out. "I'd rather die single."

Maa gasped and started praying, making us laugh.

I turned to my phone, and after a moment's hesitation—or perhaps excitement—I opened Kriti's biodata. I might as well check it out.

BIODATA
Name: Kriti Pandya
Height: 5' 6"
Birth Date: 12th March 1996
Birth Place: Laxminagar
Birth Time: 9:30 p.m.
Religion: Hindu
Caste: Brahmin
Education: Bachelor of Science (B.Sc), Bachelor of Education (B. Ed) from Sarangpur Teacher's College
Career: Teacher at Laxminagar Secondary and Higher Secondary School
About
I'm an easygoing person who knows basic housework. I love my work, especially when I can convince a family to let their daughters continue their education. My life's goal is to educate as many girls as I possibly can. I value and respect our culture but do not lead my life solely based on them. I wish to bring friendship, companionship, and, hopefully, happiness to my future husband and his family.
Family Background
Father: Saurabh Pandya, Business
Mother: Reshma Pandya, Housewife
Expectations:
A loving, kind partner with a sense of responsibility toward his family. Independent and career-oriented with a sense of humor. Someone who wants a wife to be his partner and a friend. Last, someone who is patient and willing to learn more about me.

THAT WAS ONE LONG BIODATA. It wasn't often that I came across biodata where the woman stated her expectations. Usually, it was a list of generic terms laid out by the family: a guy with a government job, nondrinker, nonsmoker, vegetarian, a minimum salary requirement, and a family man. But this one was a little more interesting. It still had the generic terms, but it read like something she wanted for her own. It made me want to know her more.

As we neared Kriti's house, Maa pulled out her compact from her purse and dabbed some powder on her cheeks. "Aakar, be good. Smile a little at the girl. Do not make her nervous. And when we send you to talk in private, please talk for at least fifteen minutes, even if you're not interested. It's rude if you return in five minutes."

"What am I supposed to talk about if the girl only answers in one or two words? It's not like I have many questions."

Maa glared at me as she stuffed her compact in her purse. "We are looking for your future wife. You must have questions. Are you even taking this seriously?"

God, I was so done with this same conversation. It took every effort not to roll my eyes at her. "Maa, I wouldn't be meeting so many women if I wasn't serious. And I'm tired of getting the same answers every time I ask them what they want from me as a husband or from the marriage. But I'm trying. Okay?"

Maa nodded and muttered, "We're almost there. Look happy."

Abhi snorted from the front, helping me relax. Leave it to Maa to ruin my perfectly good mood and then expect me to revert to a happy face. I unlocked my phone to Kriti's biodata, and her face popped into my mind. I almost smiled. I wasn't going to ask Maa to forward me her picture. Absolutely not. She'd make a big deal out of it.

I was just going to meet the woman, talk about her job and interests, have some chai, and be on my way to Meera's place. This was just like every other meeting.

Then why did my hands shake as I combed my hair?

And did I just comb my hair? For a meeting?

I quickly put the mini-comb back in my pocket and looked up at the house where we parked the car.

Control. I was in total control as I stepped out of the car.

And I would keep repeating that mantra until my heart stopped pounding.

2

Song: Do Anjaane Ajnabi
- *Shreya Ghoshal and Udit Narayan*

Kriti

The guy's family didn't even need to wait after ringing the doorbell because my mother had already seen their car arriving and taken her position in the entryway within seconds. Her glare at me, my siblings, and my father was enough to get us in our positions without any arguments. I stood near the end of the sofa—where I would sit, adjacent to the other sofa where Maa would invite the guy to be seated—ready for the show. My siblings stood behind the sofa, and Pappa stood with Maa in the foyer.

The moment the bell rang, Maa opened the door, beaming. "Shilpaji, Aakar Kumar, please come in. I hope it wasn't too difficult to find the house." Ji and Kumar are honorifics used to show respect.

A few namastes were exchanged in the entryway, and everyone moved into the living room within the next minute.

Maa entered first, followed by a woman in a light pink saree wearing a necklace with a large teardrop-shaped green pendant resting on her chest. Behind them came the man I was to get acquainted with.

With jet-black hair, short on the sides and perfectly gelled on top, he wore a light blue shirt that stretched over his broad shoulders, gray pants, and a large watch on his left wrist. His well-groomed beard was slightly longer than in his picture, but it only made him more handsome. All in all, he looked prepared, polished, and, dare I say, hot. His photograph did not do him justice.

His eyes met mine, and for a second, he paused in his conversation with Pappa. I gave him a small smile, and his lips barely lifted in return. Maa called his name and led him to sit on the sofa adjacent to mine, our knees almost touching. After we sat, he gave me another small smile, and my stomach fluttered.

My attention was pulled away from Aakar when introductions started. Maa introduced me and my siblings, and we said hi to the young people, whereas namaste to Aakar's mother. Aakar's mother started introducing their family.

"Kriti Beta, I am Shilpa, and this is Aakar, my eldest son."

Aakar looked at me and nodded, his eyes warm, with a hint of a smile on his lips. I clutched my dupatta on my lap, nerves heating my cheeks, and nodded back.

Shilpa Auntie continued, "This is my youngest son, Abhi. My daughter, Akira, studies in America." Then she pointed at another young woman who sat beside Abhi and said, "That's Ria, Aakar's cousin. We all live together in a joint family of fourteen people."

I must not have been able to hide my reaction because Maa

quickly said, "Our Kriti is very adjusting. She's always wanted to live in a big family. Isn't that right, Kriti?"

That wasn't right at all. The more people in a family, the more opinions they would have about my life. And I was barely prepared to take care of a husband and his parents, let alone a family of fourteen. How many of them were kids? How many were older people?

"Right," I said out loud, giving a polite smile to everyone.

"What do you do, beta?" Shilpa Auntie asked.

"I am a teacher at one of the schools in the village."

"What do you teach?" The question came from the man sitting on my right. Aakar. His deep and resonant voice commanded my attention. I was shocked—not by his voice, but by the fact that he had spoken at all. Men rarely participated, or even cared, to talk to me when their mother was already speaking. He looked at me, waiting for my answer, without looking away in awkwardness or hesitation. He was like a rock, steady and patient. I tried to find my bearings.

"Uh...I'm the teacher for a ninth-grade class. I teach science to high school students and English to primary grade students."

Aakar nodded, and I could feel all the eyes trained on us, especially Maa's. At this point, I'm sure she was dreaming about our wedding, just because he made conversation in front of everyone.

Shilpa Auntie added, "That is wonderful, Kriti. So you must speak great English, right?"

Well, I was a teacher in the subject. "Yes, Auntie," I said politely. But when my eyes met Aakar, his smile was a little wider than before. Was he reading my mind?

Maa turned to where Rati and Kartik stood. "Rati, Kartik, get the chai and snacks, would you?"

With a nod, they shuffled to the kitchen. Maa looked at Pappa and tried to have that silent conversation with her eyes as if none of us could see her. I turned to Aakar to gauge his reaction. The glimmer of amusement in his eyes indicated he was all too familiar with these antics and knew what came next.

Right then, Maa looked at Shilpa Auntie. "Shilpaji, I was wondering if it would be okay if the kids talked for a little while in private?"

Shilpa Auntie, clearly expecting this, answered, "Of course."

Maa turned to me. "Kriti Beta, why don't you and Aakar Kumar go to the porch outside? I'll send some chai and snacks to you."

I nodded, and Aakar and I stood together. With little space between the sofas and the coffee table, Aakar stepped aside and let me lead the way. I opened the front door and led him to the porch, taking a seat on the wooden, hand-carved jhula—a wide swing for two. When I looked at Aakar, he sat beside me, leaving several inches of space between us.

As if by mutual understanding, we moved our legs to swing the jhula slowly. The low creak of the metal bar at the top of the swing was the only sound between us. Back and forth we went, the silence growing more painful by the second. If he didn't start talking about something—anything—in the next thirty seconds, I would reject this guy. Too bad, he really was handsome.

I started counting down from thirty, looking everywhere but at him. At the count of fourteen, Aakar cleared his throat. "So I read your biodata."

Turning to him, I found him watching me. "Oh. That's good."

He chuckled. "It was interesting."

I couldn't help but smile at him. "What did you find interesting?"

He lifted a finger and opened his phone. "I really liked your *About* section, but what I found especially interesting were the last two lines of your expectations."

It had been a while since I'd prepared my biodata. Maa had been circling the same piece for the past two years. I might've looked confused because Aakar held up his phone and read aloud. "Someone who wants a wife to be his partner and a friend. Last, someone who is patient and willing to learn more about me."

He raised his eyebrows as if to say, *Remember?*

"Aah. Well, wouldn't you agree?"

Aakar looked at me, and our eyes held for a beat. "I agree. I'm glad you think so too. It's not often that people mention that they want *a partner* in their biodata. It's usually a list of demands like a government job or private business, someone who is spiritual, and other ridiculous expectations."

"Well, a woman has to leave her family, her world, and go live with a whole new family. I guess she can have as many expectations as she wants, no matter how ridiculous they are."

He raised his eyebrows at me, perhaps shocked that I disagreed with him. He should be glad I only said that much and didn't mention how his biodata didn't even have the *Expectations* section.

"I agree. I apologize for my insensitivity. I did not think."

Now, I was shocked.

He chuckled. "What? I can admit my mistake and apologize when I'm wrong."

My cheeks flushed. "That's good to know."

Before I could think about what to ask him, he took the lead once again. "If you don't mind me asking, why did you decide to become a teacher?"

His voice was steady and calm, and genuine curiosity shone in his eyes, causing warmth to bloom in my stomach. Not a lot of men cared enough to want to know about my job, my passion. I thought about my students and my classes, and my lips automatically stretched into a smile. "Well, we spent our entire childhood at school, made our best friends there, and still remember our favorite teachers. It's the most important period of our lives, even though our memories of school fade as time passes. When I was attending, so many girls were taken out of school. People often forget the importance of education and how it brings security and stability to our lives, especially for women. I just had to be a part of it. I wanted to teach in a way that made learning enjoyable, instilled discipline and manners in my students, and helped prepare them for what's to come in life."

I knew I surprised him with my answer because his eyes were wide with wonder, making me proud of my work. "That's very admirable. I always thought people went into teaching because they couldn't succeed in anything else. How wrong I was."

I rolled my eyes at that. "You're not the only one who thinks that. So many relatives constantly advised me to go into engineering and get a traditional job at some company. I had no interest in that."

He groaned softly, and a warm sensation rose in the pit of my stomach. "C'mon, Kriti, please don't compare me to your relatives. I'd like to think I must be better than them."

Hearing him utter my name for the first time had heat rushing through my body.

I gulped as my brain tried to form words. "I really hope you are."

His laughter washed over me. "I'll just have to prove to you that I'm better than them."

Pressing my lips in a small smile, I asked, "What about you? What do you do?

"I run my family's textile business. We produce and manufacture different fabrics, working on various designs, dyes, and finishes. I'm involved in almost every aspect of the business from quality control of the products to handling distribution to our clients, marketing and strategy for bringing in new clients, financial management, and researching new innovative and eco-friendly practices."

He sounded so confident, so authoritative, as he talked about it. "Do you enjoy what you do?"

He chuckled lightly, a hint of doubt in his tone. "Well, I am the oldest. It's always been my responsibility."

"That wasn't my question," I said softly.

He sighed at that and looked straight ahead. "It's a little more complicated than a yes or no answer."

Aakar seemed so self-assured, like he had everything in control, like he was sure of what he wanted out of life. "How so?"

He cleared his throat. "Now that I've been at our company for five years, my dad and uncles rely on me. I feel more responsible. I like certain aspects of working at our company, like researching the market industry, preparing reports on what to order, how much to order, making the marketing strategy, and executing it. I want to expand it, bring in sustainable technology, and handle things my way. But is working and expanding our business my true passion? No. Doesn't mean I don't enjoy it or get a sense of satisfaction from it. I know I'm good at it and enjoy seeing the company grow. Working there makes my family happy and secure for the future. And that makes me happy."

His life revolved around his family. "Spoken like a true eldest child."

He snorted and gave an embarrassed chuckle. "Do you believe that a person should always follow his passion? What if a person has no passion?"

I must have hit a nerve. I looked down at my lap as I thought about his question. He didn't rush me at all and simply waited. "I do believe that a person should always follow his passion. But I don't think that passion must always translate to a source of income. People can be passionate about different things—family, friends, traveling, reading, or simply collecting random items. Every person is passionate about something. Your passion seems to lie in your family's happiness."

Aakar looked at me with such intensity and something akin to gratefulness that it was difficult to meet his eyes. "Thanks, Kriti." He nodded. "I'm not like my siblings. Akira is spreading her wings, being independent, and falling in love in America, and Abhi seems to be exploring his options. I just want to support my siblings and family and be there for them when they need me. I want my siblings to achieve their hearts' desires, but I don't want my father and uncles to have no one to rely on in their old age. They've worked so hard to build the company. I just...I just need everyone to be happy."

An ache bloomed in my chest at his words, his love for his family so evident that, despite knowing him for all of ten minutes, the words flew out of my mouth. "I know you will keep everyone happy."

Just then, the front door of my house opened, and Rati walked out with a tray. I quickly got up and took it from her.

"How's it going?" she whispered, her eyes lit with excitement after far too many meetings.

"Later," I whispered back.

I placed the tray of snacks and two cups of chai on the jhula between us. I picked up a cup, placed it on the saucer, and handed it to Aakar. He took the chai and said, "Thank you."

Manners and a thank you? Aakar was earning points in my book.

"You're welcome."

"So enough about me. Tell me about your expectations from a husband?"

This was the moment. If and when someone asked me this question, my answer often had them running away. It was shocking that few guys even bothered to ask this simple question. But sadly, that was the society we lived in.

I took a sip of my chai and placed the cup on the saucer. "Aakarji, I must be honest," I began but was interrupted when he said, "Please, just call me Aakar."

Oh my. Clearly, he was a city boy. I nodded at his request and continued, "Aakar. I actually have three conditions my future husband must agree to before I would agree to marry him."

His eyebrows rose high, interest clear in his eyes. He placed the chai back on the tray, turned his body to face me, and gave me his full attention. "Let's hear them, then."

I cleared my throat, mostly because his gaze was fixed on me, and I needed a second to meet his eyes. I took a breath, pulling in all the authority and defiance I could muster, remembering the men I'd previously met telling me how unreasonable my conditions were and how I would forever stay alone.

Fire burned within my heart, my jaw hardened, and I faced him head-on. "First, I will continue working even after marriage and having kids. Second, I won't have sex with you for at least the first six months of the marriage. And third, I will have full control over the money I earn. Whether I spend it on my family, college fees for my siblings, donate it, or spend it on myself and things that make me happy, that's my call. It doesn't mean I won't discuss it with you or share my plans with you. I'd welcome your opinions and thoughts, but in the end, I should be free to do what I want with my money."

∽

Aakar

Kriti's eyes burned with defiance as if daring me to mock her. Her words, spoken with such conviction and power, made my heart beat faster. How could I ever mock her? And what was there to mock? Her conditions were perfectly reasonable.

"Are you going to say something?" she asked, an edge in her tone.

"Yes. Sorry, I was just thinking."

She raised her eyebrows, clearly telling me to get on with it. I couldn't stop the chuckle that escaped me. She looked gorgeous in her beautiful light pink dress and dark pink dupatta. Her dark pink painted lips, which had me struggling to focus on her words, were now pursed tight, and her eyes, lined with a thick line of kohl, narrowed with impatience and frustration. How quickly she transformed from a sexy goddess to Goddess Kali, the Goddess of Death, I'll never know.

I cleared my throat. "I mean, these seem like good requests."

"They're not requests. They're conditions. Request implies that you have the power to say no in the future."

Her eyes were narrowed to slits, almost as if she would soon shoot fireballs from them. How much must she have heard about her conditions to make her so defensive and hardened about this topic? "Of course. Conditions. I didn't mean to imply otherwise. I am sorry you had to put these wishes as your conditions."

Her shoulders loosened a little, her hand clutched her dupatta, and a hint of softness came over her face. She looked at me with such hope, such relief, when she asked, "So you don't think these conditions are unreasonable?"

Unreasonable? What sort of guys had she been meeting?

"Of course not. They are perfectly reasonable. Your conditions concern your life. Your work. Your body. Your possessions that you have earned. No other person has a right to any of it."

She met my eyes, not with defiance but with something positive. Something light. Something that warmed my chest. And this time, her voice was barely a whisper. "Thank you."

"Has it been that bad for you when you stated these conditions?"

Now that she knew I was on her side, she rolled her eyes and picked up her cup of chai. After taking a sip, she said, "It has been awful. There hasn't been a single guy who has agreed to all three conditions. Some didn't even have an opinion and had to consult their family before giving me an answer."

I picked up my own cup and took a sip. "It's a really good chai. And if you don't mind, can I ask which conditions were unacceptable to other men?"

She smirked. "Why do I feel that you think it was condition number two?"

A loud laugh burst out of me. She wasn't shy. "Was it?"

She chuckled and shook her head. "That was the least of their concerns. Some wanted me to leave work after having kids. Some couldn't handle the fact that I wanted the choice to handle my money. Some wanted me to contribute to their household income or give it to the head of the family. Not many even bothered to discuss the topic of physical intimacy. Some just ignored that fact, while others scoffed and said it was one of my many duties to my husband."

I put my cup back on the tray, unable to stomach anything at the moment. It wasn't that I was unaware of how the men in our society were. It was just hard to hear the list of sacrifices that came with marriage for women. "I'm really sorry you've had to meet such men."

She gave me a small smile. "Frankly, I thought you would say, 'Not all men are the same.'"

I couldn't help but chuckle at that. "Honestly, I was going to say that. But it felt like a cop-out. And I knew you would glare at me if I did."

She laughed loudly. The sound of her laughter, the way her eyes lit up, and how gorgeous she looked with her lips stretched wide in delight had my heart hammering in my chest.

As she placed her cup back on the tray, I said, "I have grown up with my sister, Akira and my cousin, Ria. I never want them to have to lay out such conditions for marriage. Thankfully, Akira already has an American boyfriend who worships her. And Ria, well, she can handle her own. But I don't know what I would do if their partners had issues with even the tiniest of their wishes."

Kriti smiled at me, her gaze drifting toward the street outside their porch. "You're a good brother."

"I try. It all comes with being the eldest, I guess. I mean, Ria is a year older than me, but I *feel* older."

She looked at me, curiosity in her eyes. "So, Mr. Good Brother, what are you looking for in a wife? You didn't exactly include much in your biodata."

Her raised eyebrows, wide eyes, and smile screamed *gotcha*.

Heat warmed my cheeks, and before I could answer her, Kriti's sister, Rati, opened the main door to their house and poked her head out. Without meeting my eyes, she told Kriti, "They're calling you back inside."

Already? We've barely talked.

Kriti looked at me, and she must've seen the disappointment on my face because she turned to Rati and said, "Tell them we'll be there in a bit."

Rati nodded and quickly went inside.

With a grateful smile, I said, "Thank you."

She gave me a beautiful smile in return. "You were saying?"

Ah. The age-old question. What did I want in my wife?

I looked at Kriti—her large earrings entangling with a few locks of her hair and her eyes trying to read me—and I *wanted* to share my answer with her. "I don't have a list. But I'm looking for a solid connection. Someone with whom I can share my feelings with ease, someone with whom I can joke around, someone who is passionate and kind, and someone who genuinely wants to know me and be with me. Someone I can consider a friend. Someone I'm excited to go home to."

Kriti looked entranced. "How would you know you found that person?"

I turned to her and met her eyes. "I'll know."

She nodded and gave me a small smile. "Want to head back in?"

I gasped. "Back to the riveting conversation between our parents?"

She chuckled. "I could probably recite their conversation verbatim at this point."

I nodded, but both of us got up and shuffled inside.

On the way to their living room, I looked at my watch, and a little more than half an hour had passed.

Huh. Time just flew by. That was a first.

Kriti's long hair almost brushed the middle of her back, her dupatta enhancing every one of her generous curves. She walked with confidence, authority, and grace. My eyes were riveted to her every movement.

The spell, however, broke as soon as we stepped into the living room. Maa, Abhi, and Ria looked at me, trying to decipher my interest in Kriti. And if I looked at Kriti's family, I'd find them doing the same. For the next fifteen minutes, we sat making idle conversation while I tried to sneak a glance at Kriti, doing exactly what my family was doing to me: trying to decipher her interest.

Maa cleared her throat, and I understood the telltale sign. It was time to leave because the parents had run out of conversation. My eyes met Kriti's, and I gave her a small smile.

Maa, Abhi, Ria, and I stood in tandem, and Kriti's family followed.

We slowly started to walk out of the house, exchanging obligatory *goodbyes* and *we'll talk soon*, while Kriti and I kept exchanging glances. A rush of excitement, nervousness, and some foreign emotion churned in my stomach.

As soon as we got in the car, all three started in on me. I specifically took the driver's seat to avoid the grilling.

"You guys were out there talking forever," Ria stated.

Maa added, "Do you like her, beta? Kriti's father couldn't stop praising her."

"Is she going to be my bhabhi?" Abhi teased. Bhabhi meant sister-in-law.

She certainly was the most interesting person I had met so far. But if I said that to Maa, all she would hear is *Get the invitation cards printed*. Silence was my only option.

I turned the car around at the next intersection to drop Abhi at our friend Meera's place so he could help care for Hari, Meera's younger brother.

After enduring Maa's nonstop questions and Ria and Abhi's encouragement, I turned to the three of them and said what I always say when I meet a girl. "I'll think about it."

Maa rolled her eyes and looked at Ria for support. "Ria, will you tell him that I don't enjoy looking for a girl for him if he's going to give me the same answer every time."

Smiling, Ria raised her eyebrows at me in mock anger.

Maa caught Ria's look and huffed in frustration. "Both of you are just hopeless. See if I care the next time I get a rishta proposal for you, Aakar."

"Oh, I will," I said.

I dropped Abhi off, then drove to our village house to drop Maa and Ria off before returning to Meera's place. Maa did not need to witness the possible debacle waiting to happen. She would just turn it into gossip, and Meera and her mom would not like that. At all.

For the rest of the drive, Maa asked, pleaded, and ordered me to tell her all about my private conversation with Kriti. And when I didn't budge, she told me all about the praises that Kriti's parents had sung about her. Usually, I never gave those praises any mind.

This time, though, I couldn't hear enough of them.

3

Song: Saagar Jaisi Aankhoon Wali
- *Sreerama Chandra*

Kriti

The moment Aakar and his family left our house, I rushed out the door to head over to Meera's place. I called out to Maa and told her that I'd talk to her after I returned home. If I stopped to hear her out even for a second, she wouldn't leave me alone until she got every little detail about my conversation with Aakar. I ran to my two-wheeler, pulled off my dupatta to tie it around my face, and, with a quick start, drove off.

Today, Meera was paying off the loan that had been hanging over her head for years. After the loss of her father, Meera's mother had refused to sell their farm. But after years of healing, forgiveness, and dealing with the grief, she finally asked Meera to sell it. Fortunately, our friend Surbhi needed more space to accommodate the widows and children of farmers who had committed suicide. Surbhi ran a nonprofit organization helping the families of deceased farmers, and Meera's father had been one of those farmers.

Just last month, Meera told Surbhi about her land for sale, and Surbhi proposed to buy it. Today was the big day. Meera had called all her friends and family to witness her paying off her loan to Baldev, the sleazy loan shark her father had borrowed money from.

I zoomed past a few slow-moving two-wheelers, past a few cars that seemed to think the road belonged to them, and took the turn at the street that led to Meera's house. The uneven bumps on the road slowed me down a little, but soon, I drove through the little gate of her house's compound. A few two-wheelers and a car were already parked.

Removing the dupatta from my face, I draped it over my shoulder, checking my reflection in the tiny mirror of my vehicle. My hair was all right, but I was overdressed. Maa just had to arrange the meeting with Aakar today. But I couldn't even complain. It was one of the few good meetings I'd had.

Putting it out of my mind for now, I ran inside her house. "Am I late?" I asked.

I turned to Meera, who stood at the doorway to her kitchen, and she shook her head. "Uh. No. Baldev hasn't arrived yet."

"Thank God," I said, realizing that everyone stared at me, their mouths open, a teasing smile on Meera's face. I should've changed before running out of the house. Trying to regain some semblance of control, I said, "What are you guys looking at? Maa roped me into a sudden meeting with a man. Apparently, they were only going to be in the village today."

Before anyone could comment on it, I rushed into the kitchen. I would only come out when necessary. The delicious aroma of tomato, garlic, and herbs engulfed me as I stepped inside. I looked at the giant pan filled with pasta and couldn't help myself. I grabbed a small bowl from a cupboard and served some.

I know I had just had some chai with Aakar, and samosas and kachori before he arrived, but the pasta smelled delicious.

Before I'd taken three bites, Meera, Surbhi, and Luke walked in.

"How did the meeting go?" Meera asked.

I hadn't had much time to think about that. Maa was going to ask me many more questions. Just thinking about it put a sour taste in my mouth. But Meera's question was easy yet difficult to answer. "Actually, not bad."

"Is that a bad thing?" Surbhi asked.

I turned to her and tried to explain the disaster that awaited me. "I don't think so. It's just...it's easier when things don't go well in these meetings. It's an easy no. Now, if the guy is interested, we'll have to talk again and deal with all the questions and rushing from the parents."

Luke went back to spreading butter on his fancy bread while Meera, Surbhi, and I talked about Meera's plan for today. Just a few minutes had passed when the doorbell rang. Meera quickly turned to walk out and said, "That must be Aakar. Let's go to the living room. Baldev must be arriving soon."

Her words dropped like bombs at my feet.

Sweat coated the top of my lip, and I was sure Surbhi could hear my heart pounding. My hands shook as I carefully placed the half-eaten pasta bowl on the kitchen counter. Did she just say Aakar?

I couldn't help but follow Meera out of the kitchen. My eyes met Luke's, and he raised his eyebrows in question. I shook my head and offered him a smile. He put down his half-glazed bread and followed us.

And there he was when I stepped foot in the living room.

Aakar.

He had a gentle smile on his face as he talked to Meera's mother. He turned his head to look toward where all of us had gathered, a smile on his face, when our eyes met.

His eyes widened in shock for a second, but he collected himself far quicker than I had. "You," he said, his face turning slightly red as he looked around at all of us.

"You know Meera?" I asked, wondering how I didn't know that Meera knew Aakar.

He walked toward me, his eyes moving across everyone. He closed the distance between us and stood right across from me, nodding. "Um...yeah, family friends. How do you know Meera?"

"She's my best friend," I said without taking my eyes off him.

"That's good to know."

"You came for Meera all the way from the city?" I asked. I liked to believe that if a man came for a friend when she needed it, he had to be a good person, right? And Meera wouldn't have asked for help from someone she didn't deem honorable and kind.

Aakar nodded. "I did. That loan shark wasn't on his best behavior the last time I was here. People like him often tend to take advantage of their position. So Meera thought it would be better if I was here as a witness. In case he gets a little mouthy, Luke and I could handle it. Since Luke barely understands Gujarati, I felt like I could help."

I was about to thank him for coming when Meera said, "Baldev's on the way here."

Aakar straightened, and as if we realized how close we stood to each other, we each took a step back. I felt Aakar's eyes on me, but I fixed my gaze on Meera.

Meera lifted the double-sized mattress in her living room and pulled out a big pouch of money from underneath it. She turned to all of us, and asked, "Ready, everyone? Luke, Aakar, and I will meet with Baldev out front, and you guys will stand on the porch. Just so he knows that everyone saw us exchange the money."

Once we all nodded, Meera, Luke, and Aakar took the lead, and the rest of us followed them. As Baldev approached the house, the three of them stepped forward to meet him in the middle. Meera stood in the center, with Luke and Aakar on either side. Meera's mom held my hand as we watched the scene unfold. Baldev looked at them, then back at us, clearly confused by our presence.

We could hear them talk in Gujarati, but we were too far away to understand what they were saying. As soon as Meera handed him the packet of money, he turned nasty. He said something to Meera, and she landed a solid punch on his nose. The next moment, Luke held Meera in his arms, holding her back, while Aakar stepped forward and slapped Baldev across the face. Aakar's volume rose as he uttered a few profanities that made Meera's mom worry even more, then slapped Baldev twice more.

You'd think a punch would've been more powerful, but a slap just looked way more disrespectful. As if Baldev didn't even deserve something as solid as a punch. That nasty little worm could be eradicated just by a tight slap to his cheek and his pride.

YES. YES. Hit him. My mind inwardly cheered him on. If Meera raised her hand, Baldev must have said something really awful to her. I moved forward to intervene, but Meera's mom and Surbhi pulled me back. Poor Luke looked confused by the words getting exchanged between Meera and Baldev, but Meera bellowed, "Leave me, Luke. I'm going to kill him."

"Even I want to punch him, but I can't if I'm holding you back," he shouted at her in English.

Meera's mom couldn't understand their conversation in English, so I told her what they said. She looked about to cry, so I quickly told her in Gujarati, "Don't worry, Auntie. Aakar is holding Baldev back."

I didn't know why I said that or why I had so much faith in those words. Before Aakar could slap Baldev once more, Luke pulled Baldev away from Aakar and punched him on the nose, right where Meera had hit him. Blood sprayed out on the ground, and Baldev dropped to his knees.

Luke bent over him and said something none of us on the porch could hear.

Slowly, Baldev got up and wobbled away, carrying the money under his arm. As his car left the compound, I stood there, then rushed inside the kitchen. I opened the freezer, wrapped some ice cubes in a few hand towels, and ran outside to hand them to Meera and Luke.

This moment, this day, was for Meera. It was the first time in almost six years that she was debt-free. Her knuckles were red, and her hair was a mess, but she wore the biggest smile. Luke looked at her like his life revolved around that smile. Not once did he turn to anybody else—not when I had them sit on the cot, not when I handed them their cold packs, and not when we moved back inside to give them a moment alone.

Because my friend was finally free. Free of all the burdens that had chained her to this village, her farm, and kept her apart from Luke. And now, she could fly. She could dance, jump, and ride off into the sunset with the love of her life. And finally, *finally* live.

I turned around one more time to look at their moment, so full of love, in envy and in hope. How lovely would it be to have that one person devoted to me, who cared about my happiness above all else, who had faith in me and respected me? Because I too deserved that kind of love.

Aakar

Kriti walked into the kitchen as I washed my hands and face at the sink. I needed to be rid of the filth that was Baldev. It pained me to imagine Meera having to deal with the likes of him for so many years without my family knowing about it. As I wiped my hands with the kitchen towel, I felt Kriti move closer. Her eyes on me had my heart beating faster. Her scrutiny unnerved me.

What did she think of me after seeing me raise my hand at someone and hearing the profanities that came out of my mouth? For some reason, I cared about what she thought of me.

She cleared her throat, and despite my nerves, I steeled myself and turned to her.

"Do you need an ice pack for your hand?" she asked.

Ice pack? I followed her gaze to my hand, raising it so she could look at it. "Um...I actually slapped Baldev. So my knuckles are fine. Uh...so are my palms."

She looked at my hand, and I turned it so she could see my knuckles. A breath escaped her lips, and she gave me a big smile. "Thank God. Meera's and Luke's hands are all red."

She didn't mind that I'd beaten up a man? I usually didn't get into fights, but as the eldest brother in the family, I could handle fights, conflicts, complaints, and bullies pretty well. But I just had to confirm Kriti's feelings for myself. "So you don't mind?"

Kriti started reheating the pasta, giving it an occasional stir. "Mind what?"

I was glad she wasn't looking at me with that unbending, teacher-like gaze. To avoid meeting her eyes in case she turned to me, I went to the stainless steel rack on the wall and got the plates out. "That I slapped Baldev?"

Her loud scoff made me turn around. She had one hand on her waist, her eyes wide in disbelief, and her lips were stretched in a huge smile. "Mind? I was about to join in, but Surbhi and Meera's mom held me back. That rascal deserved worse."

Rascal? Holy shit.

My face must've revealed my emotions because her eyes narrowed at me in suspicion. "Do *you* mind?"

And I couldn't help but chuckle. "Definitely not."

"Good," she said, continuing to stir the pasta.

This woman. Her eyes. Her manners. She exuded a confidence, a self-assuredness, that left me floundering behind her. And that rarely happened. She looked like she could handle it all with a smile. Even now, after the drama and the fight, she already had the injured settled and was on her feet getting the food ready.

She was quiet while I was lost in my head. The moment I got home, Maa would bombard me with questions. She'd demand an answer. Yes or no. To this day, I've never struggled to answer.

No. That was always my response.

Why? Maa would ask.

Because we don't fit.

But did I want to give Maa the same answers for Kriti? A big resounding *No* came from somewhere deep within me. I wanted to talk to her more. I liked that she was so assertive in her choices and so confident that she didn't try to impress me. That was refreshing and quite relaxing.

But I didn't even want to say *Yes* to my mother. She would have us engaged and married in three months. God, this was confusing. I thought meeting women was stressful. I never thought about what would happen when I didn't want to say *No* for a proposal.

Shit.

"Uh...Aakar," Kriti said, pulling me out of my thoughts.

She looked at me with her eyebrows raised in question. *Where were you lost?*

I shook my head and asked, "Sorry, did you say something?"

A teasing smile played on her lips. "Food is ready. Let's go outside so we can all eat together."

As we all ate, celebrating, laughing, and basking in the relief Meera and her mother felt, my thoughts circled back to Kriti. Before Maa got the chance to ask me anything, I needed to have a conversation with Kriti. I needed to know if she was interested in talking to me again. There was no point in wondering what I would tell Maa if Kriti wasn't interested in getting to know me more.

As much as the thought sat bitterly in my stomach, I needed to be ready to face Kriti's answer, even if it was a no. Even if that would disappoint me deeply.

Once we finished lunch, Meera was about to join Kriti in cleaning the kitchen. But since I really needed to talk to Kriti, I asked her if I could help instead. Meera got a teasing smile on her face, but thankfully, she said she needed to talk to Surbhi about something and let me be.

I carried the remaining plates and glasses to the kitchen and found Kriti soaping up the dishes. Upon seeing me and the dirty plates in my hand, she said, "Oh, just put them on the counter. I'll get to them."

"Let me help. I can rinse the dishes since you're already soaping them up."

I quickly rolled up the sleeves of my shirt and walked toward her. As I neared her, I noticed the slight blush on her cheeks. Slowly, she made space for me, and I stood beside her, our shoulders almost touching. I turned on the tap and began rinsing the dishes.

"Do you often help out like this at home?" she asked.

This would score me some major negative points. But

maybe I could get some points for honesty. "Well, not really. Since we have a full-time helper, I guess I've never needed to."

She nodded. "I see."

What did that mean? Did she want me to expand on that? Had she already judged me? "It's not that I'm opposed to helping. But I leave for work at nine and usually don't come home before nine o'clock. Some days, the only person left to have dinner is me. So I just haven't had the chance to help out at home."

"That makes sense," she said. A smile played on her lips, yet she didn't meet my eyes as she continued, "Can I ask why you're helping me out right now?"

I never had to ask a woman if she liked me enough to see where it could go just after one meeting. Well, technically, two now. But there was no other option than to be straightforward.

"Kriti, you and I both know that the moment we go home, our parents will bombard us with questions."

When she nodded, I continued, focused on rinsing the utensils, "Well, to be frank, I've never really said an outright yes for a woman before. I've had a few second meetings when the woman's family asked for it, and I didn't have any reason to deny it. But I don't really want to say *No* to my mother when I go home this time."

At that, she stopped scrubbing the dish, and I paused as well. The only sound was the tap running. After a beat, to keep from making things awkward, I resumed rinsing the plate as she processed my words.

"Are you planning to say yes?" she asked.

"That's the thing, Kriti. We don't know each other well enough for me to say yes either. I want to talk to you more and get to know you better. But if I ask my mother for a second meeting with you, or God forbid, a third meeting..." I paused.

"They would expect a final answer, or more like a yes, after that," she finished my sentence.

"Exactly. And I don't want either of us to feel that pressure. But before we get into it, I need to know if you even want to get to know me more. Because if you're already planning to reject me, there really is no point in discussing this further."

This time, I looked at her. She ran her fingers through the suds of soap on the plate. My stomach twisted into knots in anticipation as I continued rinsing the plates.

After what felt like hours, she said, "Aakar, unlike you, I have said yes to second and third meetings before. Clearly, they didn't pan out. And good riddance for those. But it isn't often that I meet someone who believes my conditions shouldn't even have to be conditions or someone I've seen support a friend in need. You have all my respect and admiration for that. Frankly speaking, I've agreed to second meetings for less than that."

A relieved breath rushed out of me. Why did I feel so happy? I couldn't even hide my feelings as I smiled at her. "I'm glad to have raised the bar for you."

She chuckled. "That you did."

Now that I knew she was open to getting to know me, I said, "So if you also don't want to get roped into the pressure of giving our parents the final answer in just three meetings, I have a proposal for you."

She raised one eyebrow in question. One. "How did you do that?" I asked, trying to copy her.

She laughed at my failed attempts. I must've looked ridiculous, but she was clearly having fun. "Like this?" she asked, doing it again.

"I am going to learn this little trick. You just wait and see."

She laughed out loud with a big snort, making me laugh with her. "Stop now. What was your proposal?" she asked, air-quoting the word proposal.

I raised *both* my eyebrows at that. "Well, at home, we

somehow try to delay giving them an answer. And what if we exchange phone numbers right now and get to know each other behind their backs? We can take as long as we need to decide if we suit each other. And in the end, if we do, we can tell our families. If we don't, no harm, no foul."

Just to mock me now, she raised *one* of her eyebrows. "That is an idea. I don't see much harm in that. Worst-case scenario, my mother will be ready to hear about our meeting the moment I step inside my house and demand an answer right away. In the best-case scenario, I ask her to give me some time to think, and she will continue arranging meetings with other guys in the meantime."

The thought of Kriti meeting other men and potentially getting a *Yes* from them churned my stomach. A mix of jealousy and insecurity washed over me, but I knew I had no right to exclusivity. It was painful to say, but I sighed. "Well, I might be able to delay my mother from showing me other women, but you do what you have to do. We'll figure it out along the way."

She seemed to mull over everything as she scrubbed the last of the utensils. She passed me the soapy dishes, washed her hands at the sink, and wiped them with the kitchen towel. I quickly finished up my part as I waited for her.

"Deal," she said and pulled out her phone.

She raised her one eyebrow with an evil smirk, goading me. I tried not to laugh but ended up chuckling as I recited the last two digits. My phone vibrated in my pocket with a message notification.

I pulled out my phone and opened the message.

> Unknown: This should be fun.

I quickly saved her number and replied.

> Me: Can't wait 😊

> Kriti: Lol

She chuckled at the one eyebrow-raised emoji I sent her. She gave me a quick salute and walked out of the kitchen, leaving me staring at her retreating form.

This should be fun indeed.

4

Song: Sawaar Loon
- *Monali Thakur*

Kriti

Being a teacher was my lifelong dream. Ever since I was a kid, I would pick up my old books and play pretend teacher. I'd buy a red pen, wear Maa's saree, sit at my desk, and put fake remarks, checks, and grades in my old notebooks. Once Rati and Kartik started their school, I'd drag them to be my pretend students, making them do their very real homework, call me "Kriti teacher," and even dole out punishments like sit-ups, the silent game, and being a chicken for ten minutes.

For the past five years, I have been living my dream. Not only was I a teacher of my favorite subjects, but I was also the class teacher, aka the homeroom teacher, of a ninth-grade class.

The best part of being a class teacher was my sense of accomplishment and pride when my students scored well, topped the class, or won in school sports. Also, when my kids felt they could come to me with any problem, they believed that I wanted the best for them, and we formed lifelong bonds. But the worst part of being a class teacher was parent-teacher meetings.

Like the one I was in right now.

They were a different kind of hell when the parents of one of my top students were hell-bent on stopping her education this year. This wasn't a surprise for me. Every year, I encountered two to three parents who wanted their daughters to quit studying after ninth grade to help their fathers at the farm or learn household chores. My job was to convince them to let their daughters finish tenth grade, the first milestone for every Indian student. My ultimate goal was to convince them to let their daughters complete their undergraduate education. But for parents who were adamant about pulling their daughters out of school, tenth grade was sometimes the most I could achieve.

"Teacherji, Rani has no use for studying anymore. We need her to learn more chores and farming so she can help her husband and in-laws. She needs to keep them happy," Rani's mother, Pramila, said.

Rani stood between her parents, staring at the floor. Her shoulders hunched, quietly losing her hopes for her future.

"Pramilaji, Rani is a brilliant student. Her grades in mathematics and science are exceptional. I understand that a woman should keep her husband and in-laws happy." I rolled my eyes internally but continued, "But if she finishes her tenth and twelfth grades, her life will be so much more secure. What if something were to happen to her future husband or family? What if they refuse to support Rani? Without any education, she would be helpless. If she finishes her twelfth grade or even a college degree, she will be able to support herself."

At that, her father said, "Look, Teacherji, if Rani knows how to work a farm, how to work a household, she would be a better help to her in-laws and a better support to her husband. If she is a perfect daughter-in-law, there is no way they would refuse to support her. In fact, they would rely on Rani for everything."

Such parents made my blood boil. How could they refuse to see the value of education? Why were they so scared of an unmarried daughter but had no problem supporting an unmarried son?

Steeling myself, I bolstered my authoritative teacher gaze and looked at them. "Rani is your daughter first. Raise her and support her as *your* daughter, not a daughter-in-law to some unknown people. Please, I request you, let her finish her schooling. You never know what kind of a husband she would have. One never knows. Give her the ability to leave him if and when she needs. Make her capable enough not to just support herself but to also support you and her future family. Don't you want that for her?"

I never enjoyed telling parents how to raise their children, especially in front of the children. But sometimes, the kids, the girls, needed to know they were worthy and deserved to be treated better.

Silence. That blessed silence when the parents had no logical argument to counter with. They were considering giving their daughter a chance. They just needed that little push.

"Do you have any sons, Pramilaji?" I asked. I never addressed fathers directly—they always took everything as a challenge.

Pramilaji shook her head. "No. Just five daughters."

I knew it. That was usually the pattern. "Rani is the oldest?" I asked.

The father said, "Second oldest."

So if my assumption wasn't wrong, the oldest was already taken out of school and married at a very early age.

Rani didn't look up as her parents talked. But her hands tightened into fists.

I could feel her anger.

I looked at her parents. "That can be tough. Having to marry off all the daughters. Dowry for all of them. I can understand your situation. But consider this: What if your brilliant daughter finishes her education? What if she earns enough to support her siblings? To support you? And when she marries, she will be capable of supporting her in-laws too. In fact, she might earn her own dowry. And if she finds a good family, a good husband, he wouldn't ask for a dowry."

Rani's father's eyes shone with unshed tears. He joined his hands and said, "Don't give us or my daughter false hopes and dreams, Teacherji."

"These are not just hopes. This could be a very real life for your daughter if you let her finish her education. Don't worry about the education of all your daughters at once. The younger ones are already studying for free. Soon, Rani will help you with the education of your other daughters. Just have faith in your daughter."

At that, like a well-timed machine, Rani looked up at her parents, her eyes pleading. "Please let me study, Baba." And she proved her brilliance.

Finally, the parents crumpled. "Okay, beta. But we will take one year at a time. If you don't score well in school, then no more school for you."

Well, they didn't entirely crumple. But I didn't need to worry about Rani. She was the topper of the class. And the joy on Rani's face right now was the only reason I needed this to work. She clutched my hands, tears running down her cheeks. "Thank you, Kriti teacher. Thank you."

"You're welcome. Now go tell the news to your friends."

After she ran off, I asked the parents to fill out the customary forms and bid them goodbye. Days like this kept me going. If I could help even a few girls from being forced to drop out, I would gladly work this job forever.

Since Rani's parents were the last to leave, I looked at my empty classroom and took a breather. I drank some water and opened my phone. There was a notification of a message.

> Aakar: Hey, all good on your end with your parents?

A smile instantly spread across my face when I saw his message. I had received it about two hours ago but hadn't had the time to open it in the middle of discussing grades and performance with parents.

I thought back to when I'd asked Maa to give me time to think. She'd balked at first, then started ranting about how Aakar was the best rishta proposal I'd ever received. She claimed she wouldn't be able to find someone better, so we needed to be quick and say yes to the guy before he got snatched up by someone else.

It had been a long and tedious discussion, but in the end, she'd given up arguing and granted me two weeks to decide whether I wanted a second meeting.

> Me: Hey.
>
> Me: Well, I told her you were good. But I needed some time before I agreed to a second meeting. I was given two weeks. What about you?
>
> Aakar: Told Maa I'd think about it. That should last me a few weeks.
>
> Me: Great! Hopefully, my maa stays patient.
>
> Aakar: How is your day going?
>
> Me: Just stopped a girl's parents from pulling her out of school. Phew. You?

Before I could overthink it, I hit send. After packing all my things into my big purse, I headed toward the staff room, nodding to other teachers and students along the way.

The school day was almost over. The primary and secondary level students finished school at 12:30 p.m., whereas the higher secondary level students were dismissed at 1 p.m. Since I taught the former levels, I always had to wait half an hour for Rati and Kartik to finish so we could go home together.

When I reached the staff room, most of the teachers who didn't have any lectures to take in the last period had already left, including Meera. I quickly packed a few homework assignments I needed to check and sat in my chair to wait for Rati and Kartik.

My phone beeped with an incoming message, and my face stretched into an involuntary smile.

> Aakar: Wow. You've had quite a day. I'm glad everything worked out. My day was certainly not as interesting.

> Me: So tell me about your uninteresting day.

I cleaned up my desk a little, arranging the homework assignments and classwork in separate piles by grades. Right then, my phone pinged with a new message.

Quickly, I opened it and roared with laughter. Aakar wrote these paragraphs instead of sending short sentences in quick succession.

> Aakar: Sat in three meetings discussing emerging market trends and a potential partnership with a new client. Followed up with a few inventories that have been delayed. Did two interviews for the new assistant manager we need to hire.

> Me: Wow. That sounds incredibly boring and exhausting.

Aakar: Lol. You have no idea.

Me: How many people do you employ?

Aakar: About 50.

Me: Wow. That's impressive.

Aakar: Thank you! Enough about my boring day. Since you're living your dream job, tell me about your dream vacation.

Me: I haven't given it too much thought.

Me: But I would love to go spend a few days at a beach someday.

Aakar: So you'd choose a beach if given the choice between beaches and mountains?

Me: Ha. Definitely.

Me: The sound of the crashing waves, the feel of the cool water and the sand at my feet, the smell of the ocean.

Me: What about you? Beaches or mountains?

Aakar: Mountains. Definitely.

I burst out laughing.

Me: What? Why?

Aakar: I love driving. The long, winding roads. How the views of the horizon change at every curve, the crisp air at a higher elevation, the feeling that you're on top of the world.

Me: Stop it. I'm not changing my answer.

> Aakar: I didn't ask you to. But I'm sure you'll fall in love with mountains once you come to one with me.

> Me: You haven't come to the beach with me before. Pretty sure you'd forget all about your precious mountains.

Just the thought of sitting in the car with Aakar while driving along the long, winding roads had me blushing down to my toes.

I got up and made my way to the school parking lot, knowing that the last bell was about to ring. I was almost at our two-wheeler when it rang. I quickened my pace before the hoard of running students stampeded me. It was like we were their jailers, and they were being let free after years of torture.

As I waited for Rati and Kartik to appear, my phone pinged again.

> Aakar: We'll just have to see about that.

> Me: Tea or coffee? Preferred beverage?

> Aakar: Is that even a question?

I chuckled, knowing that the majority of Indians had tea in the morning.

> Me: Coffee, then?

> Aakar: Haha. Funny. You do not want to see me before I've had my chai.

> Me: Noted ;)

Right then, Kartik jumped in front of me, almost causing me to drop my phone. I lightly slapped his back in reprimand.

"You almost made me drop my phone."

"Didi, shift back. I'm going to drive today."

I scoffed. "Not before you turn eighteen. You can practice later around the house. But no way are you carrying me and Rati all the way home. Now, get back."

I quickly typed a message to Aakar.

> Me: On my way home. Driving. Ttyl.

Rati placed her schoolbag at the front of the vehicle. She got behind me, and Kartik took a seat behind her. In no time, we were on our way home. We always traveled in triples. It used to be easier when the twins were younger, but the past two months had me thinking about buying a car. But Maa, being Maa, had refused because she wanted me to invest in gold for my marriage. Her words were, "Once you're married, your siblings can use the two-wheeler. None of us need a car."

By the time we got home and freshened up, Pappa was home from his office for his lunch break. He was a government civil engineer in a good officer position and enjoyed plenty of benefits, including the luxury of coming home for lunch. Maa had already eaten before the rest of us came home.

Once we were all seated at the table, Maa served us while Rati and Kartik talked about their day and the loads of homework they had. Both of them were studious, and this year, being their twelfth grade, they were taking their studies very seriously.

I recounted today's school incident as I devoured the aloo gobi, rotli, dal with mango pickle, and buttermilk on the side. I opened the rotli container to get one more rotli when Maa clicked her tongue in disapproval. "Kriti, you've already had three rotli. Do you really want to have more? If you keep eating like this, no man would want to marry you."

I slammed the container shut. This was becoming an

everyday headache. I used to love my mother. But as I grew into a "marriage age," my relationship with her seemed to have deteriorated.

"Could you get me some water?" Pappa asked Maa.

Maa nodded and went into the kitchen. Quickly, Pappa handed me one of his rotli, which was the one with extra ghee. He gave me a sly wink that lightened my sour mood. I quickly devoured half of it before Maa returned.

But of course, Maa figured it out because she turned to Pappa and said, "You keep spoiling her like this, and it will be on you if she doesn't get married."

I kept my head down and ignored her rambling until I'd finished every bit of my lunch. I didn't care if I was fat by marriage standards. So what if my clothes came from the large and sometimes extra-large rack? I loved my body. I was healthy, my curves were plenty sexy, and my body kept me functioning just fine. In fact, I was up on my feet all day. I helped out Maa when she needed, helped the twins in their studies when I could, paid for their coaching classes, and exercised every day. I was happy with what I had.

If a man was to marry me for just my body, I didn't want that man.

I was perfectly capable of staying single for the rest of my life rather than living a life of misery and judgment.

Once finished with lunch, I cleared the dining table and washed all the dirty dishes. I didn't utter a word to anyone except for a smile for Pappa when he left to return to work.

I got to my room and picked up one of my favorite romance novels for some mental relief. After reading a few pages without the hero or heroine succeeding in lifting my spirits, I checked my phone.

Aakar: Okay. Talk soon.

And I must have been truly out of my mind because I just had to ask him.

> Me: Tell me something, Aakar. Why does every man in these arranged marriages need a slim and trim wife?

∽

Aakar

I was in the factory basement where we stored all our textile samples when my phone pinged with a notification. Hoping it would be Kriti because I had been irrationally waiting for her message since I last texted, I quickly opened the message app.

And my feet stopped moving.

> Kriti: Tell me something, Aakar. Why does every man in these arranged marriages need a slim and trim wife?

Where did that come from? Did something happen? Did someone say something to her? What the fuck.

Kriti wasn't "slim and trim," as she put it, but she was fucking gorgeous. She had curves that had me reeling the first time I saw her. Every dip, every curve of her body, made it so fucking difficult for me to sleep at night. If I wasn't thinking about her messages, about our conversations, I was thinking of *her*. Her *body*.

I dreamed about the filthiest things that I wanted to do to her. I woke up unsatisfied and frustrated and *hungry*. How could she be shamed for a body that had me constantly burning with need?

That wouldn't do at all.

I rushed back to my office and closed the door behind me. I

turned on the air conditioner because either it was too hot right now or this message had me boiling with rage.

Since we were communicating through modern technology, I could see she was online, and she would've already gotten those blue tick marks informing her that I'd seen the message.

Before she could say anything else, I typed the first thing that came to my mind.

> Me: Who told you that?

> Kriti: Don't act stupid. There's a reason we have a section on weight and height in the biodata. I just didn't put mine in because, clearly, it was too much for my mother.

I flinched. Yeah, I'd forgotten about that. Not wanting to spook her or appear as a creep, I decided to go with a more objective answer on what "men" must be thinking.

> Me: I guess when you don't really know anything about the other person, you sort of create an image of a wife from the media you consume around you. And these days, all the heroines in our movies are very slim and trim.

I prayed that this was a proper answer.

> Kriti: This implies that the men see themselves as the hero. If you want Alia Bhatt or Deepika Padukone, you must be on the level of Ranbir Kapoor or Ranveer Singh. And I've never met such smoking hot men. Including you.

I burst into laughter. She was honest. And very mad right now. What I wouldn't give to see her face.

> Me: Lol. If I was that smoking hot, I wouldn't be working in my family's textile business. But give me a month, and I can grow a beard as good as Ranveer Singh 😉

Kriti: Ha. I shouldn't have been rude. Ignore me. I'm just a little mad.

She might be a *little* mad, but I was raging fucking mad. Nobody had a right to make her feel inadequate. And I wanted to know what caused her this insecurity. More like *who* made her question this. My fists were clenched so tight I had to pry my fingers open to be able to text her.

> Me: And who told you to get slim and trim?

Kriti: Who else? Every girl's best friend and her biggest enemy. My mother, of course.

I snorted. I'd heard my aunt asking my cousin Ria to eat less on occasion too. But Ria had the genes of her father. She never gained any weight. But I understood how mothers got a little crazy if their daughters weren't married by twenty-five.

> Me: You never asked me if I preferred slim and trim women.

Kriti: Didn't want to know.

> Me: What? Why?

Kriti: Mostly because I don't care. I've seen myself. And I love my body.

This woman could make me smile and my cock rock hard with just three sentences and a no-fucks-to-give attitude.

Kriti: I just asked that question because I wanted to know if slimness is genuinely something that men care about, or have all the mothers and women created this stigma that only slim women are beautiful?

Kriti: And I wouldn't have liked any of your answers.

Kriti: If you'd said you like slim women, I would have been a little mad and a little hurt.

Kriti: If you'd said you don't like slim women, I would have felt like you're just interested in me for my body.

She clearly had a lot of thoughts on the matter. I read and reread her messages. And yes, from her perspective, it made sense. And her confidence. *I've seen myself. And I love my body.* I read that line over and over again, need pumping through my veins to see her for myself.

And I loved that she loved her body. Nothing made me more attracted to her than her confidence.

Me: You're amazing, you know that?

Kriti: That's it? I typed so much. You just give me five words?

Kriti: And thank you. 😊

Me: You do remember that I asked for your number, right? I had the best time talking to you then, and I've had the best time talking to you today. Even though you are a little scary when mad. And I'm glad you don't care about my opinions on your body. It is your body after all.

Kriti: Exactly.

But why did I desperately want her to know that I really

found her attractive? Would she appreciate a little flirting? Would she consider it too much too soon? I didn't want her to get affected by her mother's opinions again.

> Me: But if you ever want to compliment my looks, you are always welcome to make me feel better.

Kriti: Lol. You know you're good-looking.

> Me: So do you. But I'm glad you find me good-looking. Thank you.

Kriti: You're welcome. 😊

> Me: If you want me to return the compliment, just say the word. I'm ready. 😊

Kriti: I'm not going to fish for compliments.

> Me: You're not. I'm pleading you to allow me to compliment you.

Kriti: Fine. I'll take some.

> Me: Not all? 😊

Kriti: Save some for later.

> Me: Fine. You're fucking gorgeous, and I couldn't stop looking at you the day we met.

No response for a few seconds. Did I take it too far?

Kriti: Thank you... 😊

Kriti: Don't you have any work?

I looked outside the glass wall of the office. The inventory was ongoing. I could make a few calls for shipment and invoices. I knew I was becoming an irreplaceable pillar of our company since I was involved in almost every tier of the work.

My father and uncles were entirely reliant on me and even asked me to hire more people to whom I could delegate more menial tasks that took up much of my time.

I had plenty of work lined up. But nothing that I actually wanted to do right now except chat with Kriti.

> Me: Don't you?

Kriti: <attachment> I do.

She sent me a picture of piles of notebooks and her younger siblings studying in the background. I took a picture of the view of the office and people working and sent it to her with a message.

> Me: Same. Talk later?

Kriti: Yes. Bye.

I looked around my office. The thought of my impending task of verifying the accounts versus the inventories and cataloging the reports the employees prepared was already giving me a headache. I could only hope that Kriti's day was going better than mine.

It was late when I got home, so I quietly entered the house. I removed my shoes at the entry, put them on the shoe rack, and went to the living room. I found Abhi, my younger brother by eight years, and his childhood best friend, Karan, watching football.

The moment he noticed me, he asked, "What took you so long?"

I dropped beside him on the sofa, Karan on his other side, and checked the teams playing and the scores. Without removing my eyes from the screen, I answered, "Got held up by some work. Everyone asleep?"

He hummed in agreement as he munched on popcorn.

The three of us watched the match for a while in silence when Abhi said, "Mom was talking. Wondering what you thought about the last girl you saw."

I thought about Kriti and her last reply. I hummed and said, "Let's see."

Abhi scoffed, shared a look with Karan, and turned to me. "You're just stalling, aren't you? You don't want to have an arranged marriage at all, right? Do you have a girlfriend or something?"

I frowned. "I mean, I know I started looking because of the promise I made to Maa after letting Akira run away to Sam, but it's not all bad. Where else am I going to meet someone?"

Karan shrugged and piped in, "I don't know. Ideally, in college. Maybe at work. Or friends' friends."

I couldn't help but roll my eyes, discarding all the possibilities.

"What about you?" I asked Abhi.

He turned to football, not meeting my eyes, acting all casual. "What about me?" he asked.

"Have any girlfriends?" I asked.

He shrugged. "Nope."

I looked at Karan next, who was already smiling and shaking his head. "Nope."

I nodded and remembered what Dad had asked me to ask Abhi. "Since it's your last year of undergrad, do you have any plans for the future?"

Abhi looked at me, his stare blank. "Is that you asking or Pappa?"

I chuckled. "Whoever you want it to be. For now, just me."

Abhi was currently pursuing a Bachelor of Business

Administration (BBA), a course he easily convinced our dad to allow him to do.

Abhi nodded, shared another look with Karan, and said, "I was thinking I could do my MBA in Mumbai or something."

I couldn't help but sit straighter. "Are you serious? Do you not plan to join the business? And why Mumbai? Ahmedabad has good MBA colleges."

Abhi didn't meet my eyes, just grumbled as I tried to catch his words. "Don't make a big deal out of it. I'm still thinking."

I pretended to relax and sit back because the idea of Abhi leaving the house was crippling. I loved my brother and sister. And I loved living together. Seeing them grow, being there for them when they needed me, and just having them around soothed something deep within me. With Akira in America, losing this one more connection had my heart racing. "Do you plan to start your MBA right away after graduation, or do you wanna have one or two years of work experience?"

Now that I hadn't disregarded Abhi's idea, he turned to me. "I don't mind having some experience. You think I should start spending some hours at our office?"

A wave of relief flooded over me. Sharing some of the god-awful accounting responsibilities with Abhi would free up my time to work on something I enjoyed, and it had me doing a happy dance in my mind. "For sure. If you want to come to the office on your free days or for a few hours each day, I can show you some of our accounting stuff. I would love your help."

"Really?" Abhi asked, eyes wide, disbelief on his face.

"Of course."

"Cool. I'll let you know." Ending the conversation, he returned to watching his game.

Tired of the day and needing to chat some more with Kriti, I got up from the sofa. I wished the boys a good night, got a cold bottle of water from the fridge, and took it to my room. Yes, I had a personal room. Ria and Akira used to share a room, but since Akira went to New York, Ria, too, got a room to herself.

Once in my room, I quickly turned on the AC, locked my bedroom door, and went to the attached bathroom for a quick shower. Once I got into my bed, I picked up the phone.

> Me: If you're awake, good night. If you're asleep, and you see this in the morning, good morning.

Kriti: Did you just get home from work?

> Me: Oh, you're awake. Yeah. Just got home. Had a lot of work.

Kriti: Had a lot of work, or is this your way of stalling your mom?

> Me: Potato, Pah-ta-to.

Kriti: Lol. You don't need to sacrifice rest and sleep for our getting-to-know-each-other scheme.

> Me: Guess I'll have to face her questions soon enough.

Kriti: Anyway. I'm off to sleep. Talk to you tomorrow?

> Me: Ofc. Good night!

Kriti: Good night.

5

Song: Tu Hi Hai
- *Ali Zafar, Arijit Singh, Amit Trivedi*

Kriti

The loud murmurs and laughter echoed down the hallway of the school in the early morning. I walked quickly to my class, thankful for my low-heel sandals that complemented my pink-and-green salwar kameez, and greeted the teachers I passed.

The moment I stepped into my ninth-grade classroom, the entire class stood and greeted me with a good morning in the same tune that seemed to be passed down through generations. It sounded cute when the kids were in first grade, but they looked completely ridiculous when they crossed seventh grade. Yet nobody ever tried saying good morning in a different way. The same singsong tune always made me want to sway my head in its rhythm.

I greeted them with my normal good morning and quickly took their attendance before the prayer bell rang. I was just done noting all the present students when a short bell rang, and everyone stood. Every school decided their own prayers, but every school in the country had at least a fifteen-minute prayer time. A crackle came over the overhead speaker in the class, and soon, the prayers began.

I walked between the rows of benches, occasionally glaring at the students who thought that closing their eyes and joining their hands in prayer wasn't cool anymore. Once the prayers were done and the bell for the first period rang, everybody pulled out their science textbook to the chapter "Reflection of Light." I pointed at a random student and asked her to start reading the chapter out loud.

I always made my students read the chapters because I would be the only one paying attention if I started reading. As the student read each paragraph, I explained the concept of reflection of light, how an image is formed on a mirror, and how light travels. I drew diagrams on the blackboard, and the students noted everything in their notebooks.

This was what I loved—teaching something new to my kids every single day. People often forgot how important the job of a teacher was. We shaped our students. They spent six to eight hours every day for over ten years in these rooms. Their minds, their knowledge, and their behavior developed in these rooms. It was a teacher's job to teach something new, something valuable to their students every single day.

And they did it not because they couldn't find any other job but because they chose to be teachers. It brought us joy to watch the kids grow and learn. I put every bit of my energy into engaging the students, getting them to ask questions, and making them laugh.

By the time my first period was over, I was ready for the next class with the eighth graders and the one after that with the *mature* tenth graders.

The recess bell rang after the third period, and finally, I had time to breathe. I walked to the staff room and dropped beside Meera, who was busy texting on her phone. As soon as I sat on my chair, she turned to me.

Her eyes widened, and she clutched my hand, looked around, bent closer to me, and whispered, "Are we not going to talk about how you and Aakar met? You have to tell me everything."

"First, how come you never talked about Aakar with me?"

She shook her head, wondering the same thing. "I don't know. After Pappa passed away, Aakar's dad mostly came to help us. And then, Aakar would occasionally check in. Only after Luke came to live with me did Aakar show up a little more. And I was barely able to accept his help, let alone talk about it."

I squeezed her shoulder. Meera hated accepting help from anyone. You just had to start helping her and force her to deal with it. "It's okay. I'm just glad that you know him. I need all the details."

Since Meera already knew Aakar, I needed to know whether talking to him behind my parents' backs was safe. We picked up our tiffin boxes and stepped out into the little courtyard outside the staff room. We sat in a cozy alcove in the corner and laid out our lunch between us. Since my mother was hell-bent on sending me salads, I was on a mission to feed half of it to Meera while I ate half of her lunch. Today, she'd brought pulao, while my lunch was a salad of cabbage, carrots, beets, cucumbers, tomatoes, and a half-cut lemon to squeeze over it. Well, it did complement the pulao.

We only had twenty minutes for the break. While it wasn't enough for a word-by-word explanation, it was plenty to give Meera the basics.

"So you guys have been chatting for a week now? Every day?" she asked as I ate a spoonful of her delicious pulao.

I nodded and, after swallowing the bite, said, "Yeah. Some

days, we chat a lot, and some days, it's just a few words. But pretty much the whole week."

Meera's smile widened, and her eyes had this teasing glint that every best friend gets when talking about men. "So," she stretched out the word, waggling her eyebrows, "are you having fun?"

Just the thought of Aakar had a stupid smile spreading across my face. "I'll be honest. He is one of the best men I've ever met through these arranged meetings. He's smart, handsome, and hardworking, and so far, very forward-minded."

She chuckled at that. "I'm not surprised he didn't bat an eye at your three conditions."

"You're not?"

Meera shook her head. "He was born and brought up in a big city. His sister studies in America and has an American boyfriend. He helped his sister run away from home when their parents were being difficult. And time and again, he has helped me. He is a pretty stand-up guy."

My heart warmed at the thought of Aakar helping his sister run away from home. Of course, he wanted a love like that. Listening to everything Meera said about Aakar, I couldn't help but feel a small ray of hope. Maybe being married to a man who believed in love, who helped two people get together, wouldn't be the worst idea after all.

The bell rang, indicating the end of recess, and we rushed into the staff room, picked up our respective books and purses, and left for our classes. The rest of the day flew by as I spent a lot of time laughing and shouting at my students, and even more time waiting for the school day to be over so I could text Aakar.

THE MOMENT I stepped inside the house, with Rati and Kartik two steps ahead of me, I knew something was up with Maa. The three of us exchanged glances, not wanting to get roped into her rants, so we tiptoed to our rooms while Maa kept talking loudly. I was pretty sure she was on the phone with her sister. By the time we'd all freshened up and made our way to the dining area for lunch, Maa had already set the table and was still on the phone.

I sat at the opposite end of the table from my mother, with Rati and Kartik seated along the sides. When she met my eyes, I raised my eyebrows in question. She mouthed her sister's name, confirming my suspicion. We waited for a few minutes for Pappa. As soon as we heard his scooter pull into the gate, Kartik started stacking rotlis on his plate. By the time Pappa had washed his hands and taken a seat on my right, Maa bid goodbye to Sunita Masi—Masi being a term of respect for the aunt who is the mother's sister—and gave me a hard look.

My hand stopped midway as I was about to take a bite of rotli and tindora sabji. "What?" I asked, quickly eating the bite.

"How was your meeting with Aakar?" she asked.

Maa had cornered me with this exact question the moment I returned home from Meera's place on the day of the meeting. I'd told her it was good. I didn't know what prompted her to ask me the same question again. My hand slightly shook as I ate another bite and tried to act nonchalant as I chewed my food. My conversation with Aakar flashed through my mind, especially when I had told him that I would just say yes for him while he would be the one to delay. And he had agreed.

I took a deep breath and said, "I told you that day. It was good. He was smart and respectful. Why?"

"Did you say anything rude or inappropriate to him?"

I gasped, feigning innocence. "Inappropriate? Me?"

Rati and Kartik laughed, and even Pappa couldn't help but

smile before quickly wiping it off at Maa's glare. "Kriti," she warned.

Relenting, I answered, "No. I was my usual self. I don't know if that's inappropriate for you."

Maa simply huffed. She turned to Pappa, then back to me, and said, "Then why haven't they called? It's been a week."

I looked helplessly at Pappa. He sighed and patted Maa's hand. "Things might happen differently in the city. What do we know? Maybe they will call in a few days."

Maa nodded, a hopeful spark back in her eyes. "You don't think I should just give them a call myself?"

"We're not that desperate, Maa," I snapped.

Maa snapped back at me. "You are twenty-eight. I'd say we are desperate."

There was no point arguing with her when she brought up my age. I shook my head and got back to eating. I had no idea why she was so desperate to marry me off. I wasn't living off their money; in fact, I contributed to the household income and bought my own things. Even though I lived with my parents, I liked to believe I was completely independent. And I would gladly move out like people do in other countries if it weren't for the "what will society say" drama that Maa would bring up.

Once everyone finished lunch, Pappa left for work, Maa went into the living room for her afternoon TV serials, Rati and Kartik went upstairs to study, and I cleaned up the dining area and the kitchen. After all the dishes were done and everything was spotless, I was sweating and tired.

I went to the living room and sat on the unoccupied sofa across from Maa, turning my attention to the TV serial she was watching. Her eyes were glued to the screen, nodding and shaking her head at the actors, and I couldn't help but smile at her. She wasn't all bad, my mother.

I was lost in the drama unfolding on the television when my phone beeped.

Aakar: Hey.

My heart began to race, and a tingling feeling grew in the pit of my stomach. Anticipation. Excitement. After our last conversation and hearing all the good things about Aakar from Meera, I was thrilled to receive his message.

Me: Hi...How are you?

Aakar: Same old. Work. It's my lunch break. Thought I'd message you.

Me: What are you having for lunch?

I cringed at my message. I wish I had something interesting to talk about. But how was I supposed to come up with exciting topics out of thin air?

Aakar: Ugh. Lukewarm rotli, reheated aloo gobi sabji, and cucumber carrot salad.

A chuckle escaped me, and without looking at me, Maa chided me with a swish of her hand. I hummed at her and got back to texting.

Me: What's the ugh for? Salad? Aloo gobi?

Aakar: All of it.

Me: Haha. You don't like rotli sabji?

A few seconds passed before his reply came. And instead of watching the TV serial drama, my eyes were glued to the phone while he typed.

Aakar: I like it just fine. But I hate eating out of a tiffin. Everything tastes awful from a tiffin.

> Me: Oh. That's too bad.

Aakar: What else is up with you?

I looked at Maa, who was busy nodding along with the drama, her lips slightly parted. I thought back to the conversation during lunch. Should I mention it to Aakar? It certainly wouldn't hurt him. And maybe it would be good if he knew what was going on.

> Me: Maa asked me if I was inappropriate during our meeting.

Within two seconds, Aakar's reply popped up. I loved his fast replies.

Aakar: What? Why?

> Me: Lol. She's worried because she hasn't heard back from you or your family.

Aakar: Ohh...

> Me: Yeahh...What's up on your end? Any questions? Pressure?

I saw some typing. Then it stopped. It started again. My eyes couldn't keep up with the disappearing dots. Finally, after five whole minutes of staring and trying to turn the dots into an actual text, I got a reply.

Aakar: Can I call you?

And my heart stopped.

~

Aakar

My hands shook as I held the phone, waiting for her response. Maybe I shouldn't have asked her. What if she thought I was too forward? Maybe she only wanted to know me through messaging. But I wanted to talk to her, listen to her voice. And, honestly, it's really difficult to eat rotli sabji with one hand while texting with the other.

With great difficulty, I put the phone on my desk beside my half-eaten lunch. Our office had a small dining area where my father, uncles, and other employees ate lunch. Sometimes, I joined them. But other days, I liked to take the hour for myself. So I sat in my office on the second floor of our two-story building, looking at the bustling city outside during the lunch hour as the noise of traffic filtered through the closed window.

What if I ruined everything?

That thought caught me by surprise. I didn't want to mess up whatever was going on between us. It had been a while since I had a friend, a woman, to talk to. And it was so easy to chat with her. For some reason, she seemed to understand me.

The idea that my message might have made her uncomfortable bothered me deeply.

I tried to take a few bites of my food, my eyes glued to the unresponsive phone. I unlocked it and stared at my last message. The two blue check marks at the bottom of the message taunted me. If someone walked in and asked me what I was eating, I wouldn't be able to answer them. I tasted nothing. God, this was ridiculous.

I quickly locked the phone again and looked at my laptop screen. I ate a few more bites, pretending not to care about the lack of response. I willed myself not to check it again when I heard the notification.

I dropped the bite in my hand, quickly wiped my fingers with a paper towel, and picked up my phone.

Kriti: Yes.

A sigh of relief escaped me. One word. Just one word had me smiling like a fool.

Before she could change her mind, I plugged in my earphones—so I could eat while we talked—and pressed the call button. After two rings, she picked up.

For a moment, there was nothing. I stopped breathing, and it seemed like the world around me paused. Then I heard her soft voice. "Hello?"

I finally took a breath. "Kriti."

A soft exhale, and she said, "Aakar. Hi."

"What took you so long?" The question slipped out before I could stop it.

She chuckled. "It wasn't that long."

I couldn't help but scoff. "Believe me, it was."

A breathy laugh came from the other end, and I saw the reflection of my big smile on the black screen of my laptop. "So?" I asked again.

"Well, when you messaged me, I was sitting with Maa in the living room. I had to go to my room upstairs, and I found Rati and Kartik studying there. So I am on my roof right now."

I could imagine her walking through the house, looking for a spot. To talk to *me*. "Wow. You've had quite a journey."

She snorted. "And now you better have something really interesting to talk about after making me climb up on the roof."

I laughed. "I'm really sorry for that. Next time, I'll warn you and give you enough time to find a spot before calling."

"Please do." Her voice sounded amused.

I looked at my half-eaten food and realized I wasn't even hungry anymore. I cleared my throat and said, "Well, about what you asked me earlier. Maa kept asking me about you the day we came to meet you. The entire way, and the following morning, she was relentless."

Kriti laughed at that, and it made me smile.

"It wasn't funny then. I told her to give me some time to think. And every day for the past week, I've been leaving home early and returning home late. So, to answer your question, I haven't given Maa much chance to ask me anything about you."

"Must be nice," Kriti said.

"Only during the first few days. She'll soon remember I'm single and will go and organize three more meetings with women."

She went silent after that. "Kriti?" I asked.

"Sorry. I was just thinking. What are we going to do? Maa keeps worrying as to why she hasn't heard from your parents. And I can only hold her off for so long before she just calls your mother. I just had to warn you."

Right then, the door to my office burst open. I almost dropped my phone, but it was just Abhi.

With no care in the world, he entered my office, noticed the air conditioner was on, and quickly closed the door behind him. He raised an eyebrow at the phone in my hand and dropped into the chair across from me.

"Aakar?" I heard Kriti's voice in my ear.

"Ah. Sorry. My brother just walked in. And yes, I heard you," I said, trying to keep my words vague so Abhi wouldn't know who I was talking to.

Kriti chuckled. "Got it. So we're going to make our mothers wait as long as possible. Is that correct?"

I did my best to keep a straight face. "Yes, that is correct, Mr. Kirit."

She roared with laughter. "Kirit, huh? Is your brother still in front of you?"

I looked at Abhi, who was staring at his phone while he waited. "Yes."

"Okay then, I'll let you get back to work. Talk to you later."

Before she could hang up, I asked, "What would be the best time to call you?"

Kriti hummed. "I usually have to wait for half an hour for Rati and Kartik after I'm done with school. Since they're in a higher grade, they are dismissed half an hour later than me. So how about 12:30? Would you be able to get away from work then?"

I usually had my lunch around two, like right now. But maybe I could take a little break. I tried not to let my desperation show on my face. Abhi might appear clueless, but his ears would be glued to my conversation. "I think I can make it work."

"Great."

"Thank you, Mr. Kirit. Talk soon."

She ended the call with a laugh, and my heart burst with joy.

Abhi raised his brows. "Who was that? And what are you smiling about?"

I shook my head and, to divert the topic, I said, "Nothing, just work. What're you doing here?"

He straightened in his chair and frowned. "Didn't you say I should come to the office for a few hours and get some experience?"

Honestly, I never thought he would take me up on my offer. Abhi was, to put it mildly, a laid-back person. I rarely saw him angry, upset, or in a rush. So when he showed up at the office, I just assumed he needed something from me.

I straightened in my chair and put away my tiffin. "Well, welcome to the office."

He gave me a wide grin. "So put me to work."

I got up and raised a finger, asking for a moment. I took my dirty plate to the office kitchen, washed it, and put it on the drying rack beside the sink. After drying my hands, I grabbed two packs of masala chaas, or buttermilk, from the fridge and headed back to my office. I handed one to Abhi and inserted the mini-straw into my container.

"Thanks," Abhi mumbled, gulping down his buttermilk while I pulled up a few accounting files on my computer.

"You've brought your laptop?" I asked.

When he nodded, I motioned for him to pull up his chair beside me so I could get him started on something small.

"Let's get to work," I said, beyond excited to have my little brother with me.

The day passed by in a blur, with Abhi's nonstop questions, catching up on all the shipments and deliveries, and getting updates on clients from Dad and my uncles.

That night, when I went to bed, I saw an unread message waiting for me in the inbox.

> Kriti: I was actually nervous to talk to you on the phone. I've never had a man call me just to talk. But I'm glad you did.

My heart warmed at that, and I wanted to call her again. Right then. Listen to her voice. Her laughter. Her verbal jabs and quick wit. Her amused chuckles.

> Me: I'm glad you said yes.

And I pushed a pillow over my face just to stop my stupid smile at the thought of her.

6

Song: Do Dil Mil Rahe Hain
 - *Kumar Sanu*

Aakar: Are you a morning person or a night owl?

    Kriti: Night owl. That's the only time I feel like I get for myself.

Aakar: Same.

    Kriti: Do you have a favorite sibling?

Aakar: *Gasping emoji GIF* I ask you a simple question, and you drop bombs on me like that.

    Kriti: C'mon.

Aakar: You go first.

    Kriti: It's my question.

Aakar: Ugh. Fine. Honestly, I felt closer to Akira when she was here. Abhi is eight years younger than me. Growing up, we were in very different stages of life. But ever since Akira has left, Abhi and I seem to have gotten a lot closer. And you're evil. Now you go.

Kriti: I can't pick. They're both my favorite.

Aakar: 😵

Kriti: Kidding. I'll answer.

Kriti: I guess I'll go with Rati. We share a room, and we tell each other nearly everything. Teenage brother is a bit too moody.

~

Kriti: How many kids do you want?

A few moments—and Aakar coughing up his water—later...

Aakar: Give a guy some warning, would you?

Kriti: So...

Aakar: Haven't thought about it.

Kriti: Bullshit.

Aakar: A little girl would be nice.

Kriti: ONLY ONE?

Aakar: How many do you want?

Kriti: At least four.

Aakar: 💀 DEAD

> Kriti: Just kidding. But at least two kids for me.

∼

> Kriti: Who're you closer to? Mom or Dad?

Aakar: Mom

Aakar: By the way, she is HOUNDING me about you.

> Kriti: Oh! And how are you dealing with it?

Aakar: My usual - "I'm thinking about it."

> Kriti: Lol. Wish it worked for me.

Aakar: I was thinking…

> Kriti: Oh no

Aakar: Hush now. I want to meet you again.

> Kriti: Oh

Aakar: Is that a bad oh or a good oh?

> Kriti: A good oh

Aakar: Let me rephrase that. I want to meet you without letting the family know.

> Kriti: Even better. But how?

Aakar: I'll come to meet you. Would you be able to sneak out or hide it from your family?

> Kriti: Ha. What are best friends for? I'll be hanging out at Meera's place when you come to meet me.

> Aakar: Let's do it then. How about I come tomorrow for lunch, and we'll hang out till late afternoon?

> Kriti: Perfect. Since it's Sunday, using Meera as an excuse would be perfect.

Kriti

"I can't believe you're sneaking out to meet a guy," Meera said while we sat on her porch waiting for Aakar to arrive. He'd called and told me that he was almost there.

"Me neither."

I was beyond nervous. This wasn't just any guy. This was Aakar. The first guy I had met who was so handsome that my heart started to go haywire just thinking about him. Even if he hadn't been so handsome, the fact that he was so fun to talk to, he believed in my three conditions, and he was so devoted to his family was enough to make me swoon.

I adjusted my fancy dress shirt that I bought just yesterday for this meeting.

"You look amazing, Kriti," Meera said, her eyes shining with delight.

My cheeks reddened. "The jeans aren't a bit much? I don't want him to think I only wear traditional clothes."

"It's perfect. You look sexy, if I say so myself."

I couldn't stop the giggle that escaped me. Meera had come

out of her shell after meeting Luke. "Thanks, Meera. And you're sure your maa won't gossip about me going to meet Aakar?"

"I'm sure. She's not the gossip kind."

And she really wasn't. She usually minded her own business and didn't care what others said about them.

Right then, Aakar's car arrived at the gate of Meera's house. I quickly got up from the porch, grabbed my purse, and made my way to the car.

"Have fun on your date," Meera shouted as I made my way closer to the car.

I turned and glared at her, wondering if Aakar had heard her. She just winked and ran inside her house.

When I neared the car, Aakar was out the door and running toward the passenger door. Quickly, he opened the door for me. Our eyes met as I approached the door, and for a second, everything around us disappeared for me. It was just him and his soulful dark brown eyes, the way he looked so powerful and downright sinful in his olive-green shirt that stretched so deliciously across his chest and shoulders. His eyes flared as he took me in, his gaze causing goose bumps to erupt across my skin.

"Hi," I said, my voice coming out in a whisper.

He cleared his throat and gave me a small smile. "Hey, yourself."

As soon as I sat in the car, he closed the door behind me and ran to the other side. Once he was in, he quickly started driving and pulled the car on the main road.

I quickly stole a glance at him and, to my surprise, found him doing the same. We both burst out laughing, breaking the sudden awkwardness at seeing each other again.

As he drove, Aakar drummed his fingers on the steering wheel. "You look beautiful."

My heart fluttered and gushed, and I couldn't stop the red

blush heating my cheeks. I gulped. "Thank you. You look great too."

He gave me a wide smile, his neatly trimmed beard accentuating his jaw. God, he was so sexy. "Thanks, Kriti."

"So where are we going?"

"Well, considering that we're sneaking out, how about we go for lunch in the nearby city?"

"Good idea. I don't need any relatives or friends of my mom or dad to catch me."

He chuckled, and I was riveted. His hoarse sound, the way his eyes crinkled at the corners. I wanted to keep making him laugh. "Feels like we're in high school," he said.

"For you, maybe," I muttered. "I was just busy studying and being a good girl."

He coughed. "That's...good."

After a minute of silent driving, he said, "I'm glad you agreed to meet me."

Since I did not need to focus so much on the road, I turned in my seat and sat with my back leaning against the door to look at Aakar properly. His eyes widened when he saw me adjusting in the seat, and he quickly shook his head with an approving smile.

"Honestly, I'm glad you asked. I wouldn't even have thought about it. I've never made plans like these with a guy before."

"So no ex-boyfriends that I need to be worried about?" he asked, sneaking a glance at me before turning back to the road.

I chuckled. "Nope. What about you, the hotshot city boy? Do I need to be worried about any ex-girlfriends?"

He shook his head. "Nope, nothing to be worried about. I haven't dated in a long time."

I cleared my throat, nervous about asking him this. "So you've dated before?"

A light blush coated the top of his cheeks as his fingers

tightened on the steering wheel. "Not much. But yes. I've dated some."

Well, that was vague. What did *some* even mean? Two girls, ten girls, twenty girls?

Not needing to know more about it for now, I asked the most important question circling through my mind. "Um, would you call today a date?"

For the life of me, I couldn't look at him. I stared out at the road ahead of us as I felt his eyes on me.

"Kriti," he said, "would you please look at me?"

His polite words had me turning to meet his smiling eyes, and I instantly blushed. "What are you smiling about? It wasn't a funny question."

He chuckled. "I know. And I'm sorry if I wasn't clear on the texts. But yes, this is indeed a date, if you want it to be."

"What if I don't want it to be?"

His grin was even wider as he sneaked yet another glance at me. "Well, then it is two new friends grabbing lunch together."

That definitely wasn't what I wanted. So, with my heart pounding out of my chest, I mumbled, "A date it is."

This time, he didn't turn to look at me, but a wide smile stretched across his face, causing me to smile in return.

The silence in the car was broken when "Ajj Din Chadheya" started to play. I noticed it wasn't on the radio but on his playlist. He must've started the music from his steering wheel.

"Oh, I love this song. So you love 2000s Bollywood songs too?"

"Best era of music, if you ask me."

I chuckled. "What? It wasn't better than the old classics. But compared to what's been coming out these days, I'd agree. The 2000s were so much better."

The song talked about yearning for that one love the man was pining for, begging God to get him his love. The soulful singing by Rahat Fateh Ali Khan, the tune, and the smooth sailing of the car on the road—the drive completely enchanted me.

It felt so good to know that Aakar was such a peaceful driver. He didn't get mad at the traffic or the rash driving by others. He wasn't in a rush, nor did he get irritated by the honking of other vehicles.

He didn't even fret when there weren't any parking spots when we reached the restaurant. We drove a little farther to park and walked back to the restaurant, talking about our favorite singers.

Once we were seated, the server handed us each a menu. I looked at Aakar as he read it, his eyes focused on the menu, his hair styled in a way that looked as if he'd run his hands through it a few times, and the way his beard accentuated his jaw had me sweating.

"So what do you want to order?" he asked, looking at me and catching me staring at him. His lips turned up into a bashful smile.

I averted my eyes and looked at the menu. After a glance, an idea struck me. I met his eyes and found him looking at me. I couldn't help but smile. "How about we each pick our favorite dish and share?"

"Sounds perfect."

Considering we were at a multicuisine restaurant, I had plenty of options. When the server came to take our orders, Aakar said, "I'll have a spicy paneer burger. Make it a meal, please, with fries and a vanilla milkshake."

I couldn't help but rejoice at his order. I was already waiting to split the burger with him. When the server turned to me, I said, "I'll have a Manchurian dry and chili garlic noodles with a Coke on the side, please."

The moment he was gone, Aakar said, "I don't think a better order combo exists."

I laughed. "Definitely not."

As I took a sip of the water, I wondered about a question that had been plaguing my mind ever since I met him.

"Spit it out, Kriti. I can see you thinking about something real hard."

I chuckled and rolled my eyes. "Fine. I've been wondering why a guy like you is going for the arranged marriage option when you could have any girl you want."

Light red blush coated his cheeks. "You keep flattering me, Kriti. I don't know if you'll like this answer, but the main reason I agreed to meet women from these arranged proposals was because I promised my mother I would if she agreed to let Akira date her then American boyfriend, now fiancé, Sam."

My jaw hung open. Was he getting forced to marry through an arranged marriage? My horror must have been etched on my face because Aakar quickly added, "I only promised to *meet* the women. Not marry them."

"So is this all just an obligation to you?"

He drank a sip of water, probably trying to gather his thoughts, while I sat in bubbling anxiety. He met my eyes head-on as he said, "To be honest, it started out that way. I've met plenty of women since I agreed to my mother's condition. I realized early on that it wasn't a bad way to meet new women. It's not like I was actively dating or had anybody in my life. I was too busy with work and had no time to actively seek women. This just became a convenient option."

"Well, it kinda makes sense." It still made me feel like a second option. I mean, it wasn't like arranged marriage was *anybody's* first choice. Who wanted their parents to find a life partner for them? But most people like me, who were never allowed to date during college, who never even cared to secretly date, who didn't see any prospect at work, didn't have many options.

He looked me straight in the eyes when he said, "For the first time, I'm really glad I agreed to these meetings."

Heat rushed through my body at his admission. "Now you're just trying to flatter me."

He smiled. "I'm just being honest."

I rolled my eyes, but I still couldn't wipe the smile off my face.

"And it's not like I agree with the whole process. That's why I asked for your number. That's why I asked you to meet me secretly. I don't want to be bound by our parents' and society's systems of how an arranged marriage should be. If we're interested in each other, we should be able to talk and get to know each other as much as we want. I would also say we should be able to meet each other as much as we want, but considering you live four hours away from me, that proves to be a bit of a challenge."

"What you're saying sounds very much like dating."

"And what's wrong with that? Our parents did their part by introducing us. Now, we make the rules of how we get to know each other. Wouldn't you agree?"

I couldn't believe I was talking to a man who was so sure of his thoughts and beliefs. I admired that so much. I rarely, if ever, met men who weren't mama's boys or unorthodox in their beliefs. Someone who wasn't afraid to speak his mind. Someone who genuinely wanted to get to know me and made the effort to do that.

"I couldn't agree more. You have no idea how refreshing it feels to actually get to know a man on my own terms. Thank you for giving me that choice."

He simply nodded. "Just remember, you will always have a choice when it comes to me. If you don't want to talk or chat, just say so. If you don't want to get to know me anymore, just tell me. The moment you say no, I'll back off. It's your choice."

Just to test him, I asked, "What if I want to say yes?"

Aakar

Her words instantly sent me into an internal panic. "I mean, of course. Umm..."

She instantly burst out laughing. "Just kidding. I know it's too early. But good to know where your mind's at."

"Funny woman."

Right then, our order arrived.

My heart rate was still high as I drank some of my milkshake. Her words came back to me. *What if I said yes?*

"Dig in," she said, serving up the Chinese food on each of our plates. I divided the burger in half as I thought of her question.

Honestly, my panic wasn't because I wasn't ready to say yes. It was because of how much I liked hearing her *yes*. I barely knew her, but watching her take that big fucking bite of the burger, her silky shirt clinging to every one of her delicious curves, her large earrings and wavy hair framing her beautiful face, had me going rock fucking hard. And I knew her *no* would crush me.

We ate in relative silence as I got my dick under control and tried not to stare at her too much.

Once we'd eaten and I'd paid the bill, we walked back to the car. She moaned about being too full.

"I don't think I'll be able to have dinner. Those noodles and that burger were divine."

"We didn't even have dessert."

Once we were seated, I started driving as she grumbled about not having enough of an appetite for dessert.

Deciding to humor her for now, I kept driving along the long, winding road.

"Where are we going now?"

"You'll see."

"Oooh, a surprise."

"You like surprises?"

"I'm liking it right now. I haven't been surprised before."

"What? Never?"

I couldn't believe it. One would think people would keep doing special things for her just to see her beautiful smile.

"I mean, Rati and Kartik surprise me at midnight with cake every year. But I wouldn't call it a surprise. It's more of a tradition at this point."

"Makes sense. Akira and Ria constantly used to surprise me for my birthday. Not a midnight cake. That would've been too easy. Once, they decorated the office and turned it into a glitter fest. Another time, they called me home a day early, panicking that something had happened to Maa. I came rushing home, and boom, a hundred guests shouted *Happy Birthday* at me when it wasn't even my birthday."

She roared with laughter. "That sounds hilarious and terrible."

"Laugh away. It was horrible."

"Please tell me the place we're visiting won't scar me for life."

I smiled at the thought of where we were going. "You're going to love it."

"So confident," she teased.

We each took turns playing our favorite songs on the way when I took the final turn that clued her in.

"The beach?" she shrieked. "Oh my god. Oh my god."

I couldn't stop looking at her absolute delight and excitement. Her eyes shone like a million stars lighting up the midnight sky. Her smile and the sheer joy on her face could kill a man.

Fuck, I was getting poetic on her.

She'd already removed her pretty sandals by the time I parked the car.

She jumped out of the car as soon as I turned off the engine and literally started to power walk to the sand.

The waves crashing on the shore, the fresh smell of the ocean, the warm sand at my feet, and the white cranes flying nearby instantly relaxed me. Moisture clung to my skin as we started to walk—more like Kriti power walked, and I jogged—closer to the water.

The moment we were close to touching distance of water, Kriti bent down—holy fuck, she was sexy—and folded her jeans up. I guess we were going in the water. I followed her and did the same as she said, "If you'd told me before, I would've worn a skirt or a dress."

The thought of Kriti in a skirt—the ocean breeze making it cling to her curves and the ruined possibility of seeing her bare legs—had my heart crushing. Stupid, stupid, stupid. Fuck, I was so stupid. I looked at her, and I was sure she could see the utter disappointment on my face. "The biggest mistake on my part, and believe me, something I won't repeat."

Her cheeks reddened, and she stepped into the incoming wave, shaking her head.

We stood side by side, her breathing in the ocean breeze, the wind sweeping her hair, and a soft, beautiful smile etched on her face. She was simply breathtaking.

She looked at the incoming waves, the sunlight turning the water into sparkling gold and orange hues, when she spread her arms as if embracing the view. My body yearned to embrace her, pull her into my arms, and hold her against my chest as we watched the sun together.

"Beautiful, isn't it?" she said, her eyes stuck on the sparkling water.

I, however, couldn't pull my eyes away from her. "Very beautiful."

"Thank you for bringing me here."

"I'm glad I did. Seems like I do love beaches."

Her knowing smile had my heart pumping harder. She shook her head, her cheeks all red and her hair in total disarray. And I'd never been more transfixed before.

We started walking in the shallow water as waves crashed against our feet, talking for hours about everything and nothing.

It was one of the best times I had with a woman. I might not remember everything about our conversation from today. But I would always remember how her voice, her laughter, her smile, and that delighted twinkle in her eyes brought me so much more peace than the crashing waves or a long, winding drive along the mountains.

We reached Meera's place a little later in the evening, and I stopped my car outside her gate.

"So this is it," she mumbled with a hint of sadness.

And it made me irrationally happy.

I wanted to hold her hand so badly that I clenched the steering wheel tightly to stop myself from doing just that. "Don't say that," I said softly. "We'll be talking soon enough. And if you want me to come meet you, just say the word."

She looked at me with a shy smile. "I don't want to trouble you with the long, lonely drive all the way here."

I wanted to tell her I'd drive four hundred hours to meet her. But I was terrified of such a thought. "It's no trouble at all. I had the best time today. I don't even remember the last time I was on a date and had such a great time. You gave me that. So thank you."

"You gave me my first official date, Aakar. And I'm so glad *you* gave me that and made it so special and perfect."

Warmth bloomed in my chest at the thought of being her first date. Her first *anything*. I tightened my hold on the steering wheel, afraid I'd pull her into my arms. "So if you had a great time, would you still like to keep dating me? Keep talking and get to know me better?"

Her bright eyes shone, and her lips stretched into a wide smile as she nodded. "I would love it."

"Good."

"Good."

"I'm glad."

She smiled wider. "Off you go now. You have a long drive back."

My body ached with the need to pull her into my arms and kiss her goodbye. I'd even take holding her hand and kissing it. But I had to take it slow. Fuck.

I groaned in a dramatic way. "Bored of me, already?"

She shook her head in denial, her small, teasing smile getting my heart pumping a mile a minute. "Never. Just worried. Now, go."

The moment she was out of the car, she walked to my side as I opened the window. "And don't forget to text me when you've reached home," she said in a stern voice, the teacher in her coming out.

Her worry for me had me aching in an entirely different sort of way. Very few people worried about *me* rather than the other way around. "Yes, ma'am."

As I pulled away, I couldn't stop looking at her retreating form in the rearview mirror, my heart aching with a loss I didn't expect to experience. Fuck, I missed her already.

7

Song: Nazdeekiyaan
 - *Nikhil Paul George and Neeti Mohan*

Aakar

I was almost done with my work when I got a text from my school friend inviting me to an impromptu gathering at his place. I texted him that I'd be there soon, shut down my computer, and locked up the basement. I checked the two floors of the office, ensuring everything was secure before locking the doors. It was eight o'clock, and all the employees had already left. My father and uncles had gone about two hours earlier.

I got in my car, turned on the AC, and started the drive to my friend's house, blasting the latest Bollywood jams on the radio. I let out a breath, feeling the stress of the day begin to dissipate.

I had a bit of a drive ahead of me, which I welcomed. I loved driving—whether in a car, on a motorcycle, or a bike. I enjoyed watching the world pass by—the lights, the vehicles, the buildings, people racing through their lives. Everyone was going somewhere—some in a rush, some just enjoying the journey. At every red light, I looked around. I saw a family arguing in their car, a woman embracing her lover on a bike, and poor children rushing to beg, tapping on the windows of cars and two-wheelers. Some shooed them away like bugs, while others handed them a few coins.

As one of the beggar kids banged on my closed window, I grabbed the pack of Parle-G biscuits I kept in the dashboard for these purposes. I opened the window and gave him one. Seeing that, other kids rushed to my car, and I handed out the rest of the pack. I tried not to give them cash because you never knew if the kids got to keep it or what they ended up buying.

Soon, I pulled up outside my friend's house. A few vehicles were parked near the gate. As I opened the metal gate, the main door swung open, and my friend Varun stood at the entrance. I quickly jogged up the steps and gave him a quick handshake and a hug.

"How was the drive? Any traffic?" he asked.

"Same as always. Am I the last to arrive?"

He chuckled as I removed my shoes in the foyer. "Yeah, man. Everyone's here."

Varun was one of my few friends who didn't live with his family, so most of our gatherings were at his place.

"Pizza and drinks are in the dining room. Grab some," Varun said, going toward the living room where everyone had gathered. I lived in a dry state, but people always found a way to arrange some alcohol, especially for house parties.

As I grabbed a paper plate, my phone buzzed with a notification. Quickly—because I was pretty sure I knew who was texting me—I pulled out my phone and opened the message.

Kriti: What's up? How was your day?

Would I ever not smile when I got her message?

> Me: Nothing much. At my friend's place. Day was fine. The usual. Yours?

I quickly pressed *send* and grabbed three slices of pizza. I was famished. Before joining the rest, I clicked a picture of my plate and sent it to Kriti. I grabbed a soda—because I needed to drive—and went to the living room.

We were a group of five friends, three of whom were already married. Varun had a love marriage, while our friends, Soham and Nitesh, had an arranged marriage. Zayan and I were the only single ones in the group. Varun sat on the floor near the coffee table, his back against the sofa where his wife, Komal, sat. The rest were spread around the three sofas. Not wanting to sit in the middle spot, I sat down on the floor across from Varun, put my plate and soda on the coffee table, and dug in.

As everyone talked about random things and family updates, Soham's wife, Rashmi, got up, took the empty plate from his hand, and went to the kitchen. She returned with a glass of drink for him and took a seat beside him. Soon after, Varun stood and got himself another slice of pizza and refilled Komal's drink.

I wondered if Soham, who had an arranged marriage, would have done the same for his wife. What was it about an arranged marriage that always seemed to give men the upper hand, the privilege to be served by the wife? And why did it seem that there was always a little more affection, a little more openness between couples in a love marriage? Or was it just my assumption that every arranged marriage had a little less love, openness, and happiness?

Right then, I got a message from Kriti. I wiped my hands with a tissue and opened the message.

> Kriti: Wow. Now, I'll have to order some pizza soon. And is it a bad time right now? We can chat later.

I looked around and found everyone busy in conversation.

> Me: Keep talking. I meet them often enough.

I got up and disposed of the paper plate in the dustbin under the kitchen sink. After washing my hands, I saw Kriti's message.

> Kriti: So, what do you want to talk about?

I joined the rest of them and sat back on the floor, leaning against the sofa. I wondered for a second about whether I should ask her what I was thinking earlier.

> Me: Do you think people in love marriages are happier than the ones in arranged marriages?

I saw the blue ticks that indicated that Kriti had read my message. *Kriti is typing* showed up on the screen, and my heart started to beat faster, almost afraid of the answer. I didn't know what I wanted her to say. A minute passed, then two. She was still typing. I tried to appear more engaged in conversation with my friends, but I had no idea what they were talking about. My entire focus was on my screen, waiting for Kriti's message to pop up.

After what felt like hours, her message appeared.

> Kriti: I do think so, yes.

> Me: That's it? How come it took you so long to reply with four words? And why do you think so?

> Kriti: It's based on what I've seen. Like if I see Meera and Luke, they certainly seem happier than my own parents.

> Me: Maybe it's a generation thing?

> Kriti: I guess so. Maybe it depends on the people involved. It depends on what they want out of their marriage. And I wouldn't say it is just the man's or just the woman's job to bring happiness and love in an arranged marriage. So many men out there just want a wife to take care of them and make them happy. Have you ever heard a man say that he wants a wife because he wants to care for someone, support someone, love someone? It is always the other way around. And we women are always taught that it's our job to support our husbands, take care of them, do what makes them happy. There is always a power imbalance when it comes to most arranged marriages.

That was a very long message for her. I read it again. I looked at Varun and Komal, noticing the ease with which they sat close to each other and how Varun's arm casually hung over Komal's knee. In contrast, Soham and his wife sat a foot apart, his wife holding the empty glass of the drink that Soham had handed to her.

It hurt my heart to imagine myself in a relationship like Soham's. Did I truly want that? No. We all wanted the relationship that Varun had. That casual and honest comfort between two people. The secret smiles. The unconscious touches.

> Kriti: ????

Shit. I'd totally forgotten to reply.

> Me: Sorry, I got to thinking. That was powerful. And true. I need to leave and go home. Text you later?

Because I honestly had no words. If I wanted a marriage full of love like Varun and Komal, why was I going through the arranged marriage process?

"Aakar, you with us?" Komal asked.

I tuned back in to the conversation, and apparently, I'd missed a lot. "Sorry. I was thinking. What were you saying?"

She laughed. "I was saying, if you've not found any woman through an arranged marriage, I can set you up with my friend. I have two in mind."

She wiggled her eyebrows as if that would entice me.

I chuckled and joined my hands. "Please don't. My mother is enough. Don't you start now."

Everyone laughed, and before they could get into asking me about arranged marriage or actually set me up with someone, I got up. I stretched my arms and legs and said, "Okay, guys, I'm taking leave."

After dodging a few protests, I quickly ran out the door. I was wearing my shoes when Zayan turned up in the foyer, loudly saying bye to everyone.

At my raised eyebrows, he said, "The moment you ran, they were onto me with the marriage talks. It's like a crime to be single in a group these days."

I waited for him as he wore his sandals, and we were out the door.

"You want to go for some chai?" I asked, knowing I needed someone to talk to. Zayan was one of my best friends, and I valued his opinion.

"Sure. Meet you at High on Chai near S.G. Highway?"

"You got it."

We quickly got in our cars and arrived in a few minutes.

After grabbing a table, I placed an order of two chai as Zayan got out of his stuffy suit jacket and folded his sleeves to his elbows.

"So what's up?" he asked, getting straight to the point. That's what I liked about him. He rarely beat around the bush, always targeting the heart of the matter.

"So I met a girl through an arranged marriage meeting."

His eyebrows raised in surprise. "Okay..."

My stomach churned with nerves at having to put my feelings out there. "Well, usually when I meet women through these meetings, it's been a simple no, you know. It's just that this girl, though. I couldn't, for the life of me, say no."

His jaw dropped in surprise. "You said yes to her?"

"No, no. Not yet. We've been talking behind our parents' backs. I wanted to get to know her more but without all that parental pressure."

"And?" He leaned forward in his seat as if my premarital journey was the juiciest story he ever heard.

"And I'm fucking confused. You see Soham and his wife. Varun and his wife. Fuck. I don't want a marriage like Soham. I'm terrified of what my life would be like if I went through with an arranged marriage. It's not like I have too many great examples of an arranged marriage."

"And how does the girl you met through one of these meetings come into play?"

I rubbed my hand along my forehead. "She's the first girl who I genuinely enjoyed talking to. So much so that I drove back to Laxminagar and took her on a date."

Zayan pursed his lips in thought. "If you're enjoying talking to her, does it really matter how you met her?"

I took a sip from my chai. "But I did meet her through our parents. There is a certain time limit within which we need to decide. There's only so much you can know about a person in a limited time. And there are so many more expectations from our families when they actually *arrange* it."

"Man, forget about all of that. If you met this girl through someone else, if there were no families and their time limits and expectations, if it were just the two of you, would you be interested in dating her?"

There was only one answer to that question. "Hell fucking yeah. She's the dream girl."

He slapped me on my arm with all of his excitement. "That's my boy. Then go date her. Focus on the two of you and see where it goes. It's not like you need to make a decision right away."

"I'm trying to drag it out as long as possible."

"You'll figure it out. Just treat this as a regular dating experience. Forget about how you met."

I nodded, and we sipped our chai in silence for the next few minutes. We bid goodbye, and I promised to keep him posted about my relationship status.

Once back home, I quickly turned on the AC in my room, locked my bedroom door, and went to the attached bathroom for a quick shower. As soon as I got into my bed, I picked up the phone, reread Kriti's message, and sent her a reply.

> Me: Can I be honest?

It didn't take her long to reply.

> Kriti: Please.

> Me: I have never aspired for the kind of relationship I usually see in arranged marriages.

> Kriti: Has anyone ever?

> Me: Yet we're both looking for a partner through an arranged marriage.

> Kriti: I am. Life revolves around hope. And I hope to find love in an arranged marriage. I'm not opposed to a love marriage, but I haven't yet met anyone outside arranged marriage meetings.

> Me: Like you said in your previous message, it's about what you want in an arranged marriage.

> Kriti: What do you want from your future partner? From your arranged marriage?

I thought about it. I thought about what Kriti said about why arranged marriages end up how they do. The thoughts and expectations men have from arranged marriages. And how I desperately did not want that. I did not want what my parents had, what my uncles and aunts had, or what Soham and his wife had.

> Me: I don't know. But I definitely want someone to love.

> Kriti: :) Guess that's all anyone needs. Good night, Aakar.

> Me: Good night, Kriti.

8

Song: Tera Fitoor
 - *Arijit Singh*

Kriti

The loud bell signaled the end of the school day, and, as always, chaos erupted in the classroom. Some students had already packed their bags, some ran with a book or two in hand, and a few of my patient students quietly packed their bags, let the crowd pass, wished me goodbye, and walked out of the class. Usually, I loved my patient students, but today, I cheered for my rowdy bunch who didn't like to stay in after the bell.

I checked my watch—it was twelve-thirty. Quickly, I plugged my earphones into my phone and put in the earbuds. We hadn't decided who would call whom, and I didn't want to waste a minute of our half hour, so I dialed Aakar's number. After just two rings, the call connected.

"Just hold on a second, Mr. Kirit," Aakar said.

I couldn't help it; I giggled. I'd never had a man talk to me in secret and make up lies on the spot for me. "Take your time, Mr. Aakar. I'm on my way out of the class."

I put my notes and pens in my purse and checked the classroom for any missing items, all the while hearing Aakar moving around on the other side.

"Just a minute," he whispered, and my heartbeat sped up. It sounded oddly intimate. Closer.

I mumbled, "Don't worry about it."

Soon, I was out of the classroom, and Aakar said, "I'm here. So sorry for that."

The hallways were almost empty as I walked toward the exit. "It's okay. Were you busy? We can talk later if you'd prefer."

His response was quick. "No, no. I had assigned some work to Abhi, and he had a few questions. And when it comes to Abhi, I'm afraid he would lose interest in the work and stop coming to the office if I don't help him out properly."

"He would leave? Just like that?"

He chuckled. "Well, he just joined the office to get some experience. He's helping me out with some accounting, which I hate. So I don't want to run him off too soon."

I laughed as I stepped outside the school and stood under the covered steps leading to the parking lot. "Smart. I make Rati prepare charts and drawings for my schoolwork, and Kartik makes the best chai in the house."

He laughed out loud on the other end. "Some of the few perks that come with being an older sibling."

Leaning against the wall, I waited for Rati and Kartik with my lips stretched into a constant smile. "Right? How is your day going? Other than putting the little brother to work?"

He scoffed, and I could feel his smile in his words. "Same old, same old. I can work on more pressing matters now that Abhi is handling some accounts. What about you? How was school?"

"Same old for me too. But still, pretty good."

"What's the plan for today?"

"Nothing special. Go home, have lunch, correct some assignments, and maybe go for a movie with Rati and Kartik. They've been on me about it for the past two days."

"What kind of movies do you like to watch?"

Well, there was only one answer here. "Romantic movies, of course."

He groaned loudly in my ears. I knew it wasn't anything sexual, but his groan sent tingles up my spine. "No, Kriti. C'mon. They're so dramatic and cheesy and ridiculous."

I gasped dramatically. "How dare you? They're emotional and romantic and with the best grand gestures that make me believe in the soulmate love."

"There's no such thing as soulmates."

"Of course, there is."

"Nope. That instant attraction is just dopamine and serotonin. It's just science."

My hand tightened around the phone. "I'll show you *science*."

His loud laughter in my ears had blood rushing up to my cheeks. *I* did that. I made him laugh, and that made me unreasonably giddy.

Just to keep the conversation flowing, I asked, "What do *you* like to watch?"

"Comedy movies if it's Bollywood and action if it's Hollywood."

I scoffed. "Of course. You're such a guy."

"If I must tell you, those movies also have a lot of emotions in them. And romance."

"Sure there is."

"I'm gonna make you watch some of them so you believe it."

"Ha. Only if you watch some of my recommendations."

"Deal. Text me a list of your favorite movies, and I'll text you mine. We'll compare notes later."

"Deal."

Despite having such opposing choices, I realized I was smiling. Aakar wasn't mean or condescending about my preferences, which made it easier for me to share more of myself with him. I realized that I really wanted him to know me. And every little thing he shared about himself with me just made me greedier for more.

We talked about random things, debating and laughing about our opposing views for the next few minutes when the loud bell indicating the end of school for Rati and Kartik rang, silencing any conversation for a few seconds.

Once the bell stopped ringing, Aakar said, "I think our time's up for now."

A herd of students came rushing out of the main staircase, pushing each other out. I tried not to show my disappointment at having to end the call. "Yeah. Talk soon?"

"Yes. I'll text you."

His words brought this giddy joy inside me that I'd never experienced before. "Can't wait."

After a goodbye, we ended the call.

I saw Rati and Kartik walking down the stairs when a message popped up.

> Aakar: Since you couldn't wait ;-) Thanks, Kriti. I can't wait to talk to you more. Half an hour wasn't enough.
>
> Me: :-) Soon...

When Rati asked why I was smiling, I had absolutely no answer.

The three of us drove back home on my two-wheeler. Rati

and Kartik bickered nonstop in the background as my conversation with Aakar played on an endless loop in my mind.

Half an hour was certainly not long enough.

～

Aakar: Did you ever want pets?

> Kriti: Nope

Aakar: What? Why?

> Kriti: Duh. Cuz I'd be the one who would've had to take care of it. Rati and Kartik would just play with it. All the feeding and bathing and pooping responsibilities would fall on me.

Aakar: But how cute would a dog be?

> Kriti: Would gladly play with somebody else's cute dog.

Aakar: What if I wanted a dog in the future?

> Kriti: Well. Umm. Who would take care of it?

Aakar: Both of us? Equally?

> Kriti. What if I say no? Would you take responsibility?

Aakar: You drive a hard bargain, Kriti.

> Kriti: You're the one who wants a dog, Aakar.

Aakar: Fiiine. I'll take care of it. You can just play with it. We can also get Abhi and Soham and the kids to take care of it too.

> Kriti: Now that sounds like a great idea.

Kriti: What makes you angry?

Aakar: That's a broad question.

Kriti: Not really. Except if there's a whole lot of things that make you mad.

Aakar: Not a whole lot of things.

Aakar: I guess I hate it when people lie to me or hide things from me.

Kriti: Speaking from experience?

Aakar: Yep. Akira. She didn't tell me when she started dating her boyfriend.

Aakar: She didn't tell me when she got serious about him.

Aakar: She didn't tell me she was planning to announce it to the whole family.

Aakar: I would've helped her had I known. I would've been able to plan it better. I wouldn't have been left behind to put out fires that could've been avoided.

Kriti: That sucks.

Aakar: Yeah, well. What about you? What makes you mad?

Kriti: Umm. When people start making judgments without even getting to know me.

Aakar: Speaking from experience?

Kriti: A hundred experiences.

Kriti: Especially when you're a curvy girl. People just assume that I'm a lazy couch potato.

Kriti: I've been given countless advice on how to exercise. How to diet.

Kriti: There's also me being more focused on my job than finding a husband.

Kriti: Trust me, I hate it when I'm the topic of someone's judgments and comments. If you truly want to know me, just talk to me. If you want to give me advice, just think if I really want your advice, especially if it doesn't affect you.

Aakar: I'm with you.

～

Aakar: Animal movie - Yes or No?

Kriti: NOOO

Aakar: Lol. Yes. C'mon, the action sequences?!!

Kriti: The story 😜

Kriti: Yeh Jawaani Hai Deewani - Yes or No?

Aakar: Eh.

Kriti: EH???? It's a BIG YES. The most romantic movie in recent times.

Aakar: Predictable and cheesy and the main leads were barely together.

Aakar: Andhadhun - Yes or No?

> Kriti: YES. It's a masterpiece.

Aakar: Thank God.

∼

Aakar

I'D BEEN WORKING on expanding our business in more directions than my dad and uncles. In today's day and age, it was crucial to keep changing and evolving per market trends. It wasn't just working on innovative ideas regarding our business. The first step had been convincing Dad and my uncles to approve new ideas. Sometimes it took more time to convince them to accept emerging trends and ideas than to implement those ideas in practice. Those were the challenging days at work.

By the time Abhi and I got home around nine o'clock, I was exhausted.

I removed my shoes in the vestibule and could already hear the loud volume of the television and the chatter from the living room. Walking in, I found my grandparents engrossed in a soap opera where the heroine could turn into a snake. Maa was sitting at the dining table with Ekta Kaki, talking on a video call, probably with Akira, while Ria was having dinner beside them, occasionally joining in the conversation.

Before Maa could catch me, I swiftly climbed the stairs and headed to my room. After a quick shower and changing into my T-shirt and sweatpants, I headed downstairs for dinner. Abhi was already seated at the table, halfway through his meal, talking to Akira with the phone propped up in front of him.

I walked behind him and bent down a little to fit into the video camera. Akira's eyes brightened, and she said, "Bhai, all good?"

I smiled at her and gave her a thumbs-up. "First class. You?"

As she updated me on how busy she was, I grabbed a bite of paneer paratha from Abhi's plate. He groaned, making Akira laugh. I was about to grab another bite when he shouted at Mom, "Maa, Aakar Bhai keeps taking all my food."

Just then, Maa came out of the kitchen with a plate piled high of paneer parathas. I quickly grabbed the plate from her hands—because I was famished—and took a seat beside Abhi while Maa sat on the other side. I added some yogurt, coriander chutney, and ketchup to my plate and dug in.

For the first few bites, I completely lost track of what Abhi, Akira, and Maa discussed. Only when Abhi knocked his elbow against mine did I notice both him and Maa staring at me with expectant looks.

I swallowed my bite. "What?"

Maa rolled her eyes as Akira laughed on the phone. "See how he completely ignores me?" Maa said, looking at Akira.

Maa turned the phone to face me, and Akira said, "Aakar Bhai, come on. Tell us."

"Tell you what? I didn't hear the question. I was eating."

She rolled her eyes. "Well, what did you think about the woman you met? Kriti. Remember?"

Kriti's name had my heart racing, and it took a solid effort not to let it show on my face. Inside, my mind scrambled to find a proper response to the three very expectant faces.

I cleared my throat, took a sip of water, and said, "Well, I remember."

"And?" Maa asked, her eyes wide, voice impatient.

"Well, she was good. Decent."

"Do you like her? Are you gonna meet her again?" Akira asked.

She was way too interested in my arranged marriage situation, considering she was sitting in America with an American boyfriend. I glared at her, warning her with my eyes to keep her excitement in check so as not to get Maa overly excited.

But it was clearly too late because Maa too joined in. "Should I give them a call to arrange a second meeting? We need to make quick decisions here, Aakar. We don't want to lose this opportunity if you're remotely interested."

"Yeah, bhai. Maa is right." Abhi jumped in, clearly missing out on all the fun. I glared at him, earning a reprimand from Maa from over his shoulder.

I should've said no. I should've delayed giving them an answer. But all I could think about was a chance to meet Kriti again, to talk to her in person. And for the life of me, I couldn't deny myself—or my mother.

"Fine," I said, trying to sound a little put out. "You can arrange one more meeting if Kriti is interested as well."

Maa's excited squeal had both the aunts come running. Even my grandparents turned down the volume of their TV serial.

Maa turned to them with a maddening glee. "Aakar has finally agreed to meet a woman for the second time. I'll give her mother a call first thing tomorrow morning."

I rolled my eyes at the cheering from everyone, while inside, my heart pounded in excitement.

Maa took the phone from me and turned to Akira. "Oh Akira, once Aakar gets a wife, I can completely relax. She can handle Aakar, wait for him at night, serve him dinner, and care for him. And I'll finally get a daughter-in-law to help me out around the house. We can be like those cool mother-in-law and daughter-in-law pairs who shop together. It would be so much fun."

Well, it was good while it lasted.

My hand shook as I took a sip of water. Anger clouded my vision. "Handle me? Take care of me? And what if my wife is a working woman? How will she help you?"

Maa frowned at me, confusion clouding her face. "Well, beta, of course she can work. I wouldn't expect her to leave her job. It's just that she can help me around the house once she's home. And naturally, she'll be the one to take care of your needs once you're married. You don't expect me to wait around and serve you dinner when you have a wife, do you?"

She then turned to Akira and asked, "Akira, beta, am I wrong?"

Akira stayed silent, clearly not wanting to agree with Maa's outdated thoughts. So I pressed further, "What if my wife is too tired after work to help you around the house? And what if she doesn't enjoy shopping?"

Mom turned redder with every question I asked. She sputtered, "Well, why wouldn't you marry someone who can take care of you and help your family? You wouldn't mind if your wife relaxes on the sofa while your mother and aunts toil in the kitchen?"

"Are you hearing yourself? Work takes time and effort. You don't see me or Pappa helping you out when we're back from work. So if my wife comes home from a long day at work, I wouldn't expect anything from her."

Mom frowned in indignation. "If you must know, Aakar, women can manage both work and family. They even raise kids while they work. Your wife wouldn't be the only one with responsibilities toward her new family. And what happens when you have kids? Would she leave them to us at home?"

"That's it." I stood with the plate in my hand. I went into the kitchen, put the dirty dishes in the sink with the rest, washed my hands, and came out to find Mom ranting about how every daughter-in-law helps around the house.

I couldn't help but jump in. "Maa, why are you going on and on about needing help around the house? We have two helpers coming in every day, and Raju Kaka to help in the kitchen. If you still need more help, we can hire more people. I didn't agree to an arranged marriage to find you a housemaid. I agreed to find a wife for myself. If you want me to keep seeing women for these arrangements, you need to be prepared to face the fact that even if it's an arranged marriage, our choices might be entirely different. And I will only marry the woman that I choose. If that's a problem, then I won't marry at all."

I didn't wait for her response and walked back to my room.

I couldn't help but wonder if being the first child came with a curse of never escaping your parents' expectations.

9

Song: Jashn-e-Bahara
- *Javed Ali*

Kriti

It was late at night when my phone vibrated with an incoming call. Rati was busy on her phone on the twin bed beside me, with only a small nightstand separating our beds. As the vibration continued, she turned to me and asked, "Who's calling you so late?"

After a moment's thought, I decided to go with the truth. I had never really hidden anything from my sister, and I didn't want to start now. Softly, I said, "Remember Aakar? The man who came to see me a few weeks ago?"

Her eyes widened in excitement, and before she could launch into a hundred questions, I raised my phone and waved her off. I quickly picked up the call before it stopped ringing and, before Aakar could say anything, I said, "Hold on a second."

I got up and went out onto the attached balcony. Closing

the door behind me for privacy, I said, "I'm here. Everything alright?"

For a few seconds, there was nothing but silence. Then, in a thick voice, Aakar said, "Um...I don't know why I called."

He sounded tired. And a little bit sad. I couldn't help clutching my phone tighter. "Something happened at home?"

A harsh laugh escaped him. "Something like that. It's like there are all these expectations that I must live up to—be the businessman that Pappa wants me to be, bring the perfect daughter-in-law for Maa, and be the dependable older brother for Abhi and Akira. Why do we constantly have to live up to the expectations set by everyone around us? Be the perfect version for each of them, regardless of how we feel. Do you feel that too, or is it just me?"

I looked at the quiet street below the balcony, the vehicles parked along the street, the silent sounds of the night as I mulled over Aakar's words. "Sometimes I do," I said, thinking about my own family.

"I guess today just got to me. And I'm afraid that marriage isn't going to help me out either."

"What's that supposed to mean?" I asked.

Maybe he didn't sense the warning in my tone, or maybe he didn't care, but Aakar continued, "Well, after marriage, I'd be responsible for a whole new person. Be her perfect version. Keep her happy."

"Well, unlike your other family members, your wife would have the same responsibility toward you. Keep you happy. Be the kind of person you want."

He scoffed. "Believe me. That might be the least of her worries. I'm afraid she might get too busy pleasing and keeping up with my family to even care enough for me."

Now I was sure something had happened. "You do remember that you're talking to one of your marriage prospects, right? Are your words supposed to reassure me or warn me off?"

After a few beats of silence, he said, "I'd rather you not be warned off. I just asked Maa to arrange a second meeting with you."

A gasp escaped my mouth, and my heart started beating rapidly. Sweat gathered behind my neck as I asked, "Really?"

Softly, Aakar murmured, "Really."

"You have a terrible way of showing your continued interest in me."

His warm chuckle in my ears soothed something inside me. "What was I supposed to do? The moment I told her that I was willing to meet you for the second time, she went on and on about how she could relax once she gets a daughter-in-law."

Aakar told me all about his conversation with his mother, his voice becoming more animated by the second. "Kriti, it's not that I don't understand where they're coming from, but they constantly make me feel as if I'm here to fulfill their goals. And if I'm being honest, hearing my mother's words, I was more terrified for you than me."

The poor, sweet man. I couldn't help but laugh. "Aakar, I don't know if I should feel sorry for your naivety or touched by your concern for me. I am already living a life where I work, help out my mother in the kitchen, help my siblings with their studies, and deal with my mom's constant complaints about one thing or another. I've never had the luxury of putting my feet up once I'm back from work."

He huffed. "Now you're just making me look bad."

I chuckled. "Well, you were feeling responsible for me."

"Exactly. I didn't know you were a superwoman and in no need of defense."

My cheeks warmed at his compliment. "Maybe you should have more faith in the person you eventually choose to marry. You don't have to be responsible for everyone and everything. It might do you good to share your responsibilities with her rather than take everything upon yourself."

"Maybe I should."

"So I'm guessing your parents will soon give my parents a call to set up a day?"

Now that Aakar was calm, his voice came out lighter. "Yep. Pretty sure it will be the first thing Maa does tomorrow morning."

Maybe now wasn't the best time to inform him about my conversation with Mom this afternoon—more like her order, my protests, her sharp words, and my eventual surrender. Or maybe it was the darker part of me compelling me to let Aakar know that I wasn't just sitting around waiting for him. *More like Maa isn't waiting around*, my mind whispered. I rolled my eyes at myself and tried to focus on what Aakar was saying.

I made an effort to pay attention, giving appropriate responses and sounds of agreement, all the while deliberating the right course of action.

"Kriti, you alright?" Aakar's question brought me back to the present.

I cleared my throat and decided to go with it. "Umm...Yeah. Sorry, I was, uh, thinking."

"About?" he asked, his voice gentle yet curious.

I leaned over the balcony railing and looked at my half-chipped nail polish, trying to find the right words. "Well, whether it was appropriate to tell you that Maa has fixed a meeting with a man the day after tomorrow."

Four agonizing heartbeats later, Aakar uttered only one word, "Oh."

"Oh?"

He cleared his throat, and I heard shuffling in the background. "I mean, thanks for letting me know, I guess. And, of course, it's appropriate to tell me. Wouldn't you want to know if the situation was reversed?"

"Would you have told me if the situation was reversed?"

Aakar made a slightly frustrated sound. "I would like to think I would have."

Now that I'd told him, I could breathe a little easier, even though talking about it turned the conversation from friendly to uncomfortable and awkward. I could sense Aakar trying to find words. Maybe it was my guilt or a sense of imbalance that made me say, "I did tell you the day we talked about exchanging numbers that my mother was likely to line up more guys for meetings. And you told me to do what I must."

This time, his voice caused goose bumps across my neck. "I did, didn't I?"

We were silent after that, not knowing what to say, afraid that one wrong word could shake things up. And still, I didn't want to say goodbye and escape the conversation.

"Day after tomorrow, you said?" he asked.

I made a sound in the affirmative. After another beat of silence, I closed my eyes and, shaking my head in reprimand, admitted, "I did argue against it, you know."

A soft chuckle came over the line, and I could feel Aakar's smile when he asked, "Like a lot?"

I couldn't stop the blush that spread across my cheeks as I shook my head. "A lot."

"I would've done the same thing." His honesty soothed the jagged edge of vulnerability that had been poking my nerves.

"I know. You already did."

Even though he had argued with his mother about her expectations of his future wife, I knew he was terrified *for me*. Or the wife he would have. Nevertheless, it meant something to me. It was an assurance that he would stand against his mother if she were in the wrong. Aakar was reasonable and trustworthy. He was a man who would support his wife and take care of her wants and needs, even if it came at the expense of his happiness.

"Yeah, well," he murmured.

I smiled. Things felt more right now. Not perfect, but right enough. "Good night, Aakar. See you soon."

"Soon, Kriti. I'll let Maa know to schedule our meeting as soon as possible."

"Okay."

"Good night, Kriti."

"Good night, Aakar."

Even after we ended the call, I stayed on the balcony, feeling a mix of relief and trepidation. I was glad I'd told him about the meeting, but I was terrified of what came next.

∼

THE NEXT DAY, Maa practically burst with happiness. I half expected her to break into a cheesy Bollywood song about weddings as she twirled in the kitchen, informing my masi about how in demand I was. She went on and on about how a family was coming to see me tomorrow, and Aakar and his family were scheduled for Friday, the day after tomorrow.

Aakar's mother certainly didn't waste any time calling my mom once Aakar agreed to the second meeting. She had called around nine in the morning, and by ten after nine, Maa had messaged me with about twenty emoji exclaiming her joy. I just sent her a thumbs-up and returned to the staff meeting to discuss the logistics of our annual sports day in two months.

I loved and hated school functions like these. They involved endless meetings, petty fights among teachers trying to do the least amount of work, and staying extra hours to get everything in order. There were decorations, invitations to parents, gathering equipment, setting up water and snack stations, and arranging extra security.

The only reason I loved these events was the smiles on the students' faces. They always seemed to get a little relief from their studies and personal struggles. Events like these gave them a reason to let go, engage in healthy competition, and have fun with their classmates. All the extra hours and quibbling with other teachers were worth it.

The moment Rati, Kartik, and I were back home, Maa pulled me into a hug and swayed me side to side. I couldn't remember the last time she was this happy or even the last time she had hugged me. Rati and Kartik shared smiles behind Maa's back and, with a few teasing remarks, left the living room.

I pulled out of the hug and said, "Maa, you need to calm down. It's just two men, not a line outside our house."

She waved her hand in the universal sign of shut up. "You won't understand. I was losing hope just a few days ago, and look at you now. Two rishtas in two days."

I rolled my eyes at her. "Rishta implies it's a proposal. These are just two meetings in two days." And just to temper her excitement, I said, "And you need to calm down, Maa. You're making me nervous."

She gasped. "Oh no. Don't you get nervous at all, beta. I'll get the lunch set up. You go freshen up. Your father will be home soon."

I spent the rest of the day preparing charts for sixth-grade science class, checked the homework assignments of my ninth-grade students, and went to Meera's place to help her pack. She was planning to leave the village soon and move to Ahmedabad, and I wanted to spend as much time with her as possible.

The next day, I returned home from school in a sour mood. During lunch, while correcting notebooks in the afternoon, and even as I started getting ready, one thought kept playing in a loop in my mind: Aakar did not call me today. We usually talked while I waited for Rati and Kartik, and even if he couldn't call, he always texted me. Why didn't he call today? Was he busy? Upset? Did he care enough to be upset for so long? Didn't he realize that I didn't care at all about today's meeting?

It was merely an obligation.

I wasn't looking forward to it like I was to Friday. Just thinking about seeing Aakar again caused a riot of butterflies in my stomach. I was already wondering what I would wear when Aakar came, what we would talk about, and whether I would feel the same warmth and comfort in person as I did on the phone.

With these thoughts swirling in my mind, I got ready to meet another man. This time—for the first time—I prayed it wouldn't work out.

∼

Aakar

Friday.

How could I be so stupid?

I should have told Maa that I was only available on Thursday. Maybe then Kriti's parents would have canceled the meeting with that other guy today. I wasn't usually the insecure type. I'd never had a long-term girlfriend. Not that Kriti was my girlfriend. And I was the one who had told her to do what she must. I knew how Indian moms of unwed daughters could get. I understood every valid reason for Kriti to meet this other prospect.

And still, I did not like it.

Just then, the door to my office burst open, and Abhi walked in. "Yo, bhai, we're ordering samosa and kachori. How many for you?"

I was supposed to be focusing on work and managing my new team. And here I was, lost in thoughts about Kriti. What would she wear for the other guy? Had he read her biodata? What if the other guy liked her and said yes to her?

My stomach soured at the thought.

"Bhai?" Abhi repeated, his eyebrows raised in question at my silence.

"I can't eat."

He frowned. "Why?"

"Acidity. Just count me out."

"Should I get you an antacid?"

My thoughts wandered once again. What if Kriti liked that guy back?

I quickly got up from my chair. "I'll get it myself."

Maybe an antacid was the cure for this sour taste at the back of my throat and this burning sensation in my stomach.

I went to the office pantry, grabbed some medicine from the first-aid drawer, and popped one in. As I took a big gulp of water, my gaze fell on the wall clock above the fridge, and I nearly choked. It was 5:30 p.m. This time tomorrow evening, I will be meeting Kriti.

Right now, she was probably meeting that other guy. There was a reason I didn't call Kriti today. What was I supposed to say? *Hey, are you excited about your meeting today? Hope you have a good time?* Nope. Wasn't gonna happen. And I refused to think about it anymore.

I splashed some water on my face at the sink, wiped it with my handkerchief, and headed back to my office. I had work to do.

By the time I finished an important meeting and updated a presentation, it was already eight o'clock. Abhi, Dad, and my uncles had left over an hour ago. I locked the office and got into my car, turning on my playlist and blasting the AC. The random music always helped shift my mood.

As I drove my usual route, I let the cool air and upbeat Bollywood party songs wash over me. At the traffic light, I handed out some biscuits to the beggars tapping on my car window, moving on as the signal turned green without letting the sting of pity settle in.

I refused to let thoughts of Kriti and the what-ifs bog me down. When did my feelings toward her shift from let's see where it goes to why does she need to meet other guys?

How did people in arranged marriages make the decision to marry someone so quickly? What made them say yes after just a few meetings? Was it love? A mutual understanding? A compromise?

I knew Kriti and I were seeing where it went, but the thought of her talking to another man did not sit well with me at all. I wanted to scream at her and tell her that she didn't need to talk to any other man when she had me. *I* was here.

One date and a few hundred text messages later, I was getting entirely too possessive of Kriti.

In the world of arranged marriages, I'd reached a point where meeting another woman felt wrong to me. Damn, I thought this arranged marriage business was supposed to be less complicated than love marriages.

When I reached home, Maa had already packed her bag and placed it in the foyer.

At the dinner table, I asked her, "Why the entire suitcase?"

She placed one more paratha on my plate. "I thought since we're going on a Friday, we'd stay the entire weekend. We'll visit our village temple, help Meera and her mother with some last-minute packing, see if they need anything, and stay at our village house. It's good to keep visiting the house. It keeps it warm and welcoming."

Of all the things Maa listed, I heard only five words: we'd stay the entire weekend.

Three days to meet Kriti.

Endless opportunities played through my mind, my mood shifting from sour to elated. My mind kept shouting, "In your face, other guy," to the imaginary, monstrous version of a guy it had created. A guy I'd never met, and pray to God, I never would.

After dinner, I packed my bag, paying far more attention than usual to my choice of clothes, belt, shoes, and handkerchiefs. I freshened up for bed, lay down, and stared at the slow-moving fan, the plain navy curtains, my desk bursting with ironed clothes, my desktop, notebooks, water bottle, and board games.

I stared at everything and anything except my phone.

My phone with no new messages.

She must know I hadn't texted because it would be too awkward. But why hadn't she texted me? What possible reason could she have not to text me a sweet, innocent, one-word Hi?

Fuck this.

I turned off my phone, got up, put the phone in my desk drawer, walked back to the bed, and rolled under my blanket. There, now, I won't be tempted to text or to hear the stupid vibration of an incoming notification.

With stupid thoughts and unstoppable what-ifs swirling in my mind, I went to sleep counting down the hours before I met Kriti.

～

WE ARRIVED at Kriti's place at five o'clock and were welcomed just like last time. The difference was in who all came with me. This time, to my utmost displeasure, almost all of my family members had tagged along. Apparently, since it was the first time I had willingly asked for a second meeting, my entire family was hell-bent on meeting the "miracle girl." So here we were—my parents, Abhi, Ria, her parents and her younger brother, my younger uncle and aunt, and their kids—waiting for someone to open the door.

Kriti's father opened the main door, and her mother stood in the foyer to lead us all to their living room. There, standing by the sofa, was Kriti.

Her hands clutched the edge of her dark red and navy dupatta. Her hair fell over her gorgeous curves in dark brown waves. My stomach clenched with sudden arousal, and I looked away to Maa and Abhi to prevent an embarrassing situation. But holy shit. Did she keep getting hotter and more beautiful every time I met her?

As I took a seat on the chair perpendicular to Kriti's, our knees brushed together. I didn't move away. To my pleasant surprise, neither did she. As the elders and kids settled down and engaged in customary conversation, I tried to sneak a look at Kriti. It would have been so much easier if we were seated across from each other. How was a man supposed to look at his…uh…prospective wife without alerting the adults when they were seated so close?

My mother introduced Kriti to everyone in our family, and the entire time she said namaste to each person, I watched her. Her light golden salwar kameez was almost muted by the bold red and navy dupatta. Her sharp eyes hadn't once turned to me. A big red bindi adorned her forehead, and dangling gold earrings swayed every time she talked and nodded her head.

I'd forgotten how beautiful she was.

Whether she wore traditional clothes or jeans, bindi or no bindi, or laughed at me or sat stoically without meeting my eyes, she made my heart pound.

The introductions were done. The pointless conversation was getting out of control when the elders kept finding common connections—be it friends, family, relatives, or neighbors—just to find common ground to make themselves feel at ease.

And still, Kriti didn't look at me.

I knew because I never stopped looking at her.

So many questions popped into my head. *How was your meeting with the guy? Did you like him better than me? Why didn't you call last night?* How could I be so full of questions, so angry at my desperation, and still not be able to look away from her?

Kriti's younger siblings, both sixteen years old, brought trays full of chai and snacks. Kriti and her mother helped pass them along to everyone. When she handed me the cup of chai, our eyes met for a brief second. At that moment, I saw it—hurt, repressed anger, and hard eyes full of doubts and accusations. My own eyes probably mirrored the same emotions because she quickly looked away and took a seat with her own cup of chai.

That was all I could take. I might have been patient and calm, waiting for the parents to initiate the formality of letting us talk in private, but the hurt in Kriti's eyes changed everything.

I placed the cup on the coffee table, turned to Kriti's father, and asked, "Can I take Kriti for a drive? If you don't mind?"

Everyone stared at me, their eyes wide and mouths agape. I would have laughed if I wasn't so impatient to get Kriti in my car, drive off, and hash everything out. My father looked ready to come to my defense, while Abhi seemed to struggle not to smile outright.

To my surprise, Kriti's father recovered much faster than her mother. "Uh...of course, son," he said, glancing at my family for confirmation. At my father's nod, despite the befuddled look on his face, I got up from my seat.

I waited for Kriti to get up, a polite smile pasted on my face. She didn't take long. Quickly, she placed her cup on the coffee table, stood, arranged her dupatta, and stepped forward. We made our way out of the house as everyone gawked at us in silence.

Kriti walked a step ahead of me as we exited the house and descended the three steps to the main gate. Without thinking, I lightly touched her lower back to guide her toward my car. She took a sharp breath, and I quickly backed off. "Uh...sorry about that," I murmured, feeling heat rush to my cheeks.

"It's okay," she whispered softly as I walked beside her.

"That's me," I said when we reached the car. I pulled open the passenger door for her. Once she got seated, I quickly ran to my side and climbed in.

We were silent as I reversed the car and pulled out of her housing complex. The local radio played in the background as the car gradually cooled to a more comfortable temperature. I drove in the direction of the open fields and inner roads to avoid the evening traffic.

As we moved farther away from the core village area, the traffic outside dispersed, and the silence in the car became stifling. I lowered the radio's volume, signaling to Kriti that it was time to talk. I tried to appear nonchalant and focused on the drive, not breaking the silent battle that seemed to have ensued.

I waited for a minute. Then two, as I counted the seconds in my head.

"How was the meeting with the guy?" And I broke. Fuck. "You don't need to answer that," I added quickly, trying to respect her privacy, though I really hoped she would.

She sighed as I focused on the road, deliberately avoiding her gaze. "He was certainly more communicative than you are right now."

A sound of disbelief almost escaped me, but I choked it down. "Is that so?"

I could feel her eyes on my face, my body rigid with the scrutiny. She made a soft sound of agreement. "He also lives ten minutes away from my house."

An involuntary scoff escaped me. "He's a villager, you mean."

This time, her glare hit the side of my face like daggers.

"Just like me. I won't have to change my job, and I could visit my family quite often."

My teeth ground together, and the steering wheel started to hurt my palms from my tight grip. "Great."

"Aakar," she growled at me. I couldn't help but turn to look at her. Her eyes were wild with frustration, and she looked about ready to strangle me. That just managed to bring a smile to my face.

I looked at the bend in the road, turned on the indicator to the left, and parked the car on the side of the deserted road. Just so I could see her face and talk to her. Things needed to be sorted. Now.

10

Song: Apna Bana Le
- *Sachin-Jigar, Arijit Singh, Amitabh B*

Aakar

The moment I parked the car and turned to face her, so did she. "You didn't call," she stated, her voice accusatory.

I raised my eyebrows in wry amusement. "Neither did you."

Her lips thinned in impatience, and she straightened her spine against the car door. With eyes full of fiery defiance, she asked, "What would I have even said? I was waiting for you to call."

"Can you imagine how awkward it would've been for me to call you? What would *I* have said? Hey, Kriti, you excited to meet the other guy?"

She shrugged, still a little miffed. "I don't know. We could've just talked. Like we usually do. About anything else. And after meeting Bhavesh, it got me wondering."

"About what?"

She looked at me, her eyes staring straight into my soul. "Are you genuinely considering me for a marriage? I know it's too soon, but I have to know if you actually see us going somewhere."

With those bold, unfiltered words, she had me stunned. "Are you interested in marrying me?"

Kriti rolled her eyes in exasperation. "I don't go around chatting and talking with all the men I meet through these arranged meetings."

"Me neither," I admitted. I had never chatted outside the meetings with any of the girls I had met. I never felt compelled to. But with Kriti, I couldn't resist asking for her number, couldn't stop talking to her, and couldn't get enough of her attention.

Her eyes softened, and her lips tugged up in a small smile. But a pinched look flashed across her face before she asked in a hesitant tone, "Have you met any women since we started talking?"

"I haven't. I would've told you if I had."

A small blush rose to her face, and I had to clench my hands into tight fists to stop myself from tracing her cheeks. The thought of some other guy touching Kriti, making her blush, and having these back-and-forth conversations with her made my blood boil.

"Did you really like what's-his-name from yesterday?" I asked because I had to know.

Kriti looked at me for a beat, then turned her gaze to look across the fields around us. "He is pretty perfect on paper. I should like him. He seemed decent. Has a good smile. Kind eyes," she said, then looked me straight in the eyes. "And I didn't feel a thing."

My heart pounded at her stark honesty. "Good."

Everything within me needed to touch this woman. My muscles strained against my skin, my hands ached with need, every vein in my body zinged with anticipation, and I couldn't stop myself. I leaned forward in my seat, stretched my hand toward hers where it lay on her lap, and asked, "May I?"

Her eyes widened, and for the first time, I saw a hint of uncertainty and hesitation. I was about to pull my hand back when she met my fingers. A sigh escaped me as she gasped. My heartbeat quickened, and blood roared through my veins as I slid my hand along hers, feeling the soft pads of her fingers.

Our fingers moved and explored, and for the first time, they entwined. It felt right, like they belonged.

My mind settled, and I smiled.

When I looked up from our joined hands, Kriti's soft smile met mine.

"You feel something?" I asked.

Her cheeks were bright red, and a sudden chuckle escaped her as she shook her head. "I feel everything."

I squeezed her hand tighter, causing her to gasp. "Feels right."

"What are you saying, Aakar?" she whispered, her eyes cast downward at our joined hands.

Deciding to go with my heart, I answered, without missing a beat, "I'm saying I want to meet you again. Tomorrow."

She looked at me, her eyes bright with happiness, a little mirth, and some doubt. "Third meeting, huh? You know our parents would conclude that as a big fat yes, right?"

I didn't know if Kriti was aware, but she held our joined hands in her lap now, and it was taking all my strength not to pull it toward me and kiss it. I wanted to know her taste, the feel of her skin on my lips. With great effort, I recalled her question and tried to pull words out of my clouded mind. "Yep. I'm pretty sure they would get our driver to bring my grandparents here by tomorrow."

Something akin to wonder and terror flashed in Kriti's eyes. "Wow. Okay. This is all starting to sound very, very real."

I laughed and squeezed her hand, my voice full of sincerity. "Only if you want it to be. If at any point you feel we're not a good fit, or even if we are but you're not comfortable with my family, I want you to tell me. We'll talk about it and figure out what works best for you."

"Your family seems nice. A lot bigger than mine. I know my mom keeps bragging about my excitement and openness to big families, but it's not exactly true. I'm terrified of living in a big family. Right now, I think I can manage it, but it would certainly be a challenge."

Seeing Kriti nervous made me want to comfort her and make her smile. "Kriti, if we get married, you won't be left to your own devices. We're in this together. And just because we agree to a third meeting does not mean we are committing to marriage."

Relief shone in her eyes. "What does it mean to you, then?"

"It means I want to make it work with you. Exclusively. I hated thinking about you meeting that other guy. The entire day yesterday, I kept hoping you would reject him. I want us to be exclusive and committed to each other. I want us to have whatever ceremony necessary to give us the time to meet without any conditions, get to know each other better, and talk without worrying about our families."

A big, teasing smile played along her lips, her cheeks so enticing I wanted to smoosh them together. At my raised eyebrows, she said, "That ceremony is called an engagement."

My cheeks warmed at the official term, my heart beating in terror and wild excitement as I murmured, "If that's what you want to call it."

She laughed. "I mean, I would love to be your girlfriend. But as per the arranged marriage rules, the ceremony for commitment and exclusivity equals engagement."

"Only if you want. I don't want you to agree because you think I'm your best option. I only want you to agree if you think you'll be happy with me," I murmured, running my thumb along hers.

She shivered, and her voice came out breathy when she answered. "I wouldn't mind."

"Such enthusiasm."

"You're welcome."

I chucked her chin lightly with my free hand.

I turned serious and clasped both of her hands in mine. I wasn't kidding about the meeting tomorrow. I wanted to see where things would go with Kriti. More than that, I knew I wouldn't find another woman with whom I connected so deeply. We suited each other. My heart knew I would never tire of talking to her. Time flew too fast with her, and our conversation was effortless. At this moment, I didn't care what my family thought of her, what her family thought of me, or whether we would fit in each other's lives. All I cared about was how we fit with each other.

But I needed Kriti to feel the same. "Let's meet tomorrow again. Take your time. I'm in no rush. And you don't need to rush either."

"I missed talking to you," she admitted, her eyes earnest. Her cheeks turned red under my gaze, and she shook her head as if regretting saying it out loud.

Slowly, giving her the chance to pull away at any moment, I brought our joined hands to my lips and pressed a soft kiss on her fingers. "I missed talking to you too. So much."

Her soft, smooth skin had my blood pumping hard. I could easily imagine traveling up a little farther, placing soft kisses on her wrist, her arm, her shoulder, and her neck. I nearly groaned out loud before I reluctantly let her hand go.

A deep red blush spread across her cheeks, yet her grin was wide, and her eyes shone with excitement. She adjusted her perfect kameez, trying to regain her composure. "Now, let's go back."

"Ready to go already?" I teased, noticing how flustered she was from the kiss. If she had actually looked at me, she'd have known I was just as affected by her.

Before I could turn the car back toward her house, she said, "And let's get some ice cream before they start wondering what took us so long."

I chuckled, recognizing the wisdom in her suggestion. "Ice cream it is," I agreed, and we headed off to an ice cream parlor, getting an ice cream for everyone back home.

~

Kriti

"I can't believe he asked for a third meeting already," Rati said, sitting on the floor between Maa's legs. Maa applied oil to her hair with such vigor that it seemed she believed she could make it grow by sheer force. Rati, the tough cookie that she was, simply moved wherever Maa led her head—left, right, up, down—keeping her face entirely neutral. I preferred Dad's hair oil massages far more than Maa's. His hands were bigger, but his massages were gentler, as if coaxing the hair to grow faster, unlike Maa, who probably thought pulling it out by the roots might do the trick.

Maa turned Rati's head up by her hair in the middle of the massage. "Don't put out such doubts and negativity. I'm so happy such a good man from such a great family is interested in Kriti."

She looked at me and said, "Beta, your life will be all set if you're married into a family like theirs. We won't even need to worry about Kartik and Rati."

I rolled my eyes at her dramatic dialogue. "My life is already set, Maa. With or without marrying Aakar or anyone else. And you don't have to worry about Kartik and Rati, regardless of my marital status."

"You'll understand what I mean when you have your own kids," she said, squeezing the bottle of coconut oil directly onto Rati's head.

Rati shrieked. "Maa, I told you to use less oil and more massage. I need to wash my hair tomorrow when the guests return."

That night, my mind couldn't quiet down enough for me to sleep. This was the farthest I'd ever gotten in the marriage process. For the first time, I didn't dread the next meeting. In fact, I was excited. Aakar was a good man. He cared about his family. He wanted a wife for himself, not his family. He was respectful but not shy.

I touched the back of my hand where his lips had brushed against my skin. I always thought the emotions, feelings, and kisses expressed in the romance books I read were far-fetched.

Never had I been happier for being so wrong.

Romance books merely put into words every emotion—moments leading to the kiss, the kiss itself, and the aftermath—prolonging the moment in the eyes of the reader. How I wished I could have prolonged the moment Aakar touched his lips to my hand. All I could do was remember those moments. Recall every little detail. Over and over again.

With just one tiny kiss on the hand, Aakar had me in a pile of goo. My mind had departed from the sensible department to la-la land, thinking about all he could do with his lips, his hands, and his other parts.

How would it feel to kiss his lips? Would his stubble burn? My body heated with every dirty thought that crossed my mind. And I let it. I let myself imagine every naughty thing Aakar could do to me. That I could do to him. I tested my mind and my body, waiting for any hint of rejection or unease at the thought of Aakar touching me, bringing me pleasure, or taking his pleasure from me. But none came.

My mind eased at that. If my mind and body felt comfortable—even excited—at the thought of sharing probably my most vulnerable moments with Aakar, surely that was a good sign.

His words from the evening, when he gave me the time to think and the option to call off the wedding even after an engagement, made me believe he wouldn't be selfish. And maybe it wouldn't be so bad to put my trust in him. Put my family's trust in him. His assurance that I'd be free to choose, free to take my time, and free to leave as I wish meant the world to me.

I picked up my phone from the nightstand, opened the messaging app, and sent him a message.

> Me: Thank you for being so wonderful. Can't wait to see you tomorrow.

His response came almost instantly, making me smile.

> Aakar: Can't wait to see you too. I'll try to get us even more alone time. ;)

> Me: Sounds good…Good night…

After a moment's hesitation, I sent the little heart emoji I'd always dreamed of sending to someone special someday.

> Me: 🩶

I didn't have to wait long for his response.

> Aakar: Good night, Kriti 🩶

I squealed into my pillow, clutching the phone in my hand, and fell asleep with a smile on my face.

∽

THE MOOD of the families the next day had cranked up a notch. Or a hundred. Yesterday, they seemed to be in the get-to-know-each-other phase. Today, they were in the best-friends-in-the-whole-world phase from the moment Aakar's family had stepped into our house. The ladies talked like they hadn't caught up in decades, with hundreds of stories on the tip of their tongues. The men guffawed as they ate snacks and drank cups of chai.

Aakar was stuck with the men, my father asking him about his interests and job, while Aakar's father and uncles boasted about his accomplishments. I was in charge of cooking lunch—because, of course, as the stakes go higher, so does the amount of food—with Rati and Aakar's cousin Ria helping me out in the kitchen. Aakar's mother and aunts were busy chopping vegetables, getting the dough for the puris ready, rolling the dough into puris, and preparing some salad.

Aakar and I hadn't talked once today, only exchanging a few helpless glances. Soon, all the men sat down for lunch while we ladies served them, standing in the kitchen and taking out hot, piping puris. My family usually ate together. However, whenever we had a lot of guests over, it was always the men eating first, then the kids, and finally, the women. Whether it was due to the lack of space at the dining table, the ladies wanting to finish serving and then eat in peace, or just plain old patriarchy, I hated it.

Right then, Maa handed me a container of reheated undhiyu, a mixed vegetable dish full of potatoes, brinjal, purple yams, beans, and several other seasonal vegetables. "Kriti Beta, go serve this to whoever has run out."

I didn't mind serving the food to the men. I would gladly get up in the middle of the meal to get something for someone. What irked me was that no men served their wives when it was their turn to eat. I swallowed the lump in my throat, pasted a soft smile on my face, and stepped out from the kitchen into the dining room. I started with my father, who asked for some extra, then went to Aakar's father, making the obligatory insistence on having some more. I reached Aakar and found him already watching me.

A soft smile played on his lips, as if he knew I hated doing such rounds yet was performing for everyone. I raised my eyebrows at him in question as I lifted the ladle of the undhiyu. Without stopping his smile, he said, "Just a little, if you please."

My lips twitched into a smile at his deliberate politeness. I dropped a heap of the vegetables on his plate, and he shook his head, his smile turning into laughter.

I was about to pass by him when he murmured so only I could hear, "After lunch, I'm getting us out of here."

"Good luck," I murmured back, pasting a polite smile on my face to greet his uncle with a ladle full of undhiyu.

We—the ladies—had just finished our lunch and were clearing the table, about to join the men in the living room, when Aakar turned to my father and said, "Uncle, I was wondering if I could take Kriti out for a drive."

Yesterday, my father had shown a slight reluctance to send me alone with him. But today, he was all-out beaming. He looked at Aakar's family and asked if they were fine with it. At everyone's agreement, Aakar turned to me, his eyes bright with victory and relief. I bit back my own relieved smile and got up.

In minutes, we were out the door and rushing toward his car. We stayed silent as Aakar started the engine and carefully maneuvered through the maze of other cars and two-wheelers haphazardly parked on our street. Once we got onto the main road, he said, "You hate waiting on people and serving them dinner, don't you?"

Only because he was smiling as he said it did he make me want to share my mind. "It's not like that," I began.

He chuckled, giving me a glance. "Could've fooled me. You should've seen your face while trying to be polite."

"Was it that obvious?' I asked, worried that I might have offended his family.

"Only if someone was looking closely enough."

His words sent a wave of relief as well as a rush of butterflies inside me. Heat rushed across my cheeks, and I had to stop myself from touching my cool hands to them. I swallowed the lump in my throat and said, "It's not that I hate to serve people dinner. I just find it a little demeaning having to wait on men as they finish eating while I am hungry myself. The men never even ask if the women would like to eat first or together. It's always assumed that men are supposed to be seated first, served by women, and then they retreat to the living room to chat, never offering to help when the women finally sit to eat. Their main excuse is that they bring in the income for the family. Well, so do I. But I don't get excused from serving the men."

Aakar was silent as he listened to my rant. He cleared his throat and said, "Wow. Um...It's understandable how you feel."

"We're a small family, Aakar. So, more often than not, we eat together. Even if the family I marry into doesn't eat together, I'll deal with it. It's not exactly a deal breaker for me."

"Our family is a lot more casual when it comes to lunch and dinner. Most of us aren't home during lunch, and everyone has varied dinner times. People eat when they're hungry, and some even skip it. The only time we eat together is during breakfast," he said, clearing his throat before continuing. "And if we were to marry and you continued teaching, you'd probably be leaving for school before everyone gathers for breakfast. And you're right, the ladies of the house sometimes sit with us and sometimes stay in the kitchen, depending on what we're having. In short, you're safe from being at people's beck and call all the time."

"It's not like serving food to people is a punishment or anything. I won't hate it if I have to."

This time, he clutched my hand without any hesitation like yesterday. His hand was warm and strong. He squeezed my hand in his, saying, "You don't have to do anything you don't like doing. I know you'll have to bend to our customs some days, and I won't be able to do much about it, only if it's to keep peace in the family. But I never want you to feel like you can't share your feelings with me. When something or someone bothers you, I want to know."

"I'm going to say yes if my family asks if I want to marry you." The words flew out of my mouth before I could stop myself.

Aakar glanced at me with the biggest smile I'd ever seen on his face, only for two seconds before turning his attention back to the road. "Good. Because I'm gonna do the same."

11

Song: Chaar Kadam
- *Shaan, Shreya Ghoshal*

Aakar

The moment I said that, Kriti let out a low shriek. I quickly looked at her in concern, my heart in my throat. "Kriti, what's wrong? Did I say something wrong?"

Trying to keep my eyes on the road while glancing at her to gauge her reaction, I saw her shaking her head. "Just. Oh god, really? Are we really doing this? Getting married?"

I shook my head, my heart taking its sweet time to calm down. "You scared me there for a second."

I wanted to—needed to—look at her properly and talk to her. I saw an ice cream parlor up ahead and quickly turned on the indicator to turn right. Since it was the middle of the afternoon, I had no problem finding a shaded parking spot. "Let's get some ice cream. We need to be the first to celebrate, after all."

A bright smile lit up her face, and I knew I would move mountains to keep that smile on her face forever.

I picked chocolate flavor while she picked the colorful cassata ice cream made of layers of pistachio, vanilla, and strawberry ice cream.

"It's a celebration, after all," she said as she took the ice cream from the server on the other side of the counter. Considering the time of day, the seating area was empty, so we grabbed a seat in the far corner near the window, away from the counter. We sat across from each other, and as Kriti took a bite of her colorful ice cream, I couldn't help but marvel. *This was the woman I was going to marry.*

She moaned at the giant bites she took of her ice cream, causing very inappropriate reactions in my body right in the middle of the café. I cleared my throat, shifted in my seat, and offered her a bite of my ice cream. She did the same, and we just enjoyed the delicious bites for a few minutes. Kriti tortured me with her little moans the entire time.

Swirling her spoon in the cup, she asked, "Aakar, can I ask you something personal?"

Kriti wasn't a shy person. She always looked me in the eye when she talked. But right now, she looked everywhere but at me. I took the bite of ice cream already halfway to my mouth and nodded, signaling her to go ahead.

Her cheeks had turned red as she continued to swirl the ice cream in her cup. "Um, when you said you've had girlfriends before, were they like serious girlfriends?"

I nearly choked on my ice cream, her question catching me off guard. Once I could breathe properly, I looked up at her worried eyes.

"Are you okay? I'm so sorry for springing it on you," she said, her hand halfway across the table, almost touching mine.

Gently, I placed my hand on top of hers, caressing her soft, smooth skin. Slowly, I entwined our fingers together, and when she tightened her hold, I met her eyes. Her cheeks were flushed, and as she ran her tongue along her bottom lip, I couldn't help but swipe at her lower lip. She gasped. "A bit of ice cream," I lied.

Her eyes narrowed, catching my lie, but she said nothing.

"And to answer your question, I've never had a serious girlfriend before."

Her lips curled on one side, her voice a little sharper. "So nonserious girlfriends, then?"

I shifted in my chair, trying to gauge what she wanted to hear. I cleared my throat and ran my thumb across her finger. "When I was in college, I had a couple of girlfriends. It was more about being young and not wanting to miss out on the experience. But things didn't work out. Clearly."

She nodded, her eyes thoughtful. She removed her hand from mine, and I nearly felt devastated at the loss, but then she ran her finger over my open palm. Her soft exploration sent a shiver racing down my spine. I had to cross my leg over my knee to hide the growing evidence of what the slightest touch from her did to me.

She looked at me, her eyes unreadable, and asked, "So would you say you're...um...experienced?" She barely got the words out before glancing around to ensure no one overheard us. Then she looked down at our hands.

This time, I didn't hesitate. I clutched her hand with both of mine and said, "Kriti, you must believe me. I haven't ever...um... done that with anyone else. I'm a virgin."

She looked disappointed—*What the fuck?*—and lamented, "Oh no. You too? God."

"Um...sorry, what?" I stammered. "Is it a bad thing for us to be virgins? What's going on in your mind?"

She turned her forlorn eyes to me and said, "Well, now we'll both be clueless idiots when we have to, you know, do it."

I burst out laughing. "Clueless idiots!" I laughed and

laughed until I had to take a few sips of water to calm down. Unable to resist, I reached forward and gently pulled her pouty, disappointed cheeks.

Her eyes widened in surprise, and then she blushed a deep red. "Aakar," she chided, but there was no heat in it, just a deeper blush.

"We won't be clueless idiots," I assured her.

If we hadn't been in a public place, I was pretty sure she would've wailed in anguish. It was hilarious as she murmured, "How can you be so sure? I was hoping that since you're a big-shot city boy with all this dating experience, you'd have, you know, done *it*. And I'd just have to lie back and enjoy it."

"Oh god." I rubbed my eyes, trying to control my laughter. "You were just waiting for me to say yes to marriage before bringing out the crazy, weren't you?"

She snorted. "Of course. I couldn't discuss such personal things with anyone other than my husband."

The word hung between us, making us both glance away from each other. *Husband.* I was going to be a *husband.*

I was going to be *Kriti's* husband. The thought filled me with a mix of exhilaration and terror. I would be responsible for her health and happiness forever. And that scared the ever-loving shit out of me.

But then, I looked at her. Her shy smile. Her eyes, unflinching and direct, looked too deep within me. Her trust in me to be a good husband to her seemed so unflinching that I knew I would do just about anything to make her the happiest fucking wife who ever lived.

Case in point: her ridiculous concerns about our virginity. "Of course. And just because I'm a city boy doesn't mean women are falling at my feet."

She muttered something under her breath and said, "Well, we'll just have to be prepared for a few months of bad sex."

My eyes widened in horror. "We won't have bad sex."

She glanced around the empty café as if expecting someone to jump out from under the tables and boo at us for talking about sex. Then she turned to me and rolled her eyes. "Says the virgin."

I placed both of my hands on the table and leaned forward. "Just because I haven't done it doesn't mean I don't know how. It doesn't mean I haven't thought about what I would love to do with you in a thousand different ways, a million times. You're underestimating the hunger of a starving man."

For the first time, she was speechless. Kriti's eyes dilated to pure black, her cheeks, neck, and nose flushed, and she looked hungry. So I continued, "Do you want me to believe that just because you're inexperienced, you don't feel it? The curiosity for my touch? That you don't imagine my lips touching places other than your hand? That you wouldn't know what to do with me in bed?"

The realization that I was pushing her buttons transformed her eyes from hungry to challenging. "I've read about a thousand ways to touch you. And why limit ourselves to bed? There's against the wall, in the shower, maybe somewhere scandalous when nobody's home."

Blood flowed like lava in my veins and rushed down to my cock, and all I could do was stare at her lips as she spoke, turning my world upside down with her words. Before I could get carried away in the sexual dreamland that she was weaving, I suddenly remembered her words from our very first meeting.

I looked at my melted ice cream, now more of a milkshake, and swirled my spoon in it, using the motion to regain control of my cock and get my brain functioning again. "And all of these seductive things would take place six months after our wedding, right?"

Her eyes widened in shock, and I did my best not to smile as she sputtered and struggled to compose herself. With pursed lips, she quickly collected herself. "Of course. I mean, sure.

Maybe," she murmured, blushing furiously. "I mean, I set that condition to give myself the time to feel comfortable with my husband. I didn't think that...I didn't expect to feel...uhm..."

"Hunger...attraction...need?" I supplied, my voice husky.

Her blush turned deeper red as she bit her lip. "Uh, yeah. So what I mean to say is...I'm open to trying stuff as we feel it."

I waited for her to meet my eyes. When she looked at me, I asked, "Just to be clear, you're okay with me kissing you when I feel like I'd die if I didn't feel your lips against mine?"

Her tongue licked her lips, making me feel like I was dying right then. "Yeah. That would be good."

"Good." My voice was merely a rasp as my throat dried up with the need clawing against my skin.

Right then, my phone buzzed with an incoming message, breaking my sexual haze.

"Excuse me," I said and picked up the phone.

> Abhi: You need to be back soon. Parents are getting uncomfortable.

> Me: We'll be there soon.

> Abhi: Cool. FYI, they're expecting a YES.

> Me: I know.

> Abhi: Soooo...is it? A YES?

> Me: Yes. Now, don't you dare react or tell ANYONE.

I turned to Kriti and found her already staring at me. My cheeks heated, and I shook my head. "That was Abhi. We need to head back soon. Our parents are starting to wonder about us."

She rolled her eyes and put the cup of melted ice cream to her mouth, slurping it down. Glorious, this woman.

I followed her lead and downed the chocolate milk. Once we were back in the car, I asked, "Kriti, you're 100 percent sure?"

I didn't want to say yes to the marriage if she had even a little bit of doubt about us. Before she could answer, I added, "Just so you're aware, there are some disadvantages to marrying me."

I counted on my fingers with one hand, holding the steering wheel with the other. "One, you would have to leave your job here and adapt to a new school and culture. Two, you'll be moving from a nuclear family to a joint family. Three, I'm an inexperienced virgin."

She laughed at the third, slapping my arm, chiding me. "You're thoughtful and caring. For the first time, a man is listing why he might be a bad choice for me, which just makes me trust you more. Aakar, I respect you. After talking to you for the past few weeks, I consider you a friend. And you're a *handsome* virgin. Don't forget that."

I scoffed at the last part even though my face warmed. Her words stirred a storm of undefinable emotions within me. I wanted to take her in my arms and protect her from every pain in the world. I wanted to touch her, kiss her, bring tears of laughter to her eyes, and receive her scathing glares of anger and frustration. I wanted to hoard it all. Because finally, I was looking at someone I'd call my own. My *wife*.

I parked the car on the side of the road and turned to her. "Kriti, it is difficult for me to share my feelings with someone. I'm always the one taking care of others. People come to me with troubles, feelings, anything they need to share. I like that I can come to you to share my feelings. I love talking to you, so much so that time never seems enough when I'm with you. And I'm sorry if I've never said it out loud. I realized that I hadn't when you called me handsome, but you're gorgeous, Kriti. Ever since I first saw you, I haven't been able to stop thinking about you. And the more I've talked to you, the more you enamored me. I truly feel lucky that you chose me. It isn't an obligation or a last resort or a chore for me. It is my honor to marry you."

Her eyes glistened with tears, but she quickly blinked them away. "That's all I need, Aakar. A man who understands me, respects me, wants to make me happy, finds me beautiful—"

"Gorgeous."

"Finds me gorgeous." She chuckled, then continued, her eyes turning away from me. "And hopefully, maybe, would someday fall in love with me. The rest, I can handle."

Falling in love with Kriti was inevitable. I was already halfway there.

I looked at her for a moment, then turned my eyes back to the road. I gently clutched her hand, bringing it to my lips. As I kissed her hand, I made an unspoken promise: to understand her, respect her, make her happy, and most definitely, fall in love with her.

∾

Kriti

The moment we stepped inside the house, everyone turned to look at us as if they already knew the answer. I went to sit in the empty spot beside my father while Aakar took a seat between Abhi and Ria. The parents looked at us like children awaiting their parents' return from a trip to the grocery store, eyes wide with anticipation.

I struggled to keep from laughing at their eager yet disappointed faces. Aakar and I had decided that we'd each tell our families personally, avoiding a big announcement. This way, any objections could be discussed in private.

Seeing no answers from us, Aakar's family soon left for their village home. As soon as their car disappeared, Maa, Rati, and even Pappa were on me. Even Kartik—whose head was usually buried in his phone—had his eyes fixed on me.

Before Maa could start asking questions, Pappa, for a change, spoke up. "Beta, you seem to like Aakar. You've agreed to meet him three times. Are you interested in marrying him?"

Just thinking about Aakar brought a smile to my face. I met my father's eyes and said, "Yes, Pappa."

Maa, Rati, and Kartik were silent, hooked to our conversation like never before. Pappa asked softly, "And do you know if Aakar likes you?"

I smiled, remembering the moment we agreed that we'd say *Yes*. "I'd like to think so."

This time, Maa asked, "You'd like to think so, or do you know so?"

I rolled my eyes at her. Before I could say anything, the telephone rang. All five of us just knew who that was. Maa's eyes lit up in delight, and she clutched my father's arm, dragging him to pick up the call. Pappa smiled, humoring her as he answered.

The four of us watched him as he nodded, informed them it was a yes from me, and continued nodding with a smile on his face. Maa was already beside me, clutching my hand, her grip tightening with every passing minute.

After the obligatory goodbyes, Pappa quickly put down the phone and yelled in delight, "They said YES!!"

I was pulled into the tightest, warmest, and happiest hug that Maa had given me in a very long time. It made me equal parts happy and sad. I just soaked it up. More arms came around us, and my heart tightened. I would soon leave them to go to a new house and family. I didn't know if they would ever be able to love me the same. I squeezed my mother tighter and let a few tears fall.

Pappa patted my head. "They've asked us if we want to do the Chandlo Vidhi tomorrow. At their village home. They said they would call the priest for the auspicious time if tomorrow works for us." Chandlo Vidhi, literally translated to Vermilion Ceremony, is the ceremony that solidifies the marriage decision between the two families.

Maa turned to me, her eyebrows raised in question. That took me by surprise. Usually, she would've already answered yes without a second thought.

I turned to my siblings, who wore wide, excited smiles. I looked at my mother, and if anxiety and relief could have a baby, it would be her face right now. My father, however, was the same as always: steady, relaxed, happy, and my rock. I nodded my head in agreement for tomorrow.

Pappa bent down and kissed my forehead, and in that tiny embrace, I felt his blessings and joy.

He called Aakar's family back and gave them the go-ahead. As they talked logistics, Kartik patted my cheek and headed to his room, declaring he needed to change into his pajamas. Hearing that, Rati looked at me with pleading eyes, silently asking if I minded if she left. I smiled and rolled my eyes. "Go."

She pecked me on the cheek and ran upstairs to change.

When five minutes passed, and Pappa was still on the phone, I couldn't bear it any longer. I turned to Maa with pleading eyes. She shook her head in mock exasperation. "You'll need to have more tolerance for heavy, traditional clothes in the future. You won't be able to just run into your room and change into your T-shirt and leggings all the time."

I quickly got up and gave her a peck on the cheek. "We'll see about that."

I ran upstairs before she could get started on how I would need to behave at my in-laws'.

I had a text waiting for me when I got into bed.

    Aakar: You ready to be my fiancée?

The word sent sparks of giddiness through my body, and I had to physically bite down on my pillow to stop myself from giggling.

> Me: Very, very ready. You ready to be my fiancé?

> Aakar: Counting down the hours.

～

MEERA RUSHED into my room as I was applying my makeup in a blouse and underskirt the next day. She looked beautiful in her yellow lehenga, her blouse embroidered with tiny silver threads, and the skirt's border matched the embroidery. She'd laid her dupatta on one shoulder, accentuating her curves.

"Gosh, look at you," I said, turning around and touching the soft material of her dupatta.

She gasped. "Me? Look at *you*. Just a few days ago, you were single and forcefully eating cucumbers. And today, you'll be engaged. How do you feel? Are you happy with Aakar? Does he treat you well?"

I laughed. I had kept her posted on the fact that Aakar and I talked, but we were yet to catch up on the extent to which Aakar and I enjoyed each other's company. "You've been busy with planning your move, Meera. Aakar and I have been talking a lot. He's a good man. He's also sometimes funny, he respects me, he likes me just the way I am, he shares his thoughts and feelings with me, and he considers me his friend. What more do I need from a husband?"

A slightly uncertain look crossed her face. She straightened her shoulders, held my hands, and asked, "But you always dreamed of a prince coming for you. You always talked about these heroes in your books."

"And I always said I would have an arranged marriage.

Where do you think I was going to find a boyfriend and have a love marriage?"

"Do you love Aakar?"

Her question gave me pause. I thought about all our late night and early afternoon conversations, his little jealousy, his determination to grow his family's company, and his love for his siblings. I respected him. I trusted him. But was that what love was? He caused a storm of butterflies in my stomach when he talked in that rumbly, beautiful voice, and my body heated at the thought of his hands on me. I loved the thought of us together. But still, was it love?

I looked at Meera and admitted, "To be honest, I don't know. I know I can't imagine marrying anybody else. His presence excites me, and I always pray for time to pass slower when he's with me. I really like him. And maybe I could fall in love with him."

My words seemed to have given her the assurance she needed. But she still seemed to have some doubts as she chewed her lips before asking, "What if you regret marrying him in the future?"

I squeezed her hand because who else was going to ask me these tough questions right before my engagement? "Then I would have to live with that regret. And if I trust my instincts and know the man that Aakar is, I don't believe I would regret making this decision."

Meera nodded, and her eyes shone with determination. "Okay, good. Because if he ends up hurting you, he'd have me to answer to. And Luke. And he would probably tattle to Aakar's sister, Akira, and she would bring in her fiancé, Sam. So yes. He would have a lot of people to answer to if he ever hurts you."

I laughed and hugged my best friend. "Thank you, Meera. Your friendship means the world to me."

"Same. Now, let's get you ready. We need to leave for Aakar's place in an hour."

I leaped out of her hug and got back to my makeup. It was my engagement, and dammit, I was going to look the best. She helped me drape my red saree, pleating it just the right way. I'd bought it for a special occasion, and today was as special as it could get.

I barely got ready on time, but when I entered my living room, what I found had me almost tearing up and ruining all my makeup. All my aunts and uncles and cousins were here; Meera had brought Luke, her little brother, Hari, and her mother with her. I wasn't used to so many smiles and congratulations directed toward me in a while. The last time people looked at me with such joy was when I had become a teacher and got the job at our school.

Years had passed, most of my cousins, some even younger, were already married, and people had stopped waiting for anything new to happen to my life. And today, for the first time, there were so many people to celebrate *me*. It made me feel both happy and sad. Happy that they were all here to share my joy but sad that it took my engagement for them to look this happy when they looked at me.

I let it all go and just took a deep breath. My life was going to change from this day forward, and I only wanted happy vibes and heartfelt blessings from the people around me.

It took about six cars for all of us to go to Aakar's place. And when we reached there, we found several cars parked in their large front yard. Seemed like Aakar's extended family had come too. He was the eldest sibling, even among the cousins. So naturally, this was the first big event for them.

The front porch was decorated with all the colorful flowers. Marigold and Asopalav leaves hung from the ceiling, and bouquets of white, red, and pink roses floated in large pots filled with water near the door.

Aakar's entire family stood on the porch for our welcome. Aakar was in the center, flanked on both sides by his parents and Abhi. He wore a black suit over a black shirt, his hair was styled to perfection, his beard was groomed to accentuate his sharp jawline, and I almost stumbled in my steps. His eyes roamed over me, taking in my ruby red-colored saree, heavily embroidered with golden-colored threads. Our eyes met, and I saw his approval, his admiration, and I deliberately roamed my eyes over his suit and raised my eyebrows in appreciation.

He chuckled and shook his head as we walked toward them, me at the center, with my parents on one side, Rati and Kartik on the other. All our friends and relatives cheered and hooted as I stepped on the porch and faced Aakar. Chandla ceremonies were usually not big celebratory ceremonies. But Aakar's family wanted a good celebration for their eldest son.

Maa lightly pushed me forward, and I got the hint. I went to Aakar's parents and touched their feet for their blessings, while Aakar touched my parents' feet. After that, he joined me as I got the blessings from his grandparents and his uncles and aunts.

With so many people in attendance, it took us too long just to enter their house. Inside, they had transformed the place to look like a wedding venue. Flowers and candles were everywhere. There was a beautiful rangoli in the corner, colored powder creating intricate designs of candles and flowers and everything celebration. Everyone took a seat on the empty couches and chairs set around the loveseat where Aakar and I were to sit.

I didn't know when I had left my parents behind and was walking alongside Aakar, but he softly grazed my fingers as we walked, and I tried not to show his effect on me on my face. He grazed my lower back as he led me to the loveseat, got me seated, and then sat beside me, keeping a respectful distance between us.

Rati, Kartik, and Meera took a seat closest to mine. Since

my parents would be involved in the ceremony and rituals, they went to help Aakar's parents. Abhi and Ria set up a Zoom call, and within the next five minutes, Aakar's sister, Akira, appeared on the laptop screen. She was decked out in traditional clothes with a handsome American man beside her.

With the way Aakar and I had agreed to get married, and the family's decision to get us engaged, I hadn't had the chance to talk to Akira.

While the parents were busy getting things ready, Abhi handed the laptop to Aakar. He held it so both of us would appear on the screen.

Akira screamed, "Congratulations, bhai!! And welcome to the family, bhabhi!!"

Aakar chuckled and brought the laptop closer to my face. "Akira, meet Kriti. Kriti, Akira, and her fiancé, Sam."

"Hey, guys. I wish you guys could be here."

Akira wailed at that. "I know. My brother and family have no chill. Don't you think they should've waited a few weeks for me to get there?"

I mock-gasped and turned an angry scowl at Aakar, who was busy scowling at his sister. "Aakar, how could you? Don't you care about your sister at all?"

Akira repeated my question with an even more exaggerated, sad tone.

Aakar glared at us. "You both are so going to pay for it later."

He turned serious and a little sad. "Akira, I really did ask everyone to wait for a week or two. Mom and Dad were just adamant that it was a small ceremony, and you didn't have to travel all the way from America for it. You know we'll do a much bigger celebration near the wedding."

Akira genuinely smiled at Aakar. "I understand, bhai. I'm just so happy that you found a partner. I can't wait to share all your secrets with bhabhi."

Aakar turned to me and rolled his eyes as if saying *little sisters, right?* He was about to say something to Akira when our parents and relatives were upon us.

The next few minutes passed in a blur. With the chanting and advice from the priest, our parents took turns blessing us, feeding us sweets, and giving ceremonial gifts. Soon after, our relatives came forward to where we sat. Some gave us envelopes of cash, while some gave us gifts to show us their blessings for our union.

The ceremony barely took half an hour, and my life was forever changed.

Our parents and relatives left us to distribute the sweets to other guests and make arrangements for lunch. Everyone around us was busy talking among themselves, laughing, gossiping, as if everything was just normal. As if a life-changing commitment hadn't been exchanged between two families.

My eyes met Aakar's. And I saw the same confusion reflected in his eyes.

He moved a little closer to me so our shoulders touched. He could easily hold my hand this close, entwine our fingers, and squeeze them in comfort. But he can't. Not in front of all the relatives.

"Are you okay?" he asked.

I nodded and shrugged because I had no idea how to explain what I felt. "Uh...yeah. I mean, it just feels...I don't know."

"Anticlimactic?"

My eyes widened as he gave a word to the emotions I felt. "Yes."

He smiled and looked at his hands. "I feel the same."

His words soothed the anxiety that seemed to be bubbling within me. I was about to respond when our parents arrived and called us for lunch.

They led us to their backyard, which was decorated with

garlands of flowers hanging on every available tree along the walls. They called it a backyard, but it looked like a party plot that could fit a little over a hundred people. A huge mango tree stood in one corner, garlands of roses and marigolds hanging off the branches.

Chairs and charpais were laid out across the yard for the guests. A line had already formed at the food counter, and some guests had already started eating dessert.

As we entered the backyard, shouts and whistles welcomed us. Aakar gently laid his hand at the low of my back and laughed and chatted with the guests. His silent presence and support helped me get used to the attention on me. It was disconcerting to have so many eyes on me.

Soon, Meera, Luke, and Aakar's siblings joined us. Once we'd gotten our plates loaded with food, all of us gathered our chairs together to eat. The food was simple yet delicious.

Aakar and I sat beside each other, looked at each other, but couldn't have a moment to talk to each other. I was officially engaged to the man sitting beside me, and we hadn't talked more than three words with each other. We chatted with relatives, we laughed, all the while exchanging helpless glances at each other.

The elders kept coming to talk to us to bid us goodbyes. Soon, all the guests had left, and the only people remaining were our families. The moment I was done with lunch, Maa called me to sit with the ladies of both the families.

Aakar, who still sat with our siblings and friends, turned to me. He looked at the group of ladies calling me over. I could hear his sigh all the way across the yard, or maybe it was me.

With one last helpless shrug, I made my way to my mother.

Certainly, engagements are supposed to be more romantic than this, aren't they?

12

Song: Kasam Ki Kasam
- *Rahul Jain*

Aakar

I was an engaged man. Everything was different, but to my disappointment, nothing *felt* different. Maybe the idea that I was engaged hadn't sunk in, or maybe I didn't know what was supposed to be different. But something seemed to be missing. This ceremony didn't call for an exchange of rings, so I didn't have physical evidence of being engaged.

My fiancée sat fifty meters away from me, barely exchanging a few glances with me. We hadn't had one proper conversation, and I hadn't seen Kriti be her usual cheerful self. I turned around to find her sitting beside her mother, smiling amicably at something my mother said. She, too, looked unsettled, on edge, like something was not allowing her to relax and laugh.

"Aakar." My father's voice had me turning around to find

him sitting with my uncles and the priest a few feet away. I turned to my siblings, excused myself, and got up to join them.

I pulled a nearby chair and took a seat between my dad and my youngest uncle, Sunil.

Sunil Kaka slapped me on the back in that manly, congratulatory way. "Congratulations, Aakar, how does it feel to be engaged?"

I laughed at that. *If only he knew*. "It hasn't even been a day, kaka. Ask me this question after a month."

We laughed at that, and my dad cleared his throat. I turned to him, and he had a soft smile on his face. "I feel so relieved, beta. Now that you're engaged, I can stop worrying for a while. With you choosing a wonderful woman like Kriti, and Akira having found that American boy," he said, deliberately not saying Sam's name—he was still in the process of accepting Sam as Akira's fiancé—"I can relax until it's time for Abhi to marry."

I rolled my eyes at him. "Pappa, you didn't have to worry in the first place. We'll all find the right partners when it's the right time."

Our priest nodded at that. "That is true, Aakar."

At that, Dad instantly nodded. "Speaking of the right time, panditji and I were talking about auspicious dates and times for the wedding, and he had a few options for us."

My mind instantly went on alert mode. Wedding dates? Times? Already?

At my shocked face, Dad said, "Beta, we're already in the village. It would be good to discuss such important things in person. We might as well discuss a few options with Kriti's parents."

"Dad, I haven't even been engaged for three hours yet."

Sunil Kaka slapped my back in encouragement. "Aakar, it doesn't hurt to discuss. We're not trying to force you and Kriti."

I looked at my uncles, my dad, and the priest, all of their

faces trying to be convincing and pleading for me to hear them out. I could only sigh in resignation. I knew what was coming the moment I said yes. "Fine. What are the options?"

The priest opened his little diary and said, "Today is September 16. The most auspicious dates are December 10, January 18, or February 23."

I rubbed my hands over my eyes. December was a little less than three months away. My eyes automatically turned to where Kriti sat. She was chatting animatedly with Meera, and I couldn't help but imagine her being my wife in three months.

And it did not terrify me like I'd expected. I was...excited. Thrilled even.

But I had no right or wish to make this decision before talking to Kriti first.

I turned to my dad. "I need to talk to Kriti before we discuss this any further. I'm going to take her for a drive. You can discuss these dates with her family while we're gone."

My dad nodded in agreement. "Makes sense."

Yesterday, I wouldn't have been able to outright inform him that I was taking Kriti for a drive. Just one yes and one little ceremony changed it all. Now, *this* was what being engaged felt like. Spending time with your woman without needing permission from both parents.

With the thought of all the things that Kriti and I could do together without being pushed over by our parents and the society, a sudden lightness filled my chest.

I quickly got up from my chair before they got any more new ideas and said, "I'll see you all in a while."

I made a beeline for Kriti, who saw me arriving from a distance. Her eyebrows raised in question, and since no one was looking, I winked at her. Her jaw hung open in shock, and I couldn't hold in my chuckle.

The moment I reached where all the ladies sat, I turned to

my mother. "Maa, I'm taking Kriti out for a while. Dad wants to discuss a few things with everyone."

Maa smiled at me and then at Kriti. "Sure, you guys go ahead."

It was hilarious to see Kriti's comically shocked face. I think she, too, just realized the perks of being engaged. Meera teased her a bit as she came around her to join me, and Kriti pulled her hair in return.

We made our way to the front of the house toward my car. Once we were out of sight of the family, I pulled her hand in mine as we walked to the car. Her cheeks flushed as she tightened her hand in mine. That tiny gesture was like a solid punch to my heart. The way she looked at me and her soft hands brought so much peace within me; she made me feel like a king. And I couldn't stop staring at my queen.

The moment we were both seated, I rushed us out of the main gate and onto the main street. Blessed silence ensued after hours of celebrations and conversations.

We stared at the passing roads for a few minutes before I turned to a relatively empty street and parked my car on the side of the road under the shade of a tree. Finally, I rested my back against the car door so I could properly look at my future wife.

She wore a beautiful dark red saree with intricate gold threads woven in swirls. She'd applied thick eyeliner and a dark red lipstick, her pouty lips enticing me beyond reason. I couldn't stop staring at her.

Her generous curves, how they'd feel in my arms, under me, over me. I bit the inside of my cheek to prevent a groan from escaping my lips.

"Aakar," she said, pulling my attention away from her curves, her lips, her pretty hands to meet Kriti's eyes. Her eyes that were raised in question and an unspoken knowledge that she had just caught me ogling her.

"You look fucking stunning, Kriti."

A deep red blush rose to the top of her cheeks, and she smiled, meeting my eyes. "Thank you. So do you."

I chuckled, heat warming my cheeks. "Yeah, well. How do you feel?"

Her eyes widened in relief at the question. Like she was dying to talk about this. She mirrored my position and folded her leg on my seat. "Oh god, I don't know how I feel. Just yesterday, we were two single people considering this arranged marriage option, talking to each other, and today, you've become the single most significant part of my life. I just don't know what to feel, what to do, what will happen now. My mind is just throwing these questions at me that I have no answers to."

With every word she spoke, my heart settled, and my mind calmed. Because I wasn't the only one. I leaned forward from where I sat and brought my hand closer to hers on her lap. I looked at her in question, and instantly, she moved her hand toward mine.

Our fingers touched, and I moved them between hers, feeling the soft pads, the silky, soft skin, and entwined them with mine. I looked at her looking at our joined hands, a small smile on her lips. When I squeezed our hands, she met my eyes.

I leaned slightly closer, a few inches separating us. "Would it make you feel better if I tell you that I feel exactly the same?"

She nodded and said, "It would."

She looked down at our hands and whispered, "Are you still happy with your decision to marry me?"

Slowly, I pulled her hand closer to my face, forcing her to look at me. I pressed a soft kiss on her hand, making her gasp. "I have never been happier in my life."

Her cheeks were red, her voice whisper soft. "Me too. I really hope we make each other happy."

I pressed one more kiss on her fingers—I couldn't help it. "We will. Happy engagement, Kriti."

She smiled at that, her breathtaking, bright smile that lit up my insides. "Happy engagement, Aakar."

I couldn't help but get pulled into her happiness. Her smile. I leaned closer, slowly, giving her the time to move away or push me away. Instead, she pressed forward. And when I pressed my lips to her forehead, she brushed her fingers to my jaw in a soft caress.

My body screamed to get her closer, pull her into my lap, and put my lips on hers. I breathed in her scent and rubbed my jaw to her forehead, feeling her smooth skin brush my beard. She gasped and clutched my neck.

"Aakar," she whispered.

Slowly and reluctantly, I pulled away and leaned back to the car door, keeping her hands in mine and resting them on my lap.

When our eyes met, she flushed, shook her head, and giggled. "That was..."

My mouth turned up in a smile. "Does it feel like we're engaged now?"

She laughed at my question. "That it does."

I smiled at the relief in her eyes. "Good. And now, I can visit you whenever I want, and we won't need our parents' permission."

"Thank God for that."

Now that she was relaxed and happy, it was as best a time as any to discuss our wedding date. I grazed my thumb over her fingers and met her eyes. "Now that you feel like we're engaged, I must broach a slightly difficult topic."

Her eyes widened. "Are you trying to scare me right after we got engaged?"

She tried to pull her hand away from mine, but I clutched it tighter. "No, no. I'm sorry I started the topic like that. I only wanted to talk about what the priest said to me at the house earlier. About wedding dates."

She lightly punched my arm with her free hand, her face trying to decide between being relieved and furious. "You're ridiculous. Don't scare me like that."

I chuckled, kissing her hand in apology. Her fury melted, and a soft look came over her face. "So the priest gave me three options of auspicious wedding dates. December 10, January 18, or February 23. I wanted to ask your opinion on those. And if none of these work, we can go home and discuss with the elders."

"Wow. This makes it even more serious, doesn't it?"

"Yep. I felt the same when the priest told me. That's why I had to get you out of there. The elders sort of look at us like we're just dying to get married and start a family."

She scoffed. "Right? As if we're not scared or nervous or don't have any goals or ambition in life other than to get married." Her rant turned louder and louder as she continued, "But no, none of those matter to them. Not really. Our ambitions are good enough only when we're young. But the moment you turn twenty-one, they conveniently forget all about the hard work you've put into your goals your whole life. They just want us to *simply* shift our goals to finding a husband. It becomes their life's goal. Like we're just an assignment to them, another thing to cross off their list so they can move on to the next one. And we all know what that is."

"Babies," we said together.

She startled at my voice as if she had forgotten my presence.

I raised my eyebrow, trying not to laugh at her passionate rant. Her face turned red, and she quickly averted her eyes and looked out the car window.

How she tempted me! Her words, her fierce temper, her thoughts, her pert little nose, and the way her eyes flared when she was pissed off. I just wanted to kiss her angry face and feel her passion and fire, clutch her closer to me and feel her fingers dig into my skin.

I was such a fucking goner.

If only she knew.

∼

Kriti

I didn't know what came over me, but I could not stop my mouth. One moment, we were having a conversation, and in another, I was off on my own little tirade, the conversation with Aakar long forgotten.

I could feel his eyes on me, looking at me, his amused smile burning a hole through my face. "What?" I asked; my cheeks were on fire.

"Nothing. Nothing at all. I feel pretty fired up myself."

His voice held that amused tone as if he could just burst into laughter at any moment. Although I was glad he wasn't making my little speech a big deal.

"Shut up," I grumbled and finally met his eyes.

He raised his hands in surrender. "I'm not saying anything. But if I may, you are absolutely right."

That did soothe my frayed edges. "Of course, I am. So where were we?"

Aakar composed himself and rubbed his hand along his beard. "The wedding dates."

"Yes. The dates. Well, I have some concerns."

Aakar nodded.

"I have my school children to think about."

I looked at my hand that was still in Aakar's. I'd forgotten we were even holding hands, as if it was just natural. Like a part of me. I shook my head to focus, still keeping my eyes on the way Aakar was grazing his thumb along my hand in encouragement. "The school term ends in mid-April. None of these dates would let me finish the school year. To be honest, the year has barely begun, so I guess it's simply a moot point to think about finishing this school year."

Aakar's hand tightened on mine, and I looked up to see his lips pursed in thought. "Do you want to finish the school year?"

My heart warmed at his question. I would have to delay the wedding by over eight months to finish my school year. And everything within me screamed in denial at that scenario. "I don't really want to wait that long to get married to you, if I'm being honest."

His chest visibly shuddered in relief. "Oh, thank God. I love it when you're honest."

I chuckled. My heart danced with excitement. *He, too, can't wait to marry me.*

"Well, I do feel like I'll have to quit in late November or early December if we choose to marry on December 10th. I guess the Christmas break would be soon enough, and the exams won't start till January. I could be done with some portion of my syllabus by late November. So the kids have an entire month to prepare for their exams. January could also be a good transition for another teacher."

Aakar silently listened to me talk with myself. He didn't jump in or try to give me his opinions. Only when I was done did he ask, "So, is December your preference?"

Before I said yes, I asked, "What is your preference? Your thoughts on the dates?"

He ran his hand in his hair—his thick, lush hair, longer on the top and shorter on the sides—as if hesitant to answer my question. "To be honest, I really want Akira to be a part of our wedding. And she has her college break from mid-December to mid-January. So I'm very much in the preference for the January wedding."

"Why wouldn't you say that beforehand? What if I hadn't asked you?"

He shrugged. "I just wanted to know your opinion first. I would've told you about my preferences as well."

I nodded. Like I told him, it didn't make much of a difference to me what date we chose out of the three. I wasn't going to be able to finish my school year either way. I was more concerned about joining a new city school in the middle of their school year. I might not get the job as a class teacher in the middle of the year, but getting to teach a few subjects would be great for a start.

Aakar was silent while I mulled over everything.

"What are you thinking?" Aakar asked after a few minutes passed.

"Just that I'm okay with a January wedding. I'll have to start working on applying to a few schools in your city, talk to my school's head of department to ask for a few recommendations, and talk to Meera since she's moving to Ahmedabad in a month. So hopefully, we can plan something together."

His smile grew the more I talked.

"What? Why're you smiling?"

He shook his head. "I love how passionate you are. It is very inspiring. And if you need any help or want me to look for some contacts, let me know. I'll ask around."

Of course, I needed help. So, without any hesitation, I said, "Definitely start asking around. I'll take every help that you can offer. I would hate not having a solid work plan after getting married. Because you don't know…"

I realized what I was about to say and thought better of it.

"I don't know what?" Aakar asked.

"Nothing."

"No, tell me."

"Nope. You'll judge me."

His eyes widened in disbelief. "You're deliberately being

stubborn and mysterious, aren't you? I've already decided to marry you. Why would I judge you?"

I couldn't help but smile at him. But I narrowed my eyes in suspicion when I asked, "You promise you won't judge me and think I'm a bad person?"

He squeezed my hand tighter. "I promise."

I looked at our joined hands and met his eyes. "Well, the reason I'm so adamant about having a solid work plan before I get married is that I would like to start working right when you do after marriage. My mom would insist I start after a few months of staying home and getting to know your family first. And I feel like even your parents might expect that. But I'm not going to agree to that. I'm afraid that if your family sees how convenient it is for you and everyone in the house when I'm at home full time and helping everyone around the house, they won't really like it when I return to work. They might feel that things aren't the same and later feel dissatisfied with my choices."

He was about to intervene, but I shook my head and continued, "I just don't want to give them false hope and create this image of being the epitome of a daughter-in-law. It would just be better to start working right when you do. This way, they'll know that I am a working woman and have dreams, goals, and priorities in life that are not just about serving my new family."

I didn't move my gaze away from him the entire time I spoke. I needed to gauge his reaction. But he was as solid as a rock, his hold on my hands warm and strong.

"Kriti, I understand where you're coming from. But I must tell you that you don't have to start working right away under this pressure or fear that my family wouldn't like it when you start working after being used to seeing you at home full time. If you want to live at home and get more acquainted with everyone, you will have my full support whenever you choose to start working. Be it seven days after marriage or seven months.

I won't let my family members make you feel bad for working. I'll take responsibility for them. I promise you."

My heart warmed at his promise. He seemed to be a specialist in taking on responsibilities. I nodded at him in thanks. "Thanks, Aakar. But I still would like to start working when you do."

Aakar shook his head and smiled. "Then you will. Start working on finding a new job with Meera, and I'll talk to a few of my friends and see what I find."

His words gave me the assurance that I needed to make my decision. "Well then, let's get married in January."

His smile was brighter than the sun. "January it is."

With my hand enveloped in his, he pulled me closer. I leaned into him until our faces were mere inches apart. Gently, Aakar grazed his finger on my forehead, pushed the stray strand of hair behind my ear, leaving behind sparks of heat along the shell of my ear.

He bent closer, and my eyes closed.

He grazed his cheek against mine, the feel of his beard causing goose bumps to spread all across my arm. I clutched his shirt and arched my neck, wanting to feel his beard everywhere.

A sound tore from his chest, a rumble and a groan, sending shivers down my spine.

"Kriti." His hoarse whisper along my neck had me pulling him closer.

He rubbed his bearded jaw along my throat and laid a scorching, hot kiss right on the curve of my neck.

A loud moan escaped my mouth, and I needed more of his hot kisses.

But before I could pull him even closer, Aakar slowly pulled away from me.

Our eyes met, and his pupils were dilated and clouded with dark, heated arousal. And it was all for me.

"No more, Kriti." He held me by the back of my neck, his thumb pressing at my cheek. His voice was hoarse, like it was causing him great effort to push the words out.

I tried to regain my rapidly beating heart as he looked at me with barely restrained lust. Taking a deep breath, I nodded and released my grip on his shirt with sheer force of will, leaving a nest of wrinkles behind.

"The next four months are going to be agony," he said.

And I couldn't help but agree.

"In four months, I'll be your wife."

"I can't wait."

With that, he quickly kissed my forehead and turned on the car to take us back home.

13

Song: Pehla Pehla Pyaar Hai
- S. P. Balasubrahmanyam

Aakar

Saying goodbye to Kriti to return home was torture. Not knowing when I'd see her again, hold her hand, or feel her touch again made me want to move to our village home and leave my father's company. It felt like I was leaving behind a crucial part of me—a part that made me smile and laugh.

We returned home, and within the next two weeks, I realized that the next four months were, in fact, going to be pure fucking torture. But not for the same reason that I was hoping for.

I was at work—trying to work between my mother's calls—when Kriti called me. In the next second, I was on the phone. "My mother has totally lost it, Kriti. I never knew that my mother could turn into a monstrous being that had only two words in her vocabulary: wedding preparation. For the life of me, I can't escape her. From the moment I sit for breakfast to when I return home from work, she has me cornered. I can't even escape her at work. If I don't pick up her call or reply to her within five minutes, she calls me again, and if I don't pick up her call, she calls Dad. And then he barges into my office and hands me the phone."

"Hello to you too." Her giggle had me instantly relaxing.

"Save me," I groaned, exaggerating a little bit.

Her laughter rang in my ears. "You're not the only one suffering. In fact, it's worse for me."

I swayed on my rotating chair and scoffed. "Impossible."

Right then, my office door burst open, and in walked my mother, followed by my dad, Ria, and Abhi. I couldn't stop my groan. "Maa, this is unbelievable. Now, you've come to the office?"

I could hear Kriti laughing on the other end of the call.

Maa put both of her hands on her waist, her eyebrows raised and her face pinched. "I have been trying to get you on the phone, but you haven't picked up my calls."

I waved my phone in the air. "Because I'm on the phone."

Before she could start lecturing me about the urgency of wedding preparations, I added, "With Kriti."

That instantly calmed her down. She was downright grinning now. Before I could get another word in, she extended her hand. "Hand me the phone. Let me talk to her too."

Oh shit. My eyes jumped between the phone and my mother's hand.

I knew what was coming the moment I put the phone to my ear.

"Do not hand over the phone, Aakar. Make an excuse," Kriti said. "Oh my god, I'm not ready. Do not hand over the phone."

I looked at the predatory, gleeful look in my mother's eyes and knew there was no escape from that. I cleared my throat, getting ready to act as if Kriti hadn't heard Maa's request on her end. "Kriti, Maa wants to talk to you..."

"Aakar..."

"Oh yeah, she's right here. Really excited to talk to you..."

"I'm gonna kill you."

"Here, talk to Maa."

And without waiting for another threat from Kriti, I handed over the phone to Maa.

Maa put the phone to her ear, and in the next minute, she was laughing and talking to Kriti. No matter what Kriti said, she was good at making small talk with people. I guess her experience as a teacher really makes her a good conversationalist. I was busy looking at Maa talking to Kriti when Ria and Abhi stood over me with amused expressions.

"What?" I asked.

They chuckled, and Abhi turned to Ria. "See, I told you. He's been like this ever since the engagement."

I looked between the two. "Like what?"

Ria laughed. "Mooning over our bhabhi." Sister-in-law is addressed as bhabhi.

I scoffed. Loudly. But for the life of me, no words of refute came to my mind.

So clearly, I chose to change the topic.

"Ria, why are you out and about with Maa? Don't you have any work?"

Ria looked around. Maa and Pappa had already walked out of my office with my phone. So it was just Ria, Abhi, and me.

She took a seat across from me. "Well, I took a leave."

Abhi sat beside her as I asked, "Aren't you taking a little too many days off at work?"

She shrugged her shoulders, but there was nothing casual about the way she held herself. "I'm thinking about quitting."

That had me straightening in my chair, and Abhi looking wide-eyed between the two of us. She was only a year older than me, so I never could act as an older brother to her. So I always had to tread carefully when it came to showing her my concern or support.

So I minded my words when I asked, "Something wrong at your workplace? And does your mom know? Your dad?"

Ria glared at me and ran her hand in her hair. "Of course nobody knows. I was actually going to ask for a raise at work. I called a meeting with my boss too. But before I could get a word in, he started listing things I needed to work on and how I wasn't contributing enough at the firm."

I was off the chair at that. "Bullshit."

Ria looked outside my office window, her eyes burning a hole through the glass. "I know. I've given five years of my life to that place, and this is what I get for asking for a raise."

I walked back and forth across my office. I'd never worked for someone else's company before. I'd joined our company right after graduation, so I never really had to impress a boss or needed to ask for a raise. I never knew the struggle that an employee faced. But I knew Ria. She was the most hardworking of all of us siblings.

She studied hard. She worked harder. And she was great at what she did. She was always welcome to join the company, and she knew that. But we were a textile business, and she was a chartered accountant. She had declared very early on that she wanted to make it on her own.

I looked at Ria. She wasn't one to rage out loud. You'd never know she was angry or hurting until you looked at her eyes. And right now, they were burning. She hated losing. And comments that questioned her work ethic would have bruised her soul.

I sat on my desk near her seat and slowly held her hand. "You can always quit," I offered.

At that, she looked at me. Her eyes were resolute, a deadly calm before the storm. "I already did."

Abhi burst out laughing.

Ria gave him a quick smile, looking all proud and mighty.

"You...What? Then why did you—?" I couldn't even form a proper sentence at her declaration.

She looked at me, a hint of guilt on her face. "Well, you wouldn't have reacted well if I had just told you I quit. Now you know why I couldn't continue working where I wasn't valued, even for a minute longer."

Shaking my head, I took a seat on my chair and drank some water. "You're crazy."

"I'm right."

I nodded at that, a hundred percent supportive of her. "What's your plan?"

And this is where Ria stumbled. She ran her hand in her hair and said, "I need to find a new job before Maa and Pappa find out I quit. If Maa finds out I quit before I have a new job lined up, she would grab that opportunity to get me married off somewhere, and that's happening over my dead body."

I groaned. "Arranged marriage isn't that bad."

She looked apologetic at her choice of words. "I didn't mean it that way, Aakar. An arranged marriage isn't bad when it's between two people willing to marry each other. But I am not willing. At all. And that makes an arranged marriage a forced one."

"Ahh. Okay, then. No marriage for you right now."

"Good. And you can help me find a job. Stat."

At that, my mind automatically started to surf through all my connections. "I'll ask around for an opening and let you know."

That finally brought a real smile to her face. "Thanks, Aakar."

"You never need to thank me, Ria. You'd do the same."

She nodded, and then turned her eyes to Abhi. "So, Abhi, how many times a day does Aakar talk to Kriti?"

Abhi turned his mischievous smile to me and asked, "Are we counting the times you're texting and smiling like a fool at the phone?"

That brought out a loud scoff from me. "I never smile like a fool at the phone."

At the same time, Ria laughed. "That definitely counts."

Abhi chuckled at Ria. "Then he's talking to her the entire day."

"Get out, both of you."

Right then, Maa walked in, laughing on the phone. "Of course, beta, see you on Sunday."

My heart galloped at that, and my eyes zeroed in on Maa and the phone in her hand.

And it was too late when I realized that I'd shown all my cards to Ria and Abhi, who were howling with laughter.

"I told you guys to get out."

They laughed, grabbed the phone from Maa's hand and handed it to me, then pulled her out of the office with them.

With my heart beating loudly and my smile stretched across my face, I put the phone on my ear. "Sunday, huh?"

I only heard Kriti growl at me. "I'm gonna kill you on Sunday."

I couldn't stop my laughter. "Should I bring the knife?"

"For you, my hands are enough."

"Oh, I don't doubt that." I kept my voice low and flirty.

With a growl, she cut the call, leaving me wanting for more.

Sunday couldn't come soon enough.

∼

Kriti

I was going to kill Aakar. His ill timing on the phone had cost me the only day off I got from school. And instead of relaxing with my family, who were very nice to me these days, I had to take a bus to the station early in the morning, without even breakfast. And here I stood, waiting at the station in Ahmedabad for Aakar to pick me up.

I unlocked my phone and dialed his number.

He picked up on the first ring itself. "I'm almost there. I can see the bus station from here."

"You better not be lying. It's way too hot, there are too many people, and I'm very hungry."

He chuckled. "I'm not lying. The AC is already turned on in the car, and I'll get you food in the next ten minutes."

That made me smile like a fool. I had nothing more to say, but he stayed on the phone with me.

In the next two minutes, his car pulled up right in front of me. Quickly, I opened the back seat door of his car and dropped my small bag. He was about to get out of the car, but I waved him off and got in the front seat.

The cool air in the car instantly calmed me. And the sight of my future husband in a white T-shirt and gray sweatpants had my heart pounding right out of my chest.

"Welcome to Ahmedabad, baby."

My jaw dropped open at the endearment. I turned my body to face him, uncaring of where he drove us to. I looked at his relaxed stance, the way he held the steering wheel of the car, his short sleeves showing off his biceps, his T-shirt clinging to his very flat stomach and his very wide chest, and his thighs... God, his thighs. "Have you absolutely lost your mind, Aakar?"

His eyes widened in shock, and quickly, he looked at me, then turned his eyes on the road. "What? What do you mean?"

I couldn't stop looking at him. I was burning here, and he looked entirely too unaffected for my ego. I turned the AC vents to blow directly on me, the air cooling my hot cheeks.

He had no right to look this sexy so early in the morning when I had traveled for three hours and looked like utter shit.

"Kriti? Are you okay?"

I glared at the concern on his face. "No, I am not okay. God, what are you wearing?"

He cringed at that. "I missed my alarm, and I just woke up and ran out the door. I had no time to change or get ready. Why do you sound so upset at that? I don't look that bad, do I?"

He had to be kidding me. I couldn't help the loud scoff that escaped my mouth. "Bad? Now you're just fishing for compliments."

"Compliments?"

"You've got to know how hot you look right now." I just couldn't contain the words.

"Uhh...what?" He quickly turned his face to look at me, and he looked shell-shocked.

"Well, I've only seen you in formal clothes. And this..." I waved a hand at him and continued, "This is...just...In case you didn't notice, I haven't looked at the road once."

His chest rose and fell. A dark red blush covered his cheek and neck. His hands turned white with the way he clutched the steering wheel. His eyes were hooded when they met mine.

And like I told him, I couldn't look away from him.

"You're really not joking," he said.

I laughed. "I'm really not. Imagine if I came to pick you up in my nightwear."

He groaned out loud. "Kriti...You're awful."

Before things could heat any further, I changed the topic, still fanning my face. "You promised me food in the next ten minutes. Your eight minutes are nearly up already."

"Something else is also up already," he mumbled.

"Oh my god. Aakar," I shrieked. And because he'd said it, I couldn't help but look.

And he wasn't wrong.

Having never seen a hard-on before, I quickly looked away.

But I couldn't stop myself from having another peek as he adjusted...umm...himself.

"Kriti, you need to look at the road."

"I'm looking."

"At the road."

"Right."

"It won't go away if you keep looking."

"Oh."

"Yes. So anytime now."

And because I was looking at the proof of his arousal *for me*, his gray sweatpants tightened at the front, his legs spread wide, his hands white-knuckling the steering wheel, I was soaked. My thighs clenched and hands tightened on my dupatta to stop myself from squirming.

A sudden brake of the car broke off my trance, and I quickly looked at Aakar.

His eyes burned everywhere he looked, his jaw was clenched tight, and without looking away from me, he grabbed his cock, and adjusted it not to have it tent his pants. Quite unsuccessfully, if I had to check, which I totally did.

"Should've worn jeans," I muttered.

"Thank God I didn't."

My eyes widened in shock, but a laugh escaped me at his admission. Before I could say anything else, he slowly stopped the car at a small street vendor selling chai and sweet buns. A young man came running to take our order, and in the next five minutes, I was holding two chai in my hands and two jam buns on my lap as Aakar drove us around to find a shaded place to park.

He found a spot under a tree. "My house is on the next street. We can go after we finish eating."

I loved how he always found ways for us to spend time together. He could've just as easily drove us home, and we could've had chai and breakfast at his place. But I liked that our privacy and time to get to know each other were important to him.

I passed him his chai and bun after he parked his car. The intense sexual tension that had ignited between us earlier calmed to a simmer, but I didn't miss the heated glances he sent my way. And he didn't complain when I couldn't stop sneaking peeks at him every now and then.

Between the heated moments, we had our own little breakfast, talking about our week, our work, and how our parents were getting crazier by the day.

~

Speaking of parents getting crazier by the day, the moment we stepped inside the house, Aakar's mom and aunts were upon us. By the time they'd cajoled me into having breakfast with them, Aakar had already left me alone with them. Not that I was scared of my future mother-in-law and aunties-in-law or anything. Absolutely not.

I'd barely had a few sips of chai when Aakar's mother started the conversation. "So Kriti Beta, what kind of traditional clothes would you like to wear for the wedding functions? Salwar kameez, sarees, choli?"

She sat at the head of the table. I sat on her right while the other two aunts sat across from me on her left. Before I could answer her, one of the other aunts piped in, "Didi, these Bollywood celebrities are all wearing such great clothes. I still think Virat Kohli and Anushka Sharma had the best wedding clothes."

The other aunt was quick to jump in too. "They wore too subtle colors, Ekta. I loved Deepika and Ranveer the best."

All of their eyes turned to me. Of course I was aware of all the celebrity weddings and the clothes they wore. And because the topic was familiar to me, I relaxed a bit. I placed the cup of chai on the dining table and folded my hands on the table. "I loved Vicky and Katrina's wedding. Her blouse pattern was so good."

The ladies hummed in agreement, and we talked about different styles of traditional attire we could wear for various functions. They told me about a few shops we would visit today, the clothes they want to get me, and some jewelry options.

I was engrossed in the conversation until Aakar stepped in the dining area. Aakar in a light pink shirt, blue jeans, a metal gray watch with trimmed beard and neatly combed hair was a force to be reckoned with.

Our eyes met, and my mind stopped comprehending all the words exchanged around us. Except when I heard Aakar's mother. "Aakar Beta, why are you all ready?"

I frowned. So did Aakar. "What do you mean? Aren't we going shopping?"

All the ladies started to laugh. And a sinking feeling formed in my gut. And all my excitement over shopping dropped when one of the aunts said, "*We* are going shopping. For Kriti. She's only here for a day. We need to shop as much as we can today. We can shop for you some other day."

"Don't you need me to come around with you? I can drive you all to the shops," Aakar said.

I appreciated his efforts to join us, but I didn't see it happening.

I was proved right when the eldest aunt said, "You don't need to chauffeur us around. With Ria joining us, there's no space for you."

"Oh."

All three ladies giggled at Aakar's despondent look. I quickly faked a shy smile on my face right before they turned to me. "Are you seeing this, Kriti? I'm glad you're getting married soon. Our Aakar seems to be pretty fond of you."

My face hurt with how I'd stretched my lips into a smile

when all I wanted to do was pout in sheer disappointment at Aakar for not being able to join us.

No sooner did Ria come into the dining area than I excused myself to freshen up a bit to prepare for a long day ahead. When I entered the living room where all the ladies were ready to head out, I found Aakar watching TV in his sweats.

The moment our eyes met, heat sparked in his eyes. I moved my gaze quickly over his body, causing him to smirk. Despite that, his cheeks still turned red. "Have fun, everyone," he mumbled and went back to his television.

With a quick goodbye, all five of us—Ria, me, my future mother-in-law, and the two aunts—headed out. The rest of the day was spent shopping for several traditional attires. Some of them were for the wedding ceremonies, while some were for future occasions. Even Ria joined me in trying out different clothes and got some for herself too.

I had thought that my voluptuous body would be a point of some uncomfortable conversations, but surprisingly, they never commented on my body type. We just had fun shopping, be it sarees or lehenga or salwar kameez. Later on, we stopped by some jewelers to see what would go well with my newly bought clothes, and my mother-in-law gifted me a set of gold earrings that matched my saree.

The entire day flew by, and I had way more fun than I'd anticipated. By the end of the day, we were all so tired and hungry that Maa had asked Aakar to order food from a restaurant by the time we reached home.

I sat beside Aakar at the dining table while we all had dinner together when Ria asked, "So, Kriti, if we didn't bore you too much today, would you like to come back for shopping again?"

I quickly swallowed my bite. "Ria, oh my god, I had one of the best times with all of you. And of course, I would love to join you all. But I don't think I have much shopping left to do."

Aakar's mom scoffed. "Beta, this is just the beginning. Of course there's much to shop for. And if not for you, you can always come with us when we shop for us. You have a great sense of style. I love how quick you are in matching different fabrics. Such a sharp eye."

As my mother-in-law gushed, I could feel Aakar's gaze on me. "Well, I do love shopping."

"Then it's decided. You're coming shopping the week after next. And bring your mother and sister too."

I readily agreed and got back to eating. Under the table, Aakar grazed his hand along mine. A shiver raced down my spine at his gentle, exploring touch. Not letting my expression change even a bit, I turned my hand and entwined our fingers.

Throughout dinner, we clasped our hands together, his thumb gently rubbing circles along mine, his fingers enclosing mine possessively. The moment Aakar grabbed our clasped hands and put them on his thigh, my mind nearly short-circuited. It took everything within me not to show the shock on my face with everyone right at the table.

The moment we got into the car after saying the goodbyes and a promise to return the week after next, Aakar had our hands clasped and back on his thigh. He had to let go of my hand to change the gears on the car, but he quickly pressed my hand on his thigh. "Keep it here."

I couldn't say anything but keep my shaking hand right where he instructed. All the way to the bus stop. The entire time we sat in the car waiting for the bus. And all I could remember for the rest of my journey back home was the heat of his body and the feel of his thigh under my palm.

14

Song: Tere Bin
- *Rabbi Shergill*

Aakar

The following week, I went to Laxminagar. This time not to meet Kriti specifically but to help Meera and Luke move to Ahmedabad. And it wasn't just me. I'd brought along Abhi and his best friend, Karan.

And it didn't hurt that Kriti was also at Meera's place. However, the mood at Meera's place was a little more somber than I expected. I thought everyone would rush to get everything in the mini-truck Luke and Meera had hired and reach Ahmedabad as early as possible.

But the moment I stepped foot in Meera's house, I found her and Kriti talking, tears streaming down their faces. A fierce rush to go to Kriti and take her in my arms came over me, and I almost rushed to her when Luke stepped in front of me. He rolled his eyes and dragged me outside the house. "They've been at it for half an hour. One stops and the other one starts the waterworks. It really had me worried for a second there, but I think they're just trying to delay the move."

I scoffed. "I give it five more minutes. Otherwise, I'm going in and putting them to work. If only to distract them."

Luke chuckled. "Deal."

With that, I put Abhi and Karan to work. Hari, Meera's young brother, trotted behind them, hauling smaller stuff that he could carry. It was adorable.

I gave them ten minutes. And when they still didn't come outside, I went in, crossing Luke on the way, who muttered, "All yours."

I stepped into the house, and seeing them talking, eyes shining with too many tears shed, I cleared my throat. Loudly. Both of them turned to me, now quiet, eyes swollen, and dried tear tracks on their cheeks. I only had eyes on Kriti, and she looked all soft and bitable. All I wanted to do was pull her into my arms and keep her there.

I didn't let any of it show on my face. I stared down both of them. "We could really use your help out there if we want to leave here on time and reach Ahmedabad before sunset. We'll also need to unpack everything at your new place, Meera."

Kriti turned to Meera and, with a shaking voice, asked, "Should I also come to the city with you?"

"That won't be necessary." I didn't even realize when I'd spoken the words. The moving would take us an entire day to reach Ahmedabad, and I could not, for the life of me, bear the thought of Kriti traveling back to Laxminagar all alone at night.

Both of them turned to me in shock.

I ran my hand in my hair. "I mean, Kriti, I'll safely get them settled in their new place. You don't want Meera and Luke worried about getting you home in the midst of all of this. And you're already coming to Ahmedabad for shopping next week. Meera can join you guys then."

That brought an instant smile to their faces. Kriti quickly

turned to Meera and had her in her arms. "Of course, and then I'll be getting married, and then we'll work together, and we'll be together again."

I very nearly scoffed out loud, thinking—praying—Kriti felt even a hint of desperation to be together *with me* that she had for Meera.

Just great. Now I was jealous of Kriti's best friend.

Once Kriti and Meera got their emotions under control, we got to work, and in the next three hours, we had everything hauled into the mini-truck. Luke gave Meera, her mom, and her brother some time to say goodbye to their house.

I looked around but didn't find Kriti anywhere. I walked around the house and found her washing her hands and feet at the tap in the backyard. And my feet came to a halt.

She was very methodical, her movements quick and meticulous. There should be nothing arousing about her washing off the dust and grime of old stuff, but I couldn't stop staring at her.

Couldn't stop wondering. I was looking at my fiancée.

The moment she bent over, trying to get her feet all cleaned up, I nearly bit my tongue at her glorious curves. I bit the inside of my cheek to stop any embarrassing sound from coming out of my mouth.

"I know you're there."

Her words had me coughing. "Uh...uhm...Oh. Of course. I wasn't being silent and sneaky."

"Weren't you?" Her twinkling eyes and the smirk on her lips were clear indications that she very well knew what I was looking at.

I decided to let myself be honest. "I find you really, really hot."

Her eyes widened, and she flicked her wet hands at me. "Shut up."

I couldn't help but chuckle at the way she got shy, all angry and deflecting. I walked closer to her and stopped when I was mere inches away from her. My shoes got wet from the water still running from the tap.

Her gaze never left mine, and I didn't hide how I felt about her. I raised my hand and slowly rubbed at the dust patch she'd missed near her forehead. "Remember how you felt when I wore my T-shirt and sweatpants?"

Her cheeks turned redder, and she looked away. "Wow, you really know how to push my buttons."

I smiled and didn't let her deter me. "Well, I feel the same for you every minute of the day. You don't even need to be in front of me. You're all I think about. At home. At the office. In the morning, the moment I wake up. At night, before I go to sleep. Your laugh," I murmured, keeping my voice soft to keep her looking at me the way she was. "Your eyes, the way you glare at me, the way you stare at me, and especially, when I turn you on. Your fucking curves, the way they make me lose my mind. You have absolutely no idea what you do to me."

I didn't know who moved first, but her hands clutched my shirt like it was the only thing holding her up. And my hands... My hands were around her, one hand clutching her waist and the other clutching her neck, my thumb grazing her soft cheek.

Not an inch of space separated us.

Her chest rose and fell against mine, causing all the blood to rush south.

A small smirk came across her face. Softly, she murmured, "I think I have some idea about what I do to you."

She moved her hips to brush over what was a very painful erection, causing me to groan out loud. "Do you now?"

I moved forward, causing her to take a step back, so her back leaned against the wall.

"Do you know what I really want to do to you right now?"

Her eyes were pure molten seduction. "Do *you* know what I really want you to do to me right now?"

I pressed myself fully against her. I couldn't even stop the shudder that raced along my spine. "What do you want, baby?"

She shivered against me, her hands clutched my shirt tighter, and she pulled me even closer. With our lips mere inches apart, she whispered, "Kiss. I want you to kiss me on the lips."

My heart pounded so hard that I was sure she could feel it beating against hers. "I'm glad we're on the same page."

And slowly, I brushed my lips against hers. Just the touch of her soft lips had my toes curling and my heart racing.

Knowing it was Kriti's first kiss, I placed soft kisses along her lips, the corner of her mouth, and the soft pouty part of her bottom lip. With every touch, Kriti tugged me closer, as if she couldn't get enough of me.

A lock of her hair tickled my cheek, and I brushed it behind her ear and held her cheek tighter. Just so I could kiss her deeper. Harder.

She moaned and kissed me back. Her wet lips parted, and her tongue brushed against my lips, tasting me. My cock pulsed, and my balls throbbed, every pore of my body aching to climb inside her and have her wrapped around me.

I had to quickly back off for a second, afraid I would lose control of my body. But her lips chased mine, and her soft moan had me instantly diving back for more.

I held her face with both of my hands and ran my tongue along her lips. Kriti panted like she couldn't get enough air. But the moment I would back up a bit, she kept pulling me closer by my shirt and sealing our lips. The next time her lips parted, I pushed my tongue into her mouth, gently running it along her tongue.

She went wild. She sucked and nipped and bit. I never wanted to move away from her. Kriti's arms wrapped around me, her lips on mine, and her breath against my face. Her warmth, her passion, her fire, consumed me, and I was in heaven.

I was going to be this woman's husband. She would be the only woman who would bring me this pleasure. This toe-curling, spine-tingling pleasure that was pure, blissful agony.

My body wanted more and more and more. I pulled her closer, and I couldn't help but move my head lower to kiss her neck. I took a deep breath, and the scent of her had my head spinning. My mouth watered, and I sucked. Kriti's body arched into mine at that, and her long moan had us pulling to a stop.

Her cheeks were on fire. Her hair was mussed, her eyes were clouded with lust, and her lips—dear god, her lips—were puffy and red and looked thoroughly ravaged. Her eyes took me in, and I was sure I looked the same.

Our breaths were harsh pants, my one hand still clutched her waist while I laid the other on the wall at her back, trying to keep standing on shaky legs. I gave her a tentative smile and softly wiped the corner of her wet lip with my thumb. When she still didn't respond, I licked that thumb and gave her a wink.

Her eyes widened in shock, and she burst out laughing. Her hand still clutched my shirt as she laid her head against my chest and laughed, all the while muttering, "Oh my god. What did we do? God...Wow."

I quickly kissed her head and pulled her into my arms. Her arms circled my waist, and I swayed her gently. "Did you like it?" I murmured in her hair.

She hummed in response.

"Do you regret it?"

Her head turned at that in a beat, and she looked at me shocked.

"Do *you*?" she asked in return.

"Not even for a second."

I'd never seen her smile so wide before as her eyes twinkled in delight. "Me neither. We wouldn't be waiting for us to get married before we do it again, would we?"

That had me roaring in laughter. "Not if I can help it."

She played with the button of my shirt, a crazy, satisfied smile on her face that had my heart toppling over. "Good. I quite liked it."

I scoffed at that. "*Liked it?* You were pulling me closer and moaning and..."

Her hand came over my mouth, and her eyes were trying to shoot daggers at me, but failed miserably, what with the fierce blush dotting her cheeks. "You shut up. You...You were doing all that too."

"Of course, I was. I was kissing *you*."

She was about to respond when a loud throat clearing had us jumping apart.

I looked behind Kriti to find Luke standing at the door that led from the backyard to the kitchen. He had that ridiculously annoying smirk on his face that made me glare at him. With an annoying smile, he said, "Well, we're all ready when you are."

"We'll be right there," I said through clenched teeth. All the while, Kriti wouldn't even face Luke in embarrassment.

"Take your time," he added, the sly bastard.

"Fuck off," I mouthed, and he howled with laughter as he went inside.

"Oh god," Kriti muttered.

"Hey, don't worry. Luke won't say anything to anyone."

She smiled at that. "You're right. Okay, yeah. I was just talking and kissing my fiancé. Nothing to be shy about."

"Exactly."

Knowing that I had to leave Kriti behind had my mood sinking. Every time she left me, or I left her, it felt like I left behind a piece of my heart. It was agony not to have her around me all the time. "So..." I began, moving closer to her. So close that our foreheads touched. "I'll see you next weekend."

She squeezed my hand tightly with both of hers and nodded. "And call me as soon as you get home."

Fuck, I loved how she cared. "I will."

Her eyes shone, and she looked away. "Don't you forget it," she rasped.

I brought her hands to my lips and kissed them in promise. "I won't."

With that, I left her, starting the vicious cycle of waiting to meet her again, holding her again, and now kissing her again.

∽

Kriti

I could still feel Aakar's taste on my tongue long after he was gone. I had watched the back of his car till it disappeared and had stood outside Meera's empty house long after that. My heart had pounded incessantly with this desperate need to be closer, always closer, to Aakar.

Instead of being wary about leaving my house, my family, my entire world behind, I was looking forward to it. All because of one earth-shattering, mind-altering kiss. Or maybe it was the man who gave me the kiss.

My mind replayed the moment Aakar held my cheek and kissed me. My cheeks still tingled with the way his beard had scraped and rubbed at my skin. I was never going to let him shave. His soft lips, the way his breath had quickened, and the way he had grinded on me.

I had to sit down on my vehicle before my legs gave out. All the while I drove back home, I couldn't help but lick my lips, trying to find his taste. Gosh, that was why parents didn't allow their kids to date.

One kiss, and I was all but ready to get married to the man and say goodbye to my world.

I parked my vehicle in our parking spot in a daze, wondering what it would be like if he'd kissed me on my neck more. If he'd gone farther down. If he'd clutched my waist and pulled me closer. If he'd grabbed my...

"What is wrong with this girl?" Maa's shrill voice pulled me back from my highly imaginative, romantic daydream and completely threw me off.

"Uh...what?" I looked around and found myself lying down on the sofa with a ridiculous smile on my face.

Quickly, I wiped that smile off, got my serious teacher face on, and turned to Maa.

"What were you saying?" I asked.

She raised her eyebrows and gave my father that *Are you seeing this?* look and turned to me. "I've been calling your name for the past five minutes, and you just kept sighing loudly."

"Umm. I was just thinking about Meera and how happy she was to start her new life."

If I couldn't use my best friend's name to lie, what was even the point of having a best friend?

Maa looked at me with doubt. I could almost see her mind throwing questions at her to corner me. But thankfully, she let it go, and I almost wished she hadn't because of what she said next. "Anyway, I was just waiting for you to get home. I need to start teaching you how to cook some good dishes."

With a gigantic eye roll, I rolled back on the sofa and showed her my back. "Please. God, no. I don't want to learn more dishes. I know the basics."

Maa harrumphed. "Basic dishes won't impress your in-laws."

"I don't care to impress them. They've already chosen me."

Maa sat at the seat near my feet and squeezed my ankle. "And we don't want them to regret their choice."

Okay, first of all, *ouch*.

Before I could say something, Pappa interjected, "Now, Reshma, no one is going to be regretting my daughter."

"*Our* daughter," Maa corrected.

"Glad you remember that," I murmured.

"What did you say?" Maa asked.

"Nothing." I rolled my eyes with my face pushed into the sofa seat, released my breath, and got up to face my mother.

"Maa, I know how to make basic, regular food. I don't have the time or inclination to learn all that right now, and I won't have the time to cook all the fancy, impressive dishes once I'm married."

Maa rolled her eyes, her exasperation very evident with the way she looked between Pappa and me. "When you first go to your new house, imagine how happy your new family would be if you cooked them some delicious sweets like gulab jamun or carrot halwa. Don't you want to feed your husband the sweets you cook yourself?"

"Would Aakar learn anything new to please me? Or is it just my responsibility to keep impressing my new family? What is he going to do to impress my family?"

Maa was about to answer me when Pappa cleared his throat. And when my father talked, I listened. "He will impress us by taking good care of you. By being a good and respectful husband to you. By knowing your worth and going above and beyond to fulfill all your heart's desires."

My nose tingled with the incoming tears. I blinked them away even though a few slipped by. I was going to miss him so much. No one would ever come close to loving me the way Pappa loved me.

I looked down at my hands. "Can't I impress my new family by being a good wife, being respectful, caring, loving, and supportive? Do I need to feed everyone a variety of foods?"

Maa clutched my hand, and I turned to look at her. This time, she seemed a little apologetic and a lot more loving. "*Beta,*

I know you're afraid you'll have to take over all the responsibilities of the house, and you'll lose yourself in trying to impress your new family. I'm not telling you to do that. But if your husband or any member of your family is in a stressful situation on a weekend, wouldn't you like to cook them some warm, sweet halwa to make them smile? Is that too much to do for your husband or your new family?"

That didn't sound all bad. "I mean, it doesn't hurt to know how to cook a few things, even if I don't have to make it often."

Maa smiled and squeezed my hand. "Don't be afraid, beta. Changing your lifestyle a little bit, accommodating your new family, making a few compromises, is not a bad thing. And it doesn't mean you are betraying yourself."

"It sure feels like it sometimes." Just the thought of having to learn something new or change a part of myself for my new family sent a jolt of panic within me. Not just panic, but this... this indignant emotion at being the only one who had to change so much after marriage. Did all women feel that way, or was I just too stubborn for my own good?

I shook that thought away from my mind and imagined Aakar. The thought of today's kiss, the way he looked at me—with desperate, insatiable need—and felt a rush of calm pass through me. I could learn to cook a few sweet things for Aakar. To see him smile, to see his surprise or awe.

With the thought of seeing Aakar's smile, I turned to Maa. "Let me ask Aakar what he likes. And I'll learn to cook some of that."

Maa laughed. "Why don't you surprise him with something?"

I scoffed. "What if he doesn't even like the dish that I cooked? I'm not going to waste my time learning something he doesn't even like."

Maa rolled her eyes at me and went toward the kitchen.

"Let me know what he likes, and we'll cook those dishes in the evenings."

I got comfortable on the sofa and picked up my phone.

> Me: So are you a sweet or a savory person?

It was at night that I finally received a reply.

> Aakar: Sorry, finally got home, had a quick dinner. A long shower *wink* Only because my mind kept thinking about the best kiss of my life. You're the only one to blame. And I like both. Sweet and savory. Why?

I was in my bed, under my covers, as I read his message. My cheeks were on fire, and the sharp tingling feeling between my legs had my toes curling.

> Me: You're awful!!! Also, what are your favorite sweet and savory items?

> Aakar: Why do you ask? You going to make them for me?

> Me: Well, yeah. So what do you like?

> Aakar: What are you best at making?

I scoffed in indignation. The nerve of him.

> Me: Nothing at all.

> Aakar: Oh. That's fine.

> Me: Thanks for your approval *sarcasm*

> Aakar: I didn't mean it that way 😊

> Me: Yeah, yeah. Now, are you going to answer me or what?

Aakar: You're going to learn for me?

> Me: Well, yeah.

Aakar: You don't have to.

> Me: Aakaarrrr. I know. I want to. Now, will you tell me what you love?

I saw the *typing*...on the phone. It stopped. And there was a pause before he started typing again.

> Me: Looks like a long list of items.

Aakar: Only cause you're asking. I could eat kachori all day, and if I didn't care about my health and my body, I could eat about fifty gulab jamuns.

I smiled. That didn't sound bad. And he only gave me two items. Was he trying to make it easy for me?

> Me: Just two items?

Aakar: You want more?

> Me: Well, if you love a few more items, I wouldn't mind learning them.

A moment passed before I got his reply.

Aakar: If it is any motivation for you, you're really making me blush right now.

I had to suppress my giggle so as not to wake up my sister, who was tossing and turning on the other bed.

> Me: Photo, or it didn't happen!

In the next minute, I had his reply.

> Aakar: <photo attached>
>
> Aakar: Well, you put me on the spot. And I'm not used to clicking selfies. But since you're learning to cook my favorite items for me.

I almost dropped my phone seeing the photo. He had about two pillows under him, his one hand was under his head as he clicked the picture with another. He looked tired from all the moving, but his cheeks were all red and his eyes were so soft for me that my heart ached to be closer. But it was his smile. His wide, shy smile that he couldn't seem to contain. If just the thought of me cooking for him did that to his smile, how would he smile if he loved what I cooked for him?

> Me: That was very motivating.

For a few minutes, I didn't get anything from him. I was almost going to lock the phone after staring at Aakar's beautiful smile and go to sleep when I got his message.

> Aakar: Would it scare you if I told you that I've never felt this lonely in my own bed before?

I didn't know why, or whether it made me happy or sad, but tears slipped out of my eyes.

> Me: It doesn't scare me. At all.

Why would it? When I knew there was someone who felt lonely without me. Who blushed when I decided to learn to cook his favorite food. Who kissed me like he wouldn't be able to take his next breath without me.

It wouldn't scare me at all.

It was all I ever needed not to be scared to marry that person.

15

Song: Te Amo
- *Shankar Sunidhi Chauhan, Ash King*

Aakar

Weeks passed without meeting Kriti at all. Five weeks to be precise. Our wedding was in six weeks, and I hadn't even seen my fiancée after our first kiss. I sat in the meeting, hearing Abhi describe our account reports to Dad and my uncles. And my mind couldn't comprehend a word out of his mouth.

All I heard was a humming noise, all I saw were nodding heads, and all I felt was this deep, gnawing ache inside me that simply wanted to—simply *needed* to—see Kriti. Hold her hand. Touch her skin. Feel her soft lips against mine.

But each one of the thirty-five excruciating days that we hadn't met had passed in mind-numbing tasks like shopping for endless days of functions, deciding on a menu that would please children, adults, and old relatives, preparing guest invites, and constant fighting on who to exclude and who to include.

Akira was coming home in two weeks, and all my hopes of spending some time with Kriti alone were going to pieces.

Every night, I slept with her messages in my hand and, occasionally, her voice in my ear. For the first time, I felt the coldness on the other side of my bed. And my patience was hanging by a thread.

All I wanted was to get married to Kriti and spend my days living with her, knowing every little thing about her, and making her blush the way she did when I kissed her.

Was that too much to ask for?

Someone shook my shoulder, and I almost jumped out of my seat.

"What?" I turned to find my dad staring at me, the uncles giving me quizzical expressions, and Abhi outright grinning like a fool.

"What do you think?" Dad asked.

About what? "Sounds good," I said and nodded at Abhi.

Dad's frown deepened. "So a ten percent drop in our sales in the past month sounds good to you?"

My gaze met Abhi's, who seemed to be bursting with laughter but was trying very hard to hold it in.

"Of course not." I had nothing else to say, and clearly, Dad knew I hadn't heard a word.

He sighed. "Are you okay, beta? You seem to be distracted these days."

I rubbed my forehead. "I'm fine, Pappa. Just a bit tired. The wedding preparations are frustrating. There's just no end."

Navin Kaka, my father's older brother, nodded. "Oh, it's not going to end until you're married. Wait till Akira comes."

Sunil Kaka laughed at that and piped in, "Your mom and dad will have a house full of relatives for the entire month. You know, so Akira can catch up with all the relatives. And everyone can get in the wedding mood as well."

Dad flushed. "It will be fun to have all the family together. When else do we all get to gather?"

Now, I loved my family. I would do anything to make them happy. But I was not keen on gathering all the relatives at our place and having to sit and make small talk every fucking night of the month.

Right then, Mom called. *Not again...*

"It's Maa," I said to everyone and picked up the call.

"Aakar Beta, how long will you be in the office?"

I looked at my watch. "Maa, it's three o'clock. I still have a few hours of work here."

"Can't you leave early?"

"Why?"

Please don't let it be clothing fittings.

"Beta, we need to go to the jewelers. We need to buy some jewelry for us, for you, and for Kriti. We already got a few things for Kriti when she was here, but I think it would be a nice little surprise if you could get her something for the wedding night. What do you say?"

A gift for Kriti sounded wonderful, but I really didn't want to get it with Maa and the aunties.

I sighed. "Maa, you really don't need me for your shopping. I'll go and get something for Kriti on my own."

"You wouldn't even know what to buy."

I looked at Dad, silently begging for his help. He sighed in helplessness, most likely afraid of the marriage-crazed avatar that Maa had turned into.

"Maa, not today."

Before she could start arguing, I cut the call. I looked at my dad, my uncles, and Abhi. "I need a break."

"Break?" Dad's voice cracked in worry. Whether it was for me or Maa, I didn't know. I didn't care.

I clenched my teeth and nodded. "For the past five weeks, I've been running around everywhere Maa wanted, checking off one list after another. We even spent a whole day meeting different makeup people. She wants me involved in *everything*. I'm going to be married in six weeks, and I haven't even seen my fiancée in five weeks."

"He's missing bhabhi," I heard Abhi whisper to Sunil Kaka, Dad's younger brother.

Sunil Kaka snorted while I glared at Abhi.

"You're so cute when you miss bhabhi, bhai," he teased, causing Dad and Navin Kaka to blush and Sunil Kaka to laugh.

At this point, I didn't even care. I caved. "Yes. I do. And that's why I'm going to Laxminagar for the weekend. And I'm taking tomorrow off so I can have a long weekend there. I'm leaving as soon as we're done with this meeting."

Dad sighed in defeat. He knew I was done. He pinched his brow. "What am I going to say to your mother?"

"I don't know. I don't care. And none of you are following me to Laxminagar. I'm going away to get a break. This is my only chance to spend some time with Kriti. Once Akira arrives in two weeks, it will just be one thing after another."

Dad nodded and waved his hand, dismissing the meeting.

I did not wait around.

I went to my office, closed out my files, grabbed my laptop, phone, chargers, and was out of the office before even Abhi could leave the meeting room.

After getting in my car, I put on my favorite playlist and left the parking lot. For the next four hours, I didn't pick up any calls. I simply drove, watching the trees and the people and the buildings pass by. I only had one thing in my sight. In my mind. Kriti. Only Kriti.

I had nothing else on my mind—no thoughts, no wishes, no words, just this drive to get to Kriti. And I did not stop driving until I parked my car outside her house. I opened the metal gate of their house, climbed the three steps, and rang the bell.

And waited.

In the next minute, I heard footsteps approaching on the other side, and then the door opened.

And there she was.

She'd opened the door with an absent smile, but the moment she saw me, her eyes widened, and her mouth hung open.

She didn't move. She didn't gasp. Just stared at me.

"Kriti Beta, who's at the door?" her mother shouted from inside the house.

That had her moving again.

"Aakar," she gasped, then smiled and took a step toward me.

I so badly wanted to hug her, clutch her tightly, and just breathe her in. I put my hand in my pocket to stop myself from pulling her into my arms out in the open and ran my other hand in my hair. "I just had to get out of there. I...uh...I missed you."

A wide smile came over her face, red dotted her cheeks, and she gave a soft chuckle, not meeting my eyes. Like she couldn't believe I said those words out loud. Neither could I. But I had never needed to see anyone more than I needed to see her.

It had been too long.

She shook her head for a second and then looked at me in horror. And then looked down at her clothes. And then back at me again. She whirled back to go in and immediately turned back to me in exasperation. "You...Couldn't you have called and told me that you were coming?"

I looked at her clothes. She wore a T-shirt and soft cotton pajamas. And my knees nearly gave out. I'd never seen her so casual before. All the traditional clothes hid or accentuated her curves. But this, a simple T-shirt and pajama bottoms, *showed* her curves. Her T-shirt clung to her generous breasts and her shapely waist.

"Sorry?" I asked.

She gave me a flat smile, clearly aware that I wasn't sorry at all.

"Beta, who is it?" her mom shouted again.

"It's Aakar," she shouted loud enough for even the neighbors to hear.

Her mother's shriek had me almost stepping back.

Kriti gave me a wide smile, and before I could say anything, she clutched my hand and pulled me inside.

The relief I felt at her soft, innocent touch staggered my mind. I just wanted her to keep holding my hand when I heard a rush of footsteps coming our way.

She quickly let go of my hand, and I felt the sharp sting of emptiness. I shook it off and removed my shoes at the entrance.

In the next moment, Kriti's mother and father rushed to greet me. "Aakar Beta, what a wonderful surprise," her mother gushed.

"Please, come in, beta," her dad said.

I bowed and touched their feet in greeting. "Namaste."

They gave me their blessings, and we walked in. Rati and Kartik sat at the dining table eating. Three more plates were at the table.

I quickly turned to all of them in embarrassment. "I'm sorry to intrude on your dinner."

Her mother shook off my apology. "Oh no. Join us, beta. I'm sure you haven't had any dinner if you drove right now."

I hadn't, and my stomach gave a loud rumble that had Kriti bursting into laughter.

"Kriti," her mother chided her as if I wasn't there.

She rolled her eyes at me in exasperation, and I couldn't help but chuckle at her. "C'mon, let's eat," Kriti said, and I obeyed.

Kriti went into the kitchen, got me a plate, and handed it to me. She was about to get back on her seat right beside me when her mother cleared her throat. Both of us turned to look at her, and her mother smiled and looked at Kriti. "Kriti Beta, serve Aakarji food, won't you?"

Kriti gave a quick but scary death stare to her mother. Who, in turn, gave her an equally terrifying *mom* stare.

"No worries, Auntie. I'll help myself."

I felt Kriti soften slightly. She looked at her mom and said, "He said he'll help himself."

Her mother gave me the biggest fake angry smile and said, "I insist, Aakar Beta."

Well, I tried. And I had no interest in jumping between mother and daughter when my stomach caved in on itself in hunger.

Kriti sighed and took my plate. She served me the theplas, potato bhaji, sweet pickle, and some buttermilk on the side. The moment she sat beside me, I squeezed her hand under the table lightly. Quickly. Enough for her to smile again.

I continued to graze my hand along hers every now and then while we all ate.

I looked at the twins. They looked nothing like each other. Kartik sat quite taller while Rati was shorter and slightly chubby. I could imagine Kriti at Rati's age, all cute with a soft teenage face. I smiled at Kartik when our eyes met. "So, Kartik, Rati, how's school?"

Rati flushed while Kartik met my eyes. "It's okay. Normal." And he got back to eating. I looked at Kriti, and she gave me a teasing smile as if she could see I was trying.

Right then, Kriti's father cleared his throat. "So, Aakar Beta, what brought you this way?"

Well, I missed your daughter to distraction, and I couldn't stand a moment without her. So I dropped everything I was doing and drove here, hoping to kiss her again.

Since I couldn't say all that to him, I said, "Well, Uncle, since Akira is coming in two weeks, I thought I'd come meet Kriti this weekend before I get even busier with the wedding preparations. This way Kriti and I could spend some time together and get a bit of a break from all the wedding preparations."

He smiled softly in approval. "Good idea. Kriti Beta, I don't think Aakar has seen our entire house. Do give him a tour after dinner."

"So, are you here for the next three days?" Kriti's mom asked.

"Yes, Auntie. If it isn't a problem."

I didn't even hear her response because, right then, Kriti tightly squeezed my hand under the table. And before she could let it go, I entwined our fingers together.

I didn't let it go when Rati dropped her spoon on the floor.

Not even when she bent down to pick it up.

Not even when she had a big smile on her face when she came up.

And when our eyes met, I simply winked at her, making her giggle.

I liked my sister-in-law.

∼

Kriti

"So this is my room." I opened the door to my bedroom with a flourish. And instantly regretted it.

Rati hadn't made her bed. Her books, lap desk, laptop, and headphones were all strewn across her bed. My bed wasn't any better either. Piles of my students' books were stacked in the order of the roll numbers and subjects. I had my system. But together, it all looked like a mess.

But before I could even do anything, Aakar had closed my bedroom door behind us and pushed me against the door. He stood so close I could feel his clothes brush against mine. He didn't touch me. No. He placed both of his hands on the door behind me, caging me in.

Heat radiated from his body, and I desperately wanted to pull him closer.

I looked up and met his eyes.

They looked at me with such intensity, such longing that I couldn't help but touch the button of his shirt. He took a step even closer and clutched my hand at his chest. "Five weeks. I haven't seen you in five weeks."

My heart pounded as he traced small patterns over my hand. "Missed me?"

He stepped even closer. So close, his jaw grazed my cheeks. And then, he nodded, rubbing his beard along my cheek. Heat raced through my spine all the way down to my toes. "Aakar."

"Did you miss me?"

This time, I pulled him closer by the button of his shirt. So close, his leg stepped between mine, our bodies flush together.

He groaned, barely stopping his voice.

I gasped as I felt the very hard evidence of how much our closeness, how much *I* affected him. His hold on the door behind me tightened. "Kriti," he moaned in my ear, rolling his hips against mine.

My eyes rolled back in my head at the new, intense pleasure between my legs as his thigh rubbed me just at the right spot.

"Fuck," he muttered.

Common sense returned to me at the sharp, peaking arousal. "We really need to stop."

He nodded. "Just a minute."

At my nod of approval, he pulled his hips away from mine but pressed a soft kiss on my neck, my cheeks, and my neck again. I couldn't help but arch my neck further, begging for more.

And he gave it to me. Deep, dizzying pulls of his lips on my neck.

With another sharp curse, he was off me.

I looked at my messy bed, my heart still beating like a racehorse.

And now I had to make space for us to sit. I quickly turned to him. "Just a sec."

I quickly went about moving the piles of books in a neat stack on the floor near my cupboard. In the meantime, Aakar was silent as he looked at the several pictures tacked on the softboard, all thanks to Rati.

I went and stood beside him. "If I'd known you were coming and were going to see my room, I'd have been prepared."

He chuckled, and his voice was still a little heavy from earlier when he said, "And miss young, cute Kriti? Or your messy bed?"

He was now looking at a ridiculous picture of the three of us—Rati, Kartik, and me, playing Holi. The photo was taken at least seven years ago. I was covered from top to bottom in magenta, blue, yellow, and green colors, and I was holding back the two water guns that young Rati and Kartik had aimed at me. And I was chubby.

It had taken me a while to start working out and gain a positive outlook on my body. And it had taken even longer to start loving my body.

Color rose to my cheeks. "It's not messy. It's organized."

"Sure." His teasing smile infuriated me and made me want to mess up his already messed-up hair.

His eyes moved across my room and stopped at my bookshelf.

He walked toward it and stood staring at the hundreds of

colorful paper-covered books. Aakar's eyebrows were bunched in confusion. "What is this?"

Just to mess with him, I said. "Uh...they're called books?"

His dead, flat stare had me laughing. "Fine. I like to read. And I don't want my parents to know exactly what I like to read."

A teasing smile came over his face. And before I could warn him off saying the dreaded words, he asked, "Is it *Fifty Shades*?"

Oh dear. With a very confident tone, I cleared my throat and said, "Yes, I have read those."

He smiled wider and stood closer to me so our shoulders brushed. "Really? So all of these books are like that?"

I took a step away from him that he very well noticed. "Well, most of them, yes. And not exactly like that. But yes, most of them are romance books."

He turned to me. "Are you ashamed of reading these romance books?"

"Not at all."

"Then why are they covered like that?"

I folded my hands, glaring at him. "Well, I'm not ashamed of reading them. But I'm afraid of my mother. I already deal with her constant commentary on my life on a regular basis. Imagine how she would react if she saw the cover of the books I read. She'd burn them. And I really have a lot of love for my books."

He chuckled. "I also like to read every once in a while."

"Really? What do you enjoy reading?"

"More crime, thrillers. Not romance." His tone was instantly defensive.

I didn't even stop myself from rolling my eyes at him. "Have you even read a romance book?"

He ran his hand through his hair. His eyes were a little more serious, probably catching up on my souring mood at his inquisition. "Well, no. I have no interest in it."

"How do you know you have no interest in them if you haven't read it?"

He shrugged. "I just know it. I don't care about the emotional drama or cheesy dialogue. They all sound the same to me."

My jaw dropped. "You do know that it's still not too late for me to say no to marriage, right? We're not married yet."

This time, his jaw dropped. "What?"

I crossed my arms. "Well, I have no interest in marrying someone who is so condescending to my interest."

This time, he showed true nervousness. "Umm...I didn't mean to offend you."

"Yes, you did."

He gulped. "Well, I kinda did. But it was all in fun."

"No, it wasn't."

"Well, okay. Fair point. But in my defense, I just don't see what one could gain by reading these books."

I looked at him. "Well, you'd have to read a few of these to know that, wouldn't you?"

He stepped back and sat at the edge of my bed, a guilty smile playing across his lips. "You want me to read your romance books?"

I shrugged my shoulder. "Clearly, you know nothing about them yet passed judgments. It's only fair you read one."

"Fair enough. Give me one."

My heart soared at that. "You're not kidding, are you? You'll really read it?"

This time, he smiled wide at me. "I'll read it. Tonight itself. It's not like I've anything to do at my village house. It'll pass my time."

I quickly went through my color-coded bookshelf. And it took me ten whole minutes to give him one book.

He took it from my hands, and the first thing he did was

pull off the red-color cover. A big, teasing smile came over his face. "Eight-pack abs, huh?"

I poked his ribs with my elbow. "Shut up. Just read it."

He put the cover back on, and we made our way downstairs. He held my hand until we reached the living room.

He left for his house with a promise to my parents to have dinner at our place the next day.

Hardly two hours had passed since he left when I got his message.

> Aakar: This hero is such an asshole.

I couldn't stop my loud laughter even if I tried.

> Me: I know, right?

> Aakar: Do I need to act like an asshole to seduce you?

Like he needed to seduce me anymore.

> Me: He'll change. You just wait.

I didn't get anything for a while. I was almost asleep when my phone beeped.

> Aakar: NINE INCHES???????

And I died laughing.

Before I could even respond, another message popped up.

> Aakar: FOUR TIMES IN A NIGHT????!!!

His messages kept popping up.

Aakar: Are you awake?

Aakar: Already asleep?

Aakar: This won't do at all. How will we fuck (as the book quite eloquently put it) four times if you can't stay awake?

Me: 😂😂😅

I slept with the biggest and the most ridiculous smile on my face.

16

Song: Tum Jo Aaye Zindagi Mein
 - *Rahat Fateh Ali Khan, Tulsi Kumar, Pritam*

Aakar

The following evening, I reached Kriti's place a little—a lot—earlier than dinnertime for two reasons. One, I wanted to see Kriti, talk to her, just be near her. And two, I was really hungry. So when Kriti texted me *I'm back from school. What're you doing?*, I quickly replied, *Bored and hungry.*

Kriti was quick to invite me for a late lunch and an invitation to stay for dinner. I was not going to kick a gift horse in the mouth.

"Aakar Beta, here, take one more roti." Kriti's mother put a roti dripping with ghee on my plate.

My eyes met Kriti's, who sat right across me. Kartik sat beside me and Rati across from him. The three of them had returned from school and decided to wait a little for me to arrive so we could all eat lunch together. Kriti's father had apparently taken a tiffin with him and didn't plan to return before the evening.

We were almost done with lunch when Kriti's mother returned with a big pot and placed it on the table.

Kriti instantly turned beet red.

My eyebrows rose. "What's in the pot, Auntie?" I turned innocent eyes to Kriti's mother.

Her mother got a pleased glint in her eyes as she went and stood behind where Kriti sat. "Kriti told me you love gulab jamun. She's been practicing day and night to perfect them. Right, Kriti?"

With every word that Auntie spoke, Kriti kept turning all red. Without meeting my eyes, she mumbled, "Only when I get some time."

My heart was beating so loud I was sure Kartik could hear it beside me. She had told me she was going to learn to cook my favorite food. But I had no idea what it would do to me to eat the food she'd prepared for me after *practicing* it repeatedly. For *me*.

"Wow. That's...Thank you."

I so badly wanted to pull her closer and kiss those hands. Instead, I slid my legs under the table and pulled hers between mine. A small smile came over her lips, something her family would've missed. But I only cared for her reaction. So I noticed.

And at her smile, I caressed her leg with mine.

With her face still stretched in a smile, she quickly got up and served me three gulab jamuns. Without any hesitation, I put an entire piece in my mouth.

The sugary sweetness exploded in my mouth, the texture so soft I barely needed to chew it. Before I had even swallowed the first one, I put the second one in my mouth and deliberately moaned loudly, making everyone laugh.

Even Kartik smiled a little as he shook his head. "They're not that good," he mumbled.

Kriti glared at her brother. "Why don't you stop eating them, then?"

His smile widened. "They're not that bad either."

Before Kriti could respond, I interrupted, "They're the best gulab jamun I've ever had. Really."

And they were. I didn't know what Karik was saying. I had never tasted a better gulab jamun in my life.

Kriti instantly softened but didn't stop from making a face at her brother.

She served me three more before I could even get up. I raised my eyebrows. "If I eat any more, I'm going to crash."

After lunch, Kriti's mother went to watch her TV serial in the living room while Kriti and I cleaned up the table, and I helped her do the dishes. It very much reminded me of the day I'd met Kriti, and we'd decided to talk behind our parents' backs. That one impulsive decision had changed my life forever.

Since it was the weekend, Rati and Kartik seemed to be uninterested in studying. And I had nothing to do except spend time with Kriti. So I asked Kriti if she would like to go to the movies along with her siblings. Before she could respond, Rati and Kartik were up and running to get changed.

Kriti told her Maa that we would be back by dinnertime.

Once inside the theater, Rati, my amazing and favorite new sister, pulled Karik to the farthest end of the seat and sat between him and Kriti, letting me sit on the other end to give us some semblance of privacy. I would really have to gift her something. That girl was a romantic at heart.

During the movie, Kriti and I sneaked in some hand-holding and occasional soft brushes of lips on the cheek. I was desperate to get her all to myself, but even these tiny morsels of her time and her touch were enough to soothe my craving heart.

By the time we reached home, Kriti's dad was back from

work already. So, while Kriti went to help her mom get dinner ready, and Rati and Kartik went upstairs to study, I sat on the sofa across from Kriti's father.

He was a man of few words. In all the times I've been here, I haven't heard him talk a lot. He's more of an observer. "How was the movie?" he asked.

I smiled at him. "It was pretty good, Uncle. How was your day at work?"

He shrugged. "The usual."

I nodded, and a few minutes of awkward silence followed where neither of us said anything and kept our eyes fixed on the news.

When the commercial break appeared on the TV, Uncle turned to me. "Everyone at home okay?"

"Yes, everyone is good. Busy with the wedding preparations."

A smile appeared on his face. "I'm happy you came to see Kriti. I know it made her happy too."

I couldn't stop the blood rushing to my cheeks. "It had been a while since we'd seen each other. And with the wedding preparations going on, it is getting more difficult to spend some time together and get to know each other."

He nodded. "That was thoughtful of you. My daughter has always worked hard to achieve whatever she set her sights on. She's always dreamed big. Be it her studies or getting a job. Anything she puts her mind to, she gives it her everything. Day and night. She'll work hard to achieve her dreams."

I was riveted to every word that Uncle said. I wanted to know everything about Kriti. "That's very admirable. I know how passionate she is about her work here and fighting for girls' education."

A proud smile came over his face. "That she is. She's so worried about them. She's afraid that without her, no one would fight for her students. That she is letting them down."

I never knew she felt that way. When I nodded in acknowledgment, he continued, "That's why she's personally involved in interviewing and finding the right teacher to replace her after...uh...after she leaves."

I could feel the love and pride he had for his daughter. And I never wanted to let him down by not treating Kriti right and not making her happy.

I met his eyes, and with all the truth in my heart, I promised him, "Uncle, I will keep Kriti happy and treat her with all the respect, kindness, and love that she deserves."

His eyes turned glassy. "My daughter is headstrong and blunt and a little forward minded. She doesn't shy away from speaking the truth. She likes to talk. She also gets a little shy in front of new people. But if she has to stand up for herself, she will. She always has. If she hadn't, she would have been married for a long time. But she always stood up to her mother. And believe me, Aakar Beta, it wasn't easy for her. And she has been fighting her mother about marriage matches for a very long time now."

I really didn't like to think about Kriti having to fight her mother or having a hard time in life. "She'd told me about that a little bit."

He gave me a pleased smile. "I'm glad. So imagine my surprise when she agreed to a second meeting with you. A city boy who lives a few hours away from our home, for whom she would have to uproot her entire life. Believe me, I'm quite pleased with who she chose but know that it wouldn't have been an easy choice for her."

I nodded, listening to every word.

"And Aakar Beta, I believe in my daughter's choices. She hasn't made a wrong choice in her life. I just pray that you will not make her regret her life choices. Believe me when I say this, beta. I love my daughter more than anything in this world. More than the society. So if you break her heart, if you make her sad, if you make her question her choices and her life, I *will* take her away from you."

My heart ached at the thought of someone taking away Kriti from me. But I couldn't help but feel a sense of relief that Kriti had her father watching her back. That unlike a lot of parents, unlike her own mother probably, Kriti's father cared for her above everything else. She deserved that, and more.

I quickly nodded. "Since the first time I met Kriti, I have admired her. Her sense of self-worth, her ability not to back down from tough conversations, and also how kind she is. She is going to be my wife, but I already consider her a very good friend of mine. She has my highest regard and utmost respect. And I promise to never let her down. And never let you down. I only want to make her happy and be her support and a friend in her life."

Uncle nodded. Tears shone in his eyes. "Good, good."

Right on cue, Kriti entered the room. "Dinner's served."

Our eyes met, and there was a softness in them. And I knew. I knew she heard our conversation. If not the whole, at least in part.

Once her father walked ahead of us toward the dining area, I gave her the same reassuring smile that I gave her father.

She shook her head but clutched the sleeve of my shirt as she led me to dinner.

∼

Kriti

Time flew by as the wedding got closer. One week to go.

I was done with all the shopping. Pappa and I had gone and booked the wedding party plot, chosen the decorations, all the invitations were sent out, and the menu for all the days of the celebration was set.

I just needed to decide on my official replacement at school.

I walked into the staff room, and before I could escape to my first class, the school principal, Shradda Madam, caught me. *Shit.*

"Kriti, you do realize I don't need to wait for you to choose the new teacher, right? But since you've had such an impact on the lives of our students, I want to give you the opportunity to choose and train the new teacher."

My heart pounded at her words. I was terrified to leave the school and my students in the hands of another person. Would they care for their education as much as I did? Would they fight for my girls like I did?

I nodded at the principal. "Yes, ma'am. I really appreciate that I'm involved in the process. I'm just confused between two candidates."

The principal nodded but gave me a stern look—the look that had our students shaking to their bones. "I need the name of the person you'd like to replace you by the end of the day, or I will choose one myself."

I clenched my fingers around the books in my hands to hide their tremble. "Yes, ma'am. I will get you the name."

"See that you do."

With that, she turned back to her office, and I rushed to my class.

The moment I stepped in, the students burst into loud cheers and hooting. I turned around to see if someone was behind me, but no one was around.

But then the words "happy" and "farewell" rang in my ears, and my heart started to beat faster. My jaw dropped, and my feet stopped moving. I could only just stand at the entrance of my class and stare at the happy, excited smiles on the faces of my students.

Big banners of "We will miss you, Kriti Teacher" hung on the walls of the class, a few students had a bunch of balloons in their hands, and a few students at the back held a "BEST TEACHER" banner.

I blinked my eyes faster not to let the tears stream down my face. The students wouldn't be able to handle their teacher crying.

My lips stretched into a wide smile, and I made my feet move to the closest bench. I lightly touched Madhvi's cheek in thanks and messed up Jay's hair, causing him to whine. The students whooped and clapped.

I stood in front of the class, like always, and took in all of my students. My kids. I wanted to bawl like a baby at having to leave them halfway through the year. I really, really hated Aakar right now for taking me away.

I just wanted to stay and do right by the kids. They deserved the best teacher in the world. A teacher who would not just teach them important subjects but also shape them into good human beings, instill discipline and empathy in them, fight for them, and stand by them.

Before I could get them to quiet down so as not to disturb other classes, five other teachers entered the class with a big cake in their hands. And to my surprise, the principal followed them with a big smile.

This time, a few tears slipped out. I quickly turned toward the blackboard and wiped them off.

The overwhelming love from my kids threatened to buckle my knees in guilt. And when the kids rushed around me, waiting for me to cut the cake, I wanted to pull them all into a hug, squeeze them all into tiny size dolls, and take them with me to Ahmedabad.

I quickly cut the cake, and another round of applause rang in the classroom. I kept cutting small pieces and feeding them to each of my children, thanking them, asking them to work hard, my mind begging them not to forget me.

Once everyone had a cut of the cake, and the teachers had

left, the students took their seats, and I stood at my desk, leaning my hip on it.

Each student still had wide smiles etched across their faces. Before I could even say anything, one of my most talkative students, Nidhi, asked, "Teacher, how did you like our surprise?"

And right on cue, the chorus of the same question rang in the class.

I hushed them to get a word in. "Thank you so, so much, kids. How and when did you all plan this? I didn't even know that you were going to have such an amazing surprise for me."

Nidhi, like always, took the lead. "We all decided last week. We went to the principal and asked her if we could surprise you."

My kids were in ninth grade, an age when giving surprises was their only goal in life.

"That is so sweet of you all."

Before they could get a word in, I asked, "What are we studying today?"

Just like I thought, loud groans of "teacher" echoed in the class, and I burst out laughing. "Okay, okay. No studying today. You can do whatever you want right now except leave the class or make too much noise. Nidhi, please go close the door of the class. We don't want to disturb other students."

I rounded the desk and took a seat in my chair. My knees were still shaking from the staggering amount of love I felt today. Just a few minutes passed when a few girls came to me, hands behind their backs.

When I raised my eyebrows, they handed me handmade farewell cards and letters. Some were well designed and some were scribblings. My lips stretched into a wide smile, and I had to blink really hard again not to cry.

"Teacher, these are from all of us. Everyone made a card or a letter, whatever they felt comfortable doing."

I could only nod and look around the smiling faces of the kids.

"Thank you. Thank you so much. I'll never lose these. Ever. I promise."

They whooped and cheered once more. And soon, the bell rang, and I had to leave for the next class.

The moment I got back home, I ran to my room, changed into my pajamas, and read through each letter and card I got today. Halfway through, I could barely make out any words with the big, fat tears rolling down my face.

I kept wiping them off, trying not to let them fall on the card and ruin the beautiful words that my students had written to me, and read through them all.

As soon as I was done, I video called Aakar.

The moment he picked up the call, his eyes widened, and he got right up on the screen. "Kriti, baby, what happened? Why are you crying?"

Baby. He called me *baby* again. And I couldn't help but cry harder. "I hate you, Aakar. I hate you so much right now."

His face looked tortured. I felt bad for dumping this on him, but I just couldn't help it. His voice was hoarse when he asked, "Kriti, baby, what did I do?"

I sniffled, trying to stop the tears. "You agreed to marry me. That's what."

He seemed to be walking back and forth in his office because the movement on the screen had me feeling dizzy. His eyes were scrunched up in confusion. "And that's a bad thing? You're scaring me, Kriti."

I wiped my nose on the long sleeve of my T-shirt, not caring what he thought of me. "Now I have to leave my kids and come live with you. And they will soon forget me. And I won't have such loving kids again, who would write me such sweet letters and give me these beautiful cards."

I lifted all the cards and letters up on the screen. "Why did you have to live so far away?"

A soft smile came over his face, which only made me angrier. "Stop smiling," I wailed.

He instantly stopped, and a pained expression came over his face as he resumed walking back and forth in his office. "And stop walking. You're making me dizzy."

"Sorry, sorry." He quickly sat on his chair and held his phone a little away from him so I could see his chest and shoulders. "I'm so sorry you have to leave your students, baby. Do you want to tell me what happened at the school today?"

And I did. Slowly, between the hiccups and the sobs and snorts and tears.

And he listened, all the while saying, "I'm so sorry I agreed to marry you."

I read him a few letters, and I knew I saw his eyes were shining. Or maybe they were my own tears.

Once I was done relaying everything, we sat there silently for a few minutes. "Today is the best and the worst day of my life."

His eyes turned soft, and I really, really wanted to feel his arms around me. His finger moved across the screen, and I could almost feel his warmth around me.

"Thanks for talking to me," I said.

"Anytime, Kriti."

"I need to freshen up now. And get started on packing up my things."

He nodded, and after a quick goodbye, I cut the call.

My family didn't disturb me for the rest of the day, giving me soft smiles and wide berths. Even Maa didn't call me to help with dinner but made my favorite dal makhani and jeera rice. And she even held her tongue when I ate my feelings out.

I was almost done cleaning up the kitchen when Maa called out for me from the living room. I quickly wiped the kitchen countertop and washed my hands before walking out to the living room.

When I came out, she had a small smile on her face. So did Dad when he asked, "Beta, I think I forgot my scooter keys in the scooter itself. Could you please check and get them for me?"

With the day I had, my capacity to argue was at a minimum. I just rolled my eyes, put on my slippers, tugged on my light sweater, and went out.

And there, leaning against my dad's scooter, stood Aakar. In his perfect beard, his tousled hair, his rumpled shirt, and his tired eyes. He looked so inviting, so warm.

One moment, I was looking at him, and in the next, I was tearing up in his arms. His arms came around me, and he held me like he could carry all my pain. His soft voice cooed in my ears. "Oh, baby, I'm so, so sorry."

He ran his hands in my scalp and squeezed me closer to him. His wide chest, his soft cotton shirt, and the woodsy, musky scent at his neck lulled me to a soft calm. For a few minutes, he swayed me in his arms, softly running his hands on my back.

I wiped my face on his shirt and smiled when he gave me a mock glare. "I can't believe you came."

He looked around for a second and quickly kissed my nose. "C'mon, let's go."

A smile came over my face at the way he was being playful with me. "Go where?"

He held my hand and pulled me along to his car right outside the gate of our house. "To get some ice cream."

"You're not going to come inside the house?"

He pushed me inside the car. "Nope." And he shut the door behind me.

He jogged to his side of the car and got in. In the next

minute, he had upbeat songs on the playlist and his hand on my thigh as he pulled us out on the road.

I felt warm and cherished and *loved*.

I looked at his hand on my thigh, his hold firm, occasionally squeezing it. "You okay?"

"Yes."

Soon, we were parked near the ice cream shop we usually went to when he was here.

"What do you want?" he asked, his hand back to massaging my scalp.

"A chocolate king cone."

He gave me a wide smile, and before I knew it, he pulled me into him, and his lips were on mine. He held me on the back of my neck, his hold firm, protective. His other hand squeezed my thigh tight as if he was trying not to move it elsewhere.

"Do you know how soft you look right now?" he groaned at my lips. His lips moved against mine, and I melted.

I opened my mouth and took his lips in mine. I pushed myself even closer and clutched his shirt in my fist, pulling him deeper. I needed more of his taste, his tongue moving against mine.

The blood in my veins burned, each nerve ending screaming in desire. My legs clenched together, wanting his hands between my thighs, needing them to move where I needed him the most.

I didn't know when I'd squirmed and moved my legs, but his hand was now trapped between my thighs. I squeezed them together, feeling his knuckles at my clit, and moaned.

His loud groan reverberated in my mouth. "Kriti, baby." His desperate plea had me moving against his hand.

"Fuck." He pulled his hand from between my legs, leaving me moaning and feeling achingly empty.

He quickly pushed himself back in his seat, his chest heaving and his breath panting.

He tightened his fist on his very hard, very aroused cock, almost strangling himself. His head was thrown back in pleasure or agony; I couldn't tell. "Fuck. Fuck." He blew out his breath.

My pussy throbbed as I watched him trying to get control over his cock. At the way he held himself. His hand gripping his tented pants. God, what did he look like under there?

"Ice cream," he growled. "I'm getting you an ice cream, and I really don't need to be coming in my pants, baby."

I blew out a breath. My heart rate started to return to normal. "Yes, king cone."

He chuckled, and his voice was rough and a little hoarse.

He looked down at his now normal condition, and with a quick shake of his head, he untucked his shirt, rearranged his hair, and got out of the car.

Once he was back, he gave me my king cone. He'd gotten the same.

When I smiled at his choice, he simply rolled his eyes and started eating. I followed, and we sat there eating my favorite ice cream with some great music in the background.

And I couldn't stop smiling.

Aakar looked at my face and shook his head. "You really should stop smiling. It makes me want to kiss you again."

I very deliberately, very obscenely, licked the ice cream. He groaned. "You look ridiculous."

And I laughed. I knew he liked it. The evidence was pretty clear when he adjusted his dick.

As I licked the ice cream, I cleared my throat and said, "Um…I was wondering…"

He hummed, his eyes focused on the cone in my hand.

I gave the ice cream another lick and continued, "I know I made the no sex for six months condition."

His eyes instantly met mine, the hunger in them causing goose bumps to erupt on my skin. "What about it, baby?"

My heart started pounding, and blood rushed to my cheeks as I looked at him. "I put that condition so I could know my future husband better before having sex with him. I don't need any more time with you. In fact…"

"In fact?" he asked, his voice hoarse.

"You know…"

His lips turned up in a smile. "Say it for me, baby."

I couldn't help but smile at him in return. Shaking my head in mock exasperation, I said, "I don't want to wait six months before we have sex. I love what we're doing. I love kissing you. I want us to keep doing this and more once we're married."

"Fuck, Kriti. Couldn't you have told me this *after* we got married? Now I'm going to have to live with the thoughts of a million things I want to do with you and not be able to do a single one."

I looked at his tortured expression as he licked his ice cream and couldn't help but say, "I'm really glad you're marrying me."

He looked at me and shook his head. He softly ran his hand in my mussed-up hair. "Me too."

"Are you staying here for the night?"

He shook his head. "Nope. Akira arrives tomorrow morning, so I'll be heading back after this ice cream."

I gasped. "That's tomorrow? Oh god, I'm so sorry you had to come all the way here. How will you get any rest?"

Aakar touched my cheek. "I decided to come to you. And I'd do it again in a heartbeat. I'm just as excited to see Akira. It's been months. So I don't care about resting when two of the most important women in my life need me."

I simply shook my head and finished my ice cream. Very, very slowly.

I couldn't wait to marry this man. One week, and he'll be mine.

17

Song: I Love You
   - *Ash King, Clinton Cerejo*

Aakar

The next day, I stood outside the airport along with Ria, Abhi, and Luke. Why did all flights from America have to land so early in the morning? I had returned after midnight from Kriti's place and was up at five o'clock.

Luke yawned beside me while Abhi was busy on his phone. Ria stood leaning against me as I told her all about yesterday.

Right then, the door to the airport opened, and a running Akira bounded out. Before I could even blink, Abhi ran in her direction. Ria and I quickly followed, and the four of us embraced in a hug.

We held Akira for a good few minutes before separating.

I looked around to find Luke hugging his parents and Sam talking to his parents. I was glad we'd gotten three cars. Ria, Abhi, and I walked over to Sam and his family. Sam gave us all a hug, and we all welcomed the parents. Since Sam proposed to Akira last year, Dad has been waiting for them to come home so we can do an Indian ceremony as well. This way, they all could come to my wedding and also celebrate Akira and Sam's engagement.

And Luke's parents are here to spend some time with him and Meera.

We got all the parents in the respective cars. Abhi drove the car with Luke and his parents. He would drop them off at their place and come home. Ria took a car alone while Akira, Sam, and his family came in my car. It was a little too much planning for this early in the morning.

"So, bhai, when am I meeting Kriti Bhabhi?" Akira had a teasing twinkle in her eyes.

I shook my head. "We leave for Laxminagar tomorrow. We'll all get together and have some fun before the wedding. There's the ring ceremony, the haldi, mehndi, sangeet party, and wedding."

I was getting married in six days.

Since we talked in Gujarati, Akira translated our conversation to Sam and his family.

"Congrats, Aakar. Happy for you, man," Sam said.

"Thanks, Sam."

Akira turned to me. "So why aren't we keeping all these ceremonies in Ahmedabad? Why do we need to go to Kriti's place?"

"Most of these ceremonies can be done separately. We could've only gone there for the wedding. But since we already have a few relatives near the village, Dad offered to ride all our relatives to the village. Our house is big enough to fit most of the guests who are interested in attending all the ceremonies. The rest will arrive on the day of the wedding. And it would be good to have these ceremonies in the same city. In case they need our help or we need theirs, we can be there for each other."

"Makes sense. So do you love Kriti Bhabhi?"

I nearly choked on air at that casually put question. "Akira," I groaned.

"What? Why would you marry someone you don't love?"

I had no answer to that. I always wanted to marry someone for love, didn't I? But did I not love Kriti? I certainly felt things for her. I constantly thought about her. I wanted to make her laugh and smile. I wanted to kiss her. Touch her. Fuck her.

I quickly turned my thoughts away from that direction since my sister and her fiancé and his parents sat in my car.

I cleared my throat as Akira stared at me. I was so glad Sam and his parents couldn't understand Gujarati and had no idea what we were talking about. "I don't *not* love her, Akira. I certainly feel something for her. Maybe it's love. There's certainly friendship. And attraction."

"Eww."

"You asked."

"I mean, sounds good. I guess that's as good as it gets in an arranged marriage."

I stiffened at that. "What the hell does that mean? It certainly doesn't feel like I'm compromising anything by any means. It feels like the best thing in the world."

Sam was instantly up between the two front seats. "Everything okay between you two?"

Akira quickly smiled at him. "Yeah. Totally. I just made bhai a little mad."

She turned to me. "I'm sorry about that, bhai. If you're happy, I'm happy."

I softened. Of course, I did. I nodded and drove while she turned around and talked to Sam and his family.

Akira had found her life partner a different way. She was going to have a love marriage. In my experience, every person who'd ever had a love marriage always thought of an arranged marriage as a compromise. Something that we settled for. Something that we did because we couldn't find love.

But what about people who didn't find love while walking down the street? Not everybody actually had the opportunity or a place or even a chance to just meet new people. How were they supposed to find a love match?

Didn't we deserve a life partner? Companionship? Just because my parents found that person for me doesn't mean it didn't feel right. It was an arranged marriage, not a forced marriage.

There was a difference.

Was the tag of arranged marriage making me not acknowledge my true feelings for Kriti? I didn't think I was avoiding my feelings for her. I knew I was crazy for her. Her pain had me running toward her, just so I could pull her into my arms.

Her smile made my heart sing.

If that wasn't love, I didn't know what was.

Akira certainly put my mind into a spin. For the rest of the day, while everyone was busy hugging and talking to Akira and packing everything for tomorrow, my mind twisted around in a loop. Should I share my feelings with Kriti? And if so, before or after marriage? What if she wasn't even in love with me?

Well, it wasn't like she would cancel the marriage if she knew I loved her. Surely, it was a good thing for us. Wouldn't it make her happier to know that she was marrying a man who loved her?

The entire night, I tossed and turned, thinking about ways I could tell her.

The next day, I sat on the bus with around fifty of our relatives. Abhi, Ria, and my friends had decided to take cars so we'd have enough vehicles at our disposal in Laxminagar.

Akira, Sam, and his family were with Ria, while Meera, Luke, and his family were with Abhi.

The entire four-hour trip was spent talking to each person who kept congratulating me. I was happy they were all joining us for the ceremonies, but I already knew this week was going to drain me.

Mine was the first wedding among our cousins in our family. So everyone was just way too excited.

The rest of the day was spent setting up rooms and bedding for the guests, having lunch, and making sure that everyone was settled in and prepared for the next few days.

That night, we invited Kriti and her family, along with her relatives, to come for dinner. We had arranged for a campfire-like setting in our backyard so people could sit around and chitchat. We'd hired a few chefs for the week so no one had to worry about food for everyone.

At seven-thirty sharp, Kriti arrived with her family. She was dressed in a gorgeous pink salwar kameez with an orange and gold dupatta on her arms. She'd left her hair down and put on heavy eye makeup. Akira quickly came to stand by me and gave out a low whistle. "Bhai, no wonder you mentioned attraction."

She nudged my chest with her elbow, teasing me, and I lightly pushed her so she fell on Sam's lap behind her. Her squeal got Kriti's attention.

She turned, and our eyes met.

I'd just met her last night, but my heart soared at her smile. Yep, I was definitely in love.

I didn't even realize I'd started walking toward her when she met me halfway.

Everyone disappeared around me when I looked at her. "I don't think I'll be able to keep my eyes off you."

She blushed at that. "You don't look so bad yourself."

I rolled my eyes at that because I was only wearing a normal shirt and pants. I held her hand and pulled her to where Akira, Sam, Luke, Meera, Ria, and Abhi sat around the fire. "Come, I'll introduce you to Akira and Sam."

"You think she'll like me?" Tiny crinkles formed between her eyebrows.

I didn't need her to worry about that. "Of course she'll like you. *I* like you. So she likes you. It's simple, really."

She chuckled. "Whatever you say."

The moment I brought Kriti around, Akira pulled her into a hug.

And in the next minute, they were talking about their dresses and jewelry, the songs Akira had planned to perform on the sangeet night, the dance party the day before the wedding. Meera, being Kriti's best friend, had already stolen a seat beside her. Soon, Kriti had her phone open and was showing Meera and the rest of the women her mehndi design options.

Since I had no interest in getting involved in mehndi designs, I met Sam, Luke, and Abhi's eyes and nodded toward the food counter. We quickly got up, and each of us got two plates in our hands. One for ourselves and another for our wives and fiancées and sister.

And when I handed one plate to Kriti and took a seat beside her, for the first time, I felt like one half of a couple. Like I wasn't a third or fifth or seventh wheel in our group. I had someone of my own to talk to, someone who knew me, someone who I knew intimately. And I couldn't stop the smile that spread on my lips at that realization.

Under the golden glow of the fire, we ate, and we laughed, and we talked. And with Kriti by my side, I finally felt the joy and anticipation of my wedding week. Of *our* wedding week.

∼

Kriti

Aakar seemed to be in a thoughtful mood tonight. He didn't speak much. Or maybe I hadn't seen him among his family often. He hadn't talked too much when he and his family had come to see me either. He had taken me for car rides to talk.

I sat with my empty plate while I waited for Aakar to be done with his dinner. Sam and Akira had gone off with Sam's family to talk to other elders. Luke and Meera had gone to get Meera's younger brother, Hari, to get something to eat. Abhi had wandered off to his friends. Ria's mother had called her for some preparation for tomorrow's ceremonies.

"You seem to be quiet today," I said, shifting my chair slightly to look at him.

His eyebrows raised, and a soft smile came over his lips after he swallowed. "You've met my siblings, right?"

I chuckled. "They're sweet. I'm glad they're not difficult to please."

He laughed at that. "I really hope you like living with all of us. I know it's a lot for you."

Just the thought of living with fourteen people terrified me. I'd buried my head in the sand when it came to thinking about that. I would only think about it once I started living with them. One step at a time. So I just shrugged. "I can always run away if it becomes too much."

He started coughing at that, uncontrollable hacking that had me taking away the food plate from his hands and also trying to control my laughter. Poor guy. I rubbed his back.

Once he'd caught his breath, I said, "I was only kidding. If the thought of me running away makes you out of breath, I don't know what would happen to you if I did run away."

His mouth hung open, and he shook his head. And then, with all seriousness, he said, "I don't even want to imagine."

And I melted.

He took the plate back from my hand and stood. "Let's get ice cream, and I'll introduce you to my friends. They're very excited to meet you."

I chuckled and shook my head. "Oh, there's more people to please."

He laughed. "They already like you. And if they don't, their loss."

"Flatterer."

With our ice creams in hand, we went to the mini-campfire where all his friends were gathered. He introduced me to Soham & Rashmi, Komal & Varun, and the only single man, Zayan. Zayan endlessly joked about Aakar leaving him alone in the bachelor life and getting tied to me.

At that, Aakar quickly put his arms around my shoulders and pulled me closer. "Consider me a very happily tied man."

And I couldn't help but take it in a dirtier way. My mind conjured up images of a naked Aakar tied to the bed, and I almost fanned my heated cheeks.

As soon as his friends started talking among themselves, Aakar leaned closer to me and whispered in my ear, "You were totally imagining tying me up, weren't you?"

"Of course not. What kind of a woman do you think I am?"

He snorted and whispered, "A woman who reads about men with nine-inch cocks and a million ways to have sex."

"Well. Makes me more prepared than you for our first night."

His sharp intake of breath had me holding tighter to my dupatta. "Four more days."

Just the thought had my heart beating faster. Nervousness. Excitement. And a million other emotions rioted inside me.

I shushed him so as not to let my mind wander into thinking about seeing a naked Aakar and focused on his friends.

But no matter how hard I tried, I could not tell a word of what they were talking about.

My mind was lost in thinking about how slowly the next four days would pass.

People started retiring to bed as it turned late. My family and relatives had already left since we had the mehndi ceremony tomorrow morning. Aakar had promised my father he would drop me off.

All the ladies in my close and far families were coming, and all the ladies staying at Aakar's place were invited to join us for the mehndi ceremony.

Once only a few people remained in the backyard, still talking around the campfire, Aakar and I left the house and walked to his car.

He turned on the heater, put on the midnight radio that plays the most romantic songs, and took the car in the direction opposite my house.

"Where are we going?" I asked.

"Don't know. Does it matter?"

A smile touched my lips, and I realized that it didn't. As long as he was driving, and as long as he was with me, I really didn't care where we went. "No."

With a smile, he pulled my hand on the gear stick, held his hand on top of mine, and kept driving.

After a few minutes passed on the endless stretch of road in the middle of nowhere, with barely any other vehicles, he parked the car on the side of the road.

The moment he turned off the car, the music stopped. The heater stopped. There was just him, me, and silence. I could hear his shaky exhale as he pulled my hand to his mouth and placed a soft kiss on my fingers.

Every fiber of my being was attuned to the soft touch of his lips and his beard that tickled my fingers and sent sharp arousal through my body.

"Aakar," I whispered.

At that, he turned his eyes to me, my hand still clutched in his. "Kriti, I want to...I need to tell you something before we get married."

My eyes rounded, and my heart beat faster. "Oh my god, please don't tell me you have some deep, dark secret that you didn't tell me before, and now your guilt is eating at you, and now that you've almost trapped me into a marriage, you've decided to just tell me."

His mouth hung open for a second, and he quickly closed it. "Umm. No. Are you okay? Are the wedding celebrations getting to you? Are my relatives too much? Because I did not just hear you lay out a movie or a book plot when I was trying to tell you something really meaningful."

My cheeks heated at the word "meaningful," and I quickly schooled in my expression. "Of course your relatives got me."

He smiled. "Of course. Now, can I continue?"

His voice turned serious, and I nodded.

He turned in his seat so he faced me and held my hand with both of his. "What I wanted to tell you was that these past few months, meeting you, talking to you, our endless chats and messages, and meeting you for all our wedding preparations, these months have been, without a doubt, the best months of my life. I can't remember a time when I felt this alive, when I was so aware of my heart, my emotions, when I've had just one person in my thoughts endlessly."

Goose bumps raced along the back of my neck, along my entire arm and hand that was still clutched in his. He pushed my hand over his heart, and I could feel it pounding in his chest, its rhythm wild and fierce. With a deep breath, he continued, "And I just wanted you to know that I never want it to stop. You make me feel alive. Seeing you happy makes me happy, and seeing you cry makes me want to leave everything behind and just pull you into my arms where nothing can harm you. I cannot thank you enough for agreeing to marry me. There could have been no other woman for me except you. And I promise to make you as happy as you make me. I...I love you, Kriti."

I could barely see him by the time he finished his sentence. I leaped into his arms and put my lips on his. With an umph, he clutched the back of my neck and pulled me even closer. His tongue gently touched mine, and he pulled away.

I clutched the collar of his shirt in both of my hands and met his eyes. "I never thought that I would ever find the man of my dreams. And here you are. And I get to marry you, Aakar."

I couldn't help but shake him by the collar of his shirt, making him chuckle, and crashing our lips together.

Fire burned through my veins, and all I wanted was to climb into his lap and kiss him deeper. But I was wearing a very heavy salwar kameez, and I did not want to stop kissing him, even for a second. But he did. At my groan, he moved lower and tilted my head up to gain access to my neck.

With a loud groan, he nuzzled where my neck met my shoulder, causing my entire body to tremble with need. My hips rolled in my seat, wanting to be closer, needing to pull him deeper. I arched my neck further, and he bit my neck.

"Aakar."

"Fuck, Kriti. I love you."

"I love you too."

When he sucked at the underside of my jaw, I remembered and pulled him off by his hair. "Do. Not. Give. Me. A. Hickey. Four more days."

He groaned and pulled me into a deep, drugging kiss that had me almost forgetting everything.

Thankfully, he remembered and pulled back. "You mean it?"

I had no idea what he was talking about. "Mean what?"

Even in the darkness of the car, under the dim shadows of the streetlight, I could see his cheeks flush. "That you love me."

I met his eyes, and this time, without being under the influence of his wonderful, mind-altering kisses, I admitted, "Yes. I love you, Aakar. How could I not?"

"Thank you," he said and turned on the car.

As we neared my house, he said, "I always used to think that by agreeing to have an arranged marriage, I would be sacrificing something. That I wouldn't be as happy as the couples who have a love marriage."

I used to feel the same. "And now?"

He quickly stole a glance at me and smiled. "I don't care that we met through our parents, and that we're having an arranged marriage. If not through our parents, I would like to believe we would have crossed paths one way or another. I wouldn't have wanted anyone else."

And my poor little heart, who had only heard my mother's harsh words of *No one will want you if you don't lose weight* sobbed in relief and danced in delight. I couldn't speak because he had stolen my heart.

I was going to get to live my happily ever after.

18

Song: Chhote Chhote Bhaiyon Ke
  - *Kumar Sanu, Kavita Krishnamurthy, Udit Narayan*

Kriti

<u>Mehndi Ceremony</u>

A ceremony where henna is applied on the bride's hands and feet as a way of wishing the bride good health and prosperity as she ventures into her newly married life. Scientifically speaking, henna's cooling properties also reduce the bride's stress and anxiety. Its long application process gives her some time to sit still and breathe.

THE PARTY PLOT that we'd booked for all our ceremonies was transformed from a large garden into a beautifully decorated mehndi-themed event space. Pink and orange decorative pieces hung from the trees along with yellow and orange marigold flowers.

I had brought my bright pink lehenga for this very occasion. I wore my mom's diamond necklace and large earrings.

I was showered with rose petals by the women of Aakar's and my family as I walked down the baby pink carpet all the way to the bold pink couch set up under a large tree, strung with flower garlands. Two henna designers sat on a chair facing the couch, ready for me.

Surrounding my couch were several other bright yellow, orange, and pink couches where the rest of the ladies would sit to get their mehndi applied to their hands. As soon as I was seated, the fifteen or so mehndi designers were upon us.

Stick finger foods like kebabs and mozzarella cheese balls, and mocktails like spicy guava and strawberry mint mojito were passed around by the servers.

Mehndi-themed Bollywood songs played in the background, bringing all the mehndi vibes.

My hands were about halfway covered in mehndi when the commotion at the gate of the party plot had us all looking up. One after the other, the men in our families started filing in, looking around at the decorations.

In the middle of them all entered Aakar, in a dashing light pink kurta and beige salwar. He had the sleeves of his kurta rolled up to his elbows, and the first few buttons of his kurta were unbuttoned. A silver chain rested on his bare chest, twinkling as the light fell just right on it. He looked downright sinful.

All the ladies cheered as Aakar made his way toward me, smiling at his sisters. The rest of the men made their way to their respective partners or the food counters.

As soon as he came near me, he took a seat on the arm of the couch, his eyes taking me in. Slowly.

Heat gathered on my cheeks at his perusal.

The songs suddenly changed from the mehndi playlist of a girl leaving her home and getting ready for the new venture in her life to popular Bollywood romance songs. We couldn't help but chuckle at whatever sibling decided to mess with the playlist.

"You look beautiful," Aakar said, still looking at me like he couldn't stop even if he tried.

Blushing, I looked at my mehndi design. "And my mehndi?"

He turned to look at my hands to see the intricate patterns of peacocks and elephants. "Just as pretty as you."

This man was going to kill me with compliments.

Just then, the server brought some mocktails and finger foods for the groom and placed them on a little side table beside the couch.

"Did you eat?"

I gave him the best puppy-dog eyes I could muster and showed him my hands. "No."

"Oh no." He clutched his heart and quickly grabbed the mocktail with a straw. Bringing the straw closer to my lips, he pushed a stray strand of my hair behind my ear as I took a sip of the refreshing strawberry mint mojito.

"There we go," he cooed.

Woots and cheers rang from all around us.

"Watch them lose their minds now," Aakar said, feeding me a kebab with his hand.

I chuckled as even louder hoots rang in the air.

"Do you want a little design on your hand, sir?" the mehndi designer asked.

Aakar turned to me with raised brows. "Are you getting my name written on your hand?"

When I nodded, he said, "Well, I won't be left behind."

Quickly, he brought his palm forward and placed it in the mehndi designer's hand. "Just her name for me, please."

The designer quickly wrote my name on his palm with a nice heart around it.

With my name etched on his palm, he fed me the mocktails

and finger foods as all the people close to us spent their morning and afternoon getting their mehndi done as their own partners took some inspiration from the groom.

∼

Haldi Ceremony

A CEREMONY *where turmeric paste is applied to the bride and the groom to prevent evil spirits from harming the to-wed couple. Traditionally, the bride and groom celebrate this pre-wedding ritual separately with their family members. Recently, they've started celebrating this ritual together to make it more fun and have pretty pictures.*

OUR FAMILIES DECIDED to celebrate the Haldi ceremony together. Aakar claimed it would be a lot more fun to have the ritual together, and we would also save some money between the two families by sharing the expenses for the ceremony.

All the guests had arrived when Aakar and I made our entry wearing our yellow clothes. I wore a white blouse with full balloon sleeves and a flowy bright yellow skirt. Considering we would be drenched in turmeric water and milk, people rarely dressed up too much for this ceremony. Aakar, too, was wearing a plain yellow kurta, again rolled to his elbows.

The theme of the whole ritual was yellow. Literally, every relative of ours had been requested to wear yellow-colored clothes. And everyone had delivered on their promise.

The party plot had again been redecorated and transformed into a yellow wonderland. The stage was set under the giant tree with hundreds of yellow marigold garlands hanging from the branches. Two big decorative shallow pots were set on the stage with a small sitting stool inside each one.

The moment we stepped on the stage, we were both led to sit in separate pots on the little stools. The ladies of our families walked to the stage and stood in front of us.

For the next half an hour, we did the ritual ceremony that came before the tumeric-applying thing, as per the instructions from the ladies. After that, each of our close relatives came to us and applied a bit of tumeric paste on our face and hands, wishing us luck and best wishes for our wedding.

It felt like I was floating as one after the other, our family, our closest friends, and our elders, applied turmeric paste to our face and hands as we were showered by their goodwill and blessings. Everyone's eyes shone with happiness, and their joy poured through their being.

Once everyone had a chance to peacefully apply the paste on us, the ladies of the house gave the go-ahead, and all my siblings and cousins, Aakar's siblings and cousins, and all our close relatives were upon us with large buckets of warm milk and turmeric.

Aakar quickly pulled me into the same large tub so we both sat together. The moment the buckets full of milk and water showered over us, he pulled me into his arms.

Everybody's hoots and cheers surrounded us as they poured bucket after bucket of milk and water upon us, showering us with their love, joy, and blessings.

The photographer went crazy as he clicked picture after picture of Aakar holding me close to him, him laughing at me, him wooting with everyone, and making me laugh and my heart sing.

Sangeet Ceremony

A ceremony where the party really begins. It's the time for the families to come together, have fun, dance, and eat good food. It's the evening to break the ice between families or maybe have a dance-off between the families.

I wore a blingy silver sequin lehenga for the sangeet ceremony while Aakar wore a dashing black kurta and dhoti-style pants. For the life of me, I could not stop staring at him. He looked like every girl's dream man in that outfit.

Every event had me and Aakar doing an entry walk, with fireworks around us, and Bollywood music playing in the background. I've been feeling like a Bollywood heroine with the amount of attention and cheers we were getting these days.

The night was young, and every person wore a wide smile. As much as the constant makeup and getting ready was exhausting me at this point, it was all worth it to see our families having fun together.

Once we took our seats in front of the stage, Abhi and Ria got on the stage, Abhi in a sparkly navy kurta and Ria in her bold emerald-green lehenga. With a flourish, they started introducing all the uncles and aunts, including Aakar's mom and dad, as the six of them got on a stage.

The stage lights started to transform and the song "Gallan Goodiyaan" started to play, and the six of them started to rock the dance floor. Everyone wooted and cheered, Aakar and I standing up and clapping for them. None of them were perfect, with the men forgetting half the moves, but it was hilarious, and everyone was having fun.

The next were my parents, who chose a romantic song "O Maahi" and, if I must say, completely rocked their performance. Not a single mistake or misstep in their dance.

The next were Sam and Akira, who came out with a bang, performing to "Kala Chashma," with Akira wearing a bold pink lehenga and Sam in a beautiful black kurta and pajama. By the end of their performance, every one of them had joined into the dancing, considering how fun the song was.

Meera and Luke danced to "Aaj Kal Tere Mere Pyar ke Charche," bringing in the old Bollywood vibes, getting all the older generations to sing and dance along. To everyone's surprise, Luke lip-synced the hero's part, garnering loud cheers and praises.

After them came Aakar's friends who danced to "Maahi Ve" from *Kal Ho Naa Ho*. Because Aakar's friend Zayan was like the seventh wheel in their group, Ria seemed to have joined him as a partner.

The moment they all walked off the stage, the music of "Tenu Leke Main Jawanga" started to play, and from beside me, Aakar stood, surprising the ever-loving shit out of me. The moment he started to dance, my jaw dropped, and I was on my feet cheering him on.

Every time the song talked about the hero taking away the heroine and marrying her, Aakar pointed at me. At one point, he literally ran off the stage and toward me, and got down on his knees, making me dissolve into a puddle.

His performance had everyone around us jumping up to dance once again with loud cheers and hoots. The moment he was done with his performance, it was my turn.

I'd picked "Nachde Ne Saare," a song that I performed with Rati and Kartik. It had taken some cajoling from Rati and me, but Kartik had relented and joined in learning the performance. Midway through my performance, Aakar could not hold himself back and jumped on the stage and started to dance with us.

All his siblings, Meera, Luke, and Ria were quick to follow, and soon, every single relative was dancing and cheering.

We all danced and danced, one song after another, celebrating the night and the new relationships we were forging.

Wedding Ceremony

A ceremony where the husband and wife tie the knot with the blessings of their parents, their elders, and God, after which the bride leaves her parents' house—her house—to go live with the groom and his family. Not all families have their bride live with them these days. In the times when the groom lives away from the family, the bride goes to live with him, forming their own nuclear family.

"Oh my god, didi. Aakar Jiju danced for like half an hour in the baarat. All his friends and family kept dancing and dancing. Even we joined in. The ceremony finally began after the priest insisted *loudly* that the auspicious time was passing by the minute. It was so much fun."

Rati kept her commentary going as the photographer clicked my solo pictures. Meera stood near me as she righted my clothes each time the photographer asked me to turn this and that way.

"Did the ceremony finally begin?" asked Meera, tired of waiting for the groom's side to arrive and finish their dancing.

"Yeah. Aakar Jiju finally sat in the mandap with Maa and Pappa and began the ritual. They should call you to join them soon."

As I posed for more pictures, Kartik came running to call us. I walked down the aisle to the mandap with Rati and Kartik as both of them clutched my hand. My heart felt like it was shattering and bursting, and I tightened my hold on their hands. It felt like I was telling them goodbye right here, as if they were finally letting me go. I blinked rapidly as my eyes filled with tears, refusing to let them flow.

Aakar's siblings held a cloth in front of him, preventing him from getting a look at me. I hugged Rati and Kartik, letting a tear fall as I finally reached the mandap. The moment I stood in front of Aakar, the cloth separating us, the priest gave his siblings the go-ahead to remove the cloth.

Instantly, the cloth separating us vanished, and Aakar stood in front of me.

In his white sherwani, his beard groomed and hair styled to perfection, he looked unreal. His eyes took me in, and he clutched his heart, making everyone laugh and me blush.

We were each given a flower garland to put on the other. Once we stepped closer to each other, I reached forward to put the garland on him. But all his siblings and friends lifted him off the ground.

Not to be left behind, Kartik and all my distant cousins rushed on stage to lift me.

Laughing like lunatics, we put the garland on each other.

When we walked around the holy fire, hand in hand, promising our vows to each other, I smiled and rejoiced as our families showered us in flower petals.

And when I hugged my family goodbye, I didn't shed a tear in fear or loss or regret. I shed tears of farewell to my relatives, I hugged and kissed Rati and Kartik, I cried in my father's arms because I was going to miss him the most, and I shed tears of forgiveness to my mother because she was the reason I was marrying the man of my dreams.

I cried a river for the end of my time with my world, my family.

And when Aakar hugged my family, when he told my father he'd take care of me, and when he pulled Kartik and Rati into a hug and told them to come visit us all the time, I smiled with hope for my new life.

A life with my husband and his big, loud family.

19

Song: In Lamhon Ke Daaman Mein
  - *Sonu Nigam, Madhushree*

Aakar

At one in the morning, I unlocked the door to the hotel room where Kriti and I were to stay for the night. The rest of the family had returned home, and someone would pick us up tomorrow morning for the remaining ceremonies. It was our customary wedding night. A few years ago, the wedding night used to happen at home. But as times changed, families felt more comfortable sending the couple to a hotel for their first night. It made things less awkward.

The moment I opened the door, we were greeted by a path of roses leading into the main room. Kriti had a shy smile as I let her take the first step into the room.

"It's really fragrant, isn't it?"

We were still dressed in our wedding clothes, and I watched the way the folds of her white and red saree draped over her curves. One of the green-colored folds of her saree was draped on her head. She held a small bag in her hand, same as me, that carried a change of clothes. "Really fragrant," I answered, distracted by how much I loved her in the wedding dress.

I followed her inside the room, locking the door behind us.

The moment we turned into the main bedroom, Kriti gasped, and I couldn't help but stand behind her and softly put my hand on her lower back.

The entire bedroom was decorated with flowers. The bed had a big red heart made out of rose petals. The desk had a big basket of goodies.

I lightly urged her forward by the hand on her back so we could walk around the bed. "If I'd known I'd get such a nice prize by getting married, I wouldn't have waited this long."

Kriti snorted. "Right?"

I took the bag from her hand and put it on the armchair across the huge bed.

I turned to find Kriti just standing there, staring at the bed. The moment she looked at me, I had no words. And she probably had none too because she just looked at me, her eyebrows raised in expectation.

"So," I said.

And she burst out laughing. "So? That's what you have to say to me?"

I chuckled and raked my hands through my hair. I shook my head and stepped closer to Kriti. Closer to my wife.

Her smile slipped.

After the entire day of getting ready, and dancing, and the ceremonies, and the photo session with everyone, and eating, I finally did what I'd wanted to do since I first saw Kriti walking down the aisle today.

I looked at her.

I stepped even closer to her and touched the maang tikka jewelry on her forehead. I moved it aside to see the sindoor, the red vermilion, that I put on her today, the proof that she was mine. I noticed the flat gold band on my ring finger, the proof that I was hers.

I touched her cheeks that still had makeup on.

"What are you doing?" she whispered.

I kissed her nose because it was right there, and she looked adorable when she got all flustered. "Just looking at my wife."

She shook her head, but her lips were stretched in a smile. She touched the flat golden button of my sherwani. "How does your wife look?"

"Absolutely breathtaking."

I stepped back and looked at her. The way she carried her saree, her hands full of henna and laden with gold bangles. "I didn't want to stop looking at you today, but the wedding and the people constantly got in my way."

She chuckled at that. I moved around her. I couldn't stop grazing my hands along her fingers, her shoulders, and the saree fold that went from the back of her head to wrap around her waist. "So let me just look. I've been wanting to do this all day."

She turned around, her cheeks all red, her eyes shining. She stepped closer to me so our bodies almost touched. "All day?"

I pulled on her waist and closed that gap. "All day."

She raised on her toes and pulled me down into a kiss.

Our first kiss as husband and wife.

Her bangles clanked as she clutched my hair, and I was lost. Lost in her touch, in her taste, in the fact that I was kissing my wife.

With each deep kiss, my cock throbbed. Kriti moved her body against my hardness, and I couldn't stop the loud groan.

Too soon, she pulled away. "Aakar."

Her cheeks were flushed, her lips...God, those gorgeous lips were wet and soft, and my body begged me to pull her closer.

"Aakar," she said, a smile on her face.

I shook the fog out of my mind and looked at her. "Sorry, what?"

She chuckled. Then she held my hands and said, "I cannot stay in these heavy clothes for a minute longer. I need a shower and to get into my comfiest pajamas. Right now."

I groaned loudly. "Oh my god, I completely lost my mind. Yes, we definitely need to get showered." My eyes fell on the decorated bed. "And do something about all these petals."

Kriti walked on the other side of the bed and held the top bed cover. Following her lead, we slowly rolled the cover, trapping all the petals in the ball of bedsheet, and put it on the armchair.

I turned around from the armchair to find Kriti sitting on the edge of the bed. At my raised eyebrow, she said, "You'll have to help me get my hair free from this…" She waved her hand around her head area.

My eyes bulged at the monumental task that she just gave me. "Umm…I have no idea what and how they've gotten your hair like that."

She smirked. "Neither do I. They don't explain it to you, and I don't have eyes on the back of my head."

My heart raced at the thought. But Kriti patted the mattress right behind her. "Get on the bed behind me. And we'll figure it out slowly."

My lips twitched at that. I couldn't help it. She dramatically rolled her eyes at that, but she clearly had a ridiculous smile on her face. "I didn't mean it like that."

I scoffed, pulled off my own dupatta from around my neck, and got on the bed behind her. "Sure you didn't."

When she shook her head, I clutched her shoulders. "Now stay still, baby. Let me look at what we have here."

"So you'll see tons of pins."

I chuckled. "Yes. Should I simply start pulling them out?"

She hummed in affirmative, and I got to work. One after the other, I removed the pins at the saree fold pinned to her hair. After a few pins, the fold slid down her back, revealing the deep neck at the back.

My breath came out all shaky at the smooth skin, and I was painfully hard. I wanted to touch her, taste her, kiss her.

With a rough exhale, I continued to remove the pins around the flowers pinned to her head. "How did you carry all that on your head the whole day?"

"You only get married once. I wanted it all."

She does love getting all ready. And she does it so well.

I softly plucked one pin after another so as not to pull her hair. As soon as I plucked another pin, the whole bouquet and a whole bunch of hair hung off Kriti's head. And I won't lie. I shrieked as I held that hair. Oh my god, she was going to kill me. "Kriti, this is all coming out. Oh fuck."

And she bent low so her head was near her lap. Was she crying? Oh god, I was already messing up my marriage.

I moved the hair and the bouquet as she moved her head. "I'm so sorry, Kriti. Oh fuck."

With a roar that shook my poor heart, she laughed. Her head moved back toward me, my hands clutching the flowers and the hair hanging from her head. "Aakar, they're fake."

I looked at the tangled mess of hair and flowers. The flowers certainly looked real. I brought the hair closer to my face, then moved them closer to Kriti's *real* hair. "This looks so much like yours."

She snorted. "I paid good money for a proper hairstyle. Now, please keep removing the pins and get that heavy bunch off my head."

"A little warning would've been nice," I grumbled, slowly plucking the tiny black pins.

After a few more pins, I softly pushed my hand into Kriti's hair for some grip and pulled the flowers and the fake hair out.

Once out, I spread my fingers over her scalp and gave her hair a gentle shakedown to loosen up the stray pins.

At that, she threw her head back, her neck arched, and moaned loudly. "God, that feels so good."

I couldn't help it. I bent forward and kissed her neck. I gave her scalp a soft massage, causing her body to sway toward me. I continued to run my hand in her hair and pluck out each pin that I encountered.

How many pins did one need?

Once each pin was out, I ran my fingers through her hair, not wanting to stop. With every swipe of my hand, she sighed and relaxed into me deeper. My heart was beating a mile a minute. I could not believe I was sitting here playing with my wife's gorgeous hair.

A few minutes passed, and she asked, "Aakar?"

"Hmm?"

Her fingers played with her saree. "Um. Would you help me get out of this saree? The pins..."

"Yes. Of course." I didn't need any explanation or reason.

She chuckled and turned to look at me. "When did you become such a horndog?"

I pushed her hair aside and kissed her shoulder. "Months and months of talking to you and imagining you beside me." I pulled out the first safety pin at her shoulder. "Sleeping with just the thought of you in my head every night."

I pulled out another, and the folds of the saree fell. The saree pooled in her lap, leaving her in just her blouse. "I'm fucking dying for you."

She shivered, and her breath came out in a rough exhale. "That was actually the worst place to start unpinning the saree."

I pulled her head back so she looked at me, giving me a front view to her glorious cleavage, her lush breasts begging to be touched. "I'd say it was the best place to start."

And I kissed her. Her moan touched my tongue, and I shook with need and desperation to hold her closer to me. My mind was lost in a fog of lust and desire and a need so deep I could feel it in my veins.

She turned in my arms so she faced me, her legs almost dangling off the bed. I caught her in my arms and pulled her into me, all the while she kissed me. She clutched my kurta and pulled me closer. And I went deeper. My body screamed for more. More kisses. More touching. More tasting.

She gasped and pulled back, gulping a deep breath of air. Her skin was flushed, and her eyes glazed in pools of dark desire. Her fist still clutched my kurta. "You need to undress me," she said, her voice shaky, "and then we need to shower. I feel way too disgusting after the entire day to get naked right now."

My mind barely registered her words. With all the blood rushing south, my brain had nothing but air. Before I could say anything, Kriti jumped out of bed and stood facing me, her saree fold hanging down her back, some folds pulling down at various places where those pins held them.

I shook my head to clear my thoughts. Yes. Take out the pins. Shower. Shower together? Did she say that? I needed to get my bearings. It was our wedding night. She must be bone-tired after the entire day of wearing her ensemble, and here I was, jumping her bones the moment I got her alone.

Slowly, I pushed myself to the edge of the bed and sat there, waiting for her to get closer so I could start removing the pins.

She took two steps toward me so she almost stood between my legs. "I'm sorry I lost my mind there a little bit. You must be tired, and I behaved like a selfish fool."

I took out the pins from the saree draped along her waist, and she held the fabric that came off. She held my hand at her waist, so I looked at her. "Aakar, I liked it. I needed it. Don't beat yourself up for wanting me. If I wasn't trapped in two sarees, a big hairdo, a mountain of makeup, and this jewelry, we would've been in bed making out right now."

I groaned at the visual and pulled her closer so my head rested on her waist. She was all soft and lush and a perfect handful, and I couldn't help but squeeze her closer. She ran her hand in my hair and pulled my head up.

"Aakar, get me out of this saree."

I swallowed, but my throat had dried up. I nodded and got back to work. "When you mentioned we need to shower, did you mean together?"

My heart pounded as I waited for her answer. She didn't laugh at that. And when I looked up in the middle of getting a stubborn pin out, she was biting her lip, and her cheeks were flushed.

Not to spook her, I quickly got all the pins out. She turned this way and that as we got her saree out. And there she stood. Just in her blouse and the underskirt. I knew she wasn't wearing a bra because her blouse was backless, and I could see the wide expanse of her skin. I wanted to devour her.

I let her go as I sat at the edge of the bed in my sherwani suit, fully clothed, while she was nearly undressed. "Go have a shower, baby. I'll get things sorted here."

She smiled and walked to the en suite bathroom. She went inside, and I sat there, trying to get my hard-on under control.

We are not having sex today. We are not having sex today. It's 2 a.m., and we need to rest. She is tired, and sad, and emotional. She just left her family. I need to be strong and clearheaded. She needs to see that I'm on her side. And that I'll take care of her. Not lose my mind at just the sight of her alone with me. We have our entire lives to explore. Not tonight.

"Aakar." My head snapped up to find Kriti standing at the bathroom door, all her jewelry removed, her hair falling in waves. She looked glorious.

"Yeah?" My voice was barely a whisper since I'd lost my voice at the sight of my wife.

Her cheeks flushed, and she could barely meet my eyes. "Umm...would you help me wash my hair?"

My heart—and my cock—soared, and I was off the bed.

∾

Kriti

Aakar strode toward me in the next second. In under five seconds, he had pulled me inside the bathroom. With the way his fingers had brushed along my hair, my neck, and my shoulders while he removed all the pins, my heart had not stopped racing a mile a minute.

And when he'd brushed his lips along my shoulder, I melted. My body just wanted him closer and needed him to pull me into his arms. So when he let me go to shower alone, I couldn't help but feel a riot of confusing thoughts.

On one hand, I was downright terrified of what he'd think of my naked body. No one had ever seen me so entirely naked, and the thought of him not liking my rolls and my curves sent me into a mini-panic mode. But on the other hand, I really didn't want to be alone.

I wanted to be engulfed in Aakar's strong arms, be kissed and coddled. I needed to feel needed by him. By my *husband*. And it was Aakar. I trusted him to take care of me.

And if he hated seeing me naked, better to find it out now.

So when we stepped into the bathroom, and he started to remove his sherwani, I just stood there. I watched as he quickly undid the buttons and pulled off the kurta, revealing a white undershirt. He should've looked ridiculous with the white undershirt tucked into the ballooning pajama bottom, but he absolutely didn't.

Because in the next minute, keeping his eyes on mine, his eyes dilated with need and hunger, he undid the bottom and stood in his white boxer briefs. And my eyes, my shameless eyes, were stuck at the growing bulge that stretched the briefs.

"Should I pull them off? Give you a better look?"

I quickly met his eyes, embarrassment rushing to my cheeks at being caught staring. "I didn't mean to stare."

His eyes had that sharp glint that had me taking a step back. His lips curled in a smirk that got my heart racing, and he stepped closer. "Please do. You see what your mere presence does to me?"

My breath came out short, and I nodded. "Yes."

"Are you still sure about wanting to shower together?"

I was terrified, and nervous, and self-conscious, and excited, and trembling down to my toes. But I was sure that I wanted it. I needed to see more of Aakar. "I'm sure."

A downright sinful smile came over his face, and I had never felt this heat before. "Do you want me to help you take your clothes off, or do you want me to watch?"

My cheeks were burning up. Oh god, he was going to see me naked in just a few moments. Thank God, I was entirely waxed and prepped. Everywhere. Thanks to the bridal waxing package at the beauty parlor.

Before I could even respond, Aakar pulled off his undershirt and stood in his very tented white briefs. I wish I could take my eyes off it, but I just could not. His broad chest with a light dusting of chest hair made me want to rub myself all over him.

When he stepped closer, eyebrows raised, waiting for me to make a decision, I couldn't stop the tremble in my voice. "Could you go in the shower first, and I'll join you?"

His eyes softened. And he moved closer to me, so close his naked, hairy chest brushed against my blouse. He held me by the back of my neck, his firm touch assuring, and when he spoke, his breath fanned my ears, giving me goose bumps along my back. "Don't take too long."

When I nodded, he pushed his hardness along my bare stomach, causing a flood of heat between my legs. With a quick kiss on my forehead, he turned, dropped his underwear, walked into the glass shower room, and turned on the shower.

When he spun to face me, I could see his hard cock, the entire length of him, in all its glory. That was *mine*, and God help me, but I loved how he looked. Dripping wet, he moved his one hand to hold his dick, and he groaned. His head fell back, but his eyes stayed on mine. They were clouded with hunger, and he looked at me like I was the only one who could help him.

My hands trembled with the need to touch him, feel him in my hands, and learn how to bring him pleasure. Needing his mouth on mine, I removed my blouse, and my breasts finally fell free. And Aakar quickly started to wipe the fog and the water that covered the glass partition. His eyes were wild with desire. Desire for *me*. "Kriti. God, you're so fucking sexy, baby."

His hand moved faster while his other hand kept clearing the water. His words fueled me, and I removed the underskirt and got out of my panties. Aakar's loud groan, his need for me, had my pussy wet and aching. I so wanted to rub myself and push two fingers in just to relieve the ache.

I was a virgin but not short of orgasms. Romance books and English movies educated me on what an orgasm was and how I was supposed to feel. I knew what I loved, and I was dying to learn all that we could do with our bodies.

Aakar's hand moved at a firm pace. His hips jerked in tandem, and his eyes roamed across every inch of me by the time I reached the glass door of the shower.

I had barely touched it before Aakar pulled it open and dragged me inside the hot shower.

In the next breath, his lips were on mine, and he kissed me

like he would die if he didn't get to kiss me. The moment he pulled me closer, our naked bodies brushed each other, and sparks lit up every part of my body. I wanted to pull back and get closer all at the same time.

The overwhelming need his touch ignited terrified me. His warm hand held my waist and tugged me deeper. He groaned into my mouth, and I clutched his shoulder.

"Kriti, fuck." He pulled back from my mouth, drew my head back, and dipped his head to kiss my neck. His lips were soft, but his beard rubbed my neck and burned me in the most delicious way possible.

He stopped suddenly and looked at me. "Please tell me to stop if you don't like something or if you feel uncomfortable."

Water sprayed over us, running down my body. I needed his mouth back where it was, so I quickly nodded and pulled him back to my neck. And he chased the rivulets with his mouth—sipping and licking and sucking.

He leaned me back farther and stared at my breasts, his chest heaving. "Fuck, Kriti. I love your boobs. So full. Fucking perfect."

His hands slowly moved up from my waist, grazing the side of my breasts. My body thrummed with desire, pleasure and need making me arch my back, pushing my boobs against him. "Please," I moaned.

With a gruff growl, he finally touched them and gave a rough squeeze, and they overflowed in his hands. The sight looked so erotic, so filthy, a needy moan escaped my lips. Pleasure raced down my spine, and my hips jerked to get closer to the very hard erection poking at my stomach.

Aakar looked at my body like I'd fulfilled every one of his fantasies. Like I was his only desire. Every insecurity I had about not being sexy enough for him disappeared. His eyes were dark pools of hunger. He bent down and took one of my nipples in his mouth and sucked. "Aakar," I moaned, his name echoing in the room.

"Please touch me, baby. God, I need your hands on me."

He didn't have to ask me twice. I looked down between us at his thick, dark brown cock, his pink head peeking from his foreskin. Tentatively, I brushed my fingers along the pulsing vein of his length. My heart pounded as I touched a guy's dick for the first time. Aakar shivered as his hips jerked forward. A hiss escaped him as I closed my fist around him.

Our breaths mingled as we looked down at my hand clutching his cock. "You okay?" he asked, his voice coming in pants as if he'd run a mile.

My voice was barely a whisper. "Yeah," I answered and slowly tugged at his cock.

He groaned my name. "Don't, baby. This is going to be over fast. Fuck."

And it really made me happy to watch Aakar lose all his control. He was barely hanging on. But before I could move my hand, he closed his fist around mine, stopping any movement.

When I looked at him, he asked, "Do you make yourself come, baby?"

My thighs clenched, and heat rushed down my core. "Yes," I whispered.

A savage smile came over his face, and he walked me back until my knees touched the stone bench behind me. At his next step, I sat on the bench. His rock-hard cock was right near my face, with our hands still holding it.

"What are you doing?" I asked.

Aakar got on his knees so our eyes met, and with a rough voice, he said, "Will you show me how you make yourself come?"

Heat rushed between my legs, and I couldn't help but squeeze my legs tighter. Keeping his eyes on mine, he pushed my legs apart, exposing me to him. His brows raised in permission, and without missing a beat, I nodded.

My body was on fire, and his simple touch on my knees had me squirming on the cold stone bench. At the sight of me, he grabbed one of my thighs and opened me farther. "Touch yourself, baby."

I was so close to the edge, but I was also nervous. I'd never come in front of anyone. I didn't know if he'd like my orgasm face. I was pretty sure it wasn't that pretty. Nobody had a pretty orgasm face. "I don't know if I'll be able to come. I really want you, but my mind won't stop spinning."

Aakar came forward and held both of my cheeks in one hand, causing my lips to pucker up, and ravaged my mouth. My head spun. The feel of his lips over mine, his tongue moving along mine, and the sharp sting of his teeth on my lips had me arching my back.

"Feel this?" Aakar asked, his forehead against mine, our eyes watching the way he moved his hand on his cock. "Do you like it when I stroke myself?"

I quickly nodded. It was the sexiest thing I'd ever seen in my life.

"Let me watch you too. I need to see your fingers rubbing your pussy. Just the thought…Fuck."

His hips jerked, and he quickly let go of his cock. "Too close," he said, groaning as if he was in terrible pain.

He sat back on his feet, his eyes dark with desire and his cock flush against his stomach. Fuck, his balls looked tight. And all of him was mine. My hand flew between my legs and squeezed my pussy.

My body sang in relief at that first touch. "Aakar," I moaned.

He gasped, and his eyes were riveted to the way my hands moved. I rubbed myself, softly played around my clit, round and round, occasionally brushing across my opening. My back arched, wanting more. Harder. I ached between my legs, and I squeezed my breast, hard, to soothe the need.

At once, Aakar moved forward and sucked the nipple of the breast I held, and squeezed the other one in his big hand. White-hot pleasure buzzed through my veins, causing a flood of need to rush out.

Aakar moved back, and his hand was back to stroking himself. His strong hand flexed as he tugged himself. His hips jerked as if he was already fucking me, and his other hand held my thigh wide open, watching my hand move over my clit.

The moment I dipped my finger in, Aakar let out a loud groan. "Fuck, baby. I can't...I can't hold back any longer."

His hands were a blur as he pounded into his hand, his grip so tight, his cock flushed red. And with a powerful thrust, white ropes of cum landed on the tiles between us.

My body throbbed with need, and I rubbed myself harder, wanting to follow him. My hips lifted, and I pushed two of my fingers in, rubbing at the spot that I knew had me seeing stars. With my other hand, I rubbed my clit. And when I looked up at Aakar, his eyes were focused on me.

I looked down, and his cock was still half hard. "It's not going to go down anytime soon," he said, his voice hoarse.

Before I could move my fingers over my clit, Aakar moved forward and bent down so his face was right near my pussy. "Would you like to use my fingers for fucking?"

I quickly pulled out my fingers, and in the next minute, Aakar slowly pushed his middle finger in. Pleasure raced down my limbs, my toes curled, and before I knew it, I had put them on his naked thighs.

"Another," I moaned.

And quickly, Aakar pushed two of his fingers inside, and with a wicked smile that made my heart race, he bent down.

The moment his mouth closed over my clit, I screamed. My hips jerked forward, needing him deeper, and harder, and faster. I had no idea a wet mouth over my clit could feel like *that*. So warm, so fucking wet, so hot, so overwhelming.

I clutched his head by his hair and moved my hips in perfect tandem with his head. "Don't lick so fast," I panted. "Curl your fingers as if you're trying to touch my clit from the inside."

I couldn't help but keep the chant of my instructions running. And Aakar followed my directions to a T.

"Yes, Aakar, yes. Don't stop. Just like that."

He licked around my clit and moved away. "Fuck, baby. Look at you. Fuck, I can't get enough of you."

"Don't stop. Don't stop." I grabbed his head and shoved him between my legs.

He got the message and sucked my clit while he rubbed that spot in perfect harmony. And I shattered. A bright-white orgasm raced down my spine to my toes. I grabbed his hand that was inside me and pushed him deeper, holding him steady inside as I pulsed and pulsed and pulsed around his fingers.

After what felt like a few minutes, his soft lips around my thighs and belly brought me back. I hadn't realized my eyes were closed, but when I opened them, I found Aakar still between my legs, his hands massaging my thighs, my calves, my ankles.

"And you said we wouldn't have great sex." He teased me with the same words that I'd used when I found out he, too, was a virgin.

He clutched my hand and pulled me up so I sat straighter. I bent forward and kissed him, bringing him closer. "I take my words back. I think we're pretty good at this."

"Thanks to years of self-practice and porn."

"Right? And don't forget romance books," I added.

He stood, his hardness brushing my stomach, and pulled me up with him. "Can't forget that."

We stood under the slightly cooling shower, but I didn't

care. Aakar was warm, and he massaged my hair. "So what porn categories do you watch?"

He grabbed my ass and closed the gap between us. He moved his hips against mine and bent closer to me. "Depends."

He then turned around and squeezed a lot of shampoo into his hand. With his other finger, he twirled it in the classic turn-around signal. I was nearly giddy that he was going to wash my hair. "Depends on what?"

He stepped closer, his thick cock brushing between my ass cheeks. Now that I was a little more used to it, I didn't jump away. I stood still, letting him move closer as he lathered up my hair. For a second, he didn't answer. He simply massaged my scalp as I leaned my head back.

His hands were so big. So warm. So comforting. I almost forgot what I'd asked him when he pulled my head back and ran his soapy hands over my shoulders. "Depends on whether I was imagining fucking you hard or slow."

My hips automatically pushed back, wanting his arms around me. Wanting *more*.

His hands moved lower, and he held my waist from behind and moved his hips, sliding between my legs.

And just like that, under the pouring cool water, he came between my legs, and thank God he was holding my waist because he was quick to run his soapy hands between my legs and push me into that earth-shattering bliss.

Soon, we got into the lush bed in our comfortable pajamas. He pulled me into his arms and kissed my neck. The entire day soon got to me, and I was almost asleep when Aakar said, "I'm definitely getting us a hotel room for tomorrow night too."

20

Song: Gal Mitthi Mitthi
- *Tochi Raina*

Aakar

Kriti and I woke up late. More like we were woken by the constant ringing of my phone, thanks to my mother. I didn't even get the chance to admire a sleeping Kriti or fresh out of the shower Kriti or Kriti getting ready in front of the mirror. It was all *hurry up, move aside, we should've set an alarm, help me with the pleats of this dupatta.*

Still, I couldn't stop myself from smiling. I had a wife. Though she was complaining and frowning as she put on her makeup, I couldn't have been happier.

Once she was all ready for her first welcome in the house, we went downstairs to the lobby, where Maa, Pappa, and Abhi waited for us.

Maa met us in the middle and looked behind me. "Where are your things?"

I turned to Kriti, and she'd turned her face to look at

anything else that wasn't me or my mother. I couldn't hide my smile when I met my mother's eyes. "I decided to stay one more night."

Now, it was Maa's turn to blush. I left the two ladies, red in the face, and walked to Dad and Abhi. They quickly understood the lack of bags. Dad turned around to get the car, whereas Abhi coughed. With a light slap on his head, I sent him ahead. Maa quickly ran behind him while I waited for Kriti to join me.

As soon as my family was ahead of us, Kriti glared at me. "You didn't ask them if we could stay one more night? Couldn't you have informed them earlier? That was so embarrassing. What would they think of me?"

"Just that we really had the most unforgettable night and that we clearly want privacy to continue having fun."

She ground her elbow in my waist while I laughed at her flaming red face. "You are the worst. Why did I even marry you?"

I tugged her to our car, where everyone waited. "You love me. And you'll only thank me when we get back to the hotel."

"Hmph."

The entire ride home was spent with Maa informing us about the entire day's plans. We had a few ceremonies at home as a fun little welcome to Kriti. Next up was Akira and Sam's ring ceremony. Sam had already proposed to Akira in the US, but since we already had the entire wedding ceremony, Maa and Pappa asked—ordered—them to have another ring ceremony for the family, to which they readily agreed—complied.

I, too, had a small surprise for Kriti.

All of our relatives waited at the entrance of our house when we got out of the car. The moment we got out of the car, I placed my hand on Kriti's back in support, nudging her to start walking since she was rooted to the spot.

With a quick, grateful glance my way, she stepped forward,

and we stood at the entrance. Maa quickly grabbed the puja thali from my aunt and stood before us. After doing the aarti and putting a tilak on our foreheads, Kriti and I touched her feet. Akira, who was standing beside Maa, placed a Kalash pot filled with rice at the door entrance.

Kriti gave me a smile, and at Maa's advice, she nudged the rice pot and turned it over. With that ritual done, both of us stepped inside the house, from where we were led to our house temple room. There, my grandparents were already seated. Kriti and I sat near the large, deep-set plate filled with colored water.

I already knew what was coming.

But Akira brought Sam right over to us to show him the ritual and explained, "So Maa has placed a ring inside the water with all sorts of coins and other stuff. It is said that whoever finds the ring first would dominate their marriage."

Sam chuckled. "And the other person would have to forever concede in marriage?"

I scoffed, and so did Akira. "Nooo. It's just a game."

Right then, Maa and my aunts sat down around us. "Let's begin, shall we?"

Kriti looked at me, her eyes set in challenge. I gave her a wink and put my hand in the water. She was quick to follow.

Our hands clashed, and our fingers touched under the water. I believe people played this game to sort of break the ice between the couple and also between the bride and her new family. Maa cheered me while Akira and Meera cheered Kriti.

I frantically tried to find the ring but was constantly met with coins. Dammit. Kriti was as frantic, moving her hands everywhere.

And in the next second, her hand was out of the water, the ring clutched in her fingers. Akira hooted in victory, and Meera clapped with full enthusiasm and delight.

After a few more such rituals, everyone was relaxed and

hungry. We all moved to the dining area. Such ceremonies usually didn't have many people, just close relatives and friends.

But since we were also having Akira and Sam's engagement ceremony today, the guests were soon to arrive. Neither Sam nor Akira wanted a huge celebration, but Maa and Pappa were adamant that we had to invite everyone who was invited for my engagement.

So every one of us rushed to have some heavy breakfast.

Since we'd already hired caterers and servers, everyone could have breakfast in peace without having to serve anyone.

Kriti and I stood in a circle with Sam, Akira, Luke, Meera, Ria, Abhi, and his best friend Karan. Once we'd all had lunch, Kriti went off to help Maa and the aunties.

After almost half an hour, Maa called Akira and Sam to the living room.

Together, we left the dining area and found all our relatives gathering around near our sofa, which was now entirely covered in flowers. Kriti stood on one end, whereas Sam's parents stood on the other end. Maa clutched Akira's hand and led her and Sam to the sofa.

Kriti left her spot for Maa and Pappa and joined me.

Akira was radiant in her traditional yellow dress, and when she looked at Sam, love poured out of her eyes. She looked at him like he was her every dream come true. And Sam couldn't take his eyes off her, like he worshipped the ground my sister walked on. And for that, he had all of my blessings. If anybody could love Akira with his whole heart and keep her happy, it was Sam.

All of us siblings hooted and howled and showered the couple with flower petals when they exchanged the rings. Akira laughed and hooted with us, whereas Sam had turned a distinct shade of red. Still, he did not hesitate to place a chaste kiss on Akira's cheek, causing her to blush and not meet anybody's eyes for a minute straight.

After the ring ceremony, Sam and Akira went around the room, touching the elders' feet and getting their blessings. When they reached us, Akira smiled and teasingly started to bend down to touch my feet—me, being her elder and all—but of course, I stopped her and pulled her into a hug. "I'm so happy for you, Akira."

She tightened her arms around me. "We got really lucky, didn't we?"

I looked at Kriti, who stood beside me. I was pretty sure she could hear us, and so could Sam. I looked at Kriti when I answered Akira, "We really did."

When Akira pulled away, I pulled Sam into a hug. "Take care of Akira."

He nodded and slapped my back as he pulled away. He met my eyes, and in all seriousness, he said, "We wouldn't have happened without you, Aakar. And I'll never forget that."

I felt Kriti's hand on my back, and I smiled at Sam. "Just love and cherish Akira, and we're even."

Sam nodded, and with all the seriousness, promised. "Always."

With that, they moved on to get blessings from other relatives.

I couldn't have been happier for Akira. In the past, my heart would've ached with longing for such love too. But having Kriti by my side, feeling her warmth in my arms, the memory of her kiss, the anticipation of having her in my bed again, I could finally understand why Akira fought so hard for Sam.

"Are you okay?" Kriti asked.

She looked at me with concern in her eyes. I ran my hand in her hair—I couldn't help it—and gave her a smile. "I'm good."

Now that everyone around us was occupied with congratulating Akira and taking photos, it seemed the right time for my surprise for Kriti.

I softly clutched her arm and pulled her closer to me. We kept smiling and nodding at the relatives who passed us.

"What?" she asked, her cheeks turning a little shade of pink.

"I have a surprise for you."

She quickly turned to face me, her eyes wide with excitement. "What? What is it?"

She looked around me as if the surprise would pop out from behind me.

I chuckled and pulled her closer. "Let's go. And don't ask me any questions or argue. We don't want any attention from people."

I could literally see her contain her excitement and get her face to look serious. My lips twitched, and I could barely contain my own smile. I grazed my hand along hers and led the way, and she kept up with me, just a step behind.

Once we were out of the living room and climbed up to the next floor, everything was far quieter. I could hear her bangles chiming every time her hand moved, her rough exhale at having to climb up the steps in her heavy clothing.

"Where are we going?" she panted, holding the railing of the stairs to the third floor of our house.

I paused and turned around. "Our room."

Heat rushed through me at the thought of sharing my room with Kriti, imagining her sleeping beside me in my—our—bed and waking up next to her. I waited on the steps as she joined me.

I clutched her hand and pulled her up the last flight of stairs.

She looked so beautiful. Her hair fell in waves over her chest, her maroon-and-gold blouse highlighted her thick curves, and her chaniya, the long, flowing traditional skirt, molded to her hips just fucking right.

Before I opened the door to our bedroom, I pushed her against the door. It was just two rooms on the third floor. Ria's and my room were separated by the small sitting room, so we didn't share a wall and had decent privacy. And right now, it was just the two of us on this floor, so I didn't worry about anyone catching us off guard.

When I stepped closer to Kriti, she pushed herself against the door. "What are you doing?"

"Did I tell you how amazing you look today?"

She smiled her bashful smile. "You like my dress?"

I slowly moved my gaze from the tip of her toes to her eyes, stopping at my favorite spots and making her blush. "I *love* your dress. And I *love* you."

She went entirely soft on me, her eyes shining with what I hoped was happiness and love. "I love you too."

I stepped closer to her, so close our bodies touched, her hips at mine, my hard cock against her soft stomach, my nose along hers, and our foreheads pressed tight. With a slight turn of my head, I captured her lips in mine.

At the soft touch of her lips, I was a goner. Memories flooded my mind of her legs spread out on the bench, her soft pink pussy begging for my mouth, and the feel of her tongue brushing against mine. I was starving.

I clutched her waist and pushed into her, my mouth eating at her. Her moans pressed against my tongue, and her lips sucked mine. I was lost in her. Her softness, her scent, the way her tongue moved against mine, the way she rubbed her breasts against my chest, the way she clutched my hair as if to hold me to her like she was afraid I would pull away. *Not a chance.*

But too soon, she pulled me off by my hair. "Aakar," she

panted, her body still touching mine, "we need to stop. Oh god, my lipstick. People are gonna know."

Before she could freak out and move away from me, I clutched her hand. "You completely made me forget why I brought you upstairs for a second. Now, close your eyes, and just don't worry for a minute."

She rolled her eyes and closed them, but her lips were tugged up in excitement.

I turned her around to face the door to our bedroom and opened it. I gently pushed her back. "Take two steps in."

Once she did, I closed and locked the bedroom door behind us. I didn't want anyone intruding on our private moment.

She still had her eyes closed, but she had her hands outstretched as if we were playing a game and she had to catch me. She looked ridiculous. I shook my head and tried not to smile, but I couldn't help it.

Shaking my head, I said, "Open your eyes, baby."

I stood beside her to see her reaction to our bedroom and the small surprise.

∼

Kriti

My heart seized in my chest the moment my eyes opened. Right there, in front of me, was an empty white bookshelf along half the length of the wall.

Aakar came and stood beside me, his eyes glued to my face. "Since I know how much you love reading and how many books you own, I wanted this bedroom, this home, to feel like your own."

Tears pooled into my eyes and dripped down my cheeks. And before I knew it, Aakar had his arms around me, my face tucked in that perfect spot where his neck met his shoulder.

"Thank you," I whispered against his skin and placed a kiss right there.

He clutched me tighter to him. "I've asked Rati and Kartik to courier all your books here. And given them the money."

The only reason I remained standing at this point was because he held me so tight in his arms. His shirt was wet with my tears and snot, but I just couldn't care. I was busy shaking my head in disbelief. "You did all this for me. I just...I have no words."

He swayed us gently, nuzzling at my cheek and placing soft kisses on my head. "You do know I didn't build it with my hands, right? I ordered the carpenter to do it. And I really didn't think you would cry so much."

I looked at him, my palm splayed over his firm chest. "It's been a while since I've received such a selfish gift. I'm usually the one giving the gifts. You just caught me by surprise."

He placed a soft kiss on my forehead. "I'll just have to give you so many gifts that your first reaction is an unsurprised, wide smile. And delight at finding something you wanted. No more tears."

I laughed. If he thought I would ever not get teary-eyed at a thoughtful gift, he would be sorely disappointed.

I turned to my brand-new bookshelf. It had six partitions that would fit any hardcover book, no vertical partitions to mess up the number of books I could stack, and that freshly painted wood smell.

I sighed at just the thought of arranging my books on these shelves.

Aakar's arms wrapped around me from behind, and he placed his chin on my shoulder. "And you won't even need to keep your books wrapped up in that brown paper or newspapers. You can just keep them all displayed."

As if his huge family wouldn't just barge into our room whenever they pleased. Like they would not question a cover with couples in a heady embrace, or a smoking hot guy with a hockey stick in his hands, or God forbid, *two* guys in an embrace. Even Aakar didn't have a clue about all the books I read and enjoyed.

I just patted his hand at his suggestion. "We'll see."

After I had admired my new bookshelf to the fullest, I noticed the gigantic bed at the center of the opposite wall. Covered in creamy silk bedsheets and the four fluffiest pillows I could imagine, I had the insane urge to push Aakar down on the bed and roll around the sheets with him.

He must've read my mind, or we might be on the same frequency, because he stood behind me, his very excited state pushing against my backside, and murmured, "Later."

I turned in his embrace to face him, his thoughtfulness, his surprise, his gift, still a forerunner in my mind. Aakar was someone to be cherished. His need to please his family, to be this reliable pillar of the house, needed to be celebrated. Not everyone could stand to have ten people depend on them and not buckle under those expectations and pressure.

And now, he had me, and he was doing his best to make me feel at home. I cupped his face, raised on my tiptoes, and softly grazed my lips to his. "Later."

Late that evening, when everyone was done with dinner and all the relatives had left, Aakar and I rushed back to our hotel, all my nervousness about what his family would think forgotten.

The only thing I remembered that I needed was him.

The moment we entered our hotel room, I dragged him into the washroom. He quickly removed my clothes—as quickly as one could when removing Indian traditional clothes and jewelry—and pulled me into the hot shower.

Our lips met in a frenzy as the hot water washed the hectic day away, leaving behind only the passion, the need, and the hunger that had simmered the entire time.

Aakar's large hand clutched my butt in a firm hold. His words were a rough pant when they met my lips. "We leave for our honeymoon day after tomorrow. And then you're all mine for the next week."

His leg slid between mine, his strong thigh rubbing me right where I needed him the most. His lips slid down my throat, placing hot, open-mouthed kisses. His words reverberated down my spine, causing my hips to roll, seeking more friction. "Fuck yes, Kriti. Tomorrow, I'll not just kiss you everywhere."

He bent lower and sucked at the top of my breast, leaving a sharp sting of pain and pleasure. "I'll suck you and bite you. And fuck you and make love to you. I can't wait to be buried deep inside you. Every. Single. Day."

Yes. Yes. Yes. I wanted it all. Now and tomorrow and the day after that.

Before I could revel in the sensation of his lips and his tongue on my breast, Aakar turned off the shower.

He opened the glass door of the shower and brought the towel in. He didn't pause at my questioning look, simply continued to run the towel down my body quickly but thoroughly. Once done, he met my eyes and wiped his own body. "I need you in bed today."

21

Song: Aye Udi Udi Udi
  - *Adnan Sami, A.R. Rahman, Gulzar*

Aakar

I didn't let go of a very naked and very hot Kriti for even a moment as I led her to our bed. My mouth was busy kissing her, my hands clutching her as close to me as possible. The moment the back of her legs touched the bed, I caught her free fall, pulled her up the bed, and laid down on top of her.

My lips swallowed her loud moan the moment our bodies touched. My arms surrounded her, and my legs tangled with hers, all while my hardness rubbed along her stomach. Slowly.

Her feet rubbed against my calves, and red-hot pleasure sparked through my veins. "What are you doing to me, Kriti?"

My voice was hoarse, my body on fire, as she arched her neck and moaned my name. "Aakar, closer."

Her hand clutched my hair, and she pushed my face to her exposed neck.

A loud groan rumbled up my chest, and a burning spark of possession took root inside my mind. *Mine. All mine.*

My movements held no finesse as I devoured her neck. When I ravaged the soft, creamy skin at the spot where her neck met her shoulder, Kriti's body arched up to meet mine, and her nails dragged along my back.

My cock was now dripping on her soft stomach, the friction sending hot bolts of pressure down my spine.

Sweat dripped down my back as our bodies rubbed against each other.

I couldn't get enough of her. My wife. The woman I was in love with.

Her touch branded me, and her lips owned me.

My hands traveled down as I grabbed the perfect handful of her ass and pulled her dripping wetness against my cock.

She whimpered as she entwined her legs around my waist. "Yes, baby. You're soaked for me, aren't you?"

She moaned in answer.

I stopped kissing her shoulder and looked at her. I clutched her chin in my hand, and her eyes met mine. I brushed my thumb along her lips. "Answer me, Kriti. I want to hear you say it."

I moved my cock between her legs and pushed, almost brushing at her opening.

Her pussy soaked my cock, and her wetness ran down my sack.

My body arched in pleasure as I tried to think of the worst possible things to keep from coming. "You're soaked for me, aren't you, baby?"

Her cheeks were flushed, and her eyes were hooded with pleasure as she nodded. "Yes. I'm s…soaked. F-for you."

"Fuck yes. You feel how hard you make me?" I clutched her ass tighter and pushed myself against her, sliding along her wetness and drenching myself in her.

She moaned. "Yes. God, Aakar."

All I could feel were her nails dragging down my back, her teeth biting my shoulder, her thighs, her wetness engulfing my cock. With every push between her thighs, my cock grazed her wet opening, and every time, she squeezed me tighter.

Her moans were a constant chant of *More. More. More.*

Pleasure built down my spine, but I needed her to come.

She writhed underneath me, her movements turning sharper. I clutched one of her thighs, wrapping it around my waist, and with my other hand, I held her jaw and ravaged her mouth.

I swallowed her moans and whimpers as her other leg wrapped around my thigh.

Her words were unintelligible except for my name. "Aakar. Aakar, Aakar."

Her face flushed with need, her eyes heavy with desire, her gorgeous tits bouncing with each of my thrusts, and her body writhed against mine. I'd never looked at something more breathtaking in my life than my wife. "Fuck, I love you, baby."

Those words seemed to be her undoing. She arched her spine, her hands clutching my ass in both hands and pushing me so deep I felt her thighs tighten. When a rush of wetness coated my cock, pleasure raced down my spine, and I exploded between us, coating Kriti's pussy, her stomach, and her thighs.

For a few minutes, I stayed there with my face tucked in my wife's neck. I breathed her in, feeling her exhales on my shoulder as her hands ran down my back.

I could feel the stickiness between us.

Her groans joined mine as I propped myself up on my arms to put some space between us.

I could not, for the life of me, move away from her.

"You okay?" I asked, cataloging her disheveled state.

She looked at me, her eyes soft and tired.

She softly moved her hand on my back, and I barely

stopped my shiver. My cock, however, gave a helpless twitch from where it was still tucked between her legs.

Her eyes widened, and her mouth dropped in an O. "Still?" she asked, her voice raspy.

I lightly rubbed myself against her to show her my now semi-hard state. "This is not going down anytime soon around you."

Her lips curved up into a shy smile. "Good. I like it."

"You like it, huh?"

"Very much." She pulled me closer and put her lips on mine. She kissed me like she was afraid she'd forget my taste. Her tongue rubbed against mine, and I was fully hard once more, trying not to start rubbing myself against her.

We needed to sleep. We had a long day ahead of us.

But apparently, Kriti seemed to have other ideas.

Before I could move away from the hot and wet mess between us, Kriti clutched my ass and rubbed herself against my cock.

My cum and her wetness eased her way, and my cock easily slid between her folds. "Again?" I asked, already clutching her hair and tilting her neck to put my mouth at her pulse.

She let out a loud moan, dragged her nails down my back, and clutched her legs around my waist. "Again."

∼

Kriti

The following day, I officially moved into my new house. My new family was very much in festive spirits. The day passed by quickly with lots of food and conversations with the last few lingering relatives.

Aakar and I had just reached our bedroom on the top floor of the house after dinner to settle in when the door to our room burst open, and Abhi walked in. Behind him, Akira and all of the cousins followed.

Every one of them had excited smiles on their faces. I turned to Aakar in question, but he just shrugged in confusion.

The moment I turned to them, everyone shouted, "Welcome to the family, bhabhi." Bhabhi means sister-in-law.

Abhi, Akira, and Ria were the main cheerleaders, while the three younger kids— Soham, Samar, and Dhruv—stood in front of them. Sam and Luke stood behind the group, observing the Mishra family's warmth. I met Meera's eyes behind them, where she stood beside Luke, and she gave me a look that screamed *Are you sure you're prepared for this large, crazy family?*

I instantly felt the warm presence of Aakar beside me, and he wrapped his hand around my waist.

I smiled at each of them. "Thank you so much, you guys. And do you really have to call me bhabhi?"

I really wasn't digging the term "Bhabhi" for myself. I knew it was a term of respect for a sister-in-law, but it made me feel old. Again, I *was* older than almost all of Aakar's siblings, but I didn't care.

Akira and Abhi burst into laughter and did a high-five. Akira turned to me with a smile on her face. "We were just discussing the same thing before we came up here. It's the first time we've had to call someone bhabhi. We had to practice just saying that word before coming up here."

While Akira talked, everyone had just settled into our room. Sam and Luke got some chairs from the lounge outside, Ria turned on the air conditioner, Meera and Abhi had already settled themselves on the floor against the bed, while the three kids had already run off to play.

Abhi turned to me with a mischievous smile on his face. "So we don't have to call you bhabhi?"

Before I could tell him he could call me whatever he wanted, Aakar beat me to it. "You can stop calling her bhabhi the day you stop calling me bhai." Bhai was a term of respect for the older brother.

In the next second, Abhi stood beside Aakar, put his elbow on Aakar's shoulder, and with a swag only a younger brother could muster, he said, "So, Aakar…"

We burst out laughing when Aakar chased Abhi, and Abhi ran around the room and used me as a literal human shield. "Save me, bhabhi."

Aakar stopped right in front of me, his eyes shining with emotions. He quickly took my hand and pulled me away from Abhi into his arms. Everyone cheered around us, and I could only smile at Aakar.

Soon, we'd all settled around the room. Aakar and I had quickly taken turns to change into our pajamas to get comfortable. He wore an oversized, soft-looking white T-shirt and gray sweatpants. I had to try really hard not to stare at him as he bantered with his siblings.

Looking at them gave me a sharp tug in my chest. I missed Rati and Kartik. Those two would have been harassing me, just like Abhi and Akira. Both of them were at an age where they were usually glued to their phone. It was at least better than the constant fights when they'd instantly join forces the moment I scolded one. I could just imagine myself in my room, checking my students' notebooks while Rati studied.

Right then, a glass of water appeared in front of me. I clutched the glass and met the eyes of my husband. His eyes shone in understanding, and with a nod, I took a few sips of the cold water, soothing my heart that still ached with the longing for *my* family.

As the evening passed, everyone started to leave. Meera and Luke were the first to leave since they had to return to their house, and Abhi and Sam followed. Akira and Ria stayed to talk about Ria's new job for a while. Apparently, Aakar's friend had helped her get a new job after quitting the old one she hated.

The moment Aakar went to the restroom, Akira and Ria directed their focus on me.

Akira's cheeks turned a little red as she tried to say whatever was on her mind. "Um...Bhabhi, are you all prepared to leave for your honeymoon?"

I burst out laughing. "I can't believe you're asking me that."

Akira groaned and covered her face. "I'm supposed to be all cool about this, but we all know what happens on a honeymoon, and it's my older brother's honeymoon we're talking about. Ew."

Ria and I chuckled. Ria rolled her eyes at Akira's dramatics. "Ignore her. We're here for *you*, not Aakar. We just want you to know that you can talk to us about anything, Kriti. We're sisters now. I hope you love Bora Bora. It looked like a great place."

Akira nodded. "Yes, exactly what she said."

And my heart melted. I'd always had Meera to talk to about things like that, but now I get two more people to share my feelings with. "I'm all good. Don't worry. I'm quite excited."

They both waggled their eyebrows and burst out laughing.

They left after wishing me a good night.

I couldn't wait for my honeymoon.

And oh, I was very, very prepared.

22

Song: Hua Mein
 - *Raghav Chaitanya, Pritam*

Aakar

Our flight to Bora Bora was fairly uneventful, except for the feel of Kriti's head on my shoulder throughout the flight. She had made all sorts of promises about wanting to watch movies together on the flight and eating the airplane food that barely tasted like anything. But the moment the flight took off, she fell asleep. She could not even stay awake for our short flight from Tahiti to Bora Bora.

Her head lolled forward. The good husband that I was, I put my own head on hers as she slept on my shoulder.

I had to wake her when the pilot announced that we would land in Bora Bora in ten minutes.

I looked down at the way Kriti was all snuggled up, holding my arm like her personal pillow. I placed a quick kiss on her head and nudged her. "Kriti, baby, wake up."

When she didn't move an inch, I nudged her harder. "Kriti."

She jerked upright. "Huh! What? I'm awake."

I chuckled. "Sure, you are."

She looked around in a daze, and her eyes softened when they met mine. "I slept the whole way?"

"Yep. The whole way. We're almost there. I didn't want you to miss the view of the islands from up here."

She quickly raised the window shade at our seat, and I felt her awe when she gasped at the view.

Endless turquoise blue stretched along the horizon, with small and large mountains peaking from the scattered clouds. The deep waters and the vast islands had excitement rushing through my blood.

Kriti's words were a whisper. "Aakar, it's gorgeous."

"It is."

We made our way through various overwater bungalows, following the resort manager as he led us to our one-bedroom villa suite. Endless blue stretched across the horizon on one side, the fresh breeze smelling of the sea. On my other side, all I saw was my wife, her face shining with excitement, her lips stretched wide in awe. She looked breathtaking.

The manager stopped at our villa. "Sir, welcome to your room. The lunch buffet begins soon. You can also place orders through our app, and we'll deliver food to your villa at the time of your convenience. Enjoy your stay."

We thanked him and made our way into the villa we would be staying in for the next seven days.

We were welcomed into an airy living area with a full-length glass window in a central courtyard when we entered. Big potted plants were in every corner, and all the furniture was wooden.

Kriti oohed and aahed beside me, touching every little surface, marveling at the space.

Her excitement was contagious. She led the way in, and I followed her.

She opened the glass door and stepped into the courtyard that was covered on two sides. The other corner had a pool with a view of the ocean behind it.

My mind had a singular focus at that point. I only wanted—needed—one thing.

Kriti. Naked. In the pool. Facing the ocean.

And me. Behind her. Buried deep inside her. Holding her to me.

My eyes met hers. And I saw the heat reflected in her eyes as well.

I didn't know if she read my mind, but she took a step closer to the pool.

I dropped the bags from my hand and ran.

By the time we reached the pool, she'd rid herself of her purse and her phone. And I was a damn lucky man because she had the forethought of wearing a dress that hugged every delicious curve of her body when it was dry.

Now, if it was to get wet, I might just die.

Only one way to find out.

I pulled her to me and jumped into the water before she could yell my name.

My lips were on hers as we went under, her arms wrapped around my neck. It was just me, Kriti, and the blissful silence of water. I was surrounded by water, but all I felt were her soft lips on mine and the taste of her tongue. We might've been under the water for a mere few seconds, but it felt like I could spend my eternity here.

We came up in a rush, my heart pounding. My arms clutched at the glorious bare hips of my wife, her dress floating up in the water, as I dove between her generous tits.

Kriti tilted her head back and pulled my head even closer. "Oh god, Aakar. More."

My groan was animalistic as I sucked at her skin, my body trying to obey every command from Kriti's mouth.

I was entirely too greedy for my wife.

I wanted to consume her. Live under her skin. Breathe her in. And keep her tied to me forever.

Without removing my mouth from her skin, I lifted her by the hips and walked us to the edge of the pool. Her head tilted back and rested against the edge, and the view had my heart beating out of my chest.

The endless ocean beyond, orange and purple streaks of light as the sun set behind the clouds, the sound of the waves crashing mingled with the moans coming out of Kriti's mouth as she writhed in my arms, begging for more of me.

I closed the gap between us, held the edge of the pool with one hand, another holding Kriti, and crushed my lips to her. I drank her moans and sucked her tongue. I licked the water off her neck and couldn't help but suck at the delicate skin where her neck met her shoulders.

Kriti tangled her hands in my hair and pushed me deeper. "Oh god, Aakar. Harder. Suck me harder."

With a groan, I pushed down the tiny strip of her sleeve and followed the bare shoulder with my mouth. I was hungry for her taste. I kissed and nipped and sucked at her chest, her arms out of her sleeves, her dress hanging on to her breasts.

I sucked at the top of her breasts and pulled the fabric down, finally revealing her. "Look at you, baby. All for me."

I grabbed her breasts and fucking loved how gloriously they fit in my hand. I squeezed them, causing her to arch her body and push them toward me. "You want my mouth on them, baby?"

Her eyes were dazed with lust, and her lips were dark red. Every inch of her was wet and wanting. "Yes. Yes. Please, Aakar."

And I dove in. I clutched her waist with both of my hands,

squeezing her to me, her legs wrapped around my hips, right where I needed her the most, and sucked and nipped and licked at her breasts. She panted and writhed, her pussy grinding against my very hard cock, as she led me by my hair where she needed.

I alternated between her breasts, and when I couldn't take any more of her grinding, I pushed my pants down and let them float away in the water. I did the same with her panties and had her wrapped around me in the next second.

"Kriti, baby, fuck, I need you."

"Do it, Aakar. I need you inside me." She rubbed her pussy against me, shooting electric tingles down my spine. "Get inside me, Aakar."

And as much as I wanted to push my cock inside her, I had to keep a clear head. It was our first time. So I pushed my hips away from hers, keeping her clutched to me, my forehead touching hers, my breath coming in pants. "Not like this, baby. We need to get in bed. I've waited a long time to do this with you, and I'll always regret it if I hurt you."

Tears glistened in her eyes, and she pulled me in and kissed me.

A kiss that wreaked havoc inside my body.

A kiss that had my heartbeat following hers.

A kiss that touched my soul.

A kiss from my wife.

"I love you," she whispered against my lips.

"And I love you," I breathed into hers, over and over, as I dragged her out of the pool and into our bed.

∽

Kriti

One moment, I was in the pool, kissing my husband, loving my husband, and the next moment, I was on our big, fluffy white bed.

And Aakar was on top of me, his naked body rubbing against mine while he kissed me as if his life depended on it. I had never felt this wanted, loved, or beautiful in my life before.

The place between my legs throbbed and squeezed, and I could feel the wetness coating the apex of my thighs. I wrapped my legs around Aakar and moved so I could rub it on Aakar's very hard, very prominent erection.

His groan vibrated against my chest, and I couldn't help but rub myself against him. I'd never felt so wanton before, but this was Aakar. He held my thigh with his hand as he pushed his cock along the seam of my lips, coating himself even more with my arousal.

With every push of his hips, the way he held my thighs open, the way his warm, heavy body moved over me, I felt so empty. A riot of aching need and unimaginable pleasure sent electric sparks along my spine, causing my hips to rock against him, my body demanding more. "More, Aakar, please. I need you."

"You're soaked, baby. Look how easily I slide between your lips."

My moan was loud and keening as need thrummed through my veins. The need to feel him deeper, to feel him deep inside me. But he. Just. Won't. Get. In.

"Aakar, I need you inside me. Please."

His loud groan against my cheek had me squeezing my thighs around his hips tighter, trying to pull him inside me. "Fuck, Kriti. I need you to come for me, baby. Just like this. Because once I bury myself inside you, it's gonna be fucking over. I won't be able to hold back, baby."

With every slide of his hips between my thighs—his cock hit my clit, and his balls slapped my ass—mind-bending pleasure rocked through every nerve ending of my body.

His loud groan vibrated against my chest, his body shaking as if it took all of his strength to hold back from pushing inside me. "C'mon, baby. Come on my cock, and I'll push inside you."

I erupted with those words, his urgency, the way he clutched my arms, and his teeth grazing my shoulder. My muscles tightened as a surge of pleasure wracked my body, and wave after wave of euphoria had me seeing a million stars behind my eyes. I pulled Aakar deeper against me and held him there, clutching his ass as I felt my juices coating his cock even further.

Before I could come down from the high, Aakar sat on his knees and pulled my thighs farther apart, looking at the mess I'd made.

His eyes were wild, perspiration dotted his forehead, and he looked at me with hunger, passion, and unending want. He was panting so hard that he could barely get his words out. "You ready, baby? This might hurt."

Even after the orgasm, I was still aching with want. So, despite the fear of getting hurt, I quickly gave him a nod.

Without looking away from my eyes, he held his cock against me and pushed in deeper and deeper and deeper until he was fully seated. Until I could feel the throbbing of his cock inside me. Until I could feel the weight of his balls against my cheeks. Until I teetered between pressure, pain, and discomfort.

He shivered above me, his hands clutching me tighter, his jaw sharp like ice as he looked at where we were joined. "Oh fuck, just look at us, baby. Look how perfectly we fit together."

I pushed myself up on my elbows and could barely see the length of his cock as I tried to breathe through the pain.

"Please tell me when I can move, baby. Fuck. Fuck."

He vibrated and couldn't help but push a little inside me,

causing me to flinch in pain. I clutched his ass to halt his movements, but it was impossible. He couldn't stop shaking as his hips gave tiny, involuntary jerks. I breathed through the bite of pain and pushed him out a little, trying to get comfortable. "Give me a second, Aakar."

His loud, desperate groan had me clenching around him, causing his arm to push up and grab the headboard. "Oh fuck, baby. Don't do that. You feel too good."

The sudden change in his position sent a zing of pleasure through my body among the sharp tinges of pain.

I moaned, and just to try again, I clutched his ass and pushed him in deeper.

His loud growl echoed in my ears as he buried his face against my neck and grabbed the pillow beside my head.

"Oh fuck, Kriti. I can't. I can't hold on this time. Please, please let me move. I can't stop."

And I knew I wasn't close. But Aakar was losing control, and I needed to see him unhinged. I needed to see him wild with abandon, and I needed it to be *me* who made him snap.

So, despite the fact that I was nowhere near close to coming, I clutched his head and spread my legs. "I'm good, Aakar. Move."

He didn't need to be told twice.

He fell into me, his cheek against mine, his mouth at my throat sucking, as he started to move. With every wild thrust inside me, I wrapped my legs around his waist, urging him deeper. He groaned like he was dying, and I was his only lifeline.

His control burst into smithereens, pushing inside me over and over, bucking like mad. His need, and desperation, and hunger overpowered his senses.

When his cock started to hit deep inside me, all of his care for me forgotten, each of his thrusts started to shoot pleasure down my spine. After feeling the emptiness for so long, I finally felt so full, so *needed,* so one with him. I couldn't stop the moan as I clutched his neck. I clenched my pussy tight around him, wanting to keep him inside me forever, all hints of pain forgotten.

With a sharp curse, Aakar's entire body shuddered over me. I felt his cock pulse inside me as the hot rush of his cum had me burning with want. He was still shaking over me as he kept thrusting inside me, prolonging his pleasure.

Keeping a hand on his lower back, I dragged a blanket over us.

A few moments passed as I petted him, and he breathed into my neck. "You okay?" I asked.

He hummed into my chest, rubbing his nose along my breast. "I...That was...Um..."

I laughed as he tried to string some words together.

He nipped at my breast, making me squeal.

"I think you broke me, woman."

"That good, huh?"

I caressed his hair near his ear, and he nuzzled into my hands.

"I knew having sex was going to feel amazing. I had imagined a thousand ways that I would love you and fuck you. But I had no idea it would feel like this with you."

"Like what?" I asked, my voice barely above a whisper.

He looked at me, love shining in his eyes, a smile that could stop my heartbeat, and kissed me softly on the lips. "Like I was barely living before I met you. Like I could love you forever and never be satisfied. Like I had my first breath of sunshine. Like you were mine, and I was yours."

I sniffled and tried to blink away the tears pooling in my eyes.

I pushed up on my elbows and kissed him.

"You're still inside me," I said as I felt him twitch inside me.

"Who said we're done?"

And he pushed his tongue into my mouth as he slowly began to move inside me.

~

AFTERNOON TURNED TO NIGHT, night turned to days, and we spent our time between conversations, food, and sex. Lots and lots of sex. And all of those times, we did not forget to use condoms, unlike our first time. It had totally slipped our minds at the moment, but neither of us was ready for a kid.

Aakar had quickly run down to the nearest drug store—which wasn't that near after all—and gotten me a morning-after pill.

In the time between our sexual bouts, we talked about everything and nothing. We'd begun our relationship by making conversation, so it wasn't new for us. But we'd never talked so much in person, looking at each other, walking along the beach hand in hand, or when he spooned me naked and kissed my neck.

I found he loved '90s Bollywood comedy movies. And when I saw him laugh as we watched one of his favorites, tears streaming down his face, I fell for him even deeper.

I never wanted our days here to end.

It felt like a dream.

We spent our days exploring Bora Bora—going on the wildlife tour, visiting Mount Otemanu, swimming and walking along its beautiful beaches—and our nights discovering each other's bodies. In our bed, on the sofa, in our bathtub, and finally, in the pool.

"What are you thinking?" Aakar asked, pulling me out of my musings.

We were lying in the courtyard near the pool, taking occasional dips in the cool water and eating fresh fruits.

Aakar ran his fingers through my hair as he waited for me to answer. "Just that I don't want this to end."

He pulled himself closer to me and ran his nose along my cheek. "Me too, baby."

I moved my hand along his arm, brushing my fingers in the dusting of hair. "But it will. Very soon."

Aakar placed a soft kiss on my cheek. He looked at me as if he could read my mind. And maybe he could. "I understand living with a whole new family will be very different for you. Tell me what you're feeling."

No matter how hard he tried, I didn't think he could ever understand the feeling. "I feel like we do have great sex."

He chuckled. "That we do."

"I feel like I know you. I understand you. And I think I'll be a good wife to you."

He kissed my forehead this time. "You already are."

I smiled at him. "But I'm terrified that I won't be a good daughter-in-law. I'm afraid your parents won't like me. Or I'll have to change who I am to make them like me. And I hate both options. I think your siblings like me, and that's nice. But it's the elders who worry me. I don't want to change myself to make them like me, let alone love me. But what if they hate who I am?"

By the time I finished, I couldn't even meet his eyes. My gaze was glued to his strong neck, his Adam's apple bobbing as he swallowed.

He lifted my chin to meet his eyes, and all I found was understanding in them. "I'm terrified that I'll be a bad husband too."

"You are?" It was hard to believe he could be a bad husband. He's been nothing but supportive and understanding.

He nods. "I am. I'm afraid I won't be able to fulfill my responsibility as a husband. I would love you. But I'm afraid my family, my life, will be too much for you. I'm afraid you'll regret marrying me. I'm terrified that you'll leave me."

"I wouldn't regret marrying you, Aakar."

"And I'll never let you, baby. All we can do is give our best. Support each other. Understand each other. And even fight with each other. That's okay."

I could only nod because all that seemed doable. I would love nothing more than to make this marriage work with Aakar.

Aakar pulled me even closer and kissed my nose. "And as for the elders, they're going to love you. They did choose you, after all."

I shook my head. "You know it's not that simple."

He nodded. "I know. But there is no way they wouldn't love you. *I* love you. Look at you."

I slapped his chest lightly, making him laugh as he pulled me into his arms. "We'll deal with it together. I'm right here."

I breathed in his scent, closed my eyes, took in his warmth, and believed him.

Two more days of this bliss, and the real world awaits.

23

Song: Genda Phool
 - *Rekha Bharadwaj, Shraddha Pandit, Sujata Majumdar*

Aakar

On the first morning back from our honeymoon, I woke up to a cold, empty bed. I hated it. I'd gotten used to feeling the warmth and softness of Kriti in my arms, her scent that I wanted to rub my nose into, and hearing her husky good morning as she woke up.

I'd missed all of that today.

Yawning, I looked at the clock and flew out of my bed—*our* bed.

It was nine in the morning already.

I quickly freshened up and practically ran to the dining room.

Everyone was already seated at the table, so I dropped to my usual seat beside Abhi. I had a free chair right beside me for Kriti. Before I could question where she was, everyone at the table had turned to look at me with varying smiles.

Abhi waggled his eyebrows.

Dad and my uncles just gave me the usual grunt, their heads halfway stuck inside the newspaper. Dad glanced up from the paper, his attention still stuck on whatever he was reading. "You coming to the office today?"

"Yes. Maybe a little late, but I'll be there."

He grunted and went back to his newspaper.

Abhi nudged me with his elbow, his eyes glinting with his usual mirth. "How was Bora Bora?"

I nudged him back harder. "Shut up. It was great."

Before I could ask him if he'd seen Kriti, she walked out of the kitchen. She was all dressed up, wearing a beautiful red salwar kameez and looking as fresh as a daisy.

Maa was right behind her. "Oh good, you're up, beta. I was just telling Kriti to go wake you up."

My ears burned at Maa's comment. It felt like I was still her little kid. Or maybe Kriti looked so put together while I'd just rolled out of bed. I looked at Kriti when I answered, "Uh, I usually don't wake up so late."

She smiled. "It's okay. We came in late last night."

Approaching, she placed a cup of chai in front of me. "I'll get you breakfast."

She turned and was about to leave me when I clutched her hand. "Uh, where's your chai? And breakfast?"

It was Maa who answered, "We already ate, beta."

She had this smile that said, *What kind of a stupid question is that? You know we've always finished our breakfast way before you.*

Kriti was barely hanging on with a polite smile on her face. I *knew* she hated serving food like this.

I glanced at the chai in front of me and didn't feel like I could get it down.

I looked at Kriti, who stood by the empty chair beside me, and my stomach tied in knots. "Sit with me while I drink chai?"

Her eyes widened, and her cheeks turned pink. She looked

around at the shocked faces staring at us. "Umm. Let me get you breakfast."

Her eyes were practically screaming at me.

I nodded. "And then you guys can sit with us while we eat."

I kicked Abhi's foot under the table.

He instantly parroted my thoughts. "Yes, bhabhi. And Mummy, sit with us. Aakar Bhai wants to tell us all about his trip."

I absolutely *did not* want to talk about how I railed my wife for a week straight.

Kriti's face had entirely turned red.

"Sure, Bora Bora was great," I began, and Kriti flew out of there.

I barely managed not to laugh at her.

Once we were all settled around the table, Kriti right by my side, I told everyone about the beauty of Bora Bora, the water adventures we took, the hiking we did, and the food we ate—anything to keep Kriti by my side.

"Uh...Pappa, would you like more thepla?" Kriti asked from beside me. Thepla was a classic flatbread made of wheat flour, oil, and spices.

It was probably the first time she'd addressed my father as Pappa. He looked just as flustered as her but managed to give her a pleased smile. "One more should be good, beta," he said, clearing his throat.

She quickly got up and ran to the kitchen, and I looked at the proud smile on everyone's faces at the table. I didn't know whether it was for her addressing my dad as Pappa or being so active in serving the family, but I sincerely hoped it was the former.

Maa smiled at me. "It isn't easy, you know?"

"What?" I didn't know what she was referring to.

"To address your mother-in-law and father-in-law as Mummy and Pappa."

Daadi—meaning Grandma—scoffed from the other side of the table. "I remember your mother choking on Mummy for two months straight."

"And this one"—Daadi pointed at my elder auntie Sunita—"She didn't even try addressing me as Mummy for the first three weeks. She never choked, though."

She turned to my younger aunt, Radhika. "And Radhika was the fastest at calling me Mummy."

Maa laughed, her ears turning pink. She looked at Daadi. "And I remember you cooking me gaajar halwa the first time I didn't choke on my words." Gaajar halwa was a traditional Indian sweet made from carrots, ghee, and sugar. Maa's and Abhi's favorite.

Kriti had already arrived from the kitchen with Dad's thepla when Daadi was regaling us with the stories. The entire time, she had a smile on her face, her eyes twinkling when Maa talked about Daadi preparing gaajar halwa for her. I hope she makes Kriti feel special like that.

Back in the bedroom, I paced across the room, waiting for Kriti to arrive. I was about to walk back to the kitchen to drag her back when the door to our bedroom pushed open, and she stepped in.

I instantly had her in my arms, clutching her in my arms, terrified she'd be mad at me. "I am so, so sorry. I know you hate serving people. And usually, everyone does have breakfast together, and either Raju Kaka serves us, or the food is laid out on the table, and we just make our own plate when we get there."

Kriti chuckled, which had my heart calmed down a notch. "I do hate serving people like that and eating food separately. That doesn't mean I haven't served people before. We ladies were all up early today, and the breakfast was hot and fresh, so we just dug in. Everyone gathered around like an hour later. I might've hated waiting for everyone more than just eating when I was ready. And anyway, school starts tomorrow. So I'll be out of the house way before breakfast."

I caressed her back while she moved her hand across my T-shirt, feeling my chest. I flexed my muscles, and she chuckled. I leaned down and captured that beautiful sound with my lips.

Her hands moved around my neck, and she raised on her toes to kiss me the way she wanted—thoroughly and with so much passion. My legs moved, and I pushed us back on the bed.

"Whoa." She jumped up. Well, she tried, but my arms were like steel bands around her waist.

"Where do you think you're going, wife?" My voice was rough with arousal.

She whimpered. "Oh god, that's so hot."

I pulled her closer and kissed her neck. "You like it when I call you *wife*?"

She turned her head, asking for more. "Yes, *husband*."

A rough, animalistic sound escaped my throat as if pushed out from my chest that banged around like a drumbeat.

"Fuck, I need you." I pushed my hands under her top and kissed the side of her neck, taking in her rose and vanilla scent.

"Whoa." Before I could understand what was happening, Kriti was out of my arms and off the bed. My body was strung tight, ready to devour my wife, who now paced the room, fanning her face.

"What happened? Come back." I started to move off the bed to drag her back in.

She took two steps back. "Oh my god, stop distracting me with..." She gestured her hand at my body. "I need to go downstairs and help prepare lunch. We can't have sex in the middle of the day while everyone is up and awake downstairs."

She was right. She was absolutely right. She just made me lose all sense of control. I groaned and dropped back onto the bed, dragging the blanket over me.

Before I could snuggle in and try to gather some sense of control, she pulled off my blanket. It was only because I was already clutching it so tight that I still had it in my hands. "Oh my god, Kriti. What are you doing? Let it go."

She pulled at the blanket again. "Are you crazy? You can't go back to sleep. You just had breakfast."

I pulled it back harder, and she almost got dragged back onto the bed. "Let it go. I'll just rest for five minutes."

She pulled on it again. Harder. Digging her heels in and everything. "What? No. I've been up for the past three hours, hopefully impressing everyone. You don't get to keep resting. Get. Up." She pulled the blanket so hard at the last two words that I lost my grip on it, and she almost ran into the opposite wall.

Her hair was a mess. Her eyes were wide and crazy. Her lips were pulled into a tiny, cute frown, like a baby lion. Absolutely stunning. And fucking *mine*.

And she had the audacity to put her hand on her waist and stand there like the teacher that she is, firing up all my fantasies. "Are. You. Getting. Up?"

I leaned forward on the bed, and with barely restrained control, I said, "If you don't get out of the room right now, *wife*, nothing is going to stop me from dragging you back to bed and showing you what you're doing to me right now."

Her feet stumbled, her cheeks turned pink, and before I could get up, she threw the blanket on me and ran out the door, muttering, "If you're not downstairs in five minutes, I'm sending in Abhi."

The rest of the day went by pretty fast. By the time I went downstairs to go to the gym, Abhi had left for college, and Ria was ready to leave for work. Kriti sat at the dining table while Ria packed her lunch, saying, "This new job that Aakar got me is crazy hectic."

"Or you just got too relaxed and complacent in your last

job," I piped in, grabbing an apple from the fruit basket on the dining table.

I anticipated the kick coming from a mile away, so I quickly jumped out of reach from Ria. "Mind your business, Aakar. Your friend Zayan isn't much help either. Why are you even friends with the guy?"

I bit into the apple. "*The guy* helped you get the job."

She glared at me and turned back to packing, muttering, "He's making it very, very hard to remember that."

Ria hated feeling obligated to someone, especially a guy. So I know she must hate just being in Zayan's presence.

But that couldn't be helped. Zayan helped her get her foot in the door of that office. And he was one of the most stand-up guys I knew. He wouldn't harm my sister, so I wasn't worried.

I quickly finished off my apple by the time Ria left.

It was just Kriti and me in the dining area. I could hear Maa and the aunties' voices coming from the kitchen.

So I quickly dropped a kiss on her head. "I'm going to the gym."

She tried to hide how much she liked the kiss, but I saw the way she blushed.

Time flew after that. I returned, got ready, then had lunch with Maa, the aunties, Kriti, and my grandparents.

After lunch, I went to the office and spent the rest of the day catching up with everyone and everything. It was pretty clear that the office hadn't handled the past few weeks without me all that well.

Dinner was ready when I returned home with Dad and my uncles. We all sat together to eat, Kriti right by my side. My brother joked around, Ria complained, and the elders gossiped about some relatives.

I spent the night buried balls deep in my wife, quietly making love to her while she muffled her moans in my shoulder, and all was right in the world.

Kriti

I was the first one up in the house today. Quietly, I made my way downstairs to the kitchen. Aakar's house was so much larger than mine. I was used to being the first one up in my house, but today was the first time I was up this early. And with so many people living in the house, this sort of quiet in the house was spooky.

I put the pot on the stove and started preparing my chai. I made some extra in case someone woke up, and I'd need to offer it. School started today, and I had to go an hour early to get all the paperwork and introductions out of the way. Thank God Meera started working there a few months ago. In Laxminagar, I helped her get the job in our village school. And here, Meera helped me get the job as a science and English teacher for eighth and ninth graders.

I'd already started reading up and preparing notes a month ago. I knew I wouldn't find time around the wedding and honeymoon, so I had to be done way before that. The syllabus didn't concern me. But I was still a little terrified.

I sat at the dining table, reading my e-book and sipping my chai.

And just breathed.

It was the first moment I had on my own, for myself. No Aakar. None of his—*mine* now—family members. Just me, my book, my chai, my thoughts.

Just peace.

I vowed to wake up half an hour earlier now. If every day could start like this, I just might tolerate and make it through a busy school life and my abundant new family members.

I cleaned up the kitchen once I was finished with the chai and went upstairs to get ready for school. I entered our bedroom and found a sprawling Aakar, his one arm flung over his head and another very close to his hips. I so badly wanted to get under that blanket and repeat what we did last night. My cheeks heated just at the thought of what we did. How he'd moved so slow inside me, how he had to put his hand over my mouth to keep me from moaning, the way his hips had felt as they moved and flexed so deep inside me. Who knew we had it in us?

Before I jumped my husband, I quickly opened my half-arranged closet.

I used to wear a proper conservative salwar kameez at my school back home. Meera told me some teachers here wore pants and suits, some dresses, some sarees, and some salwar kameez. So, I guessed everyone was on their own.

I picked my slightly modern but simpler salwar kameez and went to shower.

My mind kept spinning over how dramatically my life had changed. Maybe the new beginning looming over my head once again caused me to just ponder. But life was certainly different back home.

And for the life of me, I was still not used to referring to my new home as *home*. Why was it still just Aakar's home for me?

My new family was pretty decent. I didn't expect a modern and nonconservative family. I knew what I was marrying into. So, I was getting the hang of their day-to-day life. Aakar's family was certainly not as modern as he thought they were.

But who was I to judge too soon? I was just happy they were okay with me working.

I quickly wore my kameez top and went out to the bedroom to wear my salwar. I didn't know how my maa and other ladies managed to wear the tight salwar without getting it wet, but that wasn't one of my skill sets.

So I took a seat on my side of the bed and started to roll them up my legs.

And I almost shrieked the room down when a warm breath touched the back of my neck.

"Good morning, baby." Aakar's raspy voice made me shiver.

"You scared me."

He ran his nose along my neck, and I stopped whatever I was doing. I turned my neck to give him more space to explore. And he placed an open-mouthed kiss right where my neck met my shoulder. "You didn't wake me up."

My heart picked up speed as he kept placing kisses along my neck. "Was I supposed to?"

His large hand moved between the slits of my salwar, under my top, and up my bare stomach. "You didn't think I would want to drop you off at school?"

Oh. School.

I quickly pushed him away with a nudge of my elbow and started wearing the tight salwar. "No time for romance right now. I need to get ready."

I must have looked something ridiculous while pulling up my salwar because Aakar wouldn't look away from me and kept smiling like an idiot.

"What?" I asked.

He shook his head, laughing. "Nothing. You look cute."

Butterflies swarmed my stomach, but I didn't let it show. I just shook my head at him and pointed at the bathroom. "If you're going to drop me off, I need you ready in fifteen minutes. I cannot be late today."

"Yes, teacher," he said, running to the bathroom, but not before stealing a kiss.

By the time I went downstairs after getting ready, I found Maa, kaki, and Daadi sipping chai at the dining table. I touched their feet for blessings.

Daadi smiled at me while Maa quickly got up. "Wait here, beta."

Kaki turned to me and asked, "All ready, beta?"

"Yes, kaki. Just a little nervous."

She waved her hand. "I'm sure you've dealt with worse. First days are always the easiest. Don't worry at all. I'm sure you'll be just fine."

Well, that gave me a little boost of confidence.

Right then, Maa came out of the kitchen with a small bowl. "Here, Kriti Beta, some yogurt with sugar. For good luck."

My nose instantly tingled with tears. I tried to blink my eyes to keep them at bay. And Maa's laugh helped me gain some control. "Now, don't go crying on me, beta. I know it's a little tough, but you're not alone. You'll do good today."

And here came the waterworks.

Right then, Abhi walked into the dining area, his hair rumpled like he just got out of bed. "Oh god, Maa. You're making your daughter-in-law cry already?"

"Did you even wash your face, Abhi?" Maa asked.

Loud approaching footsteps had us all turning to see Aakar walking into the dining area, his head in his phone, as he ran his fingers through his hair.

"Bhai, Maa made bhabhi cry," Abhi blurted.

Aakar's head instantly whipped toward his brother, then to me, and then to Maa.

His frown deepened as he looked at my tearstained face.

He quickly walked closer to me, but before he could say anything, Maa threw a spoon across the dining table straight toward Abhi's head. This must be a regular occurrence because he ducked at the perfect time.

"I just got emotional when Maa fed me the yogurt, that's all," I said to Aakar as Maa scolded Abhi.

Abhi must've predicted Aakar's actions too because before Aakar could throw the spoon that he now held in his hand, Abhi had Maa in front of him like a shield.

He still managed to give me a wink.

And I burst out laughing. Abhi reminded me so much of my own brother.

Aakar turned to me and shook his head, giving up on Abhi. He quickly brushed the stray tear off my cheek. "C'mon. We don't want to be late now, do we?"

"Wait. Wait." Maa quickly went to the kitchen and came out with a lunch box. "Here, I packed you some snacks. We'll ask Raju Kaka to keep a better, heavier breakfast packed for you from tomorrow."

Before I could start crying again, Aakar snatched the box from Maa's hand and dragged me to his car.

24

Song: Chahoon Bhi To
 - *Karthik, Bombay Jashree*

Kriti

After getting my hand squeezed at the school gate—what with all the children around—I met up with Meera, who waited for me at the entrance.

"Meera, I'm so nervous. Do I look okay?"

She smiled and led me to the staff room, where all the teachers sat. "You look perfect. Just like always."

As we stepped inside the room, the hustle and bustle of the early morning school day enveloped me in its chaotic embrace. Teachers moved around getting their things together, a few staff members were busy looking for some books or materials, and some teachers were busy discussing an upcoming event.

It felt loud and chaotic and a little different than I was used to back home, but it was still similar.

It felt like coming home.

My eyes met Meera's, and an understanding passed

between us. She stepped closer with a small smile on her face and said, "It's a little different from how we used to do things back home, but I know you'll catch on. Now that you're here, I'm going to feel like I never left Laxminagar. We'll be just fine."

And I felt that. I nodded my head. "We *are* going to be fine."

Meera showed me her desk, and I left her to get settled to meet the principal. The school principal, Bhavna Panchal, was an older and experienced teacher. She must be in her seventies, but her gaze was sharp, her demeanor cutthroat, and power exuded from every word she spoke.

"Welcome to Lotus Crest School, Kriti."

I sat across from her in her cabin. "Thank you, ma'am. I'm excited to be here."

My heart thrummed with anticipation.

She removed her glasses and placed them on her desk, shuffling some papers around. "We are a very busy school. I don't know how your days are scheduled in the school where you're from, so I must warn you. Our methods of teaching the students are highly interactive. We encourage teachers to use creative methods to teach their subjects. The homework checking and grading of the exams are under a strict deadline. We don't want the parents complaining about something so trivial. Under no circumstances do we permit verbal or physical abuse as a form of punishment. Is that clear, Mrs. Kriti?"

Her eyes were like lasers trying to fry my skin. "Yes, ma'am."

"Good. I had thought I would start you with us by letting you shadow another teacher for a week. But I had a class teacher resign unexpectedly two weeks ago, so I hope you're ready to step up. You're experienced being a class teacher of ninth graders in your previous school, so managing a sixth-grade class shouldn't be a hardship."

What!! A class teacher? How? Easier? Sixth graders were the WORST. They were children but didn't want to be treated that way. It was the grade when they learned the most in their life. The grading got tough. Crushes started developing.

Is it too late to quit? I wanted to ask. "Would this be in addition to teaching English and science to the eighth and ninth graders?"

"Obviously."

Obviously. I tried very hard not to roll my eyes. "Any special requirements for a class teacher?"

She frowned in thought. "Hmm. They haven't had a class teacher for two weeks now, so they might be a little unruly. A fair distribution of intelligent and struggling students, good and mischievous students. Try to find the right balance. Feel free to make friends. Be yourself. Students understand that and appreciate it more than you think."

"Let's begin, ma'am."

∼

I RETURNED HOME from school around three in the afternoon. I had three missed calls from Aakar, one from Ria, one from my mother-in-law, five unread messages, and a pounding headache.

I'd had no time to even hold my phone throughout the day, let alone pick up any calls or messages. Meera and I had taken a taxi back since Aakar and Luke had dropped us off. And with the way my head pounded after the most hectic day of my teaching life, I needed a chai.

A strong ginger chai.

I entered the house quietly, a little afraid of the family's reaction to my missed calls. I could've called back when I left, but I was so exhausted that I just couldn't. Now I feel like I should've at least sent a text.

I removed my sandals in the foyer and went into the living room to find my mother-in-law and the aunties sprawled on the sofa, talking softly with a television serial playing in the background.

At my entry, everyone turned to look at me. My mother-in-law—I seriously needed to start addressing her as Maa in my mind—sat up from where she had lain down.

"Please, uh...Mummy, no need to get up on my account."

"Oh, don't worry, beta, we were just talking. I'm not tired. How was your day?"

She moved a little and patted the sofa beside her.

I quickly and unceremoniously dropped myself on the sofa with a sigh. "Very, very tiring. They sort of made me the class teacher of a sixth-grade class."

She frowned. "And that's not a good thing?"

Right then, the main door of the house opened, and we heard shuffling of feet and laughter. In the next minute, Abhi and his friend Karan walked into the living room, bags slung over their shoulders. They were both done with college but were taking some classes for future studies.

Abhi's eyes twinkled in delight. "Oho, the whole ladies' party is gathered around?"

He quickly came and sat on the arm of the sofa right beside his mom and swung his arm around her shoulders.

Karan put his bag near the coffee table and sat on the floor right near Abhi.

These two seemed to be joined at the hip.

To Abhi, Maa said, "Kriti was just telling us about how the school made her a class teacher. She doesn't seem to be too happy about it."

Abhi frowned and turned to me. "Isn't that a good thing, bhabhi?"

I smiled at him. "It's a very good thing, responsibility-wise. I'll be able to prove myself faster and get more work. So maybe grow myself faster. I would get my own class to manage, which is always wonderful. But that means a little more stress in the very beginning. I had hoped I would get some time to get used to living with a new family, new city, new school, and the way things work here. But it's like being pushed into the deep end of the swimming pool."

Aakar's mom—just Mom—nodded along at my explanation. "Don't you worry at all, beta. We'll help you any way we can. And I know you can do it."

She was so nice. And did she really mean it? Would she really understand if I got very busy? If I spent more time working at home too? Time would tell, but I still appreciated her support.

"Thank you, uhm, Mummy."

She gave me a sweet smile, understanding clear in her eyes at how I struggled to call her Mummy.

Karan got up from where he sat and turned to us. "Anybody want some chai? I'm making some for myself. Auntie? Bhabhi?"

"Yes, please," I said.

All the aunties also said yes.

"You won't ask me?" Abhi asked.

Karan rolled his eyes. "You don't like chai."

"Doesn't mean you can't even offer it to me. Maybe I wanted to try it."

Karan looked at Abhi's—also my—mother and rolled his eyes at Abhi's antics. He then shook his head and looked at Abhi. "Do you want some chai?"

Abhi leaned back against his mom and shook his head. "Nah. I don't like it."

Karan jumped on him, but Abhi was fast and moved over the sofa and ran toward the kitchen. Karan was right on his heels as he tried to grab his T-shirt.

Mom shook her head and smiled. "These two have always been like this."

"They've been friends for long?"

At that, Radhika Kaki piped in, "Oh god, they've been like two peas in a pod since third grade."

The aunties and Mom regaled me with stories of Abhi and Karan while we waited for the chai. Hopefully, my headache would go away once I had the chai. Otherwise, dinnertime and all the class planning would be hell.

Abhi brought in the tray full of chai cups, and Karan handed them out to each one of us. This time, both of them sat on the floor at the coffee table. I took the first sip, and bless Karan, he'd made it strong with a good amount of ginger.

Right then, the house phone rang. Since it was right beside me on the side table, I picked it up. "Hello?"

"Why haven't you picked up any of my calls?" Aakar's voice was sharp, laced with an edge of underlying panic. Shit, I should've called him back.

"Uh...I just got back home, and a lot of stuff happened at school, and I got really busy."

"I've been calling for hours, Kriti. I was almost out the door and going to your school to find you."

I couldn't help but giggle at that. "No need to do that. I'm home and safe, and next time, I'll keep you informed. We're drinking chai right now, and then we'll probably cook dinner. I'll see you then?"

"Oh, you *will* see me tonight."

This time, I absolutely did not look up at anyone around me but simply stared at the side table. "Umm hmm."

"There's someone around you?" His voice sounded calmer than before, almost playful.

"Yes."

"Would you like me to tell you everything that I'm going to do to you tonight?"

I quickly cut the call. We did not need to be having this conversation right now.

"Who was it, beta?" Maa asked.

I tried very hard to remove every word that Aakar uttered from my memory and smiled at Mom. "Uh...just Aakar. I had forgotten to call him back, and he got worried."

Maa shook her head with a smile. "He is like that. Always been the worrier of the family. And he did call before you arrived to ask us if you'd reached home. I completely forgot to remind you to call him back."

"No worries. We'll see him tonight," I said, keeping a calm facade while my heart tried to beat out of my chest.

∽

Aakar

Today was the first time that we'd been separated since getting married. And not knowing where she was had completely messed with my mind. It didn't help that I'd suddenly remembered that this city, too, was an entirely new place for her. She could've been anywhere. Someone could've done something to her. And she wasn't even picking up her phone. I'd gone mad with fury and concern. But mostly concern.

How could she be so careless? Didn't she know I would be worried sick over her?

I walked into the bedroom later at night to find Kriti wearing her short and ridiculously sexy sleep dress while she was busy working on something at the desk. I'd stayed downstairs in the living room after dinner with Dad, Abhi, and the uncles when Kriti had quietly excused herself to get some work done.

I'd stayed downstairs for as long as I could to let her work. I knew she was swamped with more responsibility than she'd anticipated for her class, but she handled everything like a pro.

She stood bent over a large notebook, writing something

down. So as not to disturb her, I asked quietly, "What're you working on?"

She gasped and looked over her shoulder. "A little warning, Aakar. I'm preparing my class register so I can take attendance properly starting tomorrow."

I went closer to her just because I could no longer stay away. She watched me walk closer and move behind her. She turned her head back down to the register, but not before I caught the shy smile that crossed her face.

I slowly bent my head and brought my lips closer to her shoulder, not touching her skin. She shivered and slowly arched her neck, subtly asking for my lips on her.

And because the concern, the fury, the frustration was still riding me hard, I tutted. "You've been a naughty girl today, wife. You remember what you did, don't you?"

She moaned, and her fingers tightened around the pen she was holding. "Aakar, please."

I moved my hand across her waist and pulled her closer to me so her entire back caressed my front. "You want my lips, *jaan*?" Jaan means life.

She whimpered and moved her body against mine. "Yes. Oh god, you called me jaan."

I clutched her hair in my fist and gently pulled it so she looked at me over her shoulder. I really needed her to listen to the next part. "That's because you *are*. My *jaan*. My *life*. My *wife*."

And I bit the exposed part of her shoulder, causing her to moan and arch her back against me. "Naughty girls get punished, wife, not kissed. Isn't that right, teacher? Do you reward your students when they've been naughty?"

She clutched the edge of the desk where we were leaning, her body trying to get closer to mine. Her hips moved in a delicious rhythm against mine, and I'd never been harder in my life.

Arousal had my heart beating so hard I was sure she could hear it against hers. I pushed my cock against her deliciously lush backside, turning the desire into a bone-deep need. "You feel this, baby? See what you do to me?"

"More, Aakar. Please," she cried out and bit her lip, trying to keep her voice low.

"Shh. You don't want to make any more noise or mistakes, jaan, do you?"

She quickly shook her head, not uttering a sound.

And oh, what her compliance did to my cock. All my blood had rushed south, and all I wanted to do was get inside my wife and feel her all around me. I needed to know she was here and all mine.

I moved my hand lower from her waist and slowly dragged them to her hip, her soft curves fitting perfectly in my hands. I slowly pulled her dress higher and moved my hand under it to cup her between her legs.

Her hand shot back out to clutch at my sweatpants as she raised herself on her toes, trying to grind on my hand that was cupping her. "Aakar, move your hand. Please, give me something. Your finger. Your cock."

"Such dirty words, wife. Do you know what I want to hear from these beautiful lips?"

She shook her head as she continued to grind against my hand. Her underwear was soaked, and the smell of her arousal had my cock leaking inside my sweatpants. "Tell me, please."

"A promise, wife. I want you to promise me that you'll keep me informed if you'll be late. You are new to the city, and I won't be able to handle something happening to you under my watch. You're mine. And I take care of what's mine. Do you understand me, wife?"

She whimpered and nodded. "Yes, I understand."

With my other hand, I pulled her dress up from behind and

pushed my sweatpant-clad cock between her cheeks. "Do you promise, jaan?"

Without warning, she spun to face me, then held my face in her hands and looked me straight in the eyes. "I promise to keep you informed if and when I'm running late or going somewhere. But not because I'm under *your watch*. But because you care. Because I'm yours. Do you understand me, husband?"

And I kissed her like a savage. I crushed my mouth against hers as I grabbed a handful of her ass and lifted her in my arms. She squealed in surprise and clutched my hair, moving her hips against my cock that was ready to bust in my underwear.

She had me so fucking hard I couldn't even think straight. Especially the way she called me *husband*.

I dropped her on the bed and laid myself between her legs, grinding against her.

"You make me crazy, baby," I said, moving my lips against her neck. Just like she'd wanted earlier, I placed my hungry lips on her neck and sucked. Hard enough to leave a few marks.

She latched onto my neck to suppress her moans, and it only turned me on further. My body all but went into overdrive, moving against her, trying to get inside her without having to remove her underwear or my clothes.

Kriti pushed my sweats down to my thighs, freeing my aching cock, and gave it a slight tug. I groaned into her neck and couldn't help but push myself into her fist. "Fuck, jaan, stop. Otherwise, it's going to be over way too soon."

"I don't care. Just get inside me, Aakar." She quickly put me right at her entrance and moved her leg around my hip so the tip of my cock slipped inside her.

I clutched her leg and tugged it tighter around me. "Hold on, baby."

Fuck. Condom.

I quickly pulled out of her, making her whimper. "Shh... baby. We forgot a condom."

Quickly, I grabbed it from my nightstand drawer and put it on. All the while, Kriti squirmed under me, running her fingers in the hair on my chest, then moving them lower to outline my abs.

I pushed myself inside her in a single stroke. Her back arched off the bed as her nails dug into my back, causing a sharp sting of pain that only added to the heart-stopping pleasure racing down my spine.

Kriti's eyes closed, and she arched her neck in pleasure. I held her neck and brushed my lips against her. "Open your eyes, jaan. Watch your husband fuck you."

She bit her lip to stop her moans and opened her eyes. They were dark with lust, her pupils dilated, and tears shone at the corners.

My thrusts turned harder, causing her to whimper in my neck.

"Harder, Aakar," she managed to utter from between her clenched teeth.

And I obeyed. I held her by the throat, careful not to stop her airflow but just enough for her to know that I was in control right now. With my other hand, I clutched the back of her thigh tightly, leaving a few fingertip marks as I pounded into her.

Her whimpers and moans against my throat only managed to turn me feral.

I was so close to coming, but I needed to see my wife shatter on my cock.

I bent down and sucked her nipples, lightly grazing my teeth around them. She grabbed me at the back of my hair and pulled me deeper, arching her back for more. I sucked deeper as she moved her hips, causing me to go deeper. The pleasure coursed through my body, making my vision blur.

"I'm coming, I'm coming, Aakar." The bite of her nails digging into my back turned sharper, and I swallowed down her moans as her back arched, her feet dug into my ass, and she squeezed my cock like a vise.

I growled, and my hips jerked in an uncontrollable, punishing rhythm as I followed after her, waves of ecstasy crashing through my body.

I slowed the movement of my hips as we rode our high, and I simply stared at my wife as she came. She took my breath away.

Her sweat-soaked hair, the red bite marks on her breasts and neck, and her disheveled hair had me almost hard again.

I bent down and kissed her softly on the lips as we caught our breath. "Next time, you pick up my call."

She kissed me on the cheek as she ran her hands down my back and slapped my ass. "Yes, sir."

I growled into her neck and bit her sharply, making her laugh, which had me ready to go for a second round.

And I showed my wife how I needed her, how I wanted her, how I could not stop obsessing over her again and again.

25

Song: Dhiktana Tiktana Dhiktana
 - S. P. Balasubrahmanyam

Kriti

My science class with the ninth-grade students was not going how I'd expected when I prepared a poster board about the reflection of light. And my students did not seem impressed.

When the principal had told me that they needed teachers to get creative, I didn't think it would be this hard. As I explained my poster board while going through the chapter, most of my back-bencher students were already dozing. Half of the middle benchers were zoned out, and only a few first benchers actually paid attention and took notes.

I smiled at them and decided to finish this class, trying to get as many students as I could to interact and pay attention. I knew understanding the way that light travels wasn't the most interesting topic, but it was *my* job to make it fun.

And I seemed to be failing miserably at it.

When the class ended, I reminded the students not to miss their homework for their next class and started walking toward the staff room.

It had been three weeks since I started teaching. Not only did I have to think about exciting ways to teach science and English, but becoming a sudden class teacher also rained hell on my days and nights.

I sat next to Meera in the staff room and dropped my head on my desk in defeat.

Meera quickly clutched my shoulder and shook me. "Oh my god, Kriti, what's wrong?"

"I don't think I'm cut out to be a teacher here," I mumbled into the desk.

Meera squeezed my hand. "Of course you are. We all need an adjustment period."

I raised my head and looked at her. "None of my students seem to like the posters and charts I make for them. Do you have any creative ideas that could impress the students and fellow teachers?" I leaned in closer to her and murmured, "Some of them don't even smile at me when we pass in the hallways."

Meera sighed and looked around at several teachers chitchatting among themselves. "I don't care much about other teachers now that I have you with me. And honestly, since I teach students of lower grades, charts, posters, and models seem to work for me. Maybe you need to get more digital. Older children these days only have the attention span for electronic devices."

That actually was a good idea. "You think so?"

Meera dramatically rolled her eyes. "You should see Hari. Ever since Luke got him an iPad, which was against my wishes, all he's wanted to do is play on his iPad, study on his iPad, and watch movies on his iPad. His eyes are glued to that devil thing, and all I want to do is throw that thing away."

My heart gave a tiny little dance of hope as I tried to think up some new ideas. Soon, the break ended, and I headed to my sixth-grade hellions to remind them of the upcoming sports day sign-ups.

~

WHEN I RETURNED HOME that evening, the sight that greeted me had me chuckling. Maa was scolding Abhi while Ria and Karan were having chai and laughing behind Maa's back. The scene reminded me of how Rati and Kartik would laugh behind my mother's back every time she scolded me about something.

Radhika Auntie noticed me the moment I stepped foot inside the living room. "Kriti Beta, grab some chai for yourself. Abhi has prepared a cup for you too."

My savior.

I quickly went to Abhi to save him from Maa, who was still scolding him. I went to his side, wrapped my arm around his shoulders, and jokingly said to Maa, "Mummy, look at poor Abhi. I think he is really sorry."

I turned to him and asked, "Aren't you, Abhi?"

Abhi easily picked up on my help, quickly nodded at me, and looked at Maa. "I'm totally sorry, Maa. That's what I've been trying to tell you. I didn't do anything. This Karan is the real criminal."

I jabbed my elbow in his side, and Abhi quickly returned to his apology. "But I'm the one who is so very sorry, Maa. Please forgive me."

I gave Maa pleading eyes, and she *absolutely, totally* melted, waved her hand in *it's okay* at Abhi, and got back to drinking her chai.

With a light shove at Abhi's shoulder, I led him to the dining table, where Ria and Karan joined us with their cup of chai.

Once I was back with my own cup, I sat beside Ria, who was working from home today, and across from Abhi and Karan, who were discussing something over their phone.

I took a sip and turned to Ria. "How is your new job going?"

As if she'd been waiting for someone to ask the question, she placed her cup on the table with a thud and turned to me. "It's terrible."

I gasped. "What? Why? What happened?"

Even Abhi and Karan turned to us.

Ria just rolled her eyes in exasperation. "The job is just fine. But I hate Aakar's friend Zayan."

"Isn't he the one who got you this job?" Abhi piped in, not sensing the mood at all and incurring Ria's wrathful glare.

Karan chuckled as Abhi tried to hide behind his chair, making Karan his human shield.

Ria still held Abhi in her line of sight and uttered the words from between her clenched teeth. "He did not get me the *job*. He got me the *interview*. I got this job based on my qualifications, skills, and experience. Got it?"

Abhi nodded quickly, his hands raised in defeat. "I'm sorry, dear sister. Can I please have my chai in peace now? What did Zayan do anyway? I've met him a few times. He seems like a decent guy."

Again, not sensing the mood, my dear brother-in-law. Karan and I must've been thinking the same thing because our eyes immediately met as Abhi said the words, and we shared a chuckle as Ria's temper burst.

"Decent?" she yelled. "He is the most narcissistic, condescending, know-it-all asshole. The other day, our boss was just about to hand me the new project files so I could lead that project. And do you know what your precious, decent Zayan did?"

She kept her eyes pinned on poor Abhi while Karan and I couldn't stop chuckling. When Abhi silently shook his head,

Ria looked at all of us and said in an outrageous voice, "He told our boss that since I was new to the company, he thinks he should be the one to handle this particular project."

I gasped while Abhi, who still hadn't learned his lesson apparently, asked, "Why would he do that?"

Ria's eyes bulged out of her head. Karan put his hand over Abhi's mouth, making me laugh out loud, and Ria yelled, "Because, Abhi, Zayan is an asshole."

Right then, Ria's mother walked in, apparently having heard enough of the conversation. "I'm telling you, that's because he's Muslim."

Abhi and Karan groaned loudly while Ria dramatically rolled her eyes at her mom. "Maa, please. Stop being so Islamophobic. His being Muslim has nothing to do with it. It's his personality that's my problem."

She then proceeded to strangle the air as if imagining this Zayan guy's neck, making us all chuckle.

I turned to look at Abhi and Karan as they looked at something on Karan's phone. Karan said something while on the phone, and I swear I saw Abhi stare at his lips. Karan seemed oblivious, or maybe I was just delusional. Perhaps I needed to focus on my work.

And I had an idea for it. I just needed some help.

I cleared my throat, causing three heads to turn my way.

I met Abhi's gaze and said, "Umm...Abhi, I was wondering if you could help me with something if you have some time."

Abhi completely turned to face me and gave me his full attention. "Of course, bhabhi. Anything."

I ran my finger over the rim of the cup, already debating if it was a good idea to ask for Abhi's help. He was a genuinely nice guy, but to ask for help, I'd have to admit that I was struggling at school. And I really wanted to keep my good impression in front of my in-laws.

But I didn't have a laptop and absolutely no skill in creating presentations about my subjects and other creative options.

Deciding to be honest and just ask for help—because what do I have to lose—I placed my cup on the table. "So I have been struggling at the school a little."

"Do I need to beat up some teenage kids?" Abhi asked, cracking his knuckles. "Don't you worry, bhabhi. I hate little teenagers. I'll gladly beat them up for you. What're their names?"

A chuckle burst out of all of us. I met Karan's and Ria's eyes, who shook their heads with a smile. I turned to Abhi. "You don't need to beat them up. I'm struggling because students here are used to more interactive and digital learning, and I'm used to a little more traditional approach like charts and models. I was hoping you could help me prepare presentations for my subjects if you have some time? I'm not the best at coming up with these ideas on such short notice."

Abhi was on his feet. "That's it? Oh, bhabhi. Let me get my laptop. I'm an expert in making presentations. You can ask Karan or Aakar Bhai. Or even Ria Didi."

Abhi ran upstairs. In the meantime, Ria and Karan were all praises for Abhi's apparently superior presentation skills.

Ria then turned to me. "I didn't know you were struggling. You should've come to us. Does Aakar know?"

I looked down at my cup. "I should've. But I also want to create a good impression in front of my new family, and I really don't want to appear to be incompetent at my job."

Ria squeezed my hand, and I looked at her. Compassion shone through her warm brown eyes. "We already know you're competent. We also know it's a new city for you, a new culture, and a new type of school. Nobody expects you to be perfect all the time."

Either Ria was too naive or too blinded by her love for her

family. "Ria, that's literally what everybody expects from their new bride."

Before she could discuss this further, Abhi was back with his laptop. He took his seat beside Karan and called me to sit on his other side.

Once we were all seated, Abhi asked me what I wanted the presentation to be about. I quickly grabbed my science textbook and opened it to the chapter on the reflection of light.

Abhi and Karan quickly went through the chapter, turning pages and discussing and pointing out things in my book. While Karan kept the textbook in his hand, Abhi did an over-the-top action of twisting his neck and cracking his knuckles. "You ready to impress teenage little shits, bhabhi?"

As Karan laughed out loud, Ria threw a paper towel at him, shaking her head. I couldn't help but join in on the fun with Abhi. "Yes, I'll show those little shits tomorrow who's the boss around here."

Karan and Abhi both started clapping at my use of shit but then quickly turned to work.

As we went through some other online presentations and collected images and videos, Ria returned to her room to work. We'd been sitting there for about an hour, barely making some headway, when Maa and the aunties passed us in the dining room on their way to the kitchen.

Maa stopped by and asked us what we were up to, and I explained to her how Abhi was helping me with work. The only thing she said was to Abhi. "You better make a very good presentation. Karan, better keep a watch on him."

She simply smiled at me and made her way to the kitchen.

Warning bells started ringing in my head, and my mother's voice loudly scolded in my head. *What are you doing, Kriti? Prioritizing this presentation over helping out your mother-in-law and aunts in cooking dinner? You used to cook dinner at home and work.*

Yes, but I wasn't struggling at school then, was I?

Just that inner voice and warning bells had my heart rate rising, and I couldn't help it when I called out to Maa and asked, "Umm...Maa, can I help with something?"

"It's okay, beta. You carry on with your work."

I knew she genuinely meant it, but my mother's voice managed to put a seed of doubt in my mind.

I smiled at Maa and said, "Please let me know if there's anything I can help with."

Maa simply smiled and nodded.

Once she was gone, I turned to Abhi and Karan and asked, "Do you think I should go help in the kitchen? Would they be mad if I didn't help in the kitchen?"

Abhi frowned at me. "Umm...don't we need to finish this presentation tonight?"

"We do, but I'm afraid if I don't help out in the kitchen, Maa and the aunties wouldn't like it."

"But they know you have work to do. And Maa just said it was fine."

That she did. I couldn't help but wonder, though.

Before I could voice my thoughts, Abhi added, "They've been cooking without you for years and managing it just fine, right? And you've been helping out in the kitchen ever since you got here. Why would you worry about something like this?"

My heart warmed at their thoughtfulness. I nodded at the boys, and we got back to work.

For the next hour, we continued to make the presentation. Abhi and Karan were really creative. They searched for all kinds of cool images and little clips of light rays. We were in the middle of laying out the slides in the chronology of the topics when a hand came over my eyes.

I nearly screamed, but I quickly recognized the touch.

I clutched the hand at my eyes and brought it down. I looked up from where I sat to find Aakar grinning down at me.

"Hello, wife."

It had been weeks since we were married, but his *wife* still gave me butterflies. "How was your day, husband?"

Aakar placed his hand on my shoulders and gently squeezed. My eyes almost rolled back in my head at the pleasure. I so badly needed a massage. And I just knew that Aakar's big, strong hands would take me to heaven.

Aakar quickly kissed my head, all the while, Abhi and Karan pointedly kept their gaze on the laptop screen and said, "I'm exhausted. Anything that *could* go wrong today *did* go wrong."

He did look tired. His forehead had a stress line popping, and his eyes looked a little sunken. I squeezed his hand in support.

He took a seat beside me and leaned his head on his palm, elbow on the table. As he kept my hand in his, I turned to the laptop screen, knowing that Abhi and Karan were waiting for further instructions from me.

I asked Abhi to highlight the incident ray in red and the reflected ray in orange. We discussed the images to put on the slide when Aakar said, "Kriti, would you please get me some dinner if it's ready? I'll go freshen up in the meantime."

I nodded at him while he went upstairs.

I quickly gave some instructions to Abhi and ran into the kitchen.

Since dinner was ready, I told Maa and the aunties that Aakar was home. I served up the plate for Aakar, rushed out of the kitchen, put it on his spot beside me, and got back to the presentation.

I really needed to finish this for tomorrow's class and show my students that I could be cool and modern and interesting too.

Aakar returned, silently placed another kiss on my head, and ate as Abhi, Karan, and I worked. Soon, Pappa and the uncles came for dinner too, and we put the work aside so all of us could eat together.

Since Abhi and Karan were aware of the amount of work we still had to do, they quickly polished off dinner and returned to the presentation. I gave them a nod of thanks as I waited for everyone to finish dinner. Ria had also just popped in to eat a little and went upstairs right after them.

Aakar turned to me. "Could you get me some mixed pickle from the fridge?"

Irritation pricked my skin. Couldn't he get it himself?

Not wanting to make a scene or offend anyone, I nodded and got his precious pickle for him.

Once everyone was done, I helped Maa and Auntie clear the table. The house help, Raju Kaka, would clean up the table and the utensils.

Thank God for him because I had no time to help do the dishes and finish the presentation. I already felt guilty enough for roping Abhi and Karan into doing so much work for me. I might have to quickly learn how to do all of this so as to let them get back to their life. I couldn't ask them to do this for me for the whole year.

I was about to take a seat beside them when Pappa shouted from the living room. "Kriti Beta, if you've not sat down, could you get me a bottle of cold water from the fridge?"

I mean, I would've gotten it for him, even if I had taken a seat.

Abhi rolled his eyes at me, his exasperation at his father clear on his face.

I winked at him and turned to move toward the kitchen when Aakar piped in from the living room, "Kriti, could you also get some mukhwas?" Mukhwas was an after snack of seeds and sweets, often eaten as a mouth freshener and digestive.

I was so tempted to shout, *Get it yourself,* but I guess it would make sense since I was already going to the kitchen.

It's okay. He's not taking me for granted. He's just tired today.

Once getting everyone everything they needed, I sat beside Abhi at the dining table. Karan had already left, so it was just the two of us.

"You okay, bhabhi?"

I nodded. "Just a little exhausted myself. We've been at it for a while."

"Hold on," he said and ran to the kitchen.

I went through the presentation we had so far while Abhi was gone. It looked so nice and clear, and I could just imagine explaining the diagrams and discussing each topic as I went through the slides.

Abhi was back in a minute with an ice cream cup in his hand.

Aakar must've seen it as he walked toward the dining table, and he asked Abhi, "Could you get me one?"

Abhi ran, sat on the chair beside me, and met Aakar's eyes as he said, "Get it yourself, bhai. We're working."

Aakar quickly nodded. "Sorry, sorry. I'll go get it."

Once he went to the kitchen, Abhi murmured, "It's okay to tell him to get his own stuff, bhabhi. You know that, right?"

Oh, my awesome little brother-in-law. I smiled at him and nodded. "I know. He's tired today."

Abhi simply shrugged. "So are you."

And his words hit me right where that little root of irritation was growing. "I know. I just didn't want to sound rude or offensive or defiant in front of the rest of the family."

And wasn't that the truth of the matter?

I had no issue telling Aakar what I wanted or needed. But I also didn't want to sound like a defiant wife or too bold or too outspoken in front of my new family. Did their approval of me trump my own thoughts or voice? I guess you have to choose your battles when you live with fourteen people, and bringing some water or food wasn't worth any arguments. Right?

I was lost in my thoughts when Aakar sat beside me with his ice cream, so I now sat between Abhi and Aakar.

He laid his arm on my chair and leaned in to see the presentation we were making.

"Since when are you guys helping Kriti with her presentation?" Aakar asked, watching us making the last minor changes.

I turned to him. "I'll tell you all about it later. But just know that your brother and Karan have been a godsend."

Abhi waggled his eyebrows at Aakar, preening at my praise and making me laugh.

Aakar looked at me with a smile and rubbed my back in a mindless, soothing gesture. "Do you guys need any help?" he offered.

"We're almost done," I said.

By the time our ice cream was done, we'd completed the presentation.

As Abhi transferred everything to my USB drive, I chanted, "Thank you, thank you, thank you."

Abhi chuckled. "Anytime, bhabhi. I know it's all new for you, so even if you need Karan and me to make one tomorrow, don't hesitate. We're usually just gaming or copying some assignments, so it's no trouble at all."

My nose tingled at the incoming tears, and no matter how much I sniffled, a tear or two just slipped out. "Thank you, Abhi. You have no idea how much I appreciate it."

Abhi totally got awkward at that while Aakar rubbed my back and placed a kiss on my shoulder.

My new family wasn't all that bad. Dare I say, I was really starting to love them all.

26

Song: Lazy Lad
- *Richa Sharma*

Kriti

"Oh my god, Meera, my class went so well today," I whisper-shrieked as soon as I sat beside Meera in the staff room.

She instantly closed the notebook she was correcting and gave me her full attention, her lips stretched wide in a smile. "That's so great, Kriti. Didn't I tell you? It's only a matter of time."

From the moment I'd turned on the projector in the classroom and started my slide, all the students focused. Their attention was glued to me and the presentation. Some of them even raised their hands to ask questions. I turned to Meera and squeezed her hand. "It's all thanks to you, Abhi, and Karan. I wouldn't even have thought about trying the digital approach."

Meera's cheeks reddened at my gratefulness. "It's only because I've seen other teachers do it."

"Whatever the reason, you absolutely made my day. And we need to celebrate."

She chuckled and rolled her eyes. "What were you thinking?"

"Let's go to a mall after school. We'll grab some lunch and do some shopping. It's been so long since it's just been us."

Meera's eyes brightened with excitement, and she nodded. "Yes, yes. That's a great idea."

Maybe I should invite Ria as well. I turned to Meera and asked, "Do you mind if I invite Ria?"

When she shook her head, I called her.

"Hello, Kriti, everything alright?" she answered, and I realized I hadn't ever called her to just chitchat.

"Hey, Ria, everything is fine. Great, even. Remember the presentation Abhi, Karan, and I were working on? It went great."

"Oh, that's amazing. Abhi is going to lose his shit."

I laughed. "Yes, I'll tell him myself, so don't tell him anything."

"Of course."

"So I was calling to ask if you'd like to join Meera and me for some food and shopping. We're going to the mall."

She groaned at that. "Oh my god, yes. I absolutely need a break from work right now; otherwise, I'm going to kill someone."

I chuckled, and we decided on a time and place. I reminded her to tell Maa and the aunties that we wouldn't be having lunch at home and that we'd be late.

The rest of the day passed in a hazy bubble of happiness as motivation pumped through my veins. I felt more and more determined to make presentations and explore other digital ideas for all of my subjects in all of my grades.

Now, I'd just have to save up a little to buy my own laptop so I won't monopolize Abhi's time.

Meera and I arrived at the mall after school and ran into Ria near the entrance. We were all famished and went to the food court. The entire way, Ria caught Meera up to speed on how she hated her coworker Zayan.

She was still on her tangent as she slammed her food tray on our table and took a seat across from us. "And you know how that asshole dresses?"

Meera had a wide smile on her face. So did I. It was a riot to watch Ria fume and fumble and see her eyes turn into slits like a snake when she talked about Zayan. "Suit with a tie."

"And?" Meera asked.

Ria's eyes widened in outrage as she took a big bite of her burger. "Who the fuck wears a suit and tie in this heat of Ahmedabad? Even our boss doesn't wear a suit and tie. He's such a pompous, arrogant narcissist..."

Her rant continued throughout lunch and all the way through window shopping.

Right till my feet dragged me inside a shop with the prettiest dresses. Ria and Meera also looked at the dresses in wonder.

Ria gasped. "They're so pretty. We must try some of these on and get them."

Living in the village and working as a teacher never really gave me the opportunity to wear dresses. Our usual dress code was a traditional Indian salwar kameez or a saree. I wore a few dresses in my home, but that was about it. I didn't even know if they would look good on me.

Meera must've noticed my silence. "You have to at least try them on, Kriti."

I nodded and started to pick a few of them in the large size. Whenever I saw others pick a dress size smaller than me, my insecurity would rear its ugly head, preventing me from enjoying the clothes that looked nice on me. And for years, I've actively focused on noticing it creeping up and stomping on those thoughts and insecurities by deliberately trying on even more dresses. Just because only I have to find myself beautiful. If I can't love myself, how could I ever expect someone else to?

So I picked up six pretty dresses and followed Meera and Ria into the changing rooms.

The three of us took turns changing and showing off the dresses.

Meera went first. She'd always been slim with delicate curves, so she went with something flowy to add a curvy silhouette to her body. We oohed and aahed at the wonderful prints and patterns. One of them was a backless dress, and Ria and I were adamant that she had to get it.

"Luke is going to go nuts," Meera mumbled, her cheeks going red as her lips twitched in a smirk.

She was crazy if she thought he would only lose it. "Damn right, he is. He goes nuts even when you're just dressed in your usual salwar kameez. He won't let you leave your bed for the whole day. Definitely send your maa and Hari to our place for the weekend before you wear this dress."

Ria started to laugh and nodded at her. "This dress will give you guys a second honeymoon," she said, and we all giggled.

The next was Ria, and she had such a gorgeous body. She was all soft and curvy in the best places, and she knew it. She carried her body with the confidence I was determined to pull off for my own.

After trying on a few dresses she wasn't a fan of, she came out of the changing room in a beautiful blood-red dress that stopped slightly above her knees. It was a sleeveless dress with a V-shaped neck that showed just the right amount of cleavage. Meera's jaw hung open as Ria unclipped her wavy hair and arranged it to turn herself into a badass beauty.

"You look like a James Bond heroine," I marveled.

Ria turned this way and that, checking herself out, and her

lips twitched in a smirk as she said, "I'm totally getting this dress. It would knock that Zayan on his ass."

Since when did people start buying incredibly hot dresses for their enemies?

And because my mouth had no filter, I teased, "Oooh, so Zayan would like this dress, huh?"

Meera pretended to cough to try to hide her smile as Ria sputtered and said, "Umm...If that's the only way to shut him up for a few hours, it would be totally worth it."

"Ahh. Makes total sense," I deadpanned.

She rolled her eyes, but I didn't miss her smile as she quickly entered the changing room.

Once she was done trying on her clothes, it was finally my turn. As I tried on some great A-line dresses and wraparounds, Meera and Ria oohed and aahed. But then I tried on *the* dress. The dress that put all others to shame, the dress that made you feel sexy, bold, and a knockout, the dress that you just *knew* you would wear with all the confidence in the world.

I didn't even need any reaction from Meera or Ria, but as soon as I stepped out of my changing room, I heard their gasps, and their eyes widened in appreciation.

"Yes, absolutely yes," Ria said.

At the same time, Meera said, "You're buying it."

I twirled around, checking myself out, loving myself, and bought that dress.

I didn't know about Zayan, but Aakar would definitely lose his mind when he saw me in this dress.

Maybe I would give him his very own private show.

∽

I SAT at the dining table working on my next presentation when Aakar placed a soft kiss on my head and took a seat across from me with his own work. The rest of the family, excluding Abhi and Ria, watched television in the living room.

We'd already had dinner, and I'd helped in preparation, serving, and cleaning up. I was used to cleaning up after five people before the wedding, but fourteen people was so much. And with three young kids constantly running around the house, their moms busy screaming after them to get their studying done, I found more and more chores to do.

For the past two hours, I had to get up and help find Soham, Ria's younger brother, his notebook because I *must* remember where he placed it after I helped him with his homework. I had to get Pappa his mukhwas, make a mango shake for the grandparents, and get up to collect all the dirty utensils from the living room so they didn't have to get up between their soap operas. And since Aakar had come home late from work, I had to reheat everything for him, serve him as he freshened up, and pick up after him.

I was exhausted, but I still had work to do. If only people would just give me one fucking hour to focus.

And with learning to prepare these presentations, my life turned out to be one task after another. Since today's presentation went well, and my next presentation wasn't for two more days, I decided to give this one a shot myself. I wasn't really as fast as Abhi and Karan in researching great pictures or making those nice animations with the moving arrows and sliding images, but I was trying.

We were working quietly for a while when the elder auntie called out to me, "Beta, would you get a cold jug of water from the fridge?"

I couldn't help the sigh that escaped my lips. I looked at Aakar, but he was immersed in his screen, typing away something furiously.

I got up and went to the kitchen, convincing myself the whole time that she only asked me because she must be tired too, and I was closer to the kitchen. She didn't mean to make me get up in the middle of my never-ending work.

I handed her the water and was about to sit when Aakar said, "Could you get me a glass of water too, baby?"

Excuse me! Did he not see that I was working too? What was it with these people constantly asking me for things? For once, could they not get their own stuff? My mom and dad never asked me for stuff when I was working, and here I was, constantly running around taking orders from so many people.

And I could deal with the elders. But Aakar? Absolutely not.

So I met his eyes, took my seat, and said, "No. You can get it yourself."

His eyes widened, and he sputtered, "But you were just standing."

What a stellar argument. "And now, I am sitting. And working."

His jaw tightened. "I was working too."

I clenched my jaw so I wouldn't raise my voice and alert the rest of the family members who were sitting right behind the wall that separated the living room from the dining room. "If I keep running around, handing out people's orders, I will never be able to work myself."

His eyebrows scrunched up, and he mumbled, "Do we have a problem here?"

How could he not fucking tell?

He must have read the outrage on my face, so he got up and stood at my chair. "Let's go."

My eyes widened in rage and confusion. With clenched teeth, I got the words out without screaming my head off. "I'm trying to get *some* work done. That's the whole point. I need to work. I *can't* stop."

"I'll help you with your work, but we're going out. Right.

Now." He had the audacity to utter the last two words with clenched teeth in a tone that was an order laced with anger.

My stomach burned with the need to scream, and I would've slammed the laptop screen closed if it was my computer, but I lightly closed it and turned to Aakar. I raised my hand, indicating for him to go first without uttering a word. Because if I did, things would turn ugly.

He walked to the living room and said, "Kriti and I are going out for a while."

Without waiting for anyone to say anything, he picked up his keys from the key stand at the entrance and walked out of the house.

We didn't say anything to each other as we got inside the car. The moment I had my seat belt on, he floored the gas, and we were out on the street.

We lived in an area a little farther from the more traffic-laden parts of the town. Aakar took some back road that led even farther away from the main city. We didn't exchange any words as he continued to take some winding turns, eventually leading us to a secluded road and parking the car under a tree between two already parked cars.

The moment he turned off the car, a sudden silence filled the cab.

I could feel Aakar's eyes on me, but I just couldn't look at him. Instead, I stared ahead, looking at nothing.

"You've got nothing to say now?" Aakar asked. I could see him shake his head from the corner of my eye.

I couldn't stop from rolling my eyes. "Where do I even begin?"

Aakar scoffed. "How about why you were so rude to me when I simply asked you for a glass of water when you were already standing?"

I turned in my seat to face him and looked him dead in the eyes, letting him see my anger, my hurt. Rage clouded my vision at the reminder, the sharp sting of the blame hurting my heart. "Because you could get it yourself," I yelled.

His eyes widened. "I was exhausted from work, and I still had so much more work to do. And you were already standing. It would've taken you not more than two minutes. So why make such a big deal out of it?"

The fact that he was talking in such a calm voice, as if he was the rational one here, made my blood boil. I had to clench my teeth shut so as not to scream in his face when I said, "I was standing because I *had* to. Not because I *wanted* to. I was standing because your family constantly needs things and are very quick to shout out their requests. And I'm trying really fucking hard to be a good daughter-in-law and not say no."

His eyes narrowed. "I see."

I didn't think he did. "What exactly do you see?"

"That it's a burden for you to be there for my family, but are you saying your family never asked you for anything from the kitchen or other menial help?"

Oh my god. "You guys are fourteen people," I shrieked. "Fourteen, Aakar. Not four. And I only had my mom and dad, who had some requests. I had two younger siblings who were quick to run and do some chores. And my family *definitely* didn't blindly call out my name with requests when they knew I was working."

He was about to say something, but I lifted my finger and silenced him. I had no inclination to hear him out because I knew he would argue with me, worsening this situation. I could see the defense in his eyes. So I continued, "I like your family. Don't doubt that. I have no fucking issue with getting up and handing them whatever they want. But I really have a fucking problem when you become a part of that."

His eyes widened at that, and I continued because I had a thousand words choking my throat. Now that I'd started talking about it, I physically could not stop. "You seem to have turned blind in the past few days because you're not the only one exhausted from work. You're not the one struggling to impress your superiors and your students. You're not the one coming home and helping with the chores. You're not the one helping pick up after three kids. You seem to have entirely forgotten that I'm not used to such a big family. Yes, I helped out in my family. But a little of my help was enough for my parents. No matter how much I do here, there's still more to do."

Aakar kept looking at me. Instead of anger and frustration, a little bit of understanding was shining through. But I wasn't finished because the more I talked, the more my repressed emotions poured out. So I met his eyes and asked, "When was the last time you saw me simply hanging out with you and your family while you all watched TV or just chitchatted? You think I don't want to sit and relax once in a while?

"You seem to turn a blind eye to the amount of time and effort I'm putting into my work and at home. So when you ask me to do even one more task, no matter how menial, it makes my blood boil. Not because I can't manage it. But because *you* can. Because I expected help and support from you. And if you can't do that, at least don't make it worse. I can't ask Pappa to get his own water, but I can ask you. And if you wanted a very obedient wife who doesn't get mad that people are disturbing her while she's working, you should've married someone who wanted to be a housewife."

Aakar stared at his folded hands on his lap, his lips downturned.

I was finally done speaking my mind, so I simply stared out the car window. We hadn't turned on any music, so we were just sitting in silence. I waited for him to say *something* before another wave of anger showed up, and I gave him a piece of my mind.

Warmth engulfed my hand, and I looked down at my lap to find Aakar clutching it. When I looked at him, he was staring at his hand holding mine, his jaw clenching as he seemed to try to get his words out.

He pulled my hand and brought it to his own lap, holding it with both of his hands. "I never wanted to be this guy."

"What guy?" I asked, almost sure what he meant but needed to hear him say it.

He sighed and played with my fingers. "The guy who forgets himself when he gets a wife. The guy who forgets that his wife is her own person and not there to service him and his family. The guy who forgets all the promises he made to the girl to get her to marry him."

He pressed his lips tighter and looked at me. "I'm really sorry, Kriti. I forgot myself, and I shouldn't have been a selfish asshole."

My heart clenched at the apology, and I could only nod. So he continued, "I was seeing how hard you were working, and instead of being helpful, I made things more difficult for you. And I feel so stupid and like a jerk for not doing something about it."

His stupid words and his soft eyes full of guilt were softening my heart, dammit. I squeezed my hand in his. "You're not so bad, Aakar. It's not like you ask much from me." I sighed, not wanting him to feel like he couldn't ask me for any help or support. "It's just, you don't see people disturbing you or Ria or even Abhi when you are working. And I know that your family isn't intentionally trying to discriminate, but sometimes it feels that way. So I have this big bucket of emotions piling on inside me drop by drop, and when *you* even ask for a very minor thing at the wrong time, that one drop of my frustration tips over my emotional bucket. I don't know if I'm making sense."

He gave me a small smile and nodded. "Makes perfect sense to me."

I gave him a small smile in return. "I don't want you to think that you can't come to me for any help and support. I married *you* first and your family second."

He lifted my hand to his lips and gave me a soft kiss on my ring finger. "I know, baby. I will always come to you for your help and support. I'll just not partake in filling up your emotional bucket. I'll have to come with my emotional cup and start emptying your emotional bucket. I promise you. I will start taking care of you, your needs, your work, and your time more."

My nose tingled with the incoming tears, and I tried to stop them, but a silly little one just streamed down my cheek. Before I could wipe it off, Aakar was there. "That's the last one because of me."

I met his eyes and saw guilt, resolution, and promise all reflected in them.

Clutching his T-shirt, I pulled him closer. He sealed his lips on mine, showing me how apologetic he was with his soft kisses and how he would make it better with the rough pulls on my lips.

He kissed me in apology over and over.

And I kissed him in forgiveness, hoping and praying that he was right.

∽

Aakar

I clasped Kriti's hand that I'd placed on my leg as I drove us to an ice cream parlor. I ran my thumb over her fingers, lost in thought. When did I start taking Kriti for granted? Was there one particular occasion? Or did I not even realize that I wasn't exactly being a helpful husband?

My family was always in an *on* mode, and our house was always a mess with the kids playing around. But it was never supposed to be Kriti's job to run after them or clean up after them. And she was right. I never saw Maa or kaki calling Ria or me to help them out around the house. Then why did they keep disturbing Kriti? Was it deliberate, or had the societal norms subconsciously made them act like this? Because I knew Maa, Pappa, and all my family loved Kriti.

How did I become so much of an asshole that my own wife had to tell me that if I couldn't help, I should at least not make things worse for her?

My stomach recoiled at her words because I knew that every one of them was true. And I realized that it wasn't that I'd been asking too much from her, but I seemed to have not taken an active role in making my wife comfortable in her new home. Because that was what it was.

This was *her* home. *Her* family. And it was my job to make her feel at home with me and my family. And I was failing at the one job that I had as her husband. My heart pounded, and my hands turned sweaty at the thought of how much worse I could've gotten if Kriti hadn't held me accountable. What if she had chosen to suffer silently instead of speaking up?

My hand tightened around hers, and I quickly looked at her.

She stared at the road ahead, lost in her own thoughts.

Her face was a lot more relaxed than before, but there still seemed to be some lingering hard feelings as she kept silent, not initiating any conversation.

I wanted to apologize again and again, but what good would that do if I didn't back it with actions? I'd have to prove to her that I was worthy of being a good husband, that she wasn't here to serve me or my family but to be a part of it. That I would take care of her as much as I did my family.

Thinking about how hard she'd been working on her presentation, my insides burned at the thought that even my own brother might have been more helpful to my wife than me.

Never again.

I saw the ice cream parlor up ahead and gave the right-turn indicator in my car. I parked the car outside the little café and turned to Kriti. "Want to sit inside or get the ice cream and eat it in the car?"

She looked at the café and scrunched her face. How could I hurt such an adorable person? She turned to me and said, "There don't seem to be many people inside. I don't mind sitting inside the café."

I gave her a smile and squeezed her hand. "Let's go."

The moment we stepped in, the sweet, sugary aroma of ice cream greeted us. The latest Bollywood songs played on a low volume through the overhead speakers. The cool air of the air-conditioned café and the music seemed to pull me out of the heavy guilt sitting on my chest. I turned to Kriti to find her lips stretched wide in an excited smile, looking at all the different ice cream flavors.

I stood beside her, and for the first time since getting married, I hesitated before placing my hand on her back. But when she slowly moved further into my arms, my heart sang in relief, and I quickly placed a soft kiss on the side of her head. "What would you like to have?"

She tasted a few flavors, chitchatting with the guy at the counter as he handed her little spoonfuls of ice cream while I quietly stood behind her, occasionally tasting a few bites that she shared with me, giving me small smiles in between.

She chose raspberry sorbet with chocolate ice cream, while I went for a scoop of coconut flavor.

The café had warm yellow lights and was decorated with large plants in corners with barely ten wooden chairs and tables. At almost eleven at night, only one other couple sat in the café. We took a seat at the other corner, wanting some semblance of privacy.

The moment we sat with the ice creams, I clutched Kriti's

hand, and that had her meeting my eyes. "I'm really sorry, baby. I'm going to be better, I promise."

I had no excuse. No explanation for my behavior.

She gave me a small smile and looked down at our joined hands. She bit her lip as if wondering if she should say whatever she wanted to say. So I kept quiet and waited for her.

She sighed softly. "On the one hand, I'm so mad at you that you've been so obtuse and taking me for granted. But on the other hand, I feel guilty for making a big deal out of everything. I mean, I married you willingly. I knew I was getting into a large family, and I thought I was prepared to be like those kick-ass wives who can run a household and earn a living while taking care of their family. But it's just that seeing everybody sitting around, watching TV, while I'm running around the house while trying to work makes me...I don't know...disappointed, angry, and a whole lot of negative emotions. And I know they don't mean anything by it, but I can't stand it from *you*."

Every word was like a hammer to my pride. My hand tightened around hers, and I said, "Don't ever hide your true feelings from me. And as much as it makes me want to dig a hole and hide my face in it, I'm so proud of you for standing your ground."

She turned her hand so our fingers intertwined. I looked at her, watching our joined hands. I caressed her thumb softly and waited for her to meet my eyes. A beat passed, and then two, and she finally looked at me.

Her eyes still held shreds of disappointment and hurt. I brought our joined hands to my lips and softly kissed her hand, making her breath hitch.

I vowed to bring about some changes in the house because the thought of Kriti not feeling at home with me was intolerable.

Everyone had already gone to sleep when we returned home a little after midnight. I held Kriti close to my chest that night as we got into bed. Her curves, the softness of her body, and the feel of her skin against mine, like always, made me wild for her. I wanted to devour her, consume her, keep her forever tucked in my arms.

But I had fucked up. And as much as I wanted to show her how utterly mad I was for her, I needed to hold her in my arms. I needed to feel her go soft against my chest. I needed to whisper soft murmurs of apology. I needed to smell her divine rose scent as I placed soft kisses along her neck.

That night, I made a hundred apologies to my wife, and I made one promise to myself.

My wife would feel at home with me. My wife would feel comfortable enough to say no to the elders. My wife would be happy with me.

27

Song: Falak Tak
- *Udit Narayan, Mahalaxmi Iyer*

Kriti

A weight seemed to have lifted off my chest. Not because everything and everyone just changed after I shared my feelings with Aakar, but because Aakar now knew. I never wanted to carry hurt feelings and other disappointments in my chest. They only festered and created resentment.

> Aakar: I love you, jaan 🩶

I read the text that he'd sent me when I was at school. And I'd stared at those words like a smitten teenager an embarrassing number of times.

For the past few days, he'd been actively doing his own chores. He still kissed my head when he came home. I still reheated food for him when he was late from work. But he never asked me to fetch water or a pickle while he ate. He simply got up and got it himself.

I couldn't believe how lucky I'd gotten to have married Aakar. Not because he's a perfect human without any faults but because he makes mistakes, and instead of blaming others, he owns up to them. He genuinely makes an effort to change his behavior, and that's nothing short of gaining my utmost respect.

I was riding the high of reading the lovely text from my husband and things going drastically well at school when I came home. I nodded at Maa and kaki sitting on the couch and made my way upstairs to change out of my clothes when Maa called me and said, "Kriti Beta, Abhi and Karan are in his room. Could you ask them to make chai for us?"

"Sure thing," I said, and quickly climbed upstairs, remembering the present I got for Abhi and Karan for helping me out.

I went to my room first, freshened up, grabbed the present, and climbed down to the floor below us to head to Abhi's room.

I knocked on the closed door and opened it, holding the presents in my hand with a flourish. "Surpriiii..."

I came to a sudden halt, which might have lasted a millisecond.

Because I'd shut the door so fast behind me, all the while muttering, "Sorry, I'm so sorry."

Blood rushed to my cheeks, my heart pounding at what I'd accidentally discovered. Something I had no right to find out about my brother-in-law.

Panic clutched at my chest at the consequences of me seeing what I saw.

Abhi kissing Karan.

I ran to the kitchen and started making chai, needing a moment alone to get a grip and try to get my thoughts running again.

Because if I was panicking, I couldn't imagine the sheer terror coursing through Abhi and Karan at being found out.

Fuck. I was such an idiot.

Who in their right mind did not wait to enter after knocking? Shit.

Guilt sliced through my heart, and I felt the crushing need to apologize to Abhi and Karan. Not just for disrespecting their privacy so thoroughly but also for my panic-induced and horrendously insensitive reaction.

God, they must be absolutely gutted by my reaction. How could my experience of reading so many gay romances betray me like that? Fuck, I was supposed to react like a cool sister totally okay with her brother being gay.

And I was.

I was thrilled and proud and terrified for him. I wanted to support him. But I'd made an absolute mess of the situation by reacting as I did.

I was watching the chai come to a boil in the pot when I heard footsteps behind me.

Turning around, I found a terrified Abhi, his shoulders hunched, his eyes wide with panic, and I didn't give myself another chance to mess up.

I took a step closer and opened my arms for him, giving him a smile of acceptance and apology all rolled into one.

Abhi didn't miss a beat, and with a relieved sigh, he fell into my arms even though he was much taller than me.

I rocked him lightly and softly murmured, "I'm so sorry, Abhi. I shouldn't have barged in like that."

I felt his nod at the side of my head, and he sighed. I could feel his nerves, and I soothingly ran my hand down his back. "And I'm completely okay with you being gay or bi or pan or demi or however you identify. All I want is for you to be happy with whoever you end up with. I'm here for you, no matter what."

His shoulders shook in my arms, and his hold on me tightened as I heard his soft sniffles above my head. "Thank you, bhabhi," he murmured, his voice tearing up.

I slowly pulled out of the hug and looked up at him to find his eyes red-rimmed and his jaw trembling to hold back tears. I quickly rubbed my own eyes to ward off the tears threatening to spill over and met Abhi's eyes. "You have all my support however you need it. Nothing's going to change between us. You have nothing to worry about. I'm so happy for you and Karan. To have found something special with your best friend is a dream come true."

A tear ran down his cheek, and he quickly brushed it off. He gave a light cringe at the mention of Karan. "Umm, we're not exactly together, bhabhi. We're still, I don't know, complicated."

I nodded, happy that Abhi seemed to be calming down. "Oh, okay. I hope I didn't make it worse for you guys."

He shook his head and leaned against the kitchen countertop. "You didn't. Um, can you do me a favor, bhabhi?"

I quickly nodded, needing to do whatever it took to make Abhi feel at ease. "Anything."

He ran his hand through his hair, clearly nervous to ask me for the said favor. "Um, what you saw today, would you keep it between us? I'm not ready for anyone to know yet."

I completely relaxed at that. "Of course, I'll keep it between us. It's not my secret to tell. You don't have to worry about me telling anyone."

Abhi still looked doubtful. "Not even Aakar Bhai?" he asked.

I paused for a second. Not because I was thinking about telling Aakar since I had no right to share something so personal about Abhi without his consent. But I did wonder about his reaction if he found out that I knew something so personal about his brother and I didn't share it with him. I could only hope he would understand my predicament when Abhi chose to share his story with him.

So I extended my hand for a handshake. "Not even Aakar Bhai," I promised.

Abhi let out a relieved breath, tension draining from his shoulders and a small smile lifting his face as he clutched my hand with both of his. "Thank you, bhabhi."

I turned to the now boiling chai and shut the stove off. As I poured the chai into different cups, trying to return to our normalcy, I murmured. "I hope Karan does not feel awkward around me."

Abhi arranged the cups on a tray. "Don't worry, I'll tell him you're cool. He'll feel awkward for a day or two but then get back to his shy and silent, normal self."

I chuckled at his description of Karan. While Abhi was an energizer riot bunny, Karan was more silent and reserved, except when he was with Abhi.

My romance-loving heart really, really hoped these two sorted their shit out and started living their happily ever after. Not that it was going to be that easy for them.

We took the chai to the living room and soon got busy with our respective work.

Later in the evening, I was busy correcting the notebooks of my students and checking the clock every two minutes.

It was eleven o'clock on a Saturday night, and Aakar still wasn't home. I'd called him, and he'd let me know that he was gonna be late, but I...I missed him. It had been a little over two months since we got married, and I still had to pinch myself to believe it really happened.

That I was someone's *wife*. No matter how many times Aakar growled that word in my ear while fucking me, it still wasn't enough.

Just the thought had my core clenching in arousal. Where was your husband when you really needed him?

A very long half an hour passed that had me straining my neck with all the glances toward the main door. I was done correcting all the books and busy making notes for Monday when I heard the main door open.

I glued my eyes to the entrance with a glare, ready to scare or surprise my husband, whichever happened.

The moment he turned around after locking the main door and met my unblinking glare trained on him, he jumped back in shock and fright, his hand clutching his heart. "Damn, baby, you scared me."

I burst out laughing at the way his back was glued to the main door, still looking at me with fear in his eyes. "That's what happens when you make your wife wait around for hours. And on a Saturday night."

Slowly, he shook his head and walked toward me with an apologetic smile. "I'm so sorry, jaan."

He stepped up against me, clutched my waist, and pulled me closer. He slowly ran his nose along my cheek, brushing his beard against my jaw, sending electric sparks rushing along my body. "How about I make it up to you?"

I ran my hand along his broad chest, loving the way his muscles rippled as he pulled me closer. "As much as I would love for you to make it up to me, aren't you hungry?"

Brushing his lips at the pulse on my throat, he rumbled, "Oh, I'm starving."

I giggled, my heart fluttering and bursting at the need in his voice. "I meant food, Aakar."

He started to drag me toward the stairs. "I ordered some at the office. Now, hurry."

He clutched my hand in his and rushed me upstairs, both of us laughing and giggling, trying not to wake anyone on our way to our bedroom.

The moment we reached our floor, we were instantly met with a very angry Ria glaring at the phone in her hand, prowling the hallway separating her room and ours. It looked like she was talking on the phone, her AirPods stuck in her ears, and she confirmed it when she raised the phone to her lips and, with clenched teeth, said, "If you weren't my senior, I would've told you to fuck off."

Aakar stared at her in shock and murmured in my ear, "She already did."

Ria came and closed Aakar's gaping mouth with a smirk, winked at me, and looked at her phone with daggers in her eyes. "I don't care if you think I'm impulsive or loud or direct. I haven't heard you complaining about my work. And that's all that matters. You *know* I would've handled that project just fine."

And I could hear some voice before Ria cut the call on the person's reply. I was pretty sure I knew who she was talking to.

But before I could ask her anything, she turned her glare to Aakar. He automatically pushed into me as if he feared for his dear life. "Um, everything okay? Who was that?"

Ria pointed her finger at Aakar. "You. I rue the day I agreed to let you ask around for a job for me. Your friend is the biggest asshole I've ever met."

"I'm sure he's not..." I stopped Aakar from finishing his sentence with a quick slap on his back. Clearly, neither of the Mishra brothers could sense Ria's moods.

She growled in frustration, punched the air a few times, and slammed the door to her bedroom in our face.

Aakar turned to me and muttered, "Zayan is actually a pretty stand-up guy."

"I heard that." Ria's muffled voice scared Aakar and made me chuckle. "And he's not," she screamed louder.

Aakar quickly grabbed my waist and pushed me toward our bedroom, locking the door behind us. "Ria's scary when she's mad," he muttered, running his hand through his hair.

That sexy mood had passed, but I couldn't help but step into Aakar's arms as he stood leaning against the door.

The moment I laid my head on his shoulder, he pulled me even closer so not even a hair could pass between us. His strong arms, thick corded neck, warm chest, and every inch of my husband brought me a sense of belonging. Belonging to him. His family. His world.

"How was your day?" I whispered in his arms, lightly kissing his neck.

He groaned and moved his arm lower to cup my pajama-clad ass. "As usual. One meeting after the next. Trying to get Abhi to show up every day and get Dad and my uncles up to speed with emerging trends and tech. All in all, a big headache of a day."

I pressed light kisses to the center of his chest, where the top button of his shirt was open, licking up his scent and making him grind against me. "You know what would make your headache of a day better?"

Aakar clutched my hair in his strong grip and turned my head to face him, his eyes blazing with need. He bent down so his lips brushed my ear and said, "Some cold ice cream and hot maggi."

"Wh...What?" I asked, completely flabbergasted. Did he not understand where I was going?

He got a teasing twinkle in his eyes as he quickly let go of me. I instantly looked down to confirm the evidence of the mood that I thought we were in, and yep, the evidence was very, *very* prominent.

I turned back to look into his eyes and raised my eyebrows, gesturing at his pants.

He gave himself a slow stroke with a groan and said, "Jaan, that happens every time you even breathe in my direction. You *will* get this cock later. But first, let's go for a drive."

Before I could argue further, he clutched my cheeks and

pressed his lips to mine. "You go change and meet me downstairs. I'll start the car."

"But..." Before I could convince him to stay in, he was already gone.

With a sigh and a few mumbled curses, I changed into a pair of loose, high-waisted jeans and a sweatshirt.

Quietly, I climbed down the stairs. It was almost midnight, and I didn't want to wake anyone. If only Aakar had stayed and listened to me, I would've told him that we had some ice cream in the freezer, and I could prepare him the maggi. But no...who wanted to listen to the wife, who, by the way, had been in a total let's-have-desperate-lose-my-mind-sex mood all night long.

What kind of totally clueless husband...

"HAPPY BIRTHDAY!!"

Loud shouts from all around me had me falling back down on the last step of the stairs.

Shock had rendered me completely speechless and disoriented.

And when two figures came running to help me up, I very nearly fainted.

Rati and Kartik.

Oh my god. Rati and Kartik were *here*.

In front of me. My babies. I couldn't process whether to cry or laugh or faint or jump in joy or shriek in surprise. And I kinda managed to do all at once and must've sounded like a braying donkey.

But I didn't care.

I had both of them in my arms, and we were all jumping around in our little group hug.

And when two sets of arms circled the three of us, and I met the eyes of my father, I instantly burst into tears.

"How? When? Oh god, how?" The questions came flooding out of my mouth as my dad took me in his arms and Maa rubbed my back.

Maa turned to where my husband now stood beside my siblings with a bashful smile and said, "Aakar. He called us and insisted we come for your birthday. And well, he was very persuasive."

"Not that we needed much persuasion," Rati piped in, making all of us laugh.

Aakar came toward me, and right in front of everyone, he pulled me into his arms and dropped a kiss on my head. "Happy birthday, baby."

Gah. He called me *baby* in front of my mom and dad.

Before I could get the time to blush or hide away, the uncles and aunties parted, and in walked Meera and Abhi with a gigantic cake.

And here came the waterworks. Big fat tears rolled down my cheeks as I looked at every smiling face singing "Happy Birthday."

Aakar clutched my hand and led me to where Meera and Abhi placed the cake on the dining table.

With everyone surrounding me with so much love, I cut the first slice of cake, praying for moments like these to forever stay in our lives. I fed the first piece to Aakar and then to everyone else.

When Maa and the aunties started cutting pieces of cake for everyone, I sidled up to Rati and Kartik and once again hugged them. "God, I missed you guys so much."

Rati stayed in my arms as we got a little emotional, whereas Kartik kissed my cheek quickly and went to get the cake.

And when Dad came to where Rati and I were talking about my time with my new family, he asked, "Are you happy, beta?"

I thought about my new family, my husband who listened to me and treated me with respect, my brother-in-law who was a bright, shining light of my day, my new mother who treated me like her own daughter, the aunts who loved to gossip with me, and I couldn't help but smile at my luck. "Yes, Pappa, I'm happy."

We turned to look at where Maa—as in my mother-in-law—was shouting at Abhi for not distributing the cake pieces properly while Aakar and Ria were arguing about something with their youngest uncle. "Bit loud and chaotic, aren't they?" Pappa said.

And I smiled. "They're perfect."

∼

Aakar

Once the birthday celebrations were over, Kriti's parents left with Meera and Luke to stay overnight at their place, whereas Rati and Kartik occupied our guest bedroom. The plan was to spend quality time with Kriti's family and have dinner somewhere nice.

We'd just retired to our room, where Kriti had ordered me to wait for her on the bed. So here I sat, changed into my T-shirt and sweats, as I waited for Kriti to do God knew what in our restroom.

"Kriti, baby, are you okay in there? You've been there a while," I shouted.

"It's barely been three minutes, Aakar. Give me two minutes," she shouted back.

I picked up my phone and scrolled through the family WhatsApp group, looking at the photos everyone had shared of the birthday celebrations. Kriti was going to lose it when she saw them.

The sound of the door latch opening had me looking up.

And thank God I did because the sight before me had my phone dropping on my lap.

Walking out of the door, Kriti stood in a sexy-as-fuck black dress wrapped around her body like a present, just for me to unwrap. All my blood rushed so fast down my body, it left me almost dizzy.

She took a step closer to the bed, and my cock jerked, needing to be buried deep inside my wife already.

The dress. The glorious fucking dress. The way it hugged and pushed her tits together had me desperately wanting to bury my face between them and devour her. My body buzzed with a need so electric I was burning from within.

Why was she walking so fucking slow toward me?

Clutching the comforter in my fist, I groaned as her hips swayed in that dress. "Baby, you're fucking killing me."

I dragged my eyes lower, lingering on her soft, creamy thighs. My heart pumped louder, stopping at those fuck-me heels that would fucking dig into my ass as I pounded inside her.

I had to squeeze my cock to stop from embarrassing myself as Kriti moved between my legs, my thighs pulling her closer. My hand shook with need as I ran it along her thigh where the dress ended. "My god, woman, you're so fucking sexy. Where… uh…when did you get this?"

She moved even closer to me so my face was just an inch away from her tits and softly ran her fingers along my brow, making me groan out loud. "Shh…" she whispered, putting a finger on my lips, "we don't want to wake anyone up. And I got this dress a while back but just didn't know the right time to put it on. Felt like today was the best time. I wanted to thank you for being so nice and thoughtful and calling my family here to celebrate my birthday."

I ran my fingers up the back of her thighs as she talked softly, just happy that she was happy. I pressed a quick kiss right at her wrist on the hand that was now caressing my beard. "Of course, jaan."

And I couldn't wait a second longer without her in my arms.

I pulled her into my lap, with her dress pooling around her ass and my thighs.

The moment she pressed herself into me, I dragged my hands up her thighs, and my arousal kicked in to a maddening desire. "Fuck, baby, you're not wearing any underwear?"

She moaned as I dragged her over my now-soaking sweatpants. "Did I need to?" the little vixen asked, her eyes shining with delight as she bit her lip to stop her moans.

I squeezed her round ass that fucking overflowed my hands and breathed into her gorgeous tits. "Fuck no."

The moment I grazed my beard across her round globes, she whimpered and pushed my face into her deeper by the back of my head, riding my clothed cock.

Fuck.

Removing my hand from her ass, I pulled down her dress, and her pebbled nipples popped out. I quickly took one in my mouth and gave it a deep suck, just the way she liked it, making her whimper, pushing herself deeper into my mouth.

My blood ran hot along my veins, needing to be buried in my wife's soaking pussy. I quickly pushed her on her back on the bed and got rid of my clothes.

She was about to pull her dress off when I got on the bed between her knees and clutched her hands over her head. "The dress stays on, jaan. And these heels, baby. You're going to wrap your legs around my waist and dig them in my ass as I fuck you. We clear?"

She whimpered, arching off the bed and trying to get her tits in my mouth. "Please, Aakar."

I pushed her down and pressed a scorching-hot kiss on her mouth, pouring all the simmering need and burning desire into it and rubbing my dripping cock between her thighs, soaking it in her wetness. "Happy birthday, baby. I'm so fucking glad that you agreed to marry me and made me the luckiest fucking man on this planet."

She shivered as I rutted between her legs, but her eyes went all soft. She clutched my hair and gave me a whisper-soft kiss, making my heart ache. "I love you too, husband. Now fuck me like you mean it."

My cock throbbed and jerked at her words, my body drowning in the burning hot sensation, the need to push inside her downright maddening.

"Don't rush me, wife. I'm going to spend the whole night making you come," I whispered in her ear and pushed my aching cock between her folds, making her whimper.

I grabbed her breast and sucked her nipple. Arching off the bed, she pushed me deeper, moving her hips in tandem with mine.

The harder I sucked, the faster she moved her hips. "Aakar, fuck me, please. I need you inside me," she moaned, her words coming out in breathy gasps.

And how I burned.

"Come for me, wife. Give this to me, and I'll push inside you. C'mon, baby."

With that, I clutched both of her thighs, pushed them up, and started thrusting harder.

The moment she let out a loud whimper, I pushed my palm over her mouth, quieting her. "Quiet, or I'll have to gag you with my underwear."

And with her whimpers burning my palm, she jerked violently, squeezing my ass and trying to push me in deeper, as she came on my cock, soaking me with her white-hot pleasure.

I groaned into her tits, muffling my voice as I quickly moved away, trying not to come before pushing myself inside her.

Before she could come down from her high, I flipped her on her stomach and pulled her hips back so she was on her hands and knees. Her round, full ass with her black dress bunched around the waist looked so filthy, so fucking hot, that I was tempted to paint her ass with my cum.

But then she arched her back and moaned my name, and I quickly grabbed a condom from the nightstand, went on my knees behind her, bent over her, clutched a handful of her lush hair, and whispered in her ear, "You want this cock in you, don't you, jaan?"

I pushed myself right at her entrance, dipping into the hot, gushing wetness. "Please, Aakar. I feel so empty. Need you," she cried.

And I couldn't wait a second longer. I pushed inside her in one long, slow thrust until my hips met her thighs. I muffled my groan against her shoulder, need coursing through every fiber of my being. "You take me so well, baby," I said, starting to move slowly after letting her adjust.

She relaxed and arched her back for me and said, "More, Aakar."

That was all I needed to start thrusting. I loved how wet Kriti got for me. Loved how she squeezed so hard around my cock. Loved how she said my name. Loved how she was all mine. "You're mine, only mine, aren't you, jaan?"

I grabbed a fistful of her hair and turned her head so our eyes met. Her eyes were dazed with pleasure, but the look in my eyes must've been enough for her to whimper, "Yes, all yours. And you're mine."

"Wouldn't have it any other way, baby. Only ever yours."

With that, I pounded into her, my balls so heavy and ready to burst. Her breasts swung with every thrust, making her moan. I quickly put one hand over her mouth and rubbed her pussy with the other. "Come for me, baby. Give me one more."

I dragged my cock inside her just the way she liked it, rubbing her clit and biting her shoulder. I loved seeing my marks on the parts of her body only I could see. With the next thrust of my cock, she clenched tight around me, whimpering in my palm, squeezing the fuck out of my cock and pulling me right under with her.

My balls tightened to the point of pain, and my orgasm shot through me, electric pleasure racing across every vein of my body. My cock jerked inside her once, twice, and a third time, pulling out a ragged groan from my chest.

I stayed inside her, not wanting to leave my wife's body. She gently ran her hand along the back of my thigh as I rested on top of her, still panting. "Happy birthday, baby." I whispered those words along her shoulder, placing light kisses along her skin.

With a whoosh, she dropped down on the bed from her kneeling position, pushing me out. She turned on her back so she could meet my eyes and pulled me forward.

Her lips met mine softly, her tongue danced along mine, and I gently rested my body on hers. "Thank you, Aakar."

I quickly went to the washroom to clean up and dispose of the condom in the trash. On my way back to the bed, I grabbed Kriti's present and met her eyes.

She was now sitting up on the bed, naked and well fucked, her eyes glittering with excitement as she saw the gift-wrapped box in my hand.

"You got me a present?" Her words were full of wonder.

I shook my head with a smile. "Of course, I got you a present. What kind of a husband do you think I am?"

The moment I handed her the box, she tore through the wrapping. Her jaw hung open at what she found.

"It's a brand-new laptop," she whisper-shrieked. "Oh my god, it's a brand-new laptop, Aakar. It's too much."

"Baby, it's not much at all. In fact, it's a downright necessity. Now you can work as much as you want and whenever you want, without needing to borrow it from Abhi."

Tears pooled in her eyes as she hugged the laptop box. "Thank you."

I dropped a kiss on her lips, wiping the stray tear. "You're very welcome. Now, let's sleep. I'll get you all set up with your stuff and get it ready for you tomorrow."

Once she placed it right by her bedside, after giving it a few kisses, she dived into my arms, showering me with a hundred tiny kisses, making me laugh at her cuteness. "Thank you, thank you, thank you."

I adjusted us so I was holding her in my arms, softly playing with her hair. "Always, Kriti. I know I'd disappointed you by taking you for granted. But you're my partner. My *life* partner. And I'm always going to provide for you, treat you with love and respect and equality and everything that will make you feel at home with me."

Her eyes shone with tears as she ran her hand along my chest. "I love you, Aakar."

"I love you too, baby."

28

Song: Tere Bin
   - *Rahat Fateh Ali Khan, Asees Kaur and Tanishk Bagchi*

Kriti

Ignoring the signs was always pretty easy when you didn't know someone's secret. But once you knew the secret, every little action and conversation started to remind you of the secret you knew and were keeping from your husband.

Like right now. Aakar was leaving for a business trip for two weeks. So we were busy packing his bag in our room after dinner, whereas Abhi and Ria were chilling with us in our room eating ice cream.

Aakar brought three of his shirts from the cupboard and handed them to me as he turned to Abhi and asked, "Haven't seen Karan in a while, Abhi. Something happen?"

My hand shook for a second as I arranged the shirts in the suitcase, grateful that Aakar was looking at Abhi.

I turned and met Abhi's eyes, if only for a second. He gave

me a smile, turned to Aakar, and very casually replied, "No, bhai. He's just a bit busy. I'm sure he'll turn up soon."

Aakar nodded, but he still had a frown on his face. "And you're still thinking about going to Mumbai?"

Aakar had mentioned that Abhi wanted to go to Mumbai for higher studies. I had always wondered what made Abhi decide on something like that when he had such a big family and their own business to run. But now, it made complete sense.

Abhi nodded slowly. "Yes, bhai. I really want to go."

Aakar nodded, disappointment and sadness clinging to his shoulders. He then went back to his cupboard to bring more of his clothes as Abhi met my eyes and gave me a sad smile.

I gave him an understanding smile as Ria asked, "When do you want to go? You do know that you'd have to tell our parents, right?"

Abhi quickly polished off his ice cream as he nodded. "Yeah, yeah. I'm still looking and applying to colleges. I'll let them know when I actually get an acceptance or have something looking up."

Aakar brought his pants and handed them to me as he said to Abhi, "Do you want me or Ria to help you with something? I must have some friends working in business management. They could write a reference letter or something."

Abhi was very quick to shake his head in denial. "Absolutely not. I want to do it on my own."

I'm pretty sure he didn't want to consider any of Aakar's recommendations because he must not want anything he did in Mumbai to get back to Aakar. Word traveled fast here, and if Abhi wanted to live an out and proud life, he might not want to live near his brother's friends.

I was starting to understand why Abhi did and said what he did, but seeing Aakar's slumped shoulders at Abhi denying his help was heartbreaking. My poor husband loved his family, especially his little brother. And with Akira gone, he desperately wanted to feel needed. It killed me not to say anything about Abhi to him, to help him understand why Abhi wanted to leave. I was pretty sure Aakar would be cool with Abhi being gay. At least, I hoped he would be.

Seeing the disappointment in Aakar's eyes, Ria piped in, "So Aakar, this will be the first time you'll be living away from Kriti, right?"

Abhi, picking up on Ria's change of topic, sang, "Aakar Bhai is gonna miss Kriti Bhabhi."

Smiling, Aakar chucked his tie at Abhi. "Shut up."

Wanting to make Aakar smile even wider, I gasped dramatically. "You won't miss me when you're gone? Have we lost the charm already?"

Ria and Abhi burst into laughter, whereas Aakar pinched my cheek with a big smile and said, "Of course, I'll miss you."

Abhi and Ria instantly started their *awww*s and *oooh*s, making Aakar put his head in his hand in exasperation and pointing a finger at the door. "Out, both of you."

When both started wagging their eyebrows teasingly at Aakar, he quickly moved toward them, dragged them out of our room, and locked the door.

With a happy sigh, he looked at me and said, "What am I gonna do about them?"

Just to start preparing my husband for the inevitable goodbye, I gently said, "Nothing, baby. You're gonna let them live their life without worrying so much about them."

He let out a huff and moved toward me. He sat at the foot of the bed near me and laid his head on my lap. "Promise me you won't ever leave me?"

I ran my hand through his hair and pressed a small kiss on his head. "I promise."

THE FOLLOWING DAY, Aakar left early in the morning, but not before fucking me slow and deep in the middle of the night, grunting *I'm gonna miss you so much* in my ear. He had been so frantic and needy and desperate as he'd pounded into me, it had me burning up for him. I'd wanted him over me, around me, just living inside me. And when I'd told him *I'm going to miss you so much* and that *The bed is gonna be so empty without you*, he'd growled and painted my ass, my back, and my pussy with his cum. He'd rubbed it on my skin with his large hands, marking me and making me groan.

My legs squeezed at the thought of our night as I got ready for school. When I came down to the dining area, Maa caught me and asked, "Kriti Beta, would you drop this breakfast box for your pappa and uncles at the office on your way? They left way too early today since Aakar had to go, and they had some important meeting."

I had some time to spare and quickly nodded.

After packing my breakfast in my purse, I climbed on the two-wheeler I sometimes used to go to school or for some chores and started toward the office. I'd been there a few times to drop off lunch or an evening snack if Maa had cooked something nice.

The moment I made the final turn to the small building that was the office, my hand automatically hit the brakes at the sight before me.

Was that Pappa? It was still a little weird for me to address Aakar's dad as Pappa. But I couldn't believe the man smoking a cigarette against the side of the building was Pappa.

I never knew he smoked. I didn't even know if Aakar knew that he smoked.

I absolutely did not want to be here right now. My mind was pulling me in the other direction to just leave this breakfast tiffin right on the road and drive at full speed to the school.

But what if everyone knew that he smoked, and I was the clueless one?

I was teetering between reversing my vehicle or pushing forward when Pappa took a slow drag from his cigarette, and his eyes met mine. Instantly, his eyes widened, and he started hacking out his lungs.

Decision made: I accelerated and stopped my vehicle right beside him. "Pappa, are you okay? Do you need something?"

I quickly pulled out the bottle of water from my purse at the footrest and handed it to him.

Still coughing lightly, he opened the bottle and took a few sips.

His face had the same guilt as my students who hadn't done their homework but claimed to have "forgotten their completed homework at home."

Before I could even ask him if Maa or Aakar knew, he said the exact words that his youngest son had very recently said to me, "Please don't say anything to Aakar."

"Aaah, Pappa. Not this," I groaned and hung my head. "How can I not tell Aakar? Does Maa know?"

I glared at that offending little stick of death when he cringed and was about to put his cigarette to his mouth. He sighed and threw it on the ground instead. "Umm. She knew."

I frowned and asked slowly, "What does that mean?"

He shook his head. "Ah, beta, umm, I might've promised her seven years ago that I'd quit, and I might've failed in keeping that promise. So if you don't mention this to her, that would really not break her heart."

This just kept getting worse. "Pappa," I groaned. "You actually not smoking would not break her heart. It really is injurious to health, you know. And you know how much Aakar worries about everyone. How doesn't he know?"

He gestured for me to park my vehicle, and we took the breakfast tiffin and went inside the office, me following him. He pulled out a piece of gum from his pocket and put it in his mouth. He went into the office cabin where both his brothers sat, their eyes widening in surprise at seeing me there.

"Umm…" the younger uncle, Sunil, started to say.

But Pappa shook his head and said, "She knows."

Oh no, no, no. Aakar was going to pop a vein. I turned to both the uncles and gasped, "Kaka, you both know too? And you didn't stop him? Do you guys smoke too? Does kaki know?"

Questions came bursting out of my mouth, shock making me pace the cabin as the three brothers sat on their chairs, shifting uncomfortably.

My mind kept swirling at the consequences of hiding something like this from Maa and Aakar. "What am I gonna do? Aakar would kill me if I hid something like this from him. Maa and kaki would be so disappointed in me if I didn't tell them."

"I only smoke if I'm really stressed," claimed Navin Kaka, the oldest of the three brothers, as if that made everything all right.

My eyes widened as Pappa put his head in his hands in defeat.

"How?" I whispered. "How does Aakar not know?"

Sunil Kaka rubbed his face and looked at me. "Well, we don't smoke when he's around."

I clutched my hair, my head spinning with one revelation upon another. Since when did I become a secret keeper of the Mishra family? And how did all of these people manage to hide such important things from Aakar? And why, oh why, did *I* have to find out?

Fuck.

Fuck.

Fuck.

Pappa raised his head and looked at me with pleading eyes. "You won't say anything to anybody, right, beta?"

Oh god. My legs refused to keep holding me at his plea, and

I dropped on my heels right on that floor, now clutching my head in my hands, mirroring Pappa's pose. "How could you ask that of me, Pappa? It's about your health. I *cannot* encourage you guys to put your life at risk. No, not on my watch."

Sunil Kaka sucked in a breath, his voice dropping as if I'd kicked his dog. "So you'd tell Aakar and our wives?"

Pappa piped in, "Could it not be our little secret?"

Did I have a choice? Nobody liked to be a tattletale. But this wasn't a secret like Abhi's. Now that I couldn't share with anyone. That was my duty to keep it to myself.

But this?

I looked up to find all three men staring at me with pleading eyes, weakening my resolve. Fuck.

I sighed and sat on the floor, folding my legs. "Okay, first, you've made me extremely late for school. And second, I won't tell anyone..."

Three *yeses* rang in the air before I could even finish my sentence.

I raised my finger, silencing the three of them, and continued, "If you guys promise to stop smoking. And no, you don't get to smoke behind my back. You don't get to give me a false promise. You need to quit. That's the only way I can keep this to myself."

Navin Kaka, who apparently only smoked occasionally, was the first to break. "But, beta, I only smoke occasionally. Only when Aakar is out of town."

Sunil Kaka quickly nudged him with his elbow while Pappa shook his head in defeat. "Beta, we're trying. We used to smoke every day a few years ago. But we've really reduced it since Aakar joined the business."

No wonder. "You mean, Aakar made you stop."

They just shrugged in the affirmative.

"You know it would break Aakar's heart if he found out that you guys still smoke behind his back. I really shouldn't start my new marriage with a foundation of lies. And that too about something that would affect your health severely at your age."

That got them all puffing their chest, grumbling *I'm not that old. I'm pretty healthy for my age.*

I rolled my eyes and dramatically started to get up. "Ah, well. I tried. Might as well call Aakar."

"Wait, wait, wait," Pappa said.

The three of them looked at each other and sighed. "Fine, we'll quit."

Instantly, I held my hand out.

At their raised eyebrows, I said, "Cigarettes."

"Umm. Can I have a last one?" Sunil Kaka asked. Holding a lone cigarette, he turned to both of his older brothers as if they would support him.

And, of course, they did and turned their pitiful eyes on me. They were starting to look so much like my students I was tempted to bring out a ruler or tell them to get out of my class.

But I was the one in their office holding them hostage. Or maybe they were the ones holding me hostage.

God, this power play was going to make me faint.

"Absolutely not," I said and waggled my fingers, asking for their packs.

Pappa was the first one to empty his pockets. With a grumble, he picked the cigarette and the packet from Sunil Kaka's hands and dropped them in mine.

Navin Kaka was the only one in possession of his cigarettes, who, by the way, "only smoked occasionally."

When the three of us pointedly looked at him, he got up and put his packet in my hand with the saddest, most dejected face.

I opened my purse and dropped everything inside to throw it all out later and turned to the three of them. "I really don't want to break Aakar's heart, and even more than that, I really want you guys to stay healthy for our family. So I can only hope that you guys will truly quit."

Their gazes softened, and Pappa patted my head softly. "Thank you, beta. We're so glad Aakar found a nice wife like you."

Tears clouded my vision, but I quickly shook my head and gave them all my teacher glare. "Regardless, I'll still be keeping a very, very strict eye on you all. So don't think you can hide from me."

The three sighed dramatically as Pappa looked up and said, "Oh god, please let Abhi's future wife be kinder to us."

Oh, dear Lord. Poor Abhi. The lies and the secrets were gonna be the death of me.

With a universal sign of *I'm watching you*, I left the three of them and rushed to school, ready to forget today's events.

∼

I WAS busy reading one of my favorite author's romances at night in the lounge area on our third floor two nights later when Abhi walked into the open area. Ria was out for dinner with her friends, so it was just the two of us.

"Hey, bhabhi. What're you reading?" he asked, sprawling on the couch beside me.

"A romance book," I answered, giving him a smile.

His eyebrows raised, and he waggled them like a fool. "Are these those sexy books?"

I chuckled and gave him a wink. "They could be."

He twisted his head, trying to peek at the cover of the book. "Is that why you've got these ugly brown paper coverings on your books?"

I chuckled. "Kinda. The covers aren't exactly family friendly."

He laughed. "Does Aakar Bhai know?"

"Yes, of course."

"You gotta give me one of these to read, bhabhi," he said, his face completely serious.

"Hmm. I might have something of your interest."

His eyebrows raised. "My interest?"

With a small smile, trying to gauge his interest, I said, "I don't read just straight romances. I do have queer romance books too."

Instantly, he straightened up from his sprawling position. "No way."

"Yes way, dear brother. You wanna borrow one?"

He was up on his feet, ready to dash to my bedroom. "Hell yeah. Let's go."

Chuckling, I walked inside my bedroom and scanned my shelf of queer romance books. When all your books are covered in brown paper, it gets difficult to remember which book is where. So, for my own mental sanity, I have shelves assigned by tropes.

After surfing through some books, I gave him my favorite MM romance, the romance that got me reading more of MM romance—*Him* by Sarina Bowen and Elle Kennedy.

"Here, this one got me reading more queer romances," I said, handing over my book.

He was about to take it from my hand when I pulled it back, warning him, "Remember, it gets spicy. You okay with that?"

He rolled his eyes with a smile. "We're all adults here, bhabhi. And we've all done these spicy things."

"Ekta Kaki said the same thing to me," I said and gave it to him.

"Ekta Kaki is reading your romance book?" Abhi shrieked, his face round with shock.

"Umm...can't she?" I asked.

"I guess. You do realize that she might talk all about it with Maa and Radhika Kaki, right?"

Horror washed over me. "Noooo."

"Yeeeessss," Abhi sang.

I clutched my hair and dropped onto my bed. "She can't, Abhi. The book has sex scenes in it. I gave it to her because she insisted she used to read Mills and Boons books when she was younger and loved them. And that she wanted to read more modern romance books. I warned her that it has spicy scenes in it. And she was all cool about it. And what if she talks about the book with Maa and kaki? Oh my god, what if Maa *reads* those scenes? No, no, no, no, no. What if Maa judges me and doesn't approve of my books? Oh my god, what if she asks me to throw away all my books?"

"Bhabhi. Bhabhi. Bhabhi." Abhi sat at my knees and said, "Calm down. No such thing's gonna happen. Take a deep breath."

I took a few calming breaths, then asked, "You sure?"

He visibly gulped, and that gave me all the answer I needed. "I'm *almost* sure."

"Oh god."

And then, it suddenly dawned on me. "What if Aakar finds out that Maa might read my spicy books? What if he stands with Maa when she's asking me to throw out all my books?"

At that, Abhi chuckled. "I'm sure Aakar Bhai wouldn't let Maa throw out your books. He might get really mad that you let your naughty books get in Maa's hands."

At the expression of horror etched on my face, he quickly added, "But he won't. Aakar Bhai would react that way if it were *me* that let something like that happen. He would never get mad at you."

"I guess. We'll just have to cross that bridge when we come to it."

He fist-pumped at that. "That's the spirit. You're starting to follow my mantra of life, bhabhi."

That did not make me feel better.

"Anyway, I'll let you know how I like this book," he said, waving the book in his hand and bouncing out of my room.

Shaking my head, I closed the door to my room and got on my bed with my book to find a text message from Aakar.

> Husband: I miss you, jaan.

> Me: I miss you too.

Instantly, he texted back.

> Husband: All good at home?

Well, I caught your dad and uncles smoking behind your back. Your aunt is reading a spicy romance book and might possibly share it with your mom. And your brother is gay.

> Me: Everything's great!

Fuck my life.

29

Song: Aye Hairathe
 - *Hariharan, Alka Yagnik, A.R. Rahman, Mohammed Aslam*

Kriti

The days passed at a snail's pace without Aakar. I didn't realize I would miss him so much. That the bed would feel so cold and empty without him holding me in his arms as we slept. I'd gotten so used to his silent presence, his kisses on my head when he came home, and the way he would just work on his laptop while I read my book in bed before sleeping.

These little routines that seemed almost menial at that time were now like a glaring absence every day.

My father-in-law's grumbling tone snapped me out of my musings.

"Sorry, what did you say, Pappa?" I asked.

He grumbled again. "I said we don't really need to do this. Even Aakar wouldn't have made it such a big deal."

Right. We were on our way to a physician for a proper lung and chest checkup with Dad and both the uncles.

Navin Kaka, the oldest of the three brothers, looked about ready to explode as he muttered, "I only smoke occasionally. My health's fine."

Sunil Kaka was very quick to add, "I even exercise regularly. I'm sure I'm fine. This is just a waste of all our time, Kriti."

Taking a deep breath, I uttered a single sentence, "It's either this or we tell Aakar."

Pappa mumbled, "At this point, telling Aakar seems like an easier option," but didn't stop driving to the clinic.

The amount of work required to hide this from everyone in the family was astronomical. The lies kept piling up as I told Maa that I was going to a bookstore with Meera while the men told the ladies that they were off to the office on a Saturday afternoon.

At the clinic, the physician asked all the men to get a few tests done, like spirometry, ECG scan, diabetes screening, and a vitamin D blood test. Because the doctor was their family physician and had good connections, he took the samples for vitamin D and diabetes for the three of them and got us instant appointments for a cardiologist and a spirometry test.

We went around to the test centers and got all the tests taken. We were told that we would get all the reports on Monday.

We were on our way back home when I asked, "You guys promise you're all not smoking anymore?"

Pappa sighed. "We promise, beta. I'm glad you worry about us so much. But don't you worry. Everything's going to be fine."

I just hoped that he was right. Because if anything was wrong, I would not be able to stay quiet.

~

THE NEXT DAY, I was busy working on my laptop in the living room while Maa, Radhika Kaki, and Ekta Kaki lounged around on the couch, watching a soap opera. It seemed to be some sort of romantic drama, but it focused a lot on the *drama* and not enough on the romance.

My mind kept diverting at the ridiculousness of the story as I worked.

I was busy typing the bullet points for discussion in my class when Ekta Kaki sighed loudly and said, "Kriti's romance book is so much better than these TV soaps these days."

And my heart stopped.

Blood rushed to my cheeks as Ekta Kaki's eyes widened at what she said, and when I slowly turned my head to Maa, I was met with a knowing, embarrassed smile on her face.

"Oh my god," I moaned, covering my face with both my hands. "Ekta Kaki, what did you do?" I mumbled from behind my hands, unable to meet anyone's eyes.

"Kriti, beta, the book was so good I just had to share it with bhabhi. I just knew she would love it," Ekta Kaki said, looking guilty.

Maa quickly piped in, "And you don't have to worry about the romance scenes, beta. We're all adults here." Her words were mature, but her cheeks were bright red.

I groaned, hiding my face behind a pillow on the couch. "Oh god, please tell me you didn't read those scenes."

Maa and Ekta Kaki both giggled. "We sure did."

"Oh my god, please don't tell Aakar. He'll think I corrupted you guys."

Now all three ladies burst out laughing. "Relax, beta, it's not like we're inexperienced. Although, our men certainly need some lessons from this book."

I couldn't help but chuckle at the thought of Pappa and the uncles reading these books. "Maybe hold off on that thought.

I'd never be able to look them in the eye if they ever read my books."

Maa laughed at that. "You must share more of your books with us. I'm not the best at English, but I think these books will definitely help me improve. I always get so nervous when I talk to Sam. I don't want to look stupid in front of my in-laws."

Ekta Kaki nodded. "You're so right, bhabhi. I am never able to talk to Sam. I can understand what he says, but I also get so nervous speaking English that words just stop coming out of my mouth."

I never realized how much of an issue this was for them. Having an American future son-in-law came with a set of challenges for the older generation. And communication was the number one problem. Maybe sharing my books wasn't such a bad idea.

"Umm, you're right, Maa. What if we start a book club?"

At their confused faces, I continued, "So book club means every month, we pick a book to read. You get the whole month to finish the book. And at the end of the month, we sit together and discuss our feelings about the book."

Ekta Kaki cheered up at that. "That's a wonderful idea, beta. But just one thing, we all live together. And we spend our afternoons together in the living room. We can't keep our thoughts to ourselves for a whole month. We would just keep discussing what we read every day."

She was right. There was no way they wouldn't talk about it. "You're right, kaki. I'll just give you guys my books, and we can just talk about it all day, every day. And if you have any questions about the English words, you can just ask me."

All of them cheered. Once their giggling had stopped, Maa cleared her throat and said, "Beta, speaking of asking you questions about the English words, what does *fuck* mean?"

She actually said the f-word out loud. Oh my god.

Before I could groan at having to explain or hide in the

pillow to stop the heat rising on my face, a loud hacking sound came from behind me.

No. No. Oh god, no.

Three embarrassed sets of eyes looked at me. I slowly turned my face and met the storming eyes of my husband, who I hadn't seen for two whole weeks.

"Kriti, a word?" he asked through gritted teeth and climbed up the stairs.

When I turned to look at Maa, she rolled her eyes at Aakar's retreating form. "Don't be afraid of him, beta. He doesn't control us. You tell me if he says anything to you."

I wouldn't, but her words still soothed my nerves.

As I climbed the stairs to our room, I felt like the student being called to the principal's office for misbehaving. My heartbeat pounded in my chest as I climbed each step. Was he so mad that his mom said the word *fuck* out loud? I mean, it wasn't exactly my fault. Did he even know we were talking about romance books? I didn't think he was so narrow-minded that he wouldn't want his mom to read romance books.

It felt like forever until I reached our room. I knocked at the door before I opened it slowly. *Why the hell was I knocking on my own bedroom door?*

As soon as I stepped inside our room, I found Aakar walking back and forth across the room, the sleeves of his shirt rolled up to his elbows, his tie loosened, the top few buttons of his shirt undone, and his hair ruffled like he'd run his hand through it one too many times. He looked smoking hot.

But the moment he looked at me, his eyes filled with icy fury.

What exactly was he so pissed about? I hadn't done anything wrong.

So I steeled my spine and said, "If it's about Maa saying *fuck*—"

Before I could complete my sentence, Aakar picked up his

phone and handed it to me. "Care to explain what this is about?"

I frowned and took the phone from his hands. I was looking at some sort of medical report. And it suddenly dawned on me. These were the reports for the tests we did for Pappa and the uncles—spirometry, ECG scan, diabetes screening, and vitamin D blood test.

I looked at what the reports said. Looked like Sunil Uncle had everything under normal ranges, except his vitamin D, which he had a deficiency in. I opened Pappa's report next. His spirometry report indicated his lung function is at 72 percent, which fell under the "mildly abnormal" category. My heart dropped at that. We would have to consult a pulmonologist for treatments to get it back up.

Next, I opened Navin Uncle's report, and what I saw had my hands shaking. His spirometry report was worse than Pappa's. He had dropped into a lower category that was "moderately abnormal," even though he was the one constantly saying he only smoked occasionally.

"What the fuck is all this, Kriti?" Aakar snapped, his eyes now wild with increasing fury. I hated that look on him as if I'd done something to betray him.

"You might want to take a seat," I said as I prepared to tell him everything.

He must've seen the seriousness in my eyes, so he instantly dropped on the bed. His arms were folded across his chest as he glared at me with mistrust.

My anger started to rise to the surface. "First, you might want to tone down the attitude. I've done nothing wrong, so you might want to give me a chance to explain first."

"Sure, you've done nothing wrong. You seemed to have hidden something pretty fucking important. Not only that, you seem to have taken my father and uncles for tests without even consulting me. So please go ahead and tell me you've done nothing wrong."

"Do you or do you not want to know the truth?" I asked through clenched teeth, trying to rein in the anger. Sure, he was justified in his worries, but I had little patience for accusations and sore attitudes.

After promising Pappa and the uncles that I'd keep their secret, I was already battling whether to tell him the truth. But after those kinds of reports, I just had to share it. I only wish the doctor had sent the report to Pappa or me instead of Aakar. Stupid family doctors.

With fire in his eyes, Aakar gritted out, "Please, I'm all ears."

I ignored his surly attitude and sighed. "A few days ago, I think it was literally the day after you left, I caught Pappa smoking."

"What?" he snapped, shock widening his eyes.

I sighed and gingerly took a seat beside him, almost afraid he would snap at me. "Yeah. And he caught me catching him in action. When he brought me up to the office so we could talk, or more like him telling me not to tell you anything about it, I also found out that both the uncles also smoke 'occasionally.' I was hell-bent on telling you, but they emotionally blackmailed the shit out of me."

He ran his hands through his hair and groaned out loud. "Fuck, Kriti. You should've told me. No matter what."

"And what? Ruined my relationship with them? Make them think of me as a tattletale? Never let them have faith in me? I doubt it. It was a difficult situation. I made them promise they would quit smoking."

Aakar scoffed in disbelief and was about to open his big, angry mouth before I put my hand over it, shutting him up. "I know. I know their promises are just words. They claimed they'd always smoked in your absence. Now, I don't know how many days of the month you are absent or whether they smoked every time you weren't around. I don't know any of that. And that's why I took them to get those tests done. I needed to know if I should lie to you about their smoking. If I could make them stop. I didn't want you hurt by their actions."

His shoulders slumped as he sat with his face in his hands, not meeting my eyes.

I slowly put my hand on his thigh, gently rubbing my thumb along his pants to soothe him. "I really was going to tell you if the reports showed something concerning."

At that, he turned his head to look at me and asked, "And what if they didn't?"

I looked away, knowing the truth in my heart. I would've monitored Pappa and the uncles, and I would've tried my best to make them stop smoking.

"Would you have told me if the reports had turned out normal? Answer me, Kriti."

"No," I mumbled.

He stood and started walking back and forth across the room. "And that's exactly the problem. You can't hide something like this from me, Kriti. I'm your husband. Not just that, but we're talking about my father and uncles. If they're doing something harmful to themselves, you tell *me*. You don't go around keeping something like this to yourself."

"And break their trust?" I asked.

He glowered at me from where he stood. "And what about breaking *my* trust?"

"Your trust? I was trying to protect you from the pain. I was trying to share some of your responsibilities. I was trying to make them stop without adding one more worry in your life."

"Transparency and communication are the two most important foundations of any marriage. If you start hiding things from me, how can I ever trust you?"

His point made sense. It absolutely did. But I was stuck

between breaking Pappa and uncles' trust in me and Aakar's trust in me.

"I really would've told you if I had caught them smoking again. Or if there was anything of concern in the reports. I really thought I could help them stop smoking. And Pappa and the uncles were so afraid of disappointing you that they were even complying with me. Can't you see how I was stuck between choosing you or your family? I was doing what I thought was best at that time."

"And what about the books you seemed to be sharing with Maa and aunts? You seemed to have failed in sharing that with me too."

Oh. My. God. "I knew you would bring that up."

"So?" he asked.

And this time, I scoffed. Because, seriously? "You want me to inform you before I give my book to Ekta Kaki to read?"

"Considering the kind of books you read, yes."

"Oh, you didn't," I hissed.

Seeing my wild glare, he raised his hand to calm me down. "I have no issue with you reading romance books. I've read them, and they were fun. But that doesn't mean you just hand them over to kaki and Mummy. Are you kidding me? You want them to read sexy books? You want them to know the kind of sexy books you read and enjoy?"

I narrowed my eyes at him. "I would be weirded out if my mom read my collection of romance books too. But I wouldn't stop her from reading them if she enjoyed them. I would just ask her not to share her thoughts on the spicy scenes. Same goes with your mom and the kakis. If they actually enjoy them, who are you to judge them or me?"

He raised his hands in defeat. "Fine. You and my mom can read whatever you want. It wouldn't have hurt you to mention that you'd given your book to them so I wouldn't have been so shocked."

I was so done with this conversation. "Do you want me to tell you every time I lend them a book? Am I not allowed to have anything personal between me and Mom and the aunties?"

"Oh god, Kriti," he groaned. "A little sharing and transparency between us isn't going to hurt you."

"Fine, I'll keep you posted."

"Thank you," he muttered. "Now, is there anything else you'd like to tell me?"

Abhi's confession instantly popped into my mind, but I quickly discarded that. Abhi's secret wasn't mine to disclose.

"Nope," I said, meeting Aakar's eyes head-on.

"Okay. Thank you."

"You're welcome."

His eyes narrowed at me. "Are you mad at *me*?"

The gall of him. "Why would I be mad at you? You've only snapped and growled at me for trying to treat them as my own family."

He sighed and sat beside me. "I'm beyond happy you're treating them as your family. But I've been responsible for them and caring for them for so long, baby. If you keep me informed, I can also care for them better. Having lived with my family so long, don't you think I would know better ways to make them see reason? Wouldn't I know what would make them stop smoking? Wouldn't I be able to help you keep an eye on them?"

I sighed. "I was going to tell you if the reports showed any abnormalities, you know. And I was just trying to share your responsibilities. Not pile more on your plate."

He clutched my hand in his at that. "And I would appreciate it more if you just keep me informed in the future. I don't like secrets. Consider it a 'me' thing. But I really do not like the kind of secrets with the potential to blow up when I could've been prepared for it had I known."

He was going to kill me and Abhi when he found out about

Abhi's secret. I might need to try to convince Abhi to come out to his big brother sooner. I had faith in Aakar. He would be cool with it.

"I understand, Aakar. I'll try my best to keep you informed."

"Thank you, jaan," he whispered, brushing his lips across my hand. "I really missed you so much."

"Way to show it to me," I mumbled, still miffed about him snapping at me.

"I'm sorry for getting mad at you. I just panicked and couldn't fathom the reports I was seeing. Let me make it up to you," he said, laying gentle kisses along my shoulder.

I shook my head and stood, moving away from him. "I'd rather explain the meaning of *fuck* to Mummy."

He groaned at that, then quickly clutched my hand and pulled me onto his lap. "Tell me, baby. Didn't you miss me at all?"

His big, warm hands clutching my waist were making it really difficult to resist him. But no, I was mad. "I missed you. I missed you so much. I hated sleeping alone. The bed was too cold without you. I hated waking up alone. I was dying to have you back home, working beside me, giving me your heart-melting forehead kisses. I was hoping to get railed by you the entire night. Not get railed *at* the minute you stepped foot in the house."

He groaned and rested his forehead on my shoulder, clutching me tighter to him. "We reached an understanding about that. What would it take for you to forgive me and kiss me and make it all better? I'm dying to have my mouth on you. I wanna taste you. Feel you. Fuck you. I want to spend the entire night buried deep inside you."

As much as his words had me squirming on his lap, my mind was one stubborn bitch. "I'm as dry as a desert right now. I guess I just need some time. Especially when you could've approached me with a calmer attitude and kinder words. My intention was never to keep you in the dark. My intention was to help you and protect you and keep peace with Pappa and not disappoint him as well. I'm not just your wife, Aakar. I'm trying to be a good daughter-in-law too."

He sighed and gave me his forehead kisses. "I know, baby. And you're the best wife and daughter-in-law. And I'm again so, so sorry for getting mad at you."

This time, I sighed. He did look genuinely sorry. But the damage had been done. "Give me some time to get back to normal. I can't just instantly let go. I'm not built that way. Why don't you freshen up, and we'll discuss how we want to deal with Pappa's and uncles' reports? If you'd rather handle it by yourself, I'll get out of your way."

"Jaan, you're killing me. I need you by my side. Okay? All the time. For every little thing. You gotta stop punishing me. I can't handle your anger."

"I'm not angry. I'm just disappointed."

"That's even worse," he mumbled, laying a few more kisses along my shoulder.

"You'll be fine. Now, off you go. I'm going downstairs."

~

Aakar

Did I freak the fuck out when I got an email from our family physician with different reports attached, none of them looking too good? Yes. It had scared me so bad I'd broken three speed limits in my rush to get home. And the only reason I'd known Kriti had anything to do with it was because the physician mentioned it in his email, praising Kriti for getting those tests done with Pappa and the uncles.

And sadly, my first thought had been, *Why the fuck didn't she inform me?*

Maybe because I'd been responsible for everyone in the house for too long to know a helping hand even if it was waved right in front of my face. But I'd hurt Kriti with my anger. I shouldn't have blown up the way I did. Now, she thought I didn't want her to treat my family as her own, which was the last thing I ever wanted.

I was genuinely sorry that I made her promise to tell me important stuff. It wasn't her. It was my issue that I needed to be kept informed. After the mess when Akira just up and announced her relationship without sharing it with me first, I refused to let that happen again.

I thought I trusted Kriti. But my actions clearly didn't reflect that, which surprised me as much as it did her. And after seeing the disheartened look on her face, I was determined to show her that I trusted her.

After freshening up and changing into my sweatpants, I found Kriti drinking chai with the ladies downstairs, and Pappa and my uncles had also come home. Kriti must have called them from the office, knowing we needed to talk.

As I moved to sit next to her, she said, "Your chai is on the dining table."

I raised my eyebrows, my mouth twitching at seeing her mad face.

When I went to get the chai, I let out a loud, shrill whistle and shouted, "Family meeting. Everyone downstairs."

Soon, the shuffle of footsteps from the staircase came rushing down. With a cup in my hand, I walked back and forth across the living room, the report files on my phone opened. Pappa and the uncles refused to meet my eyes, whereas Maa and the kakis thought I was mad at them for talking about romance novels. Little did they know that they were going to be mad at their husbands in exactly five minutes.

Once Ria and Abhi were downstairs, they each grabbed

their cup of chai and coffee respectively, and took a seat on either side of Kriti.

After everyone was seated, I stared down my father and uncles and asked, "Do you have anything to share with us?"

And considering I was the one asking, Pappa was the one who answered, "I'd rather you talk to us in private instead of making a scene like this."

I laughed humorlessly. "Making a scene, is that what we're calling it?"

Maa was instantly by my father's side. "Aakar. Mind your language. Is this the way to talk to your elders?"

Pappa looked directly at Kriti with disappointment on his face, and not only did she look crushed, but it also had rage boiling my blood. I instantly snapped at my father, "No. Don't you look at Kriti that way. She had nothing to do with it."

When he met my eyes, I pulled out my phone. "I got a very shocking email from our doctor this morning. Diabetes report. Blood test reports. Spirometry reports. For all three of you."

Maa started to look concerned, and both the kakis were on the edge of their seat, worry lining their foreheads. "What are you talking about, Aakar Beta?" asked Radhika Kaki.

I knew I would be breaking my mother's and aunts' hearts, but I'd gladly be the villain if it got my dad and uncles to quit smoking.

"These are the tests for those people who smoke, and I received the results this morning," I announced.

The gasps echoed in the living room. Maa, aunts, Abhi, and Ria had simultaneous looks of anger and disappointment.

While Navin Kaka looked mad and stubborn, Sunil Kaka, the youngest brother, looked down in shame. Dad, on the other hand, looked at Mom and said, "We got the tests done because we quit. Ask Kriti."

Fuck. All the ladies turned their eyes to Kriti, who hid her face in her hands.

"Kriti Beta, you knew?" Maa asked, her voice laced with disappointment.

Not wanting Kriti to take any blame—and I realized the irony here—I answered, "Don't blame Kriti, Maa. Dad and the kakas made her promise not to tell anyone. That's why Kriti forced them to quit and took them to get these tests done. And thank God she did because the test results are back."

"Is...Is everything alright?" Maa asked.

I unlocked my phone and started with Sunil Kaka. I looked at Ekta Kaki as I read the test because, clearly, Sunil Kaka wasn't all that concerned about his health. "Sunil Kaka's reports are normal. Except his vitamin D."

While Ekta Kaki sighed with relief, Sunil Kaka quickly pointed out, "See, everything is fine, Ekta. I don't smoke too often and exercise regularly."

Without looking up from my phone, afraid I would glare at my uncle, I jumped to Dad's report. "The spirometry report for you, Pappa, shows that your lung function is at 72 percent, which falls under the 'mildly abnormal' category."

"Abnormal!" Maa gasped, looking at Dad with increasing worry and ever-increasing rage at the same time.

"Mildly," Dad muttered, rubbing his hand across his forehead.

And because he was my dad, I felt like I had more than enough right to glare at him. So I looked at him with my harshest glare that had our contractors shaking in their boots and said, "A few more cigarettes and that'd drop too."

And now, the most difficult report. This time, I looked at Ria and Radhika Kaki. "Navin Kaka's spirometry report shows him in the 'moderately abnormal' category, which is as bad as we want to see."

This time, Ria was off her seat and dropped beside her teary-eyed mother, glaring at her father. "Smoking, Pappa? Really? Did you ever stop after you kept promising me and

Mom all those years ago? You just hid it better, didn't you? Don't you worry about us at all? What would happen to Mom if something were to happen to you?"

"Nothing's going to happen to me, beta. These reports just say stuff. I feel completely fine."

Ria's mouth was round in shock. "Really? You feel fine? Why don't you climb up to the third floor of the house and show me if you can breathe fine. I bet you'd be panting by the time you climb just two stories."

"That's just my age."

"Bullshit."

Her father glared at her. "Mind your language, Ria."

This time, she glared back, her eyes shining with tears. "You need to mind your habits first."

I interrupted before things could escalate further between the father and daughter. "I've scheduled a follow-up appointment with the doctor for tomorrow morning. We'll all go and meet the doctor and take it from there."

Then I looked at my dad and my uncles and said, "Till then, try not to smoke."

I looked at Kriti, Ria, and Abhi, jerked my head toward outside, turned around, grabbed my car keys, and moved toward the front door. I heard shuffling behind me, and soon, the four of us were in the car. I drove to a fast food place called "Urban Chowk" and left the three couples alone for a while.

We each grabbed our own comfort food. Kriti got a big strawberry milkshake with a scoop of strawberry ice cream on top, Abhi got a kebab platter with five different dips, Ria got a Chinese platter filled with schezwan garlic noodles, fried rice, and Manchurian chili dry, and I got bhaji pav.

The moment we all had our orders in front of us, Ria twirled her fork in the noodles and asked, "What are we going to do, Aakar? How did we not know?"

I sighed as I squeezed some lemon in my bhaji, deciding to

skip the onions today. "Apparently, they only smoked when I wasn't around."

Abhi scoffed. "Yeah, right. Their reports are saying something different."

I nodded and regarded Kriti, who was busy moving the straw in her milkshake, looking completely dejected. I lightly squeezed her thigh and asked, "You okay, Kriti?"

She sighed and nodded. "I guess."

She then looked at Ria and Abhi and said, "I'm sorry I didn't tell you guys about Pappa and the kakas. I see how much you guys talking to your fathers could help them stop smoking and not pick it up again."

Ria and Abhi were quick to reassure her, as Abhi said, "It's not your fault, bhabhi. They're the ones who made you hide it for them."

He squeezed her hand lightly and reiterated, "Not your fault."

She gave him a small smile and nodded at him.

Ria was also quick to add, "Yes, it's not your fault. Our dads tend not to take responsibility for their actions or face any consequences. Easier to blame others or find excuses. This time, though. I'm going to watch my dad like a hawk. And you just see if I let him compromise on his health."

That got a chuckle out of Kriti.

She still didn't look at me or smile at me much. I was determined to get her to forgive me before we slept.

We didn't reach home until late at night. None of us wanted to get into any fights or drama, knowing that our parents would be involved in their own fights. We had no interest in being a witness to their silent battles and loud television.

As soon as we entered our room, Kriti jumped into the washroom, mumbling about needing to change her clothes. I removed my sweatpants and T-shirt, leaving myself in my briefs, and got under the blanket. I turned on the air conditioner, putting it at the coldest temperature it would go, and waited for Kriti to come out.

The room was freezing when she stepped out of the washroom, freshly showered, dressed in her shortest shorts and her sexiest, silkiest top, absolutely determined to drive me insane.

But the moment she stepped toward the bed, her skin broke out in goose bumps. And she knew exactly the game I was playing because she glared daggers at me.

"What are you trying to play at?" she hissed, rubbing her hands over her arms, pushing her gorgeous tits together and making my mouth water.

"The same thing you're playing at, baby," I said, my mouth twitching.

My cock was rock hard underneath the blanket, but when she dove under the cover, she kept a solid foot between us.

"I'm not playing at anything. Just trying to sleep after the day we had." She turned off her side of the night lamp and lay facing the other way.

Now that wouldn't do at all.

I kept my side of the light on because I hadn't seen my wife in two weeks and *needed* to see every inch of her.

Turning, I molded myself to my wife, feeling every gorgeous curve of her body against mine. I lightly pressed my lips to her neck and whispered, "I'm sorry for my reaction, Kriti. I should've listened before reacting. Please forgive me, baby."

"I really don't like being shouted at," she mumbled.

"I know, and I won't shout at you again," I whispered, placing kisses on her shoulder and pulling her to me tighter so her hips were pushed against mine.

"I hated your mad-at-me face. I can't stop seeing it."

"Then look at my very apologetic, very-in-love-with-his-wife face," I said and turned her body so she faced me.

The moment her eyes met mine, I dropped a small kiss on her lips just because I couldn't help it.

She looked so fucking beautiful, with her hair mussed up, the strap of her top dropped down to her arm, and the top of her breast pushed up. My cock was roaring hard as all of her soft curves aligned with my rock-hard body.

I groaned and buried my face in her neck, my mouth hungry for a taste of her. My teeth ached with the need to bite her soft, delicate skin and mark my wife.

I grabbed her waist and rolled us so she went on top of me.

Her hair was like a waterfall over her shoulder, and her soft thighs spread out across my hips. I pushed her hair behind her ears and pulled her closer with my other hand so only a hairsbreadth separated us. "Do you see him? The very, very apologetic husband? The desperately-needy-for-you, the dying-for-you husband?"

Her breath came in sharp pants, but she didn't utter a single word. My stubborn little wife.

I pulled her closer to me so her tits hung over my lips, tempting me to suck and nibble and bite them, leaving my marks on her skin. But I held off, placing small kisses on her breasts, slowly lapping at every inch of her skin except her nipples.

I blew a breath on the tight little peaks, and she rolled her hips on my cock. "Suck them, Aakar," she gritted out, pushing my mouth closer to her nipples.

"Do you forgive me?" I asked, gently scraping my thumb on one of her nipples and causing her to moan.

She tightened her jaw and refused to utter a word.

I pushed my brief-covered cock between her thighs, her thin scrap of shorts barely covering anything. "You see what you do to me, baby? Wouldn't you give your husband another chance? Please, baby?"

She was upright now, rubbing herself on me, desperate for me to push inside her. She looked at me and clutched her tits in her hands and gave them a rough squeeze. My cock pulsed between her legs, my back arching, needing to be inside her, dammit. "Fuck, Kriti. Please, baby?"

"What're you willing to do for it?" she asked, pinching her nipples, moaning and writhing on my lap, grinding on me. I clutched her thighs, needing to touch her. "Anything, jaan."

"You will write *I love Kriti. I trust Kriti.* a thousand times in a notebook," she said, her eyes arched in challenge.

"Deal," I said, and in the next second, I had her pinned to the bed. I quickly removed her shorts, discarded my briefs, and fell on top of her. "I would've written that five thousand times if you'd asked, Kriti teacher," I whispered against her lips and plunged inside her in one hard thrust.

Her back arched as her legs wrapped around my hips, pushing me in deeper. Her neck arched, and she grabbed her breast, pushing my mouth to her nipples. I greedily sucked it into my mouth, knowing how much nipple play turned Kriti on.

I gave her sharp pulls as I squeezed her other breast, causing her to squeeze me tight inside her. My cock was enveloped in her warm, wet pussy, her juices sliding down my balls as I slowly kept thrusting inside her.

"We forgot the condom, baby. You want me to fill you with my cum?" I asked, not really serious, but the thought had my dick getting harder.

She keened as her pussy contracted around my cock. "Don't you fucking get me pregnant, Aakar," she hissed out but pulled me harder into her body, taking my cock deeper.

I bent lower and sucked on her nipples again, her tit overflowing from my hand, her hands clutching me to her breasts by the back of my head. Her hips rocked with mine in perfect rhythm, and the moment I scraped my teeth on the underside of her nipple, she gave a muffled scream, biting my shoulder as her pussy contracted around my cock. She squeezed and pulled and milked my cock until I was mindless with overpowering lust, and my cock roared to let loose inside her. I wanted to fill her with my cum, needing to see it dripping from her as she kept squeezing me and moaning my name.

The moment she was done, I wildly pumped inside her, trying to last as long as possible, wanting to forever stay inside her, but all too soon, my balls tightened, and the tingling at the base of my spine rose to an inferno. I quickly pulled out of her, spraying my cum all over her stomach, rubbing and squeezing my cock, spurting my load on her nipples.

We were both panting as I dropped over her and started kissing her. "I'm sorry for shouting at you, baby. I'll get to writing tomorrow."

"It's okay," she whispered. "Just remember that I want the best for your family."

"*Our* family," I added, reinforcing that thought in her mind as well as mine.

30

Song: Phil Le Aaya Dil
- *Rekha Bhardwaj*

Kriti

I was working on my laptop in the kitchen when Aakar returned from work and dropped his usual kiss on my head. It had been two days since our big fight.

"Hey, jaan. How was your day?"

I gave him a small smile, my cheeks blushing every time he said jaan. "As usual. Just came home from the evening walk with Pappa and the uncles. You? All good at work?"

He pulled the chair beside mine and took a seat. "I must say, I've been extremely busy these days."

"You have?"

He opened his office bag and nodded. "Of course. I have this teacher in my house who's handed me a punishment."

My heart started to pound. I never thought he'd actually do it. "No, you didn't."

He gave me a wide smile. "Of course, I did. What kind of a husband do you think I am, wife?"

He pulled out a notepad and handed it to me.

With shock still etched on my face, I looked down at the notepad and opened to the first page. And there it was. Two little sentences. Six words. Written in one line. A thousand times.

I love Kriti. I trust Kriti.
I love Kriti. I trust Kriti.
I love Kriti. I trust Kriti.
I love Kriti. I trust Kriti.
I love Kriti. I trust Kriti.
I love Kriti. I trust Kriti.
I love Kriti. I trust Kriti.
I love Kriti. I trust Kriti.
I love Kriti. I trust Kriti.

Tears gathered in my eyes and dropped onto each page that I turned. Pages and pages of *I love Kriti. I trust Kriti.* lined the notepad. I didn't know why I was crying when he was the one who had shouted at me.

But this, I really didn't think he would follow through. I should've known better. This was Aakar. My honorable, always-keeps-his-word husband. Of course he wrote it. More tears dropped on the pages as I flipped through each one of them, tracing the words with my fingers. Aakar pulled me closer into his arms, brushed his lips against my forehead, and whispered, "I love you, baby. I trust you."

His words were as much a balm to my soul as they were like the heaviest rock lodged in my heart. Because I was terrified of what might happen to that trust if he found out about Abhi.

As the days passed, I started finding a rhythm in my new life. I woke up, got an hour to myself as I prepared my tea and read my romance books, got ready for school, went to school, came home, chitchatted with Maa and the aunties while having chai, worked on the next day's class or corrected homework, had dinner with everyone, spent time with Aakar—sometimes we had sex, sometimes we just sat and worked on our own projects —and went to sleep.

Life was good in terms of my routine.

But it had its own challenges in terms of dealing with the health of the men of the house. The doctor had given each man their dietary instructions, exercises, and a strict order not to smoke.

Every family member was on high alert, and the men were under Aakar Mishra's strict scrutiny.

Each family member was given orders and times to be on the lookout for Pappa and the uncles. Since Aakar was with the men for most of the day, he had a handle on things in the office. Abhi was under strict orders to go to the office at least three days a week.

Ria got the men to exercise in the morning while I was responsible for accompanying them on their evening walks. The ladies had taken up the dietary requirements, not budging an inch after the lies and betrayal from their husbands.

Speaking of lies, it took me a few days to gather enough courage to apologize to Maa and the kakis, and all of them were so kind, saying they knew their husbands well and how persuasive they could be. They didn't blame me at all, unlike my dear husband.

I was on a walk with the uncles and Pappa, and Abhi decided to join in, dragging Karan with him. The moment the men saw Karan, they burst into claps on his back, welcoming him into their fold, saying *Where have you been, beta? Haven't seen you in so long. Don't you stay away for so long.*

Tears gathered in my eyes at seeing Abhi watching Karan surrounded by the elders, receiving so much love and warmth. Our eyes met, and Abhi shook his head helplessly. His eyes screamed *See how much they love him? Would they show him this love if they knew the truth?*

No, they wouldn't. But I had to talk to Abhi. Had to ask him to tell Aakar. So when the elders started to walk in front of us, first, I pulled Karan into a bone-crushing hug. His bashful smile had me pinching his cheeks. "How can you hide from me so much, Karan? I'm here for you and Abhi, always."

Karan's eyes filled with so much gratitude, so many emotions, as he shakily whispered, "I know, bhabhi. I'm sorry for staying away for so long. I was terrified and embarrassed. No one in my life knows. No one except Abhi."

"I'm so sorry I barged into Abhi's room that day. I already apologized to Abhi, but I really wanted to apologize to you personally."

He quickly pulled me into a hug and said, "I'm glad you know, bhabhi. I'm glad we have someone in our corner."

"Always, Karan."

Abhi lightly coughed and started to walk behind the elders so as not to garner their attention.

Seeing that it was just the three of us, and now that I had both Abhi and Karan's attention, I cleared my throat, making them both turn to look at me, and said, "Speaking of having someone in your corner…"

"Nope," Abhi quickly interrupted. "Do not even think about it, bhabhi."

"Hear me out, Abhi."

"No, bhabhi. Absolutely not."

Karan looked back and forth between the two of us with

raised eyebrows, and when Abhi's eyes met his, Abhi muttered, "She wants us to tell Aakar Bhai."

Karan's eyes widened, and he started shaking his head. "Bhabhi, no. Abhi's right. We can't tell Aakar Bhai. He'd kill us."

I gasped, offended on my husband's behalf. "He would not. He would stand by you and be in your corner. He'd understand."

Abhi scoffed. "Bhabhi, in case you haven't noticed, all Aakar Bhai ever asks me is if I have a girlfriend."

I cringed because I had noticed that. "In his defense, he doesn't know any better, Abhi. Heterosexual men in India don't ever think about the possibility of a family member having a different sexual orientation. Aakar wouldn't even have considered the possibility that his little brother could be gay. Give him a chance, Abhi. He's seen you and Karan throughout the years. He knows how much you two mean to each other. I'm sure he'll understand. He loves you and only ever wants you to be happy."

We continued to walk a few feet behind the elders but still kept our voices low.

Abhi sighed. "I know how much Aakar Bhai loves us. He'd take a bullet for any of us. But he'd be so disappointed in me. And I really don't think I could face him if he looked at me with disappointment or even hatred in his eyes. It would break me, bhabhi."

"Oh, Abhi. He might be shocked, but surely, he wouldn't look at you with hatred in his eyes. He could never hate you."

"Please, bhabhi. I can't tell him. Especially not now, with the health of Pappa and the kakas already stressing everyone out. Aakar Bhai has already lost his mind with his army general routine. This is really not the time, bhabhi."

I looked at the three men walking ahead of us and sighed. "You're right. Now might not be the best time. But please consider it. I know Aakar. He would support you, no matter what. He'd just be sad that it took you so long to share this with him."

Karan looked at me then and asked, "Would you get in trouble with Aakar Bhai if he knows that you know?"

Abhi also turned to me at the question.

I quickly gave them both a smile. "You shouldn't worry about that. It's between the two of us. And I guess he would be sad and probably a little angry that I hid it from him, but of course, he would understand that it's not my secret to tell."

Abhi quickly put his arm around my shoulder and said, "And if he doesn't understand, Karan and I will make him. Don't you worry, bhabhi. We've got your back too."

And I knew then. I knew I didn't just love my husband. I loved his family just as much.

~

Aakar

The six-week spirometry test results for Dad and Navin Kaka arrived today. With all of our group efforts in getting them to quit smoking and putting them on an exercise routine and a healthier diet, we found some positive updates in their reports. Not only did that help Mom and the kakis breathe a little easier, but it also gave me hope that keeping them on this routine would definitely get Dad and the kakas healthier.

Abhi, Ria, Karan, Kriti, and I were in our bedroom eating ice cream to celebrate our efforts. Abhi and Karan sat on the floor leaning against the full-length wardrobe across from the bed, and Ria and Kriti sat cross-legged on the bed, while I was on the rolling chair near my work desk.

I was finally a little at peace, and seeing my entire family together and my cousins happy made something settle in my heart. It brought me a sense of accomplishment and joy that I never got when securing a client or hitting our yearly goals.

I looked at my cousins. Ria, talking and giggling with Kriti, Abhi and Karan lost in their conversation, the smiles on their faces, the days of worries forgotten. I turned to my wife, her wide smile, and the way she looked at my siblings as if they were her own, as if she loved them like her own.

"How's the job going, Ria? You and Zayan getting along?" I asked, wanting to jump into the conversation.

Kriti put her head in her hand, shaking her head at my question. And I quickly realized why when Ria scoffed loudly. "Um. No. To get along with someone, you need mutual respect. Zayan has no respect for me, nor do I him. It's a losing battle."

Zayan was one of my best friends. And I knew that he had nothing but respect for my sister. He said so when I asked him if he could recommend Ria for a position in his firm.

"Did you try getting along with him?" I asked, knowing that Zayan would never instigate any fights, and Ria was a bit more volatile with her emotions.

Case in point, she glared at me like a ferocious lioness. "Did *I* try to get along? I was nothing but nice to him from the beginning."

Before I could ask her any further questions, Abhi quickly piped in, "Don't even try, bhai. It won't end well. Trust me, when it comes to Ria Didi versus Zayan Bhai, Ria Didi is always right."

Karan and Kriti looked at each other and started chuckling, whereas Ria had an appreciative smile on her face. "You're learning, Abhi. I'm impressed. Don't you forget this when you get a girlfriend."

Abhi just shook his head with a smile. "We'll see about that."

"Maybe he's already got a girlfriend," I teased.

"Nope. No girlfriend," he said, not meeting my eyes and looking down at his phone.

Now that I thought about it, he never talked about his girlfriends.

"What's with all the secrecy, baby bro? You know you're allowed to have a girlfriend, right? I'll totally support you if Mom and Dad object. Just ask Akira." I winked.

Abhi had a small smile on his face as he rolled his eyes. "Let it be, bhai."

The way he was deflecting and not denying that there was no one made me want to know about it even more. I know we were about eight years apart, but I wanted my brother to be open with me.

"C'mon, what's the harm, Abhi? It's just us here," I added.

Ria was quick to jump in. "Yeah, Abhi. It's just us."

"Exactly, c'mon, tell us, baby bro."

Abhi slammed the ice cream cup on the floor beside him. "I said I don't have a girlfriend, bhai. You know why? Because I'm gay."

My heart stilled. My mind froze. It was like my entire body stopped functioning at those two words. Gay. Gay. Abhi was gay? No. No. He couldn't be. My eyes were focused on him but I couldn't see anything. Shock had my body in a chokehold, and I didn't know how to get out of it.

"Are you going to say something?" Abhi asked, his voice shaking.

Was I? What did one say to that? What was I supposed to say when I didn't even know how I felt about it? What was I supposed to say to make him swallow his words back?

"Fuck this," Abhi muttered, a tear rolling down his cheek, as he got up from the floor and walked out of the room.

"Abhi," Karan called out and looked between where he went and where I sat, my eyes glued to his retreating back.

Karan looked at me, and with a shake of his head, he turned around and ran after Abhi.

Ria was quick to run after him as well.

But my body was stuck. *I* was stuck. I had no words. My heart was beating a million miles a minute. My mind threw a thousand scenarios at me, showing me Abhi's life as a gay man. Who would ever accept him? What would the world say? How would he ever have a normal life? How many people would frown at him, make fun of him, and inflict violence on him? How could he? How could he put himself through that?

I felt a sudden shaking of my body, and I realized Kriti clutched my shirt collar and was shaking me.

My eyes met her dangerous glare, and I was dragged out of the spiraling abyss of possibilities and threats I was pulled under. The feel of the cool air of the air conditioner touched the nape of my neck, and I could finally hear sounds around me.

When I looked at Kriti, scathing anger laced her words as she said through clenched teeth, "What the fuck was that, Aakar?"

Guilt and shame coursed through my body. "I'm sorry Abhi's gay. You know I just found that out. I didn't know..."

She frowned, and her tone dropped as she asked, "You think I'm ashamed of Abhi?"

"Aren't you?" I asked, my mind spinning out of control. Words failed me. My mind failed me.

Only Kriti's tightening hold on my collar kept me grounded. "How could you even think that?

"I don't know what to even think anymore, Kriti." I clutched her hand that was holding my shirt, trying to infuse some of her strength in myself.

"You need to go to Abhi and give him a hug and tell him you love him. Tell him you accept him. Tell him that nothing changes."

Nothing changes? Nothing fucking changes?

That got me moving. I jumped out of my seat as I walked around our bedroom. "Nothing changes? Kriti, it changes everything. Every-fucking-thing. It changes how I see my brother. It changes the lives of every person associated with him. It would change the way people look at him. It would change the way people talk to him, talk about him. It would change the way people even associate with this family. It would destroy our family. What do you think our family would say about this? You think our family would accept Abhi, let alone someone he would love? You think people in our society know how to deal with gay people? He wouldn't be just Abhi. He would become *that gay boy*. No. Absolutely not. I can't accept that for him. I can't let Abhi live a life like that."

Kriti's eyes widened in shock. Her fists were clenched so tight with anger, but I couldn't comprehend how she wasn't on the same wavelength as me. "How can you even think that? This is about your brother and his sexual orientation. He hasn't announced this to the world. He's shared this with you. *You*, Aakar. He wants *your* support."

My heart started to beat faster at every word she spoke. My body started to heat and sweat gathered at the back of my neck at seeing Kriti so calm and collected at Abhi's announcement. How was she not freaking out? How could she be so okay? How was she not losing her mind?

My mind spun out of control at the thought. I looked at her. Looked at how she was defending my brother. Looked at how there were no signs of shock on her face. Just fight. "You knew," I breathed out.

Her eyes widened at that.

And I was sure. "Tell me, Kriti. You already knew about Abhi, didn't you?"

I didn't want to see it. I didn't want to hear her admit the truth. Yet I kept looking at her face. The way she gulped, the way she turned her eyes away from me.

"Say it, Kriti." My voice was numb. Every second of her silence was stealing all my trust in her.

I walked to her and held her shoulder. I pulled her closer to me, so close I could feel her heart pumping at my sternum. "You knew, didn't you? You knew my brother was gay, yet you hid it from me."

She turned her eyes away from me once more and mumbled, "Now is not the time for this."

Fury raced down my spine, betrayal shattering every kernel of trust I had in my wife. It took an insurmountable effort for me to get the words out when all I wanted to do was scream and rage and shut off from the world. "I can't think of a better time than this. How long have you known?"

She must've realized that it was futile to delay this conversation because she looked me in my eyes as she said, "Two and a half months."

Pain so sharp echoed in my chest. It felt like her words had cracked open my heart, and I looked down at my chest to check if blood was pouring out onto my shirt. I turned to look at where Kriti's hand lay on my chest. And I couldn't bear it.

I couldn't bear my wife's touch. Words flew out of my mouth as if they burst out from a cracked shell and not me when I looked at my wife and said, "All I've ever asked for is your trust. Honesty. After so many fights. So much discussion. So many promises. The one thing I've asked for is honesty and openness to share everything with me. You promised. You promised after what happened with Dad and the kakas. I asked and asked…"

"Aakar." Her teary voice would break me.

My own heart was shattering. "No. I don't want to hear it. I can't."

"Your brother needs you right now." Her words might've

meant well, but all I heard was *It was too late. My brother was gay. How did I not see it? How could I have stopped it? I was too late.*

"My brother needed me two and half months ago, too, but you didn't think about telling me then, did you? You just decided to deal with this yourself too, right?"

"It's not like that, Aakar..."

"Don't. Don't say my name. I can't even look at you right now." I turned around and clutched my hair, the pain in my heart expanding to my head. "Fuck," I yelled.

"Aakar, please..."

"I need you to leave." My heart cracked down the middle as I said those words. Those five words poured out of me because I couldn't pretend I wasn't hurt. My life was unraveling around me, and I felt like I didn't even know who was who anymore.

"You don't mean that," she whispered.

My vision swam as tears gathered in my eyes. "I don't even know who you are anymore. I don't know how many times I should put my trust in you. I need some time, Kriti. To think. To make everything all right. And I just can't...I can't deal with this right now. And I can't see your face knowing you knew everything. So I need you to go back to your home."

31

Song: Yeh Dil Deewana
 - *Sonu Nigam*

Kriti

There was a loud ringing in my ears. Or maybe it was the sound of my heart shattering. *I need you to go back to your home.* I thought this was my home. I thought *he* was my home.

Just nine words, and I felt like a stranger in this house.

My husband said he couldn't even look at me. And for what? For caring for his brother? For treating him like I would treat my own brother? For protecting his privacy? For loving him like I would love my own little brother?

"Don't do this, Aakar," I whispered, tears clogging the back of my throat, refusing to let a sound escape.

He stood with his back facing me, his hands clenched in tight fists.

His back expanded as his head hung low, defeat etched in

every angle of his body. "I'll drop you at the station tomorrow morning."

"You're making a huge mistake. This is not the way to deal with a fight," I said, trying to make him see reason.

His chuckle was hoarse, and when he turned around, his eyes were red-rimmed with tears, despair etched on his beautiful face. "Sure, teach me how to be better at communication."

He was beyond exasperating and unreasonable. I knew he would be disappointed and hurt when he found out that I knew, but never in my wildest imagination did I think he would be so furious that he would send me back home.

My worry grew with every second that passed because he didn't take his words back. My legs started shaking so badly that I sat on the edge of the bed, watching him move across our bedroom.

How the hell did a perfectly good evening dissolve into utter chaos and misery?

My heart was in pieces for Abhi. While I understood it must be frustrating to face the same questions over and over again, this was definitely not how I imagined him coming out to his brother.

And there I was, so confident that Aakar would support his brother, that he would be there to protect him and fight for him, no matter what. Looking back up to where my husband paced our bedroom like a caged lion, I felt so fucking sorry for giving Abhi hope. I never should've asked him to put so much faith in Aakar.

I was so fucking angry now. Angry with him for being such a dickhead, and angrier at myself for thinking he would just instantly hug Abhi when he came out.

My head started to pound, watching him walk back and forth, and I couldn't help but snap, "Are you insane? Go to your brother. What's the matter with you?"

If his glare could physically shut me up, my lips would be sewn shut. "Will you just...? I'm thinking."

"What the fuck is there to think about?"

"A million things that you couldn't even begin to understand. If you could, we wouldn't be in this position right now."

My anger rose with every word he spoke. I wanted to hit him, grab his head by his hair, and bash it against the wall to bang some sense into him. "What position? Where your brother isn't gay?"

His entire face scrunched up in a cringe. "Don't say that word."

Rage exploded in my heart and spread like a wildfire through my veins. I could feel myself burning hot, my head pounded like someone was ramming a bulldozer in my skull. "Did Abhi break you? Have you got no fucking heart?"

His glare could flay someone's skin open. "Shut. Up."

He went to his nightstand, opened the drawer, and got his car keys. Without even looking at me, he said, "I'm leaving. You better be ready to go tomorrow morning."

A gasp tore through my chest. "But..."

His eyes were dark pools of venom staring at me. "What? You thought just because I was talking to you that I changed my mind? That I can look at you in the face and not feel betrayed?"

Every word from his mouth was a punch to my chest. My heart broke. "It's that easy for you, huh?"

For a second there, his eyes flashed with agony. But he quickly froze and said, "Just as easy as it is for you to lie to me."

And it wasn't. But what about lying for his brother?

Tears pooled in my eyes, but I refused to let them drop. "Don't do this, Aakar. Don't send away your wife."

"Seven o'clock sharp."

With those words ringing in my ears, he left the room. And I let my tears fall.

Gut-wrenching agony. Betrayal. Disbelief. Anger. A barrage

of all of the emotions bombarded me. Maybe this was how Aakar felt. Tears streamed down my face freely now.

I wasn't going to try to convince him anymore.

I wasn't at fault here.

If I could go back and had to keep Abhi's secret, knowing how Aakar would react, I would make the same choice all over again. No regrets.

So with tears streaming down my face—why wouldn't they stop?—I opened my wardrobe and got my suitcase out. And I packed one dress after the next. I got my toiletries and added them. I opened my laptop and sent an email to my school requesting a leave of absence for the next two weeks. I'd deal with a further leave of absence when the time came.

I didn't pack all my clothes. I left enough not to raise any suspicion at home, mine and his. I had no intention of letting anyone in my or Aakar's family know why I was leaving. Not because I wanted to give Aakar a chance or because I was leaving with a delusion that I'd be back in two weeks. But because I would protect Abhi.

If Aakar reacted like *that*, there was no way anyone in the family would react well.

By the time I zipped the suitcase shut, tears had dried on my face. My mind seemed to be going numb, whereas my heart had never beaten faster. It had never ached more. The sharp sting of rejection felt like a knife plunged into my heart.

He told me he loved me. Over and over again.

Was this his love? So fickle? So conditional?

I lay down on the bed, not feeling the mattress or the comforter. My eyes closed, but sleep evaded me. Seconds on the clock ticked by, and my heart hardened with every tick that passed. My mind was stuck in a circle of hopes and dejection. It created endless loops of conditions. *If he asked us to stay, we'll be okay. If he lets us go, we'll never come back. If he comes to our home to call us back, we're going to be the ones to reject him.*

I did not sleep that night.

I never opened my eyes when I heard Aakar walk in or when the bed dipped at my back.

For the entire night, every minute, every second of it, I waited for Aakar to tell me to stay. He didn't. Not even once. Not even a word. And each second of his silence crushed my heart into pieces.

I woke up way too early in the morning, got ready, brought my bag downstairs to the dining area, prepared my chai, and waited for everyone to wake up.

When Maa arrived downstairs, she frowned at the bag near my feet. "What happened, beta? You going somewhere?"

I mustered up a smile. "I really missed home and thought I'd go stay with Mom and Dad for a bit."

Her eyes shone with worry, and she quickly dropped into the chair beside me. "All of a sudden? Everything okay with Aakar? Did you two fight? Did he say something?"

I quickly put my hand on hers, shaking my head in denial even though my insides were tearing into pieces. "No, Maa. Everything's fine with Aakar. It's been months, and I haven't visited my home. That's all. I talked to Aakar last night, and he said he'd drop me at the morning bus. That's all."

Tension eased from her eyes, and she gave a bright smile. "Oh, alright then, beta. I understand. The first year is always the most difficult. Especially when you live in a different city from your family. We'll miss you. So don't stay away for too long."

My voice shook as I said, "I'll miss you too. All of you."

Thankfully, before I could dissolve into tears, Aakar stepped into the dining area and stopped short.

I waited, like a stupid girl, just one last time for him to utter a single word. *Stay.*

Instead, he said, "Ready?"

No. "Yes," I said and stood. After touching Maa's feet for blessings, I wheeled the bag out the door, not looking back at the house or my husband.

~

Aakar

Life as I knew it stopped the moment Abhi came out. My mind was stuck in a vicious loop of anxiety, stress, and disbelief. Whereas my heart was feeling the moments of betrayal from my wife over and over again.

Rage was riding high in my system, and all I wanted to do was hit something. To destroy something. After dropping Kriti off, I went to the office. I couldn't bear the thought of seeing our room without her in it. I spent the rest of the day immersed in work, only talking to people when needed and checking my phone every two minutes.

I didn't know why I couldn't stop checking the damn phone. Was I hoping for her to text me something? An apology? A lashing? Just a fucking *I've reached home, Aakar*? Was that too much to ask for? *Yes*, my mind screamed at me. Rage and concern waged a battle in my chest the entire day, not letting me even swallow a bite of food.

When I returned home from the office, I went to Abhi's room to talk to him. But it was empty. He must've gone to Karan's place.

Shaking my head, I made my way upstairs to find Ria's door was shut.

I opened the door to my bedroom, and my feet halted at the threshold. Every corner I looked at had imprints of Kriti all over them. Be it her elaborate bookshelves, her books wrapped in ugly brown wrapping paper, or the dip on her side of the bed.

I didn't know why I was so fucking mad at her.

Was it because she didn't tell me? Or was it because Abhi chose to tell her and not me?

This was exactly why I sent her away. Her choices. Her actions. Her reasons. I couldn't deal with them. I couldn't deal with her.

I had to think about Abhi. My brother. My *gay* brother.

How did I not see it? How did he hide it so well? How would my brother live his life as a gay man in India? Would he spend his life in hiding and in the shadows? How else would he live his life with his head held high? How else would he protect himself? Did he have no sense of self-preservation? Did he not see the sneers and jabs that gay people had to deal with day and night? Did he realize that he'd never get to marry? What if something happened to him, and I wasn't there to protect him?

Every question had fear racing through my veins. All I could hear was my own heart beating against my chest, and my head felt like I was submerged in water, drowning in anxiety.

A loud bang of my door crashing into the wall pulled me out of my spiral.

And there stood Abhi, his eyes bloodshot, his body taut, and his hands clenched into tight fists. "Where the fuck is bhabhi?"

My eyes widened. I'd never seen him so furious.

"I think we need to talk."

"I think you need to answer my question. Where is bhabhi?"

I hardened my voice at that. "That's between me and her. Don't interfere. I'd like to talk to you about the bomb you dropped last night."

Abhi walked into my room, his eyes blazing with fury. "Maa told me bhabhi went home. Said she missed her home."

It felt like there was a knife stuck in my chest, and Abhi was bound to push it deeper and deeper and deeper. "I said I don't want to talk about it. Let it the fuck go."

His voice was barely a whisper when he said, "You sent her away, didn't you?" But his words fell on me like a bomb detonating inside the room.

My silence was my admission, and Abhi crashed into me like a hurricane. He clutched my T-shirt in his fist and pushed me against the wall. Over and over again, his teeth clenched with restrained fury as he kept repeating, "What the fuck is the matter with you?"

Two smaller arms came between us, pulling Abhi off me. Ria stood between us, her smaller body protecting me while keeping a hand outstretched toward Abhi, stopping him from jumping on me. "What the hell is going on?"

Abhi now had tears streaming down his cheeks, but his eyes were filled with fury and hatred and disgust, all directed toward me. Never taking his eyes off me, he said to Ria, "Ask Aakar Bhai where bhabhi is."

When Ria didn't say anything, Abhi shouted like he'd never shouted at us before. "Ask him, Ria Didi."

Ria's voice shook as she looked at me. "Where is Kriti, Aakar?"

Heartbreak and shame collided in my chest. "I asked her to go back to her house for a little while."

Abhi's laugh was scathing. "Hear that, Ria Didi? He sent her away for a little while. For how long, bhai? One day? Two days? A week? Two? Ten weeks? Does she know that she's in a time-out?"

This time, Ria was in my face, her jaw clenched. "Have you lost your mind? Why the hell would you do that?"

Before I could get words out of my chest, Abhi interrupted. He had a manic look in his eyes as if he'd lost control of all his emotions. "Oh, oh. Can I make a guess?"

When Ria simply stared at him, her fist clenched tight and her face shining with worry, Abhi quickly rushed to me, and with an unhinged expression, he said, "Because she knew. She knew and didn't tell you."

"Aakar?" Ria asked.

I looked at Ria, my jaw clenched tight to stop the scream building up in my chest. "She knew, Ria."

Abhi punched the wall near my head with a loud cry of frustration and stepped away. He looked away as if he couldn't bear to look at me, whereas Ria's eyes were round with shock. "And?"

Didn't she get it? I waved my hands in the air. "And she hid it from me."

"It wasn't her secret to tell," Abhi shouted, his face still turned away from me, his voice broken.

Sharp pain tugged at my chest.

Ria rushed to where Abhi sat on my bed, on Kriti's side, his head clutched in his hands. He looked at her as she softly caressed his knee. "It wasn't her secret to tell. It was mine."

He sounded like my sad little brother who cried when Maa scolded Akira or me. Or when he got a scolding from Dad for not understanding a mathematics equation, where I would pull him into a hug and take him for an ice cream.

I stepped closer and tried to put my hand on his shoulder. But he jerked his shoulder away, rejecting my touch. He looked at me, tears streaming down his face, his eyes reflecting complete dejection, as he whispered, "Is my being gay so bad? Are you that disgusted at the thought of me being interested in men?"

My knees gave out at his broken words. My ass hit the bed, and I sat slumped on my side of the bed, facing Abhi's back. Guilt and worry waged war in my chest as I extended my hand toward where he sat. "Being gay isn't bad, Abhi. And it's not disgust that I feel at the thought of you preferring men over women. I'm terrified. I'm scared shitless for you."

Abhi scoffed and turned around, his eyes red-rimmed. "Are

you scared for me, or are you scared for the family? Don't start sugarcoating your words now. Not after you sent bhabhi away."

How was one different from the other? How could he even separate those two questions? "Of course, I'm scared for the family as well, Abhi. *You* are my family. I'm terrified to just think of the hatred and violence and injustice gay people have to face every day. How am I supposed to protect you? What if something happens to you? Are you ever going to be able to live freely? Hold your lover's hand in public? Get married? I am beyond scared at just the thought of all the challenges you'd have to face by being gay. Fuck, Abhi. How am I supposed to protect you? And who all do I fucking protect you from? From the world? From our relatives? From our own parents? Do you have any fucking idea how Mom and Dad will react? What this'll do to them?"

Tears shone in Abhi's eyes as he clenched his jaw. At least he was looking at me. "I came out to *you* because all I cared about was *your* opinion. Not the world's. Not our relatives'. And not Mom's or Dad's. If I needed their opinion, I would've come out to them."

With a sad laugh that shook his chest and pierced my heart with a thousand tiny needles, he turned to Ria, who sat at the foot of the bed, clutching his knee, and said, "You know, I never even intended to tell Kriti Bhabhi. She accidentally caught me in a compromising position and figured everything out on her own. And do you know what she did when I went to her and told her I was gay?"

My heart pounded at every word Abhi spoke. I stopped breathing as I waited for Abhi to continue.

He turned his face away from Ria and looked me square in the eyes and said, "You don't deserve to know. Maybe you should've asked her. Just so you know, I don't regret her finding out about me. I'm actually glad she did. And you should be too. Because if not for her, I would've never come out to you."

He shook his head as his eyes once again filled with tears, and my body burned with agony and guilt. "You know, bhai, she was so sure that you would be accepting of me. She thought you'd stand in my corner and be there for me. She had so much faith in you. Bet she's regretting it now." He wiped his cheeks and looked at me with so much disappointment. "And so am I."

With that, he walked out of my room, not once looking back at the broken mess he left behind.

"What have I done, Ria?" My voice was a mere whisper.

Ria shook her head, her eyes shining with pity. Pity for me, the asshole who broke not one but two hearts. "What went wrong, Aakar? I never expected you to be this big of an asshole."

Shame had me looking away from her eyes. I looked down at my hands. "Fuck, Ria. I don't know. I freaked out. The only thought that kept circling my head at Abhi's declaration was that his life was fucked. The ridicule he'd have to face. The dangers he'd exposed himself to. The relationships he would shred to pieces in this house. And Kriti *knew*. She knew what would happen if Abhi was gay, and she so easily hid it from me. Did she not think about this family? About what would happen to Abhi? About the repercussions of him being gay? Aren't *you* worried?"

"Of course, I'm worried. But not about the list of things you seem to be worried about. I'm worried about Abhi, who was so brave in coming out to us. Being gay isn't a fucking choice, Aakar. And you're not the only one who realizes the rough road ahead of him. In fact, Abhi seems to have been dealing with this for quite a while now. So you need to stop treating him like some baby who doesn't know his mind."

I was getting that from our conversation just now. Thinking about Abhi's wounded face, his disappointment and heartbreak, felt like I swallowed hot coals down my throat, and I was burning from the inside. "I panicked, Ria. Just the thought of him coming out to Mom and Dad, thinking about their reaction, Abhi leaving us all, I couldn't deal."

She shook her head with disappointment. At least she didn't leave, like Abhi. She walked around the bed and took a seat beside me. "As for Kriti, you fucked up big time."

I couldn't bear to look her in the eyes. "I realize that. I should've given her a chance to explain."

Ria scoffed and got up at that. "Typical men," she spat. "Given her a chance? Are you kidding me? You should've thanked your wife for supporting your little brother. What you should've done was discuss your feelings about Abhi being gay with her. You should've kissed her feet for being so open and caring for your family and treating them with kindness, respect, and love. What you *shouldn't* have done is send her back home."

"No." My voice was a whisper. The next three words I uttered were the biggest admission of my failure as a husband. "I shouldn't have."

Tears gathered in my eyes at the thought of Kriti's face as she begged me to hear her out. Begged me not to send her away. The way she didn't tell Maa anything, despite my cruelty.

Horror washed over me at the thought of getting Kriti back. I looked at the scathing anger on Ria's face. "What have I done?"

She glared at me. "You treated her like shit. You humiliated her. In your delusional obsession about being this leader of the house who needs to know everything about everyone and having this control, you hurt the one person who was actually your biggest ally and partner and who was helping you carry this unreasonable burden. We love you, Aakar, but nobody asked you to carry the burden of this family. In trying to care and worry for your family, you hurt the one person you were supposed to put above everyone else. Instead, you showed her what you really think of her place in this family. Which is at the very bottom."

My voice was sharp as I glared at her. "That's not true."

She glared back. "Doesn't look like it. If I had a husband who sent me back home for just caring for *his* family, for treating them like my own, I'd never forgive him."

"You're not fucking helping, Ria."

"I'm not trying to help you. I'm trying to open your eyes, you fucking idiot."

After a long fucking time, I was feeling like a younger brother to Ria. She was only a year older, but today, I felt like she was far more wise and mature than me, and I fucking needed her.

I groaned, the emptiness Kriti left behind creating a gaping hole in my chest. "I know, I'm an idiot. But how do I get my wife back? Should I go to her place and bring her back?"

She laughed without any humor. "What a great move. And what would you say to her when you get there? Sorry I sent you back home. I realize my mistake, and now I want you to come back?"

At my silence, because that was exactly what I was thinking of doing, she clutched her hair in exasperation and spat, "What a load of shit. Fuck, Aakar. I thought you were smart."

"I need her, Ria. I am an idiot for putting that burden of needing to know everything on her. And it wasn't fair of me. But I want my wife back."

She shook her head, entirely done with me. "Then figure something out."

With that, she walked away, but unlike Abhi, she turned around, looked me in the eye, and said her parting words, "Just don't be an idiot."

Big sisters, always with the wisdom.

32

Song: Suna Man Ka Aangan
- *Sonu Nigam, Shreya Ghoshal*

Kriti

The constant ringing of the doorbell had me rushing out of the kitchen. My heart pounded, thinking it could be Aakar. Yet I did not want it to be Aakar. First, I was furious with him. Second, I had not told my parents that my husband had sent me back home despite their incessant questions at my surprise arrival. And third, my heart was shredded to pieces.

So when I opened the door of my house, I was shocked to see a face I did not expect.

Abhi.

With a small, guilty smile and his hands jammed into his pockets, he simply shrugged.

I quickly pulled him inside the house and closed the door.

Thank God I was the only one in the house. Maa had gone

to her sister's place, and they were going shopping. Rati and Kartik were at school, and Dad was at work.

"Abhi, what are you doing here?"

Determination filled his eyes, and his lips tightened as he said, "I'm here to take you back home with me, what else?"

I wasn't shocked by his declaration, but it still touched my heart. "Oh, Abhi. I'm sorry. But I can't."

Clutching his hair, he sat on the sofa as anguish poured out of him in waves. "It's all my fault. I shouldn't have come out to him like that. If I'd just shut up, you would still be home with us."

Slowly, I took a seat beside him and rubbed his back. "If coming out is your fault, then asking you to come out, making you believe that Aakar would be cool about it, running into you and Karan, all of that was my fault. I've just made mistakes upon mistakes, and none of it has been your fault."

"Don't blame yourself, bhabhi. The only person to blame here is Aakar Bhai. He had no right, *no right*, to send you back. You're not just his wife. You're a part of our family. And nobody gave him the right to act like a selfish asshole to you."

"Abhi..." I had no words. I loved my little brother-in-law, but I refused to step foot inside the house.

"If he doesn't want to talk to you, his loss. I can give you my room. Or you can sleep with Ria Didi. She'd happily take you in. You don't even have to talk to Aakar Bhai. Just come home, bhabhi."

I thought I'd cried all my tears dry last night, but I guess not. My eyes filled with them at the genuine love he has for me. "You have no idea how happy you made me by coming here. Makes me feel like I at least fulfilled my role as a sister-in-law well. But I'm not coming back, Abhi. I didn't deserve to be yelled at by Aakar. I didn't deserve to be thrown out of the house because Aakar didn't want to deal with me. I don't know if I can forgive him, Abhi. I don't think I even want to."

His eyes widened at my declaration, and he shook his head in denial. "I can't. I can't accept it, bhabhi. But I also can't ask you to forgive Aakar Bhai." He groaned out loud. "God, he's such an idiot and an asshole."

Despite the circumstances, despite how raging mad I was at my husband, I chuckled. "He is, isn't he?"

We were both quiet after that. "You sure you don't wanna come back home, bhabhi? You just say the word, and I'll be here to pick you up."

"I'm sure, Abhi." My voice teared up as I said in barely a whisper, "He asked me to go home."

With a jerky nod and a few curse words, Abhi walked out of the door.

From where I was standing, Aakar messed up. He was the one who hurt not one but two people. Yet it felt like we were the ones being punished. And like a fool, I was hiding what he did, what he said, from my parents and his. Despite his cruelty, I was trying to keep his impression good in front of my parents.

Why? I was mad at myself for lying to my parents for him. Because deep within me, I knew that I would go back to him. That I would forgive him. And I hated it. I didn't want to forgive him.

I scoffed at that thought. I'd have to think such thoughts when he actually asked for an apology. I didn't see him knocking down my door asking me to come back.

How could he do this to the person he claimed to love?

Was it even love if he could so easily discard me like that?

And didn't that hurt me like a motherfucking bitch. To know that the person you were in love with didn't truly love you at all.

∽

Aakar

It had been twenty-four hours since I dropped Kriti off at the bus station. Twenty-four excruciating hours where I regretted making that decision.

I'd shredded my own heart to pieces in trying to have control over everything and everyone. And now I'd ended up hurting two of the most important people in my life.

I walked down from my room and stepped into the dining area to find the usual chaos that was my family. My heart pounded at the thought of what I was about to do.

My eyes met Ria's, who sat in one of the chairs at the dining table, eating breakfast. She gave me the classic *What the fuck are you doing?* look as she saw me just standing there like a fool.

I gave her a shrug and was preparing myself to go for it when Maa looked at me as she served a hot paratha to Dad and said, "Aakar, go on. Grab a plate and take a seat. I'll get you some hot paratha."

Clearing my throat, looking at Ria's wide eyes, I turned to Maa. "Um. I actually needed to tell you all something."

Everything stopped. Ten pairs of eyes bore down on me. This wasn't the first time I was making an announcement in this house. I'd never been nervous before. My legs never shook. My throat didn't dry up at the thought of uttering words. But I'd never been more in the wrong before. I'd never been so ashamed of myself before.

"What did you want to tell us?" Abhi's voice came from behind Maa as he walked out of the kitchen carrying his plate of parathas. I'd not seen him since he walked out of my room yesterday morning.

His face was scrunched up in suspicion, his hackles raised.

Except for him, everyone else looked at me with normal worry. *Not for long.*

"Umm, Maa. Remember how Kriti missed her family and went to see them?"

Her voice dropped in confusion. "Yes?"

My heart raced, and my voice shook as I said, "She didn't leave because she missed her family. She…uh…She left because I told her to."

A laugh of disbelief and confusion escaped her as she looked around, then at Dad, at his confused face, and back at me. "Wha…What do you mean you told her to?"

Tears blurred my vision as I got the words out again. "We got in a fight, and I told her to leave and go back to her house."

A loud shriek came first, followed by a hot steel spatula swinging at me and hitting me sharply on my chest. Before I could get over the shock, a large glass was flung at my head that I barely dodged. "What did you say you did?" Her shrieking had my legs shaking.

I'd never seen my mother so mad at me. Or at anyone else. Not even when Akira announced that she was in love with an American man.

Before I could step back, Maa and Pappa rushed toward me, Maa in the front, her angry eyes an exact replica of my little brother's just a day ago.

She reached me and grabbed my T-shirt. "What could she have possibly done for you to send her back home?"

And wasn't it a kick in my ass. I met Abhi's eyes from behind Dad, then turned to Maa and said, "Nothing. She didn't share something with me that I thought was important at that time, but it turns out, it really wasn't important."

In the next second, my head jerked sideways as Maa gave me a tight slap across the face. "So you're telling me that you asked my daughter-in-law to leave this house for no reason at all?"

At my slow nod, Pappa quickly dragged Maa behind him before she could slap me again and asked, his voice dangerously low, "Was this thing that she didn't share something like a secret that we made her keep about our health?"

My cheek burned, but nothing compared to the way I burned on the inside. I wish Maa could've given me a few more slaps, if only that could help ease this guilt. Answering my dad's question, I only gave a sharp nod.

His eyes clouded with disappointment and rage. Turning to my mother, he shouted, "Look at him. Look at his obsession with needing to be in everyone's business. Constantly correcting everyone. Relentlessly advising and controlling everyone."

Turning to me, he shouted in my face, "What do you wish to gain by needing to know everything about everyone? You think your mom and I tell each other everything? You think that your kakas and kakis tell each other everything?"

My mistake, my weakness, my failure, all of it was laid bare in front of my family. In front of the people for whom I wanted to be perfect, reliable, and strong.

Maa was quick to jump in. "No, he just thinks he is needed everywhere. That without him, we wouldn't be able to do anything right. But that's not true, Aakar. We were living just fine before you were born, when you were a little kid, and when you grew up."

Every word cut me where it hurt the most. And they were my family after all. They knew what would hurt me the deepest.

My lips trembled, and I bit it sharply. "Maa, please."

Her eyes flooded with tears as she sat on the floor in defeat. Her voice broke as tears streaked down her cheeks. "Maa, what? Is this how we raised you? How could you, Aakar? Never in my life would I have imagined you disrespecting your wife like this."

Defeated, I dropped to my knees in front of my mother, tears rolling down my cheeks. "I'm sorry, Maa. I don't know what came over me. But I need my wife back. I know I messed up, but I want to get her back."

I felt a warm hand on my shoulder and looked over to find Abhi, tears shining in his eyes as well. "She said you broke her heart. And won't come back."

If my heart could stop beating, it would've stopped at those four words. "What?"

Ten other people echoed the same question at Abhi.

He looked at everyone and sighed. "I figured out yesterday that Aakar Bhai sent bhabhi home." He raised his hands in the air as everyone began to scold him and shouted, "Now it was between bhai and bhabhi, and I was mad at bhai for sending bhabhi away. So I went to Laxminagar to bring her back."

I stayed on my knees, waiting with bated breath to know more. Abhi looked at me with defeated eyes. "She was really hurt, bhai. She just kept saying that you sent her home. As if she couldn't believe you did that. She said she's not coming back."

Radhika Kaki was quick to pipe in, "Maybe she meant she wouldn't come back with you, Abhi. Maybe if Aakar went to get her?"

Everyone's eyes turned to me. With a shake of my head, I looked down at my hands. "It won't be easy. Uh. This might not be the first time I've fought with her about not being open with me and hiding things from me," I said and looked at Dad and kaka. "Remember when she kept your secret?"

Maa was now clutching her head in her hands. "Oh, Aakar. Aakar. Aakar. What am I gonna do with you? I thought you were my smartest son."

It didn't take a second for Abhi to jump in. "Maa, you think I'm the smartest, then?"

While it got a few chuckles from the kakas and Ria, Maa turned a helpless look his way and said, "Beta, if Aakar can disappoint us to this extent, God only knows what *you'd* do to us."

Knowing what I knew now, my eyes met Abhi's, and we burst out laughing.

Tears streamed down my eyes as I heard my grandfather exclaim, "He seems to have lost his mind, poor boy."

Once our laughter died down, Ria came over and sat on the floor between me and Maa. "What are we going to do, kaki? How are we going to get Kriti back?"

Maa's glare returned in full force. "Have you thought of something?"

Before I could utter a single word, she turned to Dad and, in the most disappointing tone, said, "What would he think? He didn't even think about what the poor girl would tell her parents when she showed up at her place out of the blue. Or what would she tell them when she wouldn't come back home here and stayed there for a long time."

With a murderous glare and another slap at my chest, she shouted, "You didn't even bother to think about all that, did you?"

When I shook my head in defeat and denial once again, Maa scoffed and looked away.

I clutched her knee. "I'll bring her back, Maa. I'll apologize. I'll get down on my knees and beg for her forgiveness. I'll do whatever it takes, but I'll bring her back. And it's only been a day. She'll forgive me, right?"

Radhika Kaki scoffed at that. "One day or one week or one month. It's not about time, Aakar. It's about what you did."

Ekta Kaki quickly added, "And I don't think just saying sorry is going to do anything, Aakar."

Abhi piped in, "Yes, bhai. Bhabhi was really hurt and angry."

And just because my grandma hadn't had any say so far, she

jumped in as well, "If your grandfather had asked me to go home, I would've just stayed at my home."

And it seemed like Kriti had dug herself into everyone's hearts because Grandpa gave me the nastiest look and turned to Grandma, saying, "I'm not stupid enough to tell my wife to go back home."

With a loud groan and my heart aching with regret, I asked, "What do I do? At least give me something."

After a minute of silence, Ekta Kaki cleared her throat. "Maybe you should do a grand gesture."

"Grand gesture?" I asked, utterly confused.

But apparently, I was the idiot of the Mishra family because my mother, Radhika Kaki, Ria, and Abhi exclaimed in delight, "Yes. Oh my god, yes."

Seeing my confusion, Maa asked, "Haven't you seen your wife read so many romance novels?"

"And?" I asked.

An evil look crossed my mother's eyes, which scared me to my bones. "You know what, beta? Pick any ten books from your wife's bookshelf and read them. Come to us once you're done with that, and then we'll help you."

"But..." I started to argue.

But Abhi gave a quick and hard slap on my back and said, "Wow, Mummy. You are a genius."

All the ladies of the house now had a smile on their faces, and no matter how evil, they shed a tiny spark of hope in my chest.

"We need to bring her back fast, Maa. It would take me days to read ten books, and she'll only get angrier," I tried to reason with her.

Wiping her face, Maa got up from the floor and said, "Then maybe you should read them quickly."

"Don't worry about work. We'll handle it. Don't want you to get too used to all that control and power. You're officially on leave till we get our daughter back," Dad announced, getting a round of applause from everyone.

"Do you want a few recommendations, beta?" Ekta Kaki asked, making Maa laugh.

With literally nothing better to do, and needing the help of my family to get my wife back home, I got up from the floor and moved toward the staircase.

Quickly, I turned to Ekta Kaki. "Umm. Kaki. I'll take some recommendations."

33

Song: Raat Hamari Toh
- *K.S. Chitra & Swanand Kirkire*

Kriti

Two days had gone by with radio silence from Aakar. Not even a message. Not even a call. Nothing. With every hour that he didn't attempt to reach out to me, I started to lose hope. My fear was that I'd have to admit the truth that my husband had sent me back home to my family. These emotions were minuscule compared to the hurt and anger brewing in my heart.

I had started to see worry lines on Maa's face, especially now that the weekdays had officially started, and I wasn't going back to school. Especially when it was extremely rare for me to skip school.

It was the third night since I was back home, and everyone in the house was asleep when my phone vibrated with the incoming call.

Aakar calling...

My heart beat so loudly that I was afraid it would wake Rati up.

I quickly silenced the vibration and stared at the name of my husband lighting up the screen. My fingers shook as I tried to make a decision. On the one hand, I was dying to hear his voice. But on the other hand, I was so fucking furious that I just knew if I heard his voice, I'd accidentally throw my phone out the window.

So before the call could drop, I deliberately ended the call just to drive the point home.

In the next minute, I got a notification.

> Aakar: I miss your voice, baby. I'm really sorry.

Then you shouldn't have sent me back, asshole.

A blue tick showed under the message, indicating to him that I'd read the message.

Because I didn't have anything else to say to him, I stayed quiet.

After just ten seconds of waiting, another message from him popped up.

> Aakar: I know you're extremely mad at me. As you should be. And you definitely shouldn't forgive me. I know I handled myself in the worst possible way imaginable. But please tell me there's a shred of hope left for us.

I read and reread his messages. I knew Aakar never gave apologies for the sake of it. And I did believe he was sorry. But this wasn't the first time he'd reacted so poorly, and I could only bear so much.

Refusing to reply to him, I kept the chat open, my heart waiting for more of his words. Despite the fight, despite the insults, and despite his harsh words, my heart was starving for his words. My heart was stupid like that. It only knew how to love. Now, if only it could learn how *not* to love.

> Aakar: I know my apologies mean nothing if I keep making the same mistakes again and again.

How the fuck was this asshole able to read my mind?

> Aakar: Just know that I'm working on myself, Kriti. I'm going to be better for you. All you've ever done is be there for my family, treat them like your own, and like a selfish, controlling jerk, I've stood in your way. That won't be happening ever again. I promise.

> Aakar: Please reply, baby. Even if it's one word. Or even just to tell me to fuck off. This silence is killing me.

He was a master of pretty words, my husband. And I refused to give him an inch. Nobody had ever disrespected me to this extent, and I refused to bear the brunt of his emotions that were too difficult for him to handle.

Even so, I slept soundly for the first time in two nights.

~

THE FOLLOWING two days passed with several missed calls from Aakar, or more like calls that I deliberately didn't pick up, and a constant stream of messages that popped up on my phone literally every half an hour. And with every passing day, I was getting entirely too desperate for his texts.

> Aakar: I miss waking up next to you, baby.

> Aakar: I was an asshole who let his emotions control his actions. None of which were kind.

Aakar: I'm sorry for hurting you.

Aakar: Please pick up my call.

Aakar: I need you, Kriti. In our bed. In our home. In my life.

Aakar: I hate myself.

While I was desperate for Aakar's texts, Maa and Pappa were desperate for me to return home. But how did I tell them that I was mad at my husband for being an insensitive, immature jerk and that I was tempted not to leave for the next year because I couldn't bear to look at his face?

It was the morning of my sixth day at my place, and Maa, Pappa, and I were drinking chai when Maa cleared her throat. Knowing she was trying to catch my attention, I looked at her. "What is it, Maa?"

With pursed lips, and after meeting my dad's eyes, she turned to me and said, "When are you going back home?"

With raised eyebrows, I said, "I thought I was already home."

Her glare could've eviscerated a weaker soul. "You know exactly what I mean. Has something happened between Aakar and you? Did you two fight?"

With a steady voice, I asked, "What makes you think that?"

Even though Dad wasn't saying anything, his eyes volleyed between the two of us. "Because I rarely see you talking on the phone with him. You used to talk more with him when you were engaged. And these past few days, all you do is stare at your phone."

Before I could say anything, Dad added, "You haven't smiled once since you came back."

I gave him a smile, to which he replied, "A real smile, beta. The one where your eyes light up."

This wasn't good. Dad was looking at me like he just knew I

was lying. I didn't know how to give him a real smile when I spent the majority of my day in a constant state of anxiety, hurt, disappointment, and rage. But I was terrified of disappointing my parents even more. Maa would kill me if she found out that I sucked so bad at being a wife that my husband asked me to leave.

My throat closed up at the thought of speaking the truth. The expectant look in Maa's and Dad's eyes had my heart pounding and my hands shaking when the doorbell rang.

Saved by the bell. I sighed in relief as Maa got up and went to open the door.

I shrank into myself and started surfing through my phone, just to get my dad to stop looking into my soul. I was about to ramble out all the truth on the spot with the way he was looking at me, I swear.

"Oh my god, Aakar Kumar!" Maa's shriek dropped like a bomb in my chest.

At the rise of my dad's eyebrows, I quickly schooled my facial expression, gave him a big—albeit fake—smile, and braced myself.

Walking behind my mom, my husband entered.

~

Aakar

The moment I entered Kriti's living room, my eyes found Kriti. While her lips were stretched in a polite smile, her eyes glared daggers at me. With the way that Kriti's mom welcomed me with a smile and the way Kriti's dad folded his newspaper and stood to greet me, I knew she hadn't told them anything.

And didn't that make me feel even worse of an asshole?

Keeping my stride confident, I touched Kriti's dad's feet in respect and shook his hand. Once that was done, I looked at

Kriti. She looked about ready to strike me and claw me to shreds. But knowing that she wouldn't do anything in front of her parents, feigning confidence and keeping my gait natural so as not to alert her parents, I walked to Kriti, my legs quite literally shaking, bent down, and pressed a kiss to her forehead.

The moment my lips brushed against her skin and my wife's distinct smell hit me, I finally felt at home. My heart leaped and bounced in my chest with joy, while deep within me, my soul settled.

I took a seat on the sofa right beside Kriti while Kriti's—and now my—mom and dad took a seat on the sofa right across from us.

Her mom's face was shining with delight. "So, Aakar Beta, Kriti didn't tell us you were coming. If I'd known, I would've cooked something special for breakfast."

I told Maa, "It's no problem, Maa. I didn't even tell her. It was a surprise."

"What a wonderful surprise, beta. Right, Kriti?" Maa asked, her eyes glinting with joy.

I looked at Kriti and saw a sort of calm acceptance on her face as she gave her mother a small smile. "Yep. A wonderful surprise, indeed."

While Maa looked delighted, Dad looked doubtful. I could sense that he felt the tension between Kriti and me.

So when our eyes met, he asked, "So you'll stay for lunch, right?"

And because I had promised Dad that I'd take care of his daughter and knew I had failed horribly, I quickly gave him a nod. "Definitely, Pappa."

At that, Kriti jumped out of her seat. "I'll go pack everything."

Once she left the living room, Maa went to the kitchen, leaving me with Pappa.

When Pappa didn't say a word and went back to his newspaper, I quickly opened my phone and went to our group chat.

> Me: I've arrived and told her I've come to take her back home.

Maa: What did she say?

Abhi: And?

Ria: Could you type any slower?

Dad: What are you waiting for? What did she say?

> Me: She's packing right now.

There was a beat of silence for a second before a barrage of texts started flooding the chat.

Abhi: Doesn't sound right to me. Am I the only one?

Maa: Definitely doesn't sound right.

Ria: Are you sure you heard correctly?

Ekta Kaki: I thought she would make him grovel.

Radhika Kaki: Doesn't seem like Kriti.

Abhi: Bhabhi was really mad when I went to get her. Told me she's not coming back.

Maa: You better not mess it up, Aakar.

Dad: I don't trust this boy.

Maa: I knew sending him alone was a bad idea. We should've gone with him.

Ria: Let's give him a chance, everyone.

Abhi: I don't trust bhai. AT ALL!

The sound of a throat clearing had me looking up to find Pappa staring straight at me.

> Me: Gtg.

> Maa: What?

> Ekta Kaki: What does he mean?

> Dad: This boy.

> Abhi: Maa…He means he's got to go.

After a tense silence, Pappa spoke up, "Something happened, didn't it?"

Because I didn't have the heart to lie to Kriti's father, I looked down at my feet and nodded.

"You messed up." His voice was firm yet gentle.

I looked up to meet his eyes and nodded, trying to show him how sorry I was through my eyes.

"You hurt her really bad, Aakar."

His words squeezed my heart and throat in a vise, choking me with guilt and regret.

"I did, Pappa. I'm trying to make up for it."

He nodded and folded his hands at his chest. "If she tells me she doesn't want to go back, I'm not letting you take her."

I nodded. "I know, Pappa. I'd never force her. I'm here to make up for my mistake."

He harrumphed. "You better. My daughter hasn't smiled since she got back."

Sharp pain akin to a thousand needles pierced my heart, leaving me gasping for my next breath. The guilt was drowning me, and all I wanted to do was make my wife smile at me.

And because I knew Pappa and I both wanted the same thing—Kriti's smile—I leaned closer to him and asked, "I did hurt her bad, and I'm really here to make up with her. But how come she's so agreeable? I won't lie; I expected a little fight."

That got a smile out of Pappa, albeit reluctantly. "Oh, she will definitely give you a fight."

With that, he flipped open his newspaper and returned to his reading, leaving me gaping at him.

I spent the rest of the day in blind anxiety. Every time my eyes met Kriti, I worried she would decline to return home with me. Even when Rati and Kartik returned from school, and we all sat to eat together, I feared Kriti would decide to stay after all. And what terrified me the most was how she didn't glare at me. At all. She was extremely passive, and that in and of itself was downright terrifying.

She did everything that I actually prayed she would do, that was, readily come home with me. But now that she was actually doing that, it didn't sit right with me.

> Me: She's being too agreeable. I'm scared.

> Abhi: As you should be.

> Me: Shut up, Abhi.

> Maa: Don't talk to your brother like that, Aakar. This is all your doing.

Fuck.

> Me: What do I do?

> Dad: What CAN you do?

> Maa: Just let it play out.

We said goodbye to her parents and siblings, and I put her bag in the trunk of the car.

Once I started the car and we left her house behind, the resounding silence was nerve-wracking. My throat dried up, and my hands gripped the steering wheel as I thought about how to start apologizing.

But before I could get a word out, Kriti said, "Take me to your village house."

My heart stopped. Blood rushed to my ears, making them hot. "What? Why?"

I quickly looked at her, but I found her staring out the window. "Because that's where I'd like to go."

I gulped. My heart raced as I tried to formulate a response. "But I thought you were coming home with me."

With not a single inflection in her tone, voice more frigid than ice, she said, "You thought wrong."

"Kriti..."

"Now."

One word.

One word as cutting as the sharpest sword.

One word, and I knew how much I hurt her.

One word that shredded my pride.

One word that no matter how much it hurt, I obeyed.

I turned the car around and took her to our ancestral home in the village. I realized her whole charade on our way to the house, which did give me a tiny sliver of hope. She hadn't told her family about what I did and didn't want to worry her parents now, which my mind translated to the fact that she didn't plan to stay with her family.

But Kriti was too mad at me to step foot inside our home, which only left her with our ancestral home.

When I was a kid, my grandmother used to tell me stories about kings and queens. In the stories, the king would often do something stupid, enraging the queen. The queen would have a special palace or a room called *kop bhavan*, which translated to sulking room, where she would go to brood and sulk until the king groveled to the queen's satisfaction.

And apparently, our ancestral home would be *my* queen's kop bhavan.

Once we reached the house, I quickly got out, hoping to open the car door for her. Of course, she beat me to it and started making her way toward the main door.

I rushed behind her and quickly unlocked the door to our house as she silently waited behind me.

Once unlocked, she went in while I went back to the car to get her suitcase.

Pulling out my phone, I opened the chat. Just the thought of giving the latest update to my family had me breaking out in hives. I ignored the slew of messages that had appeared in my absence.

> Me: Umm. We're at our ancestral home.

Abhi: What are you doing there?

Maa: What happened?

> Me: She refused to come back home with me. But she told me to take her to our ancestral home in the village.

Ria: I KNEW it. I knew Kriti wasn't a pushover.

> Me: How long do you think she will want to stay here?

Maa: As long as it takes.

Dad: It's not like you've got anything better to do.

Abhi: I'd be surprised if bhai manages to get bhabhi home.

I waited for Maa to defend me.

> Me: Are you not going to say something to him, Maa?

Maa: I'm afraid, beta, I'm with Abhi on this one.

Without replying in the group chat, I closed the app, got her suitcase and mine from the trunk, and went inside the house to face my very angry, very hurt wife.

The moment I stepped inside, I was met with silence. I looked around the living room and the kitchen, the dining and the bedrooms downstairs, but found nothing.

"Kriti?" I called out.

But nothing. Not a peep.

I rushed upstairs and found all the doors to the bedrooms open except for one at the end of the hallway.

I quietly walked toward it, my heart thumping in my chest. I gave a few quick raps of my knuckle on the door. "Kriti?"

A rustle came from inside, and I quickly straightened myself before the door opened, and I was met with my wife, her face devoid of emotion. Like a perfect statue. "Yes?"

The blood in my veins froze at the arctic chill in her voice. Like a fumbling idiot, I completely blanked out on what to say. "Umm. I came here to apologize."

"Don't. You're not forgiven. If there's nothing else…"

Ouch. I quickly reacted. "Of course there is. Umm. We need to eat dinner."

"I'm afraid I've lost my appetite."

I pity all the students my wife taught.

At my silence, she cocked her head to the side. "Was there anything else you needed?"

"Umm…Where would I sleep?"

At that, I was met with the slam of the door in my face.

Fuck.

It was going to be a long few days.

34

Song: Tum Tak
- *Javed Ali, Keerthi Sagathia & Pooja AV*

Kriti

> Aakar: Please join me for dinner.

I stared at the text message. I'd heard the doorbell ring about an hour ago. Aakar had probably ordered in. It was nine o'clock, and I was starting to get hungry. Why did I have to tell Aakar I'd lost my appetite? Right, because I was furious with him.

How dare he?

How dare he just drop by my house without asking me? On the one hand, my heart jumped with joy and excitement at seeing him, all haggard and tired-looking. On the other hand, I didn't want to see his stupid, impulsive asshole face again.

The moment he entered my house, my body instinctively wanted to jump into his arms. I missed us. I missed his strong presence in my bed. I missed the way he always held me and kissed my neck before sleeping. I missed the way he kissed my head in front of his entire family when he got home from work. I missed working with him. I missed the way we bantered and spent time with his siblings. I missed the way his eyes shone with delight when his mom praised Abhi or when he saw his grandparents laughing.

I knew how much he loved and cared about his family. But was I not his family as well? I did realize that he panicked when Abhi came out to him. But that still didn't give him the right to disrespect me.

My stomach growled louder. Grrr. I freshened up a bit and changed into my sexy pajama set of silky shorts and a cute top. If he was going to see me, he better suffer.

The moment I stepped foot downstairs and followed the delicious smell of some Indo-Chinese into the dining room, I realized my vast error in judgment.

I should've known when I put on my sexy pajamas. If I was here to make him suffer, Aakar had come prepared to seduce. Because my husband had reheated the food and was setting the table while wearing his soft white T-shirt that stretched across his broad chest and bulging biceps and his gray sweatpants that hugged his hips like sin.

Fuck.

Why did I think forgoing a bra was a good idea? Now, he was clearly going to see the effect he had on me.

Stupid. Stupid. Stupid.

Before I could think of turning back around to get a shrug to cover my now very erect nipples, Aakar turned and met my eyes.

Our eyes held, and then his gaze slowly traversed to my chest and my betraying nipples. His hand clenched tight around the bowl that he held as his eyes darkened with fiery lust. My thighs squeezed together to try to control the wetness seeping into my underwear at an alarming rate.

No. I was mad at him. I refused to get turned on by Aakar. No matter what he wore or how he looked at me.

His eyes were now pools of hunger and regret, so seeing how affected he was, I strode into the dining room to get to the kitchen on the other side.

"Umm. I've ordered plenty for both of us."

And because I really loved Chinese, and I really, really didn't want to cook, I sighed and grabbed a plate off the dining table. Silently, I filled my plate with Hakka noodles and some fried rice with Manchurian gravy on top of it.

I sat at the table and dug in without waiting for Aakar.

I kept my head down, refusing to look at his face. I saw his hips moving around the dining table in my periphery as he got his plate of food ready, and then I felt him sit on the chair right beside mine so I couldn't ignore his presence any longer.

Now, our legs were dangerously close to touching, and despite the intense aroma of the Chinese food right in front of me, my senses were assaulted by *his* smell of the gentle ocean breeze on a summer morning. I did not love it. At all. I hated it. So much so that I scooted my chair slightly away from him.

And of course, he followed me and sat even closer to me. So now our elbows brushed together.

An irritating growl escaped my lips as I shoveled food into my mouth faster. The faster I ate, the faster I could lock myself in the bedroom upstairs.

Thankfully, he didn't do or say anything. He let me eat in peace, letting my mind stew in its ever-growing hurt and anger.

The moment I was done eating, I got up to put the plate in the sink in the kitchen. I heard quiet footsteps following me.

"You're being creepy," I murmured.

He murmured, "I was just done eating."

Sure, he was. I'd seen his plate. He barely ate.

I washed my hands and was almost out of the dining room when he followed me. "Kriti, please talk to me."

I turned around, feeling his eyes on every part of my body. "When do you leave?" I asked.

Determination filled his eyes. "Whenever you're ready to come back home."

A harsh chuckle came out of me. "It's home now, is it?"

I quickly turned around, but his strong hand captured mine. He quickly moved behind me so his entire front touched my back, causing blood to rush through my veins. I desperately wanted to push back in his embrace, feel his heat, his warmth. But I held myself perfectly still. He gently brushed his lips on my shoulder and whispered, "It's always been your home, baby."

I pulled out of his embrace as all the hurt and the anger boiled over. "Bullshit."

I raced up to the room, with him following closely. I turned back and looked him in the eyes. "Go back to your house, Aakar."

He quickly reached me and pushed me against the door to the bedroom. "*You* are my home, Kriti. I'll be wherever you are. I'm not leaving this place. Not without you."

"And what are you going to tell your family?"

His lips pursed as if he were biting back his words. But his eyes shone with determination and resolve as he said, "The truth."

My heart beat louder with his words. "Sorry, what?"

He moved his hand from my wrist to my upper arms and neck as he held me firmly. "They know the truth."

Sudden worry for Abhi had me clutching his wrist. "You told them about Abhi?"

He quickly shook his head. "Sorry, no. Nothing about Abhi."

As I frowned in confusion, he pulled back and dragged me into the bedroom and sat me on the small couch across from the bed while he sat on the floor at my knees. His seating arrangement didn't escape my notice.

He didn't let go of my hand as he said, "I told everyone that we had a fight about something and that I asked you to leave and go to your house."

I cringed as I heard the words coming out of his mouth. The memory of his sharp words stung me even deeper. My lips trembled as I feared knowing what his family thought about me. "What...What did they say?"

Aakar's eyes had a world of heartbreak and regret in them, yet he gave a self-deprecating smile when he said, "Maa gave me a tight slap across the face."

A gasp escaped me. Aakar was the embodiment of *the perfect son*. He believed he was the responsible one. He never made mistakes. That one slap would've hurt his very soul.

And before I could process, he added with an embarrassed smile, "In front of the entire family."

"Aakar," I gasped louder. No grown man deserved to be slapped by his mother. *Maybe he does.*

He quickly bent his head and brushed a kiss on my hand. "It was very well-deserved, don't you think?"

And before I could stop myself, a tired laugh escaped me. "It kinda was. I would've loved to see that."

"If it helps my case, she also hit me multiple times on my chest."

I rolled my eyes. "That doesn't count."

"And I've been banished from the office, and Dad and the kakas have taken over all the work."

"No way." Shock had me in a chokehold as Aakar laid out one thing after another.

"I've been forbidden from doing anything until I bring their daughter home."

That did it. All the hurt, all the anger, all the crushing disappointment, and the utter humiliation and disrespect I felt, all of it tore through my chest and burst out of me. Tears poured out of my eyes as I clutched my head.

My heart squeezed in my chest, relieved and ecstatic that I had a new family who supported the truth and the right, not just their son. That they considered me as their own daughter. All my growing affection for them, my new family, and my actions to help and protect them weren't one-sided. It proved that they loved me. I truly felt like a part of my new family at this moment, knowing what they did for me despite having already left their house.

As I let all my hurt pour out of me, Aakar clutched my knees and placed kisses on my lap. He held my hand and placed kisses on top of my hand, all the while muttering, "I'm so sorry, Kriti. I'm so sorry, baby. I never should've asked you to leave."

I scoffed as a defeated chuckle escaped me. "But you did, Aakar. You asked me to go back home. Without any hesitation. Without thinking for a single second about what I would tell my family. Without thinking about my job. Without giving me any indication of how long you wanted me gone. You just sent me home."

A tear escaped his eyes as he clutched my hand as if his life depended on it. "I know. I don't know what came over me. Believe me, I don't even expect you to forgive me, Kriti. How can I when I can't even forgive myself? I want you to stay mad at me for as long as you want. Just come back home. You belong with me. Your home is with us. And I was out of my ever-loving mind for asking you to leave."

Tears steadily streamed down my cheeks. His words were everything I wanted to hear. I could see the regret in his eyes. I could feel his anguish for what he did. But he'd broken my heart. My trust in him was shredded to pieces. I removed my hand from his grip, and a wounded noise escaped his lips. I clutched my stupid silk shorts that I shouldn't have worn. They made me feel naked and hot at a really wrong time.

I got up from the couch and sat on the bed across from it, trying to put some distance between us. "What if you send me back again?"

He almost jumped off the floor as he rushed to say, "I won't."

Shaking my head, I asked, "What if there's another big secret that I hide from you? What if that secret could ruin your family?"

He clenched his hand in a tight fist, his jaw sharpened, and he shook his head. "I don't care. I trust you. You would do whatever is right for the family."

I gave a humorless laugh. "Even right now, it's so difficult for you to say those words. You don't really mean that. You wouldn't be okay if I kept secrets from you. It would kill you, and then, you'd end up hating me or blaming me."

At that, he jumped to his feet and dropped to his knees where I sat on the bed. He clutched my knees, his large, warm hands on my bare skin causing a gasp to escape my lips. He tightened his hold on me and vehemently shook his head. "Never. Yes, it would kill me to know you kept secrets from me. But that's *nothing* compared to spending a moment of my life without you in it. I'd rather you kept a thousand secrets from me than having to sleep alone in my cold, lonely bed ever again."

His words sounded so fucking earnest, so heartfelt, my own heart pounded in my chest. I traced the veins popping on the back of his hand, one of the infinite things that I loved about him, as I looked at his hands on my skin. I then looked at him as I whispered, "You told me you loved me. Even before we got married, you told me you loved me. Even after we got married, you told me you loved me. Before going to sleep, before I left for school, every time we made love, you said you loved me. I don't think you know what love is, Aakar."

"Please don't," he whispered. His voice broke, and tears flooded his eyes.

I still couldn't stop. "You can't love someone you don't trust."

He shook his head in denial, and I gently held his cheek, my heart breaking as I said the words that had been haunting me for days, "You don't love me, Aakar."

I stopped him from denying it by putting a finger on his lips, my vision blurring with the tears flooding my eyes. His eyes reflected the same pain, but I couldn't bear for him to deny this. I shook my head at him. "If you truly loved me, you would've trusted me. If you loved me, you'd have never asked me to leave. Never. Because I couldn't bear the thought of hurting you. Everything I did, I did it for you. Be it caring for your father and uncles or supporting your brother. Be it finding new hobbies with Maa and the kakis or going shopping with Ria. Every person who I tried to connect with, that I tried to support, was all for *you*. Every action and decision I made was to make *your* burdens lighter. It was to give *you* a moment of peace. It was to try to be a good partner. A good wife. A good daughter-in-law. I fell in love with your family and treated them as my own because I fell in love with *you* first. And it breaks my heart to know that the person I really love doesn't even understand the meaning of love."

With that, I climbed farther onto the bed, got under the blanket, and turned around to sleep. I didn't want to cry over Aakar. I'd promised myself not to shed a tear over him. But putting all of my feelings out there crushed me even more. The stupid tears wouldn't stop leaking from my eyes. It hurt. My heart ached so bad it felt like someone was tearing it out of my chest.

"Can I…Can I please sleep with you, baby?" His voice broke.

His request had my limbs aching with the need to be held. I

missed being in his arms at night. And I really needed to be held right now. I didn't want to be alone. "Okay," I whispered.

In the next moment, the bed dipped behind me, and I was pulled into the inferno of his hot chest and warm hands.

"Aakar," I sighed, not expecting him to do that.

He nuzzled at the junction of my neck and shoulder, the brush of his beard creating havoc inside my mind, body, and soul. "Please. Please let me hold you. Just for five minutes. Please."

And because I had missed sleeping with his arms holding me, his legs tangled with mine, his heart beating at my back, and the soft nuzzling of his face against my neck, I nodded. "Five minutes."

He brushed his lips against my neck and pulled me even closer in his embrace. My heart squeezed painfully in my chest. How could his embrace feel so much like love? Why did his arms around me, the way he clutched me tightly at the waist, feel like he'd die if I wasn't in his arms? Why did his chest collapse against my back at the first brush of his lips against my neck? Why did my eyes tear up even more when I felt wetness sliding down the back of my neck?

And why did he feel so much like home? So much so that I slipped into his warmth when I closed my eyes and finally slept for the first time in what felt like ten days.

∾

Aakar

My body roused with my hard cock flush against my wife's ass. I nuzzled into her for a second before the previous night barrelled into my brain.

Her tears. Her claims that I didn't love her. That I didn't even know the meaning of love.

Fuck that.

I loved Kriti. I loved my wife to the point of madness. I wouldn't feel like my life had lost its meaning without her in it if I didn't love her. I wouldn't feel like death would be an easier choice than leaving without her if I didn't love her. I wouldn't feel like the king of the world every time she gave me a smile if I didn't love her. I wouldn't be burying my face in her pillow just to be able to close my eyes at night if I didn't love her.

Yes, I screwed up. Royally.

But surely, I wasn't the first man in love who fucked up.

I was ready to beg every single day to convince Kriti to come back home with me.

I was ready to build her a new place if she'd rather not live with my family.

But I refused to let my wife think I didn't love her.

I loved her.

And it was time I made her believe it.

Placing a featherlight kiss on her shoulder, I quietly got out of bed and went downstairs. After freshening up, I started to prepare chai and breakfast.

I put the potatoes on to boil as I quickly prepared the dough to make aloo paratha.

As the potatoes were still boiling, I opened my phone to check what I predicted would be a hundred missed messages.

Two hundred and thirty-six missed messages.

Ignoring all of them, I sent my own message in our thread.

> Me: I have a plan. And I'll need you guys.

I didn't have to wait more than three seconds before messages started to flood in.

> Abhi: When? Now?

Maa: What's the plan?

Dad: You better tell your mother your plan before doing anything. I'm afraid you'll make everything worse.

Ekta Kaki: Is it a romantic plan?

Maa: It better be a romantic plan.

Me: I'll send you guys the details in the afternoon. I'm preparing aloo paratha for Kriti.

Maa: Do you even know how to make aloo paratha?

Abhi: Maa, there's online videos and recipes.

Maa: Still. Don't mess it up, Aakar.

Radhika Kaki: Are you making coriander chutney with it, Aakar?

Me: Um, no. I was planning to serve it with yogurt and chai.

Before they could start giving me any more culinary suggestions beyond my expertise, I got out of the chat.

Once I had prepared the potato mixture with all the spices, I rolled the dough and added the filling. After I had prepared a few parathas, I started on the chai.

Thankfully, Kriti was still asleep.

As the chai boiled on the stove, I decorated a tray with parathas, yogurt, ketchup, and some mango pickle I found in the fridge.

Once the chai was done, I poured it into a kettle that I found at the back of a shelf while I was looking for flour.

Checking that the stove was off and I'd cleaned up the kitchen, I carried the tray of food upstairs. As I entered the room, I found Kriti still asleep, her face buried under my pillow.

I couldn't have stopped the smile that took over my face even if I tried. I missed the view. I missed seeing Kriti sleeping, the way she started with her head on the pillow but would bury her face under it by the middle of the night. I gently placed the tray on the side table and climbed under the blanket.

My movement jostled her a little, and she let out an adorable moan, turned in the other direction, and pulled the blanket over her head. I lay down beside her and placed a kiss on the blanket over her arm. "Wake up, baby."

"What do I smell?" she mumbled from under her blanket.

I pulled at the blanket so I could see her face. Softly pressing my lips to her forehead, I said, "Breakfast in bed. Open your eyes."

She immediately opened her eyes, surprise and disbelief etched in the lines on her forehead.

I brushed those lines to smooth them out and smiled at how adorable and mine she looked. "Sit up."

Her lips twitched in an almost smile, and I did cartwheels in my mind.

Once she sat, her sexy-as-sin blouse barely covering her tits and the blanket pooling at her hips had my cock go rock fucking hard. I picked up the tray and placed it on the bed between us.

Her jaw was wide open as I poured the chai into two cups. "You did this?"

I brushed a soft kiss to her lips, loving the look of barely concealed delight on her face. "I did. You like it?"

She gave me the barest of a nod.

"Want me to serve you the parathas?"

"I…I'll go freshen up first."

With that, she jumped off the bed and rushed into the bathroom.

I heard some mumbling from the bathroom, and I quickly jumped off the bed and stepped on the other side of the door.

"Did you say something, baby?"

"N...Nothing."

I chuckled, knowing in the deepest part of my soul that she was impressed. That she wanted to smile.

I was ready to do whatever it took to make my wife believe that I loved her.

I quickly got back on the bed and started sipping my chai. The moment she was out, I served her the parathas, the yogurt, and the chai.

Usually, she would fill the silence with conversation.

But today, she was silent. Her eyes were on the food as she ate, and I desperately needed them on me.

I took a sip of my chai and cleared my throat. "Abhi and I had a talk after...after you left."

She glared at me, and I quickly corrected myself, hating the words coming out of my mouth. "After I sent you away."

She nodded as she continued eating and sipping her chai. "And?"

I shook my head thinking about the day. "Well, it was more like Abhi screamed and shouted at me for sending you away and broke down."

And before she could interrupt or give me her piece of mind, I continued, "You might think that I'm the biggest asshole for not accepting my brother for who he is. But that's not true."

When I met her eyes, she was looking at me. "I love my brother. I'd take a bullet for him. I'd fight the whole world for him. Of course, I don't care who he loves. It's just that the prospect of him having to face the bigotry, the discrimination, the cruelty from people who don't understand, terrified me. I couldn't bear the thought of someone hurting Abhi. Especially our own family. These are the people who could barely handle the fact that their daughter loved an American boy. These are the people who have prejudices against people of different religions. They wouldn't understand or accept Abhi. I'm terrified of what his being gay would do to Mummy and Pappa. Our family would be broken, Kriti. And I wouldn't be able to do anything."

"Abhi deserves to live his truth, Aakar."

I nodded. "I know. I agree."

"And we don't know if he plans to come out to the entire family. All he cared about was your opinion."

"And I completely ruined my response. I was terrified, Kriti. I should've listened to you then. You told me to stop thinking and just hug him. And I should've done that. I should've trusted you. And now, I'm left with a brother who can't stand me and a wife who can't trust me."

She sniffled, and her eyes shone with tears. But she didn't say a word. We ate in silence for a while as she polished off her chai and a paratha. Once we were done, I placed the food tray on my nightstand and sat facing Kriti, who was still quiet.

I hated her silence.

Gingerly, I slid my hand to where her hand rested on the blanket. When she didn't pull away, I said a silent prayer and took her hand in mine. "All my life, I've heard the phrase *Aakar, you're older. Aakar, you need to take care of your sister and brother. Aakar, you're older. We rely on you. Aakar, you're older, and you need to step into your father's shoes. Aakar, you're older, and you need to be here for the family. Aakar, if you leave the house, who's going to take care of this family.* The more I stood up for my family, the more validation I got. The better I felt about my place in the family. And the more responsible I felt for their well-being. I guess, to the point where I felt like they needed me. That I was the only one who could take care of this family.

"And then, you came along. Yes, I looked at arranged marriage as a way to appease Mom. But I chose you because *I* wanted you. For myself. For every selfish reason. Because you make me happy. You make me want to have fun. You make me want to be selfish. And when we got married, I stupidly put you in the box with my family. I included you among the people who *I* needed to care for, be responsible for. Not someone who also cared for me. Who wanted to care for my family *together*. And instead of putting all my trust in you, I hurt you. Despite making the same mistake once, I was stupid enough to make it again."

Tears streamed down her cheeks. "I'm afraid you will never be able to trust me with your family. I'm afraid of how you will react the next time I keep a secret about your family. I'm afraid these are all empty words coming out of your guilt, and nothing will change. And what I'm afraid of the most is that I'd always be afraid of your reactions. I'd always be afraid of being thrown out of your house."

Every word from her mouth was a dagger to my chest, slicing my heart over and over again. *I* made my wife afraid of me, and I hated myself for it. I climbed off the bed and circled to her side and sat near her hip. My wife looked defeated. *Defeated*. All because of my ego. I clutched her hand and got down on my knees at the side of the bed. "Baby, look at me."

Her eyes were wet with tears when they met mine.

My voice wavered when I spoke, "Every day without you was torture. Every night without you in my arms was pure hell. Food lost all taste. Work lost all its meaning. Life lost all its color. Baby, *I'm* the one who's afraid. I'm downright terrified of spending a single day without you. *You* hold all the power, Kriti. *You* could tear my entire world apart by choosing not to be with me. *You* could make me the most pathetic loser in this world by deciding to get rid of me, or *you* could make me the king of this world just by forgiving me and giving me a second chance. You say you're afraid of me throwing you out of the house again. First, I hate that I've driven you to call our home *a house*. It's *your home*. But, baby, there *is* no home without you in it. Trust me, jaan, you don't have anything to fear. I'm afraid of being stupid again. I'm afraid of hurting you again. I'm afraid you'd leave me, and I'll be broken."

Tears steadily flowed down my cheeks now, and I knew I looked ugly as fuck. Before I could count more things I was afraid of, Kriti was in my lap, burying her face in my chest and holding me against her. "I'm so mad at you," she cried.

I buried my face in her neck and squeezed her tight to me. "I know, my jaan. And I'm so sorry for messing everything up like this. I'm on my knees begging you to give me one more chance. I need you."

She clutched my T-shirt as she cried in my arms. I pulled out of her hug and held the back of her neck as I met her eyes. "You told me last night that I didn't love you. That I didn't know the meaning of love. You're wrong, baby. If there is only one thing you're wrong about throughout this entire fight, it's you thinking that I don't love you. There is no one, absolutely no one, that I love more than I love you. I'd been living my life just fine before you came into my life. And now, my life is pure fucking torture without you. What do you call it if not love?"

I held her cheeks in my hands, her tears sliding down my palms as my heart twisted painfully in my chest. "I love you, Kriti. I will always love you. Even when I'm stupid, even when I'm angry, even when I'm sad. I will always love you the most."

I closed my eyes, pressed my forehead against hers, and prayed to her. "Tell me you believe me, baby."

I felt her nod. "I believe you."

The sheer relief and happiness at those three words had me pulling her into a kiss. A needy fucking whimper escaped my lips at the first taste of her. Tears escaped my eyes as she opened herself to me and grazed her tongue against mine. Our kiss was pain and passion, hurt and a balm; it was need and hunger and desperation and thirst for more and more.

I wanted to drown in her. I clutched her to me, not leaving a breath of space between us. My need for my wife was all-consuming, needing to claim her back, dying to worship her.

But she quickly pulled away. A pitiful, needy sound escaped my chest at the feel of her loss.

Wiping her tear-stained cheeks, she climbed off my lap. "I'm still mad at you. Just because I believe you love me doesn't mean I'm not mad at you."

With that, she walked into the bathroom and closed the door in my face, leaving me mildly relieved that she at least believed in my love for her and highly desperate to make my wife smile again.

So, like a lost puppy, I stared at the closed bathroom door as she got ready. I rushed through my own shower after she went downstairs, needing to keep her in my sight. I sat near her as she scrolled through her phone and worked on her laptop. The entire time, Kriti gave me the silent treatment.

When lunchtime rolled around, I ordered her a large spicy burger and fries and ate what she ate.

She knew I was sorry and wasn't going anywhere.

Every time she moved, I straightened in anticipation that she was going to talk to me. But she didn't.

My ears ached to hear her voice. I'd rather she scream and shout at me, berate me for being an awful husband. But no, my wife stewed in silence.

So when she was about to climb up the stairs to go back to her room, I couldn't help but stop her. "Um...Would you sit with me downstairs? You can do your own thing. I'll do mine."

Her fists were clenched tight, and a flood of emotions crossed her face. I tried to give her my best puppy-dog eyes. With a sigh, she said, "Fine."

I went to the living room and took a seat on the couch. She was slower to follow but then took a seat on the sofa across from me. I needed her to talk to me, especially after this morning's emotional conversation. And there was probably only one thing that might do the trick.

I gave her a smile and casually grabbed my bag from beside the couch. I could feel Kriti's eyes burning a hole into me, but I kept it casual as I opened my bag and pulled out three of her romance books I brought.

Her gasp had me looking up.

Her eyes were round with shock as she clutched the sofa cushion tight in her fist. "What...Where...What are you doing with my books?"

I put two of them on the coffee table between us and kept my half-read book in my hand. "Oh, these? Umm. I'm reading them, of course."

She let out a loud scoff with a chuckle. "Why?"

I raised my eyebrows at her. "What else am I supposed to do the entire day when I have no work, baby?"

Her cheeks reddened at the *baby*. "You could literally do anything," she muttered.

I flipped the pages of the book and gave her a guilty smile. "Well, it wasn't my idea, to be honest. When I confessed to my family about what I did, Maa and the kakis forbade me from contacting you until I read ten romance books from your shelf. In fact, some of the recommendations came from them."

Kriti's eyes brimmed with tears. "Really?" Her voice shook.

I simply nodded. And just to make her smile, I said, "I've especially been reading a lot of grovel romances."

She burst out laughing. "Really?"

"I'd say it's a very important research material."

"That's true."

"How do you think I'm doing? I've read over ten books so far."

She turned her face away as her cheeks flushed red. She shook her head and mumbled, "It's not so bad."

I was off the couch. "Not so bad? *Not so bad?*"

"Well, if you were mind-blowing, I would be back home with you."

I gasped dramatically and clutched my chest. "You wound me, baby."

And I realized one thing. She finally called our home a home.

She chuckled at my antics and picked up one of her books from the stack on the coffee table. She flipped through the book, and her mouth hung open in shock. "You annotated them?"

Worried that she minded notes in her books, I quickly went to her and took a seat beside her. "I only put them on sticky notes. See? I didn't ruin your book."

Before I could explain further, she grabbed my T-shirt and pulled me into a kiss. I quickly took the book from her hand and placed it on the coffee table, all the while kissing her. I never wanted her to stop. I was starving for a single touch, a single kiss, a single little nip of her teeth on my lip.

Kriti's tongue tangled with mine as she pulled me closer to her. I clutched her waist, and we ended up lying on the couch, making out like teenagers. She panted at my mouth, "Did you like my books?"

I was so wound up as I dragged my hand down her body, lightly grazing her curves, causing her to shiver. "I thought getting a hard-on reading some of these scenes would just be a one-off," I said. Placing a wet kiss on her neck, I sucked the soft skin at her pulse. My pulse thundered at her scent, and I continued, "I was so fucking wrong. The agony these scenes put me through."

Her laughter touched my lips, and I captured them in my mouth. "Fuck, baby. I missed your laugh."

She sobered up at that, and I instantly regretted saying those words. Even though they were true. Softly, I caressed her face. Brushing a stray lock of hair behind her ear, I placed a kiss on her forehead. "I know you're still mad, and you've still not forgiven me, baby. Take your time. I'm not going anywhere."

She played with my T-shirt, her eyes not meeting mine. "It's not that I don't want to forgive you, Aakar. I understand your reaction. And I believe you when you say you'd never send me away again."

"Never."

"But my heart isn't quite there yet."

I placed a kiss on her forehead. "I know what's stopping your heart from forgiving me."

"What?"

I touched her chin to raise her face so she was looking at me and placed a small kiss on her lips. "It's waiting for the grand gesture."

Her eyes widened, and her mouth opened and closed with no words coming out.

I placed my finger on her lips. "Don't worry, baby. I'm gonna give you a grand gesture. You just wait and watch."

35

Song: Tujh Mein Rab Dikhta Ha
   - *Roop Kumar Rathod*

Kriti

I stared at the blades of the fan above, spinning round and round and round, just like my own mind. When I asked Aakar to take me to his ancestral home yesterday, I didn't think he would take up residence with me there.

After finding out that he had read my romance books, to my utter surprise, we actually spent the entire afternoon reading the books. Aakar even prepared coffee, and we discussed the books he'd read. When I told him one of my favorite phrases by a book boyfriend was *Who the fuck did this to you?*, Aakar, to my utter surprise, was shocked.

He'd glared at me and, for the first time since he came to take me back, shouted, "Are you insane? How could you deliberately want to get hurt enough for me to have to say those fucking words? Nope. You take that back. Pick another favorite line."

And just to rile him up further, I said, "How about *Touch her and you die*?"

He was downright glaring when he said, "Oh they *will* die. Now pick something else."

We'd talked back and forth about this for the entire evening while we had dinner at a restaurant, and even when he took me to the same ice cream shop that we went to the day we officially decided to say yes to marriage.

And when we'd returned home, he'd given me a bone-melting kiss that had left me wet and wanting. He made my heart flutter and pound and melt and shiver. I never wanted our conversations to end. He made me want to burrow myself in his arms and forgive him and go back to our home and resume our life.

But I needed some time to collect myself. I need time to think. I needed time to forgive and forget. It was difficult for me to let go, no matter how badly I wanted to.

So, here I was, sleeping alone in the bedroom while Aakar took up the bedroom right next to mine. He'd shouted, "Good night, baby, I love you," a while ago, and here I was, *I love you too* still on the tip of my tongue after what felt like hours but unable to let it out.

Yes, I knew he would apologize because that was Aakar. Even when he asked me to leave his house, I knew he would regret it and come to take me back. I knew he panicked and was out of his mind. I just didn't expect to feel so damn angry and hurt when he asked me to leave.

Seeing my parents worried about us, returning home and not hearing from him for more than a week, I started to wonder day after day whether he would return. All of it just kept building up my anger. I couldn't comprehend how he could stay away from me for so long when my stupid little heart was dying to hear from him despite being furious at him.

So when he stayed here in his house with me, I couldn't tell him to leave me alone. I missed him. I missed seeing his stupid face. I missed seeing his eyes. I missed feeling his arms around me at night. I missed his hard, warm body. I missed the way he looked when he fucked me, like he would die if he had to stay away from me. Like I was the most precious thing he held in his arms.

I loved my husband. I loved being his wife. I loved the life we had. I loved how he stayed. I loved that he literally got down on his knees. Fuck, seeing him on his knees broke me. My strong, beautiful husband cried for me. His tears were like a thousand stabs to my chest.

But he was the one who had hurt *me*. He had shown me over and over again that he didn't trust me with his family. Yes, he'd promised that he would trust me. That he *trusted* me. But all the evidence pointed otherwise. How do I put my trust back in him? I trusted him to always care for me. I trusted him to always give his everything in trying to make me happy. I trusted him with my life. I just wished he trusted *me*.

I didn't even realize when sleep took over, and the next time I opened my eyes, it was to the sound of the birds chirping and the smell of chai.

I quickly freshened up, changed into decent pajamas—because dealing with Aakar in sexy clothes just made me hotter, and I did not need that—and went downstairs to find him at the stove. His hair was in disarray, and his gray fucking sweatpants hugged his ass in a way that always left me drooling. I knew he owned other colored sweatpants, but the asshole knew what he was doing.

I stood beside him near the stove as we watched the chai.

"Good morning, jaan," he said, turning to me and placing the softest kiss on my cheek.

My hands ached to pull him closer and ask him to kiss me harder.

But I stopped myself. "Good morning."

"I have some khaman for breakfast," he said, pointing at the polyethylene bag on the kitchen countertop behind us.

I grabbed the bag, unwrapped everything, served the khaman on a plate, and poured the chutney into a big bowl. By the time I got everything served at the dining table, Aakar got us the chai.

We silently ate the breakfast as Aakar wrapped his legs around mine under the table.

I let him, needing his touch, his presence, to ground me.

I was almost done cleaning up the kitchen when the doorbell rang.

I frowned. No one in the village knew that we were here. I turned to Aakar, and he had a nervous yet hopeful smile. He came to me and held my neck, his thumb caressing my cheek, and gave me a deep kiss. "Get ready for the grand gesture, baby."

He moved toward the door but stopped midway and quickly turned around and said, "If you don't like the gesture, you gotta forget this ever happened and give me another chance. Okay?"

He looked so fucking adorable, I couldn't help but smile. "Okay."

I let out a breath and went to the door. I slowly followed him, too curious. The moment I reached the living room, Aakar opened the door.

And utter chaos flooded into the house.

"What took you so long?" Maa's voice washed over me.

My heart started to beat faster as one after the other, every single member of Aakar's—also my—family started to pour into the house.

"Were you sleeping?"

"Who takes so long to open a door?"

"That too when we told you we were almost here."

The moment they saw me standing in the living room, my

mouth wide open, I was pulled into Maa's arms. Maa held me tightly to her and said in my ear, "Don't worry, beta. We're here now. Everything's going to be just fine."

And I broke down. I clutched her back and cried in her arms, fat teardrops sliding down my cheeks. "I'm sorry I lied to you."

She patted me on the back and swayed me lightly in her arms. "You have nothing to be sorry about, beta. *I* am sorry for the stupidity of my son. But we're going to set him straight, aren't we?"

We pulled out of the hug, and I nodded at her, tears streaming down my face.

She wiped my tears, clutched my hand, and seated us on the couch. The entire family found a seat on the couches, armchairs, and some on the floor. Abhi sat on the armrest of the couch we sat on, his arm across the back of the couch, very clearly picking a side.

Everyone gave me an understanding smile as Maa turned around to glare at Aakar. "Did you apologize?"

Aakar stood alone across from us as if facing an execution. He looked down at his feet and answered, "Yes, Maa."

"Properly?" That was from Pappa.

Aakar looked at Pappa and then at me, raising his eyebrows in question. "Did I apologize properly, Kriti?"

I looked at Pappa and nodded. "He did."

"Good," Pappa said, his arms folded across his chest.

Nobody asked me if I was ready to return home. Nobody asked me if I forgave Aakar.

I looked at Aakar in confusion. He said to be prepared for the grand gesture. I didn't understand what was happening.

Aakar gave me a small smile and cleared his throat. "Kriti, I hurt you. I know I broke your trust. And I know that no amount of me asking you to trust me will make you trust me from the bottom of your heart. I know gaining your trust will take some time, and I'll be working hard every day to get you to trust me again, but I hope this is a small start."

I looked around to find pleased smiles on everyone's faces.

When I looked at Aakar in confusion, he continued, "I have asked every person to share a secret with you, something that I have no clue about and something that would...uh...that would drive me to the brink of my sanity."

My mind froze with utter shock. Abhi nudged my shoulder, and I quickly came to my senses. I shook my head in denial and looked at everyone. "Oh my god, please no. I don't want any of you to share something personal that you don't want to share. Aakar can't ask you to do that. It's a huge invasion of your privacy, and you deserve to keep your secrets."

Maa clutched my hand in hers. "Beta, stop worrying. We're going to share what we feel comfortable with. The secret would just stay between you and the person sharing the secret. None of us know what we're all going to share. We all trust you, beta. And Aakar will watch us sharing our secret with you. And it is up to you whether you want to share the secret with him in the future. Isn't that right, Aakar?"

Aakar got a chair from the dining room, placed it in the farthest corner of the living room, and took a seat.

Maa looked around the room. Everyone got up and moved out of the living room and into the kitchen, leaving Maa and me on the couch and Aakar sitting across from us.

"Keep looking at me, Kriti," Aakar said.

Aakar was bent forward on his seat, his elbows on his lap, hands folded between his spread legs. We looked at each other as Maa came closer to me, put a hand at my ear, and whispered, "I lost my driving license three years ago and have been driving without one ever since."

A gasp escaped me as my mouth hung open.

Aakar's hands tightened, his forehead creasing at my face. I didn't hide the shock on my face.

"Maa," I uttered in shock as she gave me a saucy wink, making me chuckle. How was she not caught? I looked at her and clutched her hand. "We've got to remedy that."

"I trust Kriti," Aakar gritted out from between his wide smile, his foot tapping on the floor.

Maa laughed at him. "Beta, you alright?"

Aakar stretched his legs out, feigning nonchalance. "Of course. Kriti said she'd remedy whatever you're sharing."

Poor guy looked miserable. And the vindictive part inside me rejoiced.

Maa squeezed my hand and walked out of the room.

In walked Pappa. He took a seat beside me and gave me a smile. "You ready, beta?"

I couldn't help but laugh. "Not even a little bit," I said, but moved my ear closer to him.

He bent closer and whispered, "I'm addicted to online gambling."

My brain literally glitched. "Ohmigod, ohmigod."

Aakar's eyes were round with anxiety. I tried hard to school my face, but I must've failed miserably because Pappa said aloud, "You think you could keep this between the two of us, beta?"

Aakar had started to sweat. He clenched his teeth and said, "Yes, Pappa. She won't share it with me."

I looked at Pappa, my eyes wide as saucers, and shook my head. "We'll see, Pappa. I make no promises. We're gonna have to talk about this later."

Pappa looked delighted and simply shrugged his shoulders. I was sure I looked anxious as fuck.

"You alright, baby?" Aakar asked me the moment we were alone.

"Are *you* okay?"

"Splendid."

He didn't *look* splendid.

Abhi entered next.

Aakar immediately grumbled, "You can't have any more secrets that could shock me more."

Abhi winked at him. "I'm a man of many secrets, bhai. None of which you will be privy to from now onwards."

"I am sorry how I reacted, Abhi. I love you, and I'll protect you to death. You know that, right?"

Abhi's eyes shone with tears, but he quickly shook his head and squared his shoulders. "We'll talk once we get bhabhi back."

He took a seat beside me and came closer to my ear. "Bhabhi, I have no new secret but just gasp and make a shocked face. Need to keep Aakar Bhai on his toes."

He was so devious I almost felt bad for Aakar. But I readily obeyed and gasped, "Abhi. Oh my god."

Abhi made an extremely guilty face and ran out the door.

Aakar shook his head and said, "He's never going to forgive me."

"Of course he will. You're his brother, and he loves you."

Aakar was nodding when Radhika Kaki entered. Oh god. I was starting to feel increasingly burdened with every person who came to share a secret with me. The moment kaki took a seat beside me, she asked, "You alright, beta?"

I smiled at her and nodded.

She came closer to me and whispered in my ear, "I occasionally smoke a cigarette with your kaka. Nobody else knows."

And my jaw dropped. "Oh. Uh. Okay."

I so badly wanted to control my reaction so as not to make it worse for Aakar. But our entire family seemed to have decided to drop one truth bomb after another on me, and I felt like I was getting blasted in the face.

Aakar had a hand covering his mouth, pressing his hand tightly on his cheeks.

Next came Ekta Kaki. "I might have become obsessed with

your romance book collection. And I might've read through over half of them. I might've come across some man and man books. And I might've enjoyed them."

This time around, my smile was so big, Aakar also had a big-ass smile on his face. Only kaki was blushing bright red.

So I clutched her hand and gave her a big, excited smile. "We're going to discuss."

Then came Navin Kaka. "I invested ten lakh rupees in a start-up business. I'm too afraid to tell Aakar."

Why were these men's secrets so fucking terrifying? God, this one I'd have to share with Aakar. And it did sound like he was just afraid to share it with Aakar, not that he didn't want me to share it with him.

So I simply nodded at him as he left.

When we were left alone, I quickly met Aakar's eyes and said, "You're going to hate me if I keep some of these secrets."

"Never. You can keep them all to yourself, or you can do something about them on your own, and I wouldn't mind it one bit."

"It must be killing you, though."

He simply chuckled. "Honestly, yes. It is killing me. But I'd take this a thousand times over spending another night without you. If hell existed, it would be a life without you in it."

Fuck. Tears pooled in my eyes, but I quickly wiped them away as I heard footsteps.

Sunil Kaka was next. He didn't have anything to share with me, but he must've talked to Abhi because he too asked me to just act surprised to mess with Aakar. Like the obedient daughter-in-law that I was, I gasped with a hand to my chest.

Then came Ria. "You know how much I hate Zayan. Um. I also find him extremely attractive."

I couldn't help but smile. I'd seen it coming but had kept my mouth shut. I patted her hand and said, "That's okay. We can discuss it more later."

She sighed and rolled her eyes at her situation. With a quick wink at Aakar, making him glower at her, she ran out of the room.

I was left shaking my head at her.

"What if I really don't tell you any of these secrets?" I asked him.

"Baby, you *really* don't have to tell me a single one of them. They're yours."

"And you're okay with it?"

"Yes. I trust you, Kriti. I truly do not care about any of these secrets."

"You would if you knew a single one of them. Our family is a critical case."

He laughed at that. "I know, baby. Join the Mishra Family Monitoring Club."

I laughed at that. "Are you the founder of the club?"

"Yep. And I appoint you the CEO."

I was laughing when Soham, Ria's little brother, walked in. He put his hand to my ear and whispered, "Bhabhi, I failed in two subjects on the last exam. I haven't told Mummy and Pappa."

"Soham," I groaned; the teacher in me was wailing.

He looked at Aakar, who sat there in his full big-brother mode, and ran away.

Grandma entered next. "I was not totally innocent when I married your grandfather, if you know what I mean. Even he doesn't know. Men are stupid like that."

That had me holding my head in my hands, groaning. "Dadi…"

Dadi simply laughed and walked away, leaving me groaning and Aakar laughing.

"What are you laughing at?" I grumbled.

"Your face. You're starting to look increasingly frustrated."

"It's all your fault."

He laughed. "This is the grand gesture, baby. Savor it."

"Savor it, my ass," I mumbled.

I was savoring it, though. The entire family was here for me. Every single one of them was showing their trust in me. They all willingly gave their darkest and deepest parts of themselves to me for safekeeping. Because they trusted me. They believed in my ability to care for them. Love them. They showed me that they would stand by the truth, and no matter what, I was a part of the family.

It was as grand a gesture as it could get.

Next walked in Samar, Ekta Kaki's older son, who still was only ten years old. He sat beside me and said, "I burned Mummy's saree by mistake. I've hid it back in the cupboard. But I don't remember which saree is burnt."

I couldn't help but laugh at that. Poor guy. And poor kaki. She was going to be so mad when she found out.

"Your secret's safe with me, Samar," I said and enacted zipping my mouth shut.

He laughed and ran away.

Then came grandfather. "I don't have a secret, beta. I just wanted to ask you to forgive Aakar and come back home. Sometimes boys are stupid. You should just scold them and move on. Don't put yourself through this agony. We miss you."

"I miss you all too, Dada," I said, my voice shaking as a tear rolled down my cheeks.

He patted my head and walked away.

Last came Dhruv, the youngest of the family at eight years old. "Bhabhi, I peed in my pants in my sleep last night. I changed my clothes myself and didn't tell Mummy. I hid the clothes in Aakar Bhai's cupboard because Mummy said he gave you a time-out and made you cry."

"Really?" I shrieked with laughter.

He nodded, and I pulled him into a hug. My little warrior.

"Give me a kissy," I asked him, offering him my cheek.

He placed an adorable kiss on my cheek and ran off, all the while booing Aakar.

"Seemed like a good secret," Aakar said from his seat, his eyes twinkling with laughter.

"The best one of them all," I said, getting up from my spot and walking to where Aakar sat on the chair since all of the secrets were done.

He stayed rooted to his spot as I took a seat on his lap. He held me by the waist and pulled me closer.

I grazed my hands along his cheek, feeling his beard on my fingers. I brought my lips closer to his so they were almost touching and said, "I love you."

His head bowed at that as he rested his forehead on my shoulder. The sheer relief in his eyes had him closing the distance between us and taking my mouth in a heated kiss. I held his face and pushed my tongue in his mouth, tasting his need, his love for me. "I forgive you."

I kissed his cheeks. I kissed his eyes and licked the lone tear that rolled out of them. "Take me home."

"Tomorrow," he said against my lips. "I need you alone for a little longer."

"Sounds good."

I held his face and gave him a warning glare. "And you promise to never ever send me home like this ever again."

He pulled me closer to him and looked me in the eyes. "Never. I can't promise not to get into a fight with you. But I promise to never ask you to get away from me. Not even to go to another room."

"And if you do?"

"You have my permission to tell my mom about it. Her slaps still terrify me."

I kissed his cheek. "Poor baby."

He snuggled against my neck and said, "You're never allowed to leave me. I won't let you."

I clutched him tight to me. "Sounds good."

"Good."

"Great."

"Awesome."

"Did you guys make up or not? We're dying to come in," Ria's shout came from the other side of the door.

I quickly jumped off his lap and shouted, "C'mon in, everyone."

The entire Mishra family came rushing into the room. "What happened? Are you coming back home, bhabhi?" Abhi asked.

I looked at Aakar, who looked with utmost longing at me. I kept my eyes on him and answered to the entire room, "Yes. Yes, I'm coming back home."

Aakar had me in his arms the next second and twirled me around in front of the entire family. "Yes. Yes. I love you, baby," he whispered in my ear.

I hid my face in his neck at the woots of the whole family and said, "I love you too."

He kept hugging me and very quickly, one after the other, every person formed a huddle around us.

The moment every one of us got our emotions under control, Aakar cleared his throat and announced, "Everyone, you guys are leaving after lunch. Kriti and I will return tomorrow. Or maybe the day after tomorrow."

While Ria and Abhi started to laugh, Maa and the kakis slyly smiled at each other as Maa announced, "Get up, everyone. We can grab lunch on our way home. Our job here is done."

The moment we were alone, Aakar dragged me upstairs, only pausing to kiss me against the wall, on the stairs, against the hallway, against the bedroom door. We were panting by the time we crashed through the bedroom door, and he had me sprawled on the floor itself.

36

Song: Pyaar Ki Yeh Kahani Suno
  - *Sunidhi Chauhan, Gayatri Iyer*

Aakar

We rolled on the floor as we kissed. I had her lying on top of me, as I crushed her in my arms, pushing my tongue in her mouth, needing to taste her. I moved to a sitting position as I pulled my wife on my lap, her legs on either side of my hips. I devoured her gasps and moans as she finally, finally agreed to come home.

I moved my lips to her neck, her jaw, tasting her, inhaling her scent that smelled like home. *My* home.

She moaned as I grazed my teeth at her pulse point, her hand pushing me harder against her skin by the back of my head.

She clutched me like she'd never let me go again, and my heart raced. My cock was weeping in my sweatpants, and I all but saw heaven when she pushed me lower to her breasts.

"You need me to worship these gorgeous tits of yours, baby?"

"Please," she whimpered.

"You don't ever have to plead, jaan."

I lowered the thin little strap of her bra and pulled down the cup to expose her breasts. The sight of them had me grinding up into her, causing her to tighten her legs around me.

In the next second, I had her lying on the floor as I bent down and sucked the top of her breast. Her moans echoed off the wall and reverberated in my soul. I squeezed her other tit and rolled her nipples just the way she liked. She whimpered and wrapped her legs around my hips, grinding up into me.

"Kriti, baby. Fuck."

I sounded desperate and wild and needy. But I couldn't help it. She deserved to know how pathetically I needed her.

I sucked the tight bud of her nipple as she ran her hands in my hair, moaning, "Harder. Suck it harder, Aakar."

And I obeyed. I sucked and bit and lapped at her, lost in her warmth and softness and curves. My body was an inferno as I rolled my hips between her legs, pleasure racing through my veins.

I moved down her breasts, licking and nipping down her stomach and her hips until I reached her panties. I sucked at her pussy right over them, too impatient to roll them down. She went wild the more I sucked.

She rolled her hips as she pushed me deeper into her, the silky material soaking and sticking to her pussy.

"Off, Aakar. Need them off."

I groaned, the pain of pulling off her turning me wild with hunger.

I tore through her panties and threw them behind me, then dove right back in.

I clutched her thighs as they wrapped around my shoulders and pushed my tongue inside her. She was so fucking wet, her juices were sliding down her ass. Her smell had my cock throbbing, and the moment her slick wetness rushed into my mouth, my cock fucking erupted.

Ropes of cum shot through me as I buried my face deeper between her legs, drinking her down as I jerked my hips on the floor. Pure ecstasy washed over me the more I drank her down.

"I'm coming, baby. Fuck. Fuck," I groaned, clutching her thighs tighter, my hips still jerking with a need to be deep inside my wife.

Kriti keened as her hips started to roll faster, and she tightened her thighs around my head, drowning me in her juices. Her pussy fluttered around my tongue as she came, and her fist tightened in my hair as she chanted my name.

Once our orgasms subsided, I lay down right there between her legs, resting my head on her thighs, holding on to her as she lightly ran her fingers through my hair. I was panting, yet my mind was at peace.

"Did you come in your pants, husband?" she asked, her voice scratchy.

Husband. She called me *husband.* And I couldn't help but smile. I turned my head and placed a featherlight kiss on her pussy and hummed in acceptance. "Cut me some slack, baby. I haven't tasted you in ten days."

She chuckled. *Chuckled*. And my heart soared.

We lay there as I caressed her leg, her stomach, her tits. "I missed this."

She hummed. "Me too."

Still not done with her, I dragged her toward the bathroom.

"What are you doing?" she asked.

"Let's get a shower together. Because I really need one." I gestured toward the embarrassing wet spot on my gray sweatpants. "And I'm not done with you yet."

Her eyes flared with heat, and before I realized what was happening, Kriti moved her hand right at the wet spot and cupped me right over it, spreading all the sticky cum over my cock and balls. Arousal came rushing back and roared through my veins, hardening me in her hands.

"Fuck, baby," I groaned as she massaged me through the fabric. My knees almost buckled before I pushed her against the sink and held on to its edges as she drove me to sheer madness.

Pleasure coursed through my spine as my balls tightened and my cock throbbed. More and more pre-cum oozed from my cock, wetting my sweatpants even further. Kriti whimpered at the sight as she squeezed her legs together.

I pushed harder into her hand and panted, "C'mon, baby. Take me out."

She quickly shook her head, shaking with need as her hands tightened on me, making me shiver. "Need this. Need to see you cum in your pants for me."

I groaned, the sound echoing in the bathroom. "Need you to come too. Fuck, I'm close. Ride my cock. Cover my sweatpants in your cum. Please."

She pulled me by my covered cock between her legs, and her bare pussy stretched over my sweatpants. She didn't let go of her hands, just used my cock to rub herself, spreading her wetness all over me.

The sight had my cock throbbing with need. My hips jerked with the need to push my sweats down and thrust into her, but Kriti clutched my cock as if it was her favorite toy. My own cum coated my cock, and I pulsed as she jerked me off just the way I liked it. Silky wetness coated me, my oozing pre-cum, my cum from before, and Kriti's wetness had my sweatpants sopping wet.

Kriti rolled her hips over my cock and pulled me closer by my neck so our foreheads touched.

"Look at us, Aakar," she cried out.

Her pussy rubbed over the imprint of my cock, leaving

white streaks on the now darker, wet fabric. My chest rumbled, and I groaned as I pushed harder in her hand, her grip tight around the base. "Want to bury myself inside you, baby. Fuck."

"Come for me, Aakar. Come for me, and I'll let you fuck me."

With a roar, I started to come, and Kriti instantly pulled her hand off. I groaned at the loss of her touch as I kept coming untouched, my cock pulsing, my balls tightening as my hips jerked against the fabric. Our eyes were glued to me as a new wet spot formed on my sweatpants.

My heart beat out of my rib cage, perspiration dotted my chest, and Kriti panted against me.

Slowly, she grazed her hand at my chest and moved lower. She tugged at the waistband and peeked inside. Cum trailed down my thighs as streaks of it stuck to the fabric. Her hips rolled in the air as she made a sexy, needy little noise in her throat.

I clutched the back of her neck and pulled her into a kiss. I pushed my tongue in her throat, and she sucked me in deeper. I growled as she bit my lip and sucked on them. I kissed her as she removed all my clothes. I sucked at her neck as I helped her get rid of her bra.

Turning on the shower, we climbed in, my arms clutching her. I washed her softly, placing kisses at every spot that I washed. She did the same to me, leaving me a groaning, trembling mess. I got down on my knees and ate her out again, her moans echoing off the walls.

～

Kriti

The moment we were out of the shower, Aakar had me pinned on the bed as he put his weight on me, groaning out loud, a wild desperation etched on his face. His cock settled between my legs, my pussy throbbing to feel him inside me. "I missed you so much, baby. Never. I'm never letting you go."

My hips moved against his cock, need still strumming in my veins as I pinched his cheek. "Even if you tell me to go, I'm not leaving. It's my home now. Your family is my family. I know more of their secrets. And they love me, and I love them."

Aakar's eyes filled with tears, and his voice shook when he asked, "Despite knowing their secrets?"

I wiped the stray tear with my thumb. "*Because* of their secrets."

He kissed me, pushing harder against me, his cock slick with my juices. "And do you love me?"

I wrapped my legs around him and pushed him inside me, both of us groaning with relief and pleasure. I clutched his neck and kissed him, licking and sucking at his lips. "You are the one and only love of my life, Aakar."

He groaned out loud at my words, at the pleasure, as he thrust into me harder.

Need clawed at my insides as I moved my hips to feel him deeper. Yet I talked to him. "Never in my life did I imagine I'd have a husband who treated me as his equal. I never imagined a life when my husband treated me as something precious."

"You are. Fuck, you are *everything*."

I pulled him deeper by his hips. "I never thought I'd feel the joy of feeling love from my husband, let alone his entire family. I never thought I'd fall so deeply in love with my husband that *he* would become my home."

He whimpered and pushed his tongue inside my mouth, sucking the words right out of my mouth. "You are my home, my jaan. You are my joy. You are everything fucking good in my life."

I tasted his words between every thrust. I licked his tears. I sucked the skin at the junction of his neck and shoulder, making him thrust harder and deeper inside me. Pleasure coursed through my veins, turning my moans into whimpers.

I clutched his hair and pulled his lips to my neck, and he sucked my skin with a wild abandon. He gave me exactly what I needed. The wet slide of his cock hit me at just the right spot, sending sparks of electric pleasure along my spine. My hips jerked with an aching need, wanting more and more and more from him.

I clutched his hair at the back of his head, pushing him deeper into my neck. With every lick, he thrust harder into me. The sound of the headboard banging against the wall turned me feral. I grabbed his ass, pushing him deeper into me, then wrapped my legs around his waist, getting closer and closer to the peak.

"Aakar, I'm almost there."

"Fuck. Fuck. Come on, baby. Come on my cock. Wanna feel you squeezing me. Missed this."

His words were my undoing. My spine arched as my body jerked. Pleasure unlike anything I'd experienced raced down my spine, my pussy throbbing and clenching and squeezing around my husband as a million stars burst behind my eyes. The pleasure went on and on as I slowly moved my hips, clenching around his cock, prolonging the euphoria wracking my body.

I suddenly realized then that he wasn't wearing a condom. "Come inside me," I whimpered, needing to feel him inside me.

His groan turned feral as his thrusts got wilder. He groaned in my neck, entwining his hand with mine, and his other hand clutched my shoulder, the force of his thrust bringing me closer to another orgasm.

"Come inside me, Aakar. Let me feel you," I moaned, mindless with the need to feel him.

He let out a fucking roar as he started to come, spraying hot jets of his cum inside me. He kept pushing and thrusting inside me, milking every drop of his cum until he lay sprawled on top of me, pushing all of his weight on me.

I pulled him closer to me as we regained our senses and calmed down.

I ran my finger through my husband's hair, now dotted with sweat. I grabbed a blanket and covered us, placing a kiss on his head as he snuggled deeper into me, keeping his cock notched deep inside me.

My husband wasn't perfect. Neither was I.

Looking back at the life I'd lived, and the life that was yet to come, I was infinitely happier to have Aakar by my side. I felt blessed to have *him* be the witness to my life. I wanted my future children to have Aakar as their father, who would be their biggest protector, the best caretaker, and the most loving father they could ever have. I was relieved out of my mind that I had found Aakar, that he had found me and chosen to marry me.

Our first meeting was planned for an arranged marriage. Our second meeting was our choice. Our third meeting sealed the deal.

Our marriage might have been arranged, but our love wasn't. Our families brought us together, and I'll be eternally grateful for that blessing.

By no means was marriage easy. But with Aakar, it felt more like friendship. We had laughter, and I was sure there would be many more fights to come in life, especially knowing the sheer number of secrets our family kept from us. He made life more exciting for me. With him, I looked forward to living my married life, to having those ordinary, boring days of eating, working, and sleeping, having those silent fights, feeling the passionate love, to experiencing the joy and stress of living with a large family.

Just because it was with Aakar.

Just because *he* was my husband.

EPILOGUE

Song: Jaadui
  - *Jubin Nautiyal*

Aakar

5 *months later*

"Maa, Aakar is cheating," Kriti cried out, pointing her finger at me.

"I am not cheating," I gritted out. I really wasn't.

Dad scoffed. "Of course, he's cheating, Kriti Beta. How else could he be winning?"

Kriti hummed in support.

"Because I'm good? Because I know how to play? Because I'm smart?"

Abhi winked at me and turned to Maa. "Bhai is definitely cheating, Maa."

As Maa, Dad, and Navin Kaka glared at me, I saw Abhi exchange a card with Kriti.

"Look, look. Abhi and Kriti were just cheating," I shouted.

I, for a fact, knew Ekta Kaki had seen Abhi exchange his

card with Kriti because our eyes had met right after we caught them, and she had a little smile on her face.

But the moment Maa looked at them, both of those cheaters started looking at her with all the innocence in the world. "We're not. Aakar is just trying to distract you."

Maa turned to glare at me again, leaving Kriti and Abhi to sneak in their evil laughs. I couldn't help but roll my eyes at Maa. "Maa, they're lying. Ask Ekta Kaki."

Ekta Kaki suddenly started to act all innocent as she said, "What? Who, me? I didn't see anything."

I literally gasped out loud. I pointed an accusatory finger at all of them. "It's because Kriti's pregnant, isn't it? That's why you're blatantly ignoring all the cheating happening here."

Every single one of them started to deny it.

Abhi: "Bhabhi is a great player, bhai."

Pappa: "Didn't you see her win the last three games?"

Maa: "She beat all of us. We don't need to do her any favors just because she's carrying this house's first-ever grandchild."

Navin Kaka and Ekta Kaki: "That's right."

I raised my hands in defeat. "Fine. You're right. Kriti is an exceptional player." She was not even a decent player. I could literally see Pappa grinding his teeth, trying to play his worst to help her win, which was funny as fuck.

Right then, Ria brought a large tray full of warm masala, milk full of saffron, cashews, and almonds. I got up and quickly grabbed two glasses.

I went to the couch where Kriti sat between Maa and Abhi and asked Abhi to move.

"But I want to sit with bhabhi," he argued.

"She wants to sit with me," I argued back.

"No, she doesn't."

"Of course she does."

"Ask her."

I wasn't going to ask her. Otherwise, she would just torture me by picking Abhi. Those two had joined forces to my utter frustration.

So I simply glared at him and said, "If you don't let me sit with my wife, I'm going to take her away for a long drive."

In the next second, the seat was empty for me.

I handed Kriti her milk as I sat beside her, my arm around her shoulders.

Kriti sat in soft cotton pajamas and one of my T-shirts that covered her slightly round stomach. I still couldn't believe that I was going to be a father. That I already was a father to the tiny baby growing inside my wife.

Kriti was five months pregnant, and she'd never looked more gorgeous in her life. Her cheeks had turned slightly rounder, her curves were more pronounced, her hips had become fuller, and her tits were the bane of my existence.

We found out that she was pregnant six weeks after Kriti came back home. Our make-up sex had brought us the tiny, little miracle that was growing in her belly. We did have a discussion the day after our unprotected sex sessions, but Kriti wanted to leave it up to fate. I was ready to take on the responsibility of a kid, and so was Kriti. We started using condoms later on, but we did end up being pregnant.

And not a single day did we regret our choice.

Kriti and I tried to keep it to ourselves for the first two weeks after we found out. But I might've gone a bit overboard in being cautious and caring for Kriti. It didn't exactly take our family too long to figure it out after that.

And to say I was the one who went overboard would be an understatement. Everyone had started to hog her so much that I'd had to resort to blackmailing them to get some free time with my own wife.

The doorbell ringing brought me out of my musings. The moment Abhi opened the door, in walked Luke, Hari, and Meera. A slightly more pregnant Meera. How in the hell did we sync up a pregnancy, I'd never figure out. But it was maddening and something I did not want to repeat. Ever.

I didn't even have to be told before I cleared my spot from beside Kriti. Meera gave me a sweet smile as she sat beside Kriti.

"Meera, you've grown big," Kriti cooed at Meera's stomach.

Meera chuckled. "Yeah, well a seven-month pregnant belly does that to you."

Right then, Luke handed Meera a glass of warm saffron milk and greeted my family in our native language, Gujarati.

He'd started to pick up a lot more of the language since they moved to Ahmedabad.

We spent the rest of the evening eating some spicy foods—Kriti was on a vada pav kick—and drinking warm milk. Luke and I fussed over our wives and played some card games that Kriti completely sucked at but always ended up winning.

Once everyone was gone, I asked Kriti to go upstairs while Ria, Abhi, and I cleared up the living room, dining room, and kitchen. I got some water and went to our bedroom.

I found Kriti lying on her side in her sexy silk nightgown, with very thin straps and a really, really low neckline, leaving nothing to the imagination. She wore nothing underneath, showing me the tight buds of her nipples and her slightly round stomach.

I quickly locked the door, got rid of my clothes, and pulled us both under a blanket. I pulled her closer to me, her back to my stomach as she pushed herself deeper into my arms, rolling her hips against my hard, aching cock.

I caressed her stomach and nuzzled against the back of her neck, breathing her in. "Finally. Alone at last."

She arched her neck and caressed my cheek, bringing my mouth closer to hers. She dropped a kiss on my lips. "I missed you. Even when you were right there, I missed you. I so badly wanted to be in your arms."

She nuzzled deeper into me and pulled me into a much deeper kiss. Kriti had started to express her needs more and more freely, and she got horny as all hell. I pulled her nightgown up around her waist and dragged my cock between her wet folds. She was always wet these days.

I slowly pushed inside her, and she sighed in relief. We stayed like that. Breathing each other in. Feeling each other to the point of madness. Loving each other.

Five months ago, I'd experienced ten days without Kriti.

Every day after Kriti returned home was all about growth and change. Even before we found out about being pregnant, we'd started to make changes. I shared more of my troubles with her while she started to share some important tidbits about the secrets that our family told her.

When she first found out about the pregnancy, she was worried that I'd start treating her like glass. That I'd stop trusting her and sharing important things with her. She was afraid I'd not treat her as an equal. But I promised her I wouldn't let our pregnancy affect the partnership and trust we were forging.

We were more of a team now than ever. I knew I could trust Kriti with anything. She'd be there for me, sharing my burdens. I didn't have to be too careful with her. I didn't have to worry about stressing her out. I didn't have to *handle* things for her. She was my rock, my partner, my friend, my wife.

I didn't worry about my life, about my family anymore. I knew that whatever challenges life threw our way, we'd handle it together. As a family. With Kriti by my side, I didn't watch my life pass by. I didn't fear what life would bring me. I cherished my life. I looked forward to a new day, ready to love my wife, ready to welcome our child, and ready for whatever life brought us.

GLOSSARY

-ji / -Ji : Ji is a gender-neutral honorific suffix used in Hindi and Urdu to convey respect to the individual whose name it is appended to.

Aloo: Potato

Beta/Beti: Child

Bhabhi: An honorific term used to refer to a sister-in-law

Bhai: An honorific term used to refer to an older brother

Dal: Dal is an Indian dish made from pulses such as chickpeas or lentils.

Dal Makhani: Dal makhani is a popular North Indian dish where whole black lentils & red kidney beans are slow cooked with spices, butter & cream.

Chhaas: also known as spiced Buttermilk , is a popular Indian beverage that is made by combining Yogurt (curd) with water and various spices and herbs.

Didi: a term used to refer to an elder sister

Dupatta: The dupattā, also called chunni, chunari and chundari, is a long shawl-like scarf traditionally worn by women in the Indian subcontinent to cover the head and shoulders.The dupatta is currently used most commonly as part of the women's shalwar kameez outfit, and worn over the kurta and the gharara.

Fafda: Fafda is a fried crispy crunchy tasty snack made with besan (gram flour), laced with carom seeds and black pepper.

Gobi: Cauliflower

Jhula: A swing

Kachori: a deep-fried, savory pastry filled with spiced lentil, pea, or potato filling, often served with chutney or yogurt.

Khaman: Khaman is made from ground channa daal or channa gram flour, usually with lemon juice, semolina, and curd. A final tadka can be added, using ingredients such as asafoetida and chillies

Kurta/Kurti: A loose collarless shirt or tunic worn in many regions of South Asia

Lehenga: A long skirt worn by women in South Asia that is often elaborately embroidered with beads, shisha mirrors, or other ornaments

Mehndi: Henna

Pav Bhaji/Bhaji pav: An Indian fast food consisting of a thick spicy vegetable gravy served with soft dinner rolls.

Rotli: A type of flat, round South Asian bread

Sabzi: Sabzi, or subji, is an Indian term that defines simply a "vegetable dish.

Salwar-Kameez: The salwar kameez is a traditional outfit worn by Punjabi women. It comprises a pair of trousers known as the salwar and a tunic called the kameez. Traditionally, the salwar trousers are tailored to be long and loose-fitting with narrow hems above the ankles that are stitched to look like cuffs.

Samosa: a small triangular pastry filled with spiced meat or vegetables and fried in ghee or oil

Thepla: A type of flat, round South Asian bread.Its common ingredients are wheat flour, besan (gram flour), methi (fenugreek leaves) and other spices. It is served with condiments such as dahi (yogurt), red garlic chutney and chhundo (sweet mango pickle).

Vada Pav: The dish consists of a deep fried potato dumpling placed inside a bread bun (pav) sliced almost in half through the middle. It is generally accompanied with one or more chutneys and a green chilli pepper.

Undhiyu: Undhiyu is a Gujarati mixed vegetable dish that is a regional specialty of Surat, Gujarat, India. The name of this dish comes from the Gujarati word Undhu, which translates to upside down, since the dish is traditionally cooked upside down underground in earthen pots, termed Matlu, which are fired from above.

ACKNOWLEDGMENTS

This book has taken me the longest to finish. I had the idea of needing to write an Indian arranged marriage that had all the elements of courting, a wedding, and finally living with the in-laws and the challenges it posed. But all of it in an ideal fictional world.

I'm already married and I've found my Aakar but if I had to have an arranged marriage, this is how I would've liked my story to go. I'm incredibly proud of the book that I've written.

It was when I lost my dad this year that I truly realized the importance of a big Desi family. The way every single relative came together to support us, came to live with us for a few weeks, and helped us deal with the grief and loss. Without them, we would all have been broken forever.

This book is merely a glimpse of the beauty and power a big, supportive family can hold in a person's life. So, I would like to begin by thanking my own family for inspiring the Mishra family.

I would like to thank my beta readers—Anna P, Kacey Sophia, Riya I, Kriti, Apoorva, and Gurasis Kaur for providing their incredible feedback and comments. They've made this book a hundred times better with their thoughtful suggestions. You didn't have to beta read my book, but you *chose* to do this for me, and I'll forever be grateful.

Hannah, from English Proper Editing Services, you are incredible. I absolutely loved your commentaries throughout the book. Your opinion and suggestions have been extremely valuable.

Kriti, from Swipethebook PR, you are a gem. You arrived in my life when I was at my lowest, when I'd given up on doing much for this book in terms of promotion. But you changed it all. You have handled every little aspect of my release from ARC reader management, to designing and preparing the PR boxes, to creating all the hype and a street team, to reaching out to amazing accounts for promotion. You are forever stuck with me now because there is no way I can do a release of my book without you.

Thank you to all the bookstagrammers and booktokers who've gone above and beyond to create content for my book, leave reviews, include my books in their recommendation lists, and given my books a space on their page. This wouldn't have happened without your support.

Thank you to all the people who've read my books and shown them so much love. I hope this book made you happy.

And last, but not the least, thank you to my very own book husband. You're the inspiration for all my heroes. You've made me an incredibly happy wife. Your constant support and encouragement to pursue my dreams has made my life a million times more fulfilling than I'd ever imagined.

Thank you all.

ABOUT THE AUTHOR

N.M. Patel is a passionate author who writes romance novels inspired by her love of Bollywood movies. Her books are filled with humor, steam, and plenty of love, featuring strong heroines and swoon-worthy heroes. Get ready to be transported into a world of Desi culture, unforgettable characters, and a romantic escape that will leave you feeling warm and fuzzy inside.

You can find N.M. Patel here:
  Website: https://nmpatelbooks.com/
  Instagram: https://www.instagram.com/nmpatelauthor/
  Tiktok: https://www.tiktok.com/@nmpatelauthor

Printed in Great Britain
by Amazon